THE

GLOAMING

Rise of the Stealth Vampire Elder

M L WORTHINGHAM

TABLE OF CONTENTS

Gloaming (gləʊmɪŋ) *noun*
Twilight; dusk. (old English)

MOTION

Valentin von Hahn walked a cobblestoned alley called Pijlsteeg, the rounded stones beneath his feet still shiny from the last rain as he headed toward the center of the city. He wore an untucked black Hugo Boss shirt, Scotch and Soda jeans, Van Liers on his feet, Rolex on his wrist, and tousled brown hair. The lingering summer gloaming was upon the city, and for a very long time, this had been the start of his day.

In the slowly fading light of the northern European summer, the air still and—to many—stifling with seasonal heat and humidity, people passed by him, some glancing, some not. He smelled the sweet scent of jenever, antecedent to modern-day gin distilling, in Wynand Fockink, heard the buzz of tourists high, drunk, and excited to be away from the daily grind of their real lives. Valentin loved Mokum, its warm summer embrace, refuge from the hard world outside, provider of much, and haven from the many that feared and hated.

Tonight would be like many before. Walk the public squares in search of that girl, the one. More often than not, the search would lead to a bar or club later, as fear and suspicion checked the instinct of most.

Valentin had come to terms with his life long ago. He did it well, the practice and execution down to a fine science, or was it an art? He would like to think so, but deep down he knew he was now more survivor than artist. Either way, he was known as one of the best— handsome, charming, convincing, suave, with that moneyed European air of one who maybe possessed the lineage of nobles. He knew all the responses to no, but more importantly, he knew when not to waste his time. Time, he had plenty of that, but to waste it was a sacrilege.

Tonight Valentin would meet a good girl, or a bad girl, it didn't matter which, and tomorrow night she would be all but forgotten, not because he was mean or callous, but for her own good. Sometimes he would meet a woman he wished he could see again, but only for a moment. Love was not for him, or at least not the love felt by the hoards of tourists streaming by in the street, but he was fine with that too. Almost. He didn't hate them or feel any pangs of jealousy. These tourists with their on-holiday mentality and just-this-one-time morals were what made his life easy. He loved them in his way as he walked down the street, the wet warmth of the city a blanket enveloping him.

Something about the plane actually being in the air made Steve Breckenridge relax. It wasn't that he was afraid of flying, or of the takeoff. That was for the non logical and the mentally ill, like his ex-wife Naomi. It was the tension of waiting. Waiting in line to check his luggage, waiting in line for security, waiting for his row to start boarding, waiting for the plane to pull away from the gate and start taxiing, and finally waiting for the plane to take off. Until that moment, the time felt so wasted, nothing being accomplished toward his goal of being in the next city. This time the city was Amsterdam.

Amsterdam one of those cities that didn't need to be identified by country or state, like Paris—which he could see vanishing out the window as the plane banked—or New York or San Francisco, near Steve's hometown of Sausalito. Another place whose name lived on its own.

He looked around the plane at what he considered amateur travelers, especially on a Friday afternoon, annoying him and getting in the way as he tried to do his job. Tourists from all over the world, turning their brains off for a week or more, just as Steve hoped to do in the next few hours, with a little help.

He loved Amsterdam, but the intensity, the hyper energy, the stark utility, and the crowds of summer were really draining in high doses. Propelled out of the seventeenth century like a cannon ball, shot into being the most important city in its day, Amsterdam today was little faded from that high-water mark, and held its history up like a proud champion of old, still more athlete in its middle age than most twenty-somethings. Steve, like most non-Dutch, tempered the city's edge by visiting one of its many "coffee shops," and of course the red-light district. There was nothing like pounding out a little stress on top of a hot European girl after smoking some prime bud, but that would have to wait.

He popped open his laptop and went over the next week's work—installing new routers and firewalls at two partner banks in Amsterdam as part of his company's private network. The logistics and planning of the project had been large in scope, but with just one more city to go, it was almost done, and with it a decent bonus. The stress was low on this project, and the visibility high. Based in San Francisco, Steve's company, Sterling Klein Financial (SKF), an international broker in the secondary market for asset derivatives, was conservative but paid well. All the data links were already in place, so there would be no wasted time. He wouldn't be showing up at a location with no data line, or with one installed two hundred yards—or in this case, meters—away from where it needed to be. No yelling on the phone and re-planning the visit, sometimes months later, just the satisfaction of pulling out the old equipment, installing the new, configuring, and bringing everything up, and then of course, the show of testing. Steve would know within two minutes if there was a problem, with a cable, the equipment itself, or the data link to the Telco. A simple ping with 64k packets told him all that he needed to know in 99 percent of cases. This being banking, though, he had to give the appearance that sophisticated activity was going on. Steve was good at his job as a network engineer. He double-checked his spreadsheets for IP addresses, subnet masks, and host names, glancing at the passenger next to him. *A German or Austrian,* he thought, *who probably didn't speak English; and if he did, would not have anything interesting to say.*

He closed his MacBook and sighed. Amsterdam lay ahead, with all the boring airport and airplane procedure in reverse. Steve knew he should try to reject the feeling that institutionalized time thieves were robbing him, but knowing and doing were not the same thing. Doing what you think was just as hard as "do what I say."

Veronica Thompson was the shit. She knew it, but not in a bad way. Born and raised in Montgomery, Alabama, she had been pretty from thirteen. She made head cheerleader in her sophomore year of high school, and there was never a doubt that her reign would last until she graduated. It just was, and nobody could imagine anything else. She barely missed being homecoming queen. The slightly less pretty Lauren Williams broke both her legs and an arm in the same accident that killed her boyfriend, and she got the sympathy vote. In college at Auburn, Veronica didn't go out for cheerleading because she quickly realized that in this day and age, being a cheerleader really wasn't that cool. It objectified women, and the perception was that a cheerleader was not intelligent. Someday a woman would be president, and Veronica doubted she would have been a cheerleader in college—just not résumé material.

Having recently graduated from Auburn, Veronica, her friends Sophia and Carol from the University of Alabama, and Lauren—yes, that Lauren from high school—were on their way to Europe for the summer. It was Veronica's second choice, but maybe just missing out on being a *Big Brother* cast member was a blessing. As the plane approached Amsterdam Schiphol Airport, Veronica and Lauren were catching up on missed time. Lauren was a year behind Veronica due to the physical rehab and was still attending Auburn; Veronica was considering moving to Los Angeles to get a job, and applying to UCLA for a master's degree in communications. She was officially blogging about her trip this summer for a wannabe travel app. All her friends wanted to know about the Big Brother audition, of course. What was it like, was it fun?

"A cattle call, as first calls to anything in the business are usually called, is anything but glamorous," Veronica started in the Southern drawl she cultivated both naturally and to effect. "Hundreds of people show up, you wait in line to register, and then just wait for your name to be called. When you finally do get called, despite maybe waiting three to eight hours, you have to be ready for your five minutes in front of the producers. In the case of *Big Brother*, they asked me a few questions and videotaped the response. Luckily I got a callback, which included interacting with other potential cast members and a quick confession-booth taping at the end. Eventually I got a 'thank you we're not interested' call."

The conversation eventually switched to boys, and they all told tales of fun, heartache, and, yes, one or two real men. They looked forward to meeting men in Europe and breaking the rules. If not in Amsterdam, then a Frenchman in Paris—oblivious to the fact that they would be arriving in August—when everybody that was anybody would have already fled the City of Lights. That would still leave Barcelona and London to meet the perfect bad boy. This was going to be a great summer, and they all knew it!

AMSTERDAM

Steve Breckenridge arrived at the hotel Grand Krasnapolsky around 2:00 p.m. by car, which had been provided by his company. One of the nice perks of working for a prestigious financial firm. The Krasnapolsky sits on the edge of Dam Square in the heart of Amsterdam, directly across from the royal palace. Behind the hotel, the city's red-light district begins just one hundred yards away, like a metaphor for Dutch liberal pragmatism. The hotel itself is rated at five stars, but Steve felt it could be inconsistent, from the room you got to the service. The one saving grace that always delivered was breakfast in the winter garden. *Without it, this is just a really old four-star hotel,* Steve thought. Besides the buffet being top quality, the room itself, built in 1879 and renovated in 1885, was an incredible example of Victorian architecture. Between fifty and sixty yards long and about thirty-five yards wide, the room was covered by a glass roof supported by arched steel beams.

Check in was always stressful, *will I get a good room or get fucked?,* he thought. It was the same everywhere, and Steve, at thirty-three years old having traveled all over the US, Europe, and a little in Asia, had been through this before. His experiences at the Krasnapolsky varied. What was considered a "deluxe" room seemed to change with every visit. He had been in the apartments in the Amsterdam wing and once had had a decent room that impressed his friends, and he had been in a cramped room in the middle of the hotel earlier on this trip. It was the same all over, and some of it he was sure had to do with luck.

Once he had arrived, with a reservation, at the Marriott in north Dallas, and was told they only had one room left. His first thought was that they were going to stall until they had moved the janitorial equipment out of a closet. This was Dallas, after all. They directed him to an unmarked room on the second floor. He passed it once, but doubled back and found the door. His card key worked, and he stepped into about 1200 square feet of space that included a large TV and sectional couch, an open kitchen, and a dining area with a table that could seat twelve, and that was just the beginning. To the left, behind a wall open at both ends, was a den area with another television, and to the right were three bedrooms, each with their own TV and a laundry room with a full-size washer and dryer. He figured the suite was between 2500 and 3000 square feet, and had five TVs. Steve had not owned five TVs in his entire life. He regretted he was only staying the night, and was too exhausted from a brutal four days working in Houston to enjoy the room.

"Second floor," the woman behind the desk at the Krasnapolsky informed him. "You can take the elevator or the main staircase."

Steve pulled his rolling bag to the elevator across the lobby from the front desk. Once the elevator arrived, after a long wait, he rode up to the second floor and decided that until he was checking out with his luggage, he'd take the stairs. He quickly found the room, and upon opening the door saw the best room he had ever seen at the Krasnapolsky. It was large by European standards, and its windows looked out onto Dam Square, with a view of the royal palace. The main windows opened to a faux balcony, maybe not sturdy enough for both feet, but he could definitely hang out later with one foot outside while he smoked some weed.

After hanging his clothes in the closet, Steve texted his friend Jim, of Jim and Suzy, who where flying in later that evening from London. They were all going to have dinner together. He knew both of them from school, UCLA. Married to Jim for five years, Suzy had once dated Steve. They were all friends now, no weirdness at all, and Steve was pretty much beyond all that. He rarely thought about fucking her again for the sport of it. Next he went out for supplies, which included a couple of bottles of Spa Water to supplement what the hotel provided. Then down an alley to a coffee shop called Green House Red-light District on the canal behind the hotel. He picked up a gram of Afghan Kush, which was a bit pricey at eighteen euros, and went back to the hotel. The weed would wait for later, after dinner, and especially after he caught up with work email.

About 8:00 p.m. he texted Suzy to see if they had checked into their hotel,

<Jim lost his phone. Stuck in London tonight, C U tomorrow? –

Suzy>

That sucked for his dinner plans. He had hoped to have a sit-down dinner with friends. A welcome change from the fast food and room service he got on business trips. Still, Steve was used to rolling with the punches and dealing with adversity. His job depended on it. He remembered something he'd heard John Wooden, the legendary UCLA basketball coach, had said: "Adversity is the state in which man most easily becomes aquatinted with himself." Steve wanted to believe that, but deep down he thought it was bullshit. He knew he threw himself into situations that forced him to fight his way back out as a means of escaping from the real world, a dysfunctional family, and a failed marriage. If you're forced by circumstances to act, you really aren't making a choice, except the possibly subconscious choice to get yourself into those situations. Perhaps the first few times in life, learning how you act when faced with adversity, you do become more acquainted with yourself. *But after a few championships,* he thought, *you know you can come back in the fourth quarter, and Steve supposed the losers know they can't.* He looked again at Suzy's text and shook his head. *Change of plans, whatever,* he thought.

☥

Veronica, Sophia, Carol, and Lauren sat around Veronica's room in the Amsterdam American hotel. Her room was much larger than the other girls'; enormous, really. Two levels with a loft bedroom, and a living room with a couch and two big chairs. Veronica sat in one of the throne-like chairs while her three friends faced her from the couch. They were exhausted from jet lag, and it was only 8:30 p.m.

"The website says we have to stay up until at least ten," Veronica proclaimed.

"Oh my God, I don't think I can do it," was the last thing Sophia said that night.

THE GLOAMING

Amsterdam in high summer gets dark around 10:30 p.m., with an extended gloaming that starts about 8:00. Steve had gone out for some fast food from Wok to Walk, Asian stir-fry—good but probably not something he should eat every day—sometime after 8:30 instead of getting room service. Just to feel the energy of the crowds. Now he rolled up a nice fat joint from the gram of Afghan Kush he had purchased earlier. He would smoke a little weed and then go down to the red-light district for some fun. He hung one leg out the window, resting it on the faux balcony, and sparked up the joint. He disciplined himself to just three hits, blowing the smoke out the window into the warm summer evening. He didn't want to get too high tonight and wake up hours later fully clothed on his bed. Steve had smoked plenty of weed when he'd attended Mill Valley's infamous Tamalpais High School, but today it was far and few. It had been almost two months since he'd last smoked, near the start of this trip to Europe and here in Amsterdam, where it was legal. He loved that relaxing feeling, the impending oblivion if he just took five to seven more hits, but not now. Maybe later.

So he put the joint out and hung out for a few minutes gazing over Dam Square, at the tourists wandering in seemingly random directions, or sitting on the edge of the war memorial, getting stoned like him or just talking. Bicycles raced by on every street, the single-speed bikes of his youth, and not a helmet in sight. *When a bicycle is your primary transportation a helmet just gives you "helmet hair" by the time you get into the office, and with the number of people riding on a single day probably exceeding the number of people riding in a whole month back in California, the statistics are clearly against the relative safety of helmets,* Steve thought.

Steve reached for his phone out of habit, but it was behind him in the room. He pulled his outside leg in and walked over to the small round glass table in the corner, tossed the joint down, and grabbed his phone. When he turned back to the window, she was there. His first thought was, *how stoned am I?* His second: *How did she get there?* He stared at the hot eastern-European-looking brunette out on the faux balcony, sitting on the blue iron railing like she had been there the whole time. Just three hits, of strong weed, granted, that was pricier than average at eighteen euro, but if there was weed that could make you hallucinate, it would cost more than that. This was the Dutch, after all. You paid a fair price, no bargains, but no rip-offs either.

Momentum brought him almost face to face with her. "Hi," she purred in a generic old-world accent.

"Uh," Steve managed.

"How did I get here? Why am I here? Who am I?" she asked.

"Yeah, that," Steve replied.

"I'm Karolina. Will you invite me in?"

"Did you climb up, or did you come from another room?" Steve asked, looking around.

"If you invite me in, I'll tell you," she replied with a tease in her voice.

"Is it even safe out there?" Steve asked, still confused, but trying at least to act cool.

"It's safe for me since I only weigh about fifty kilos. It would probably break if you were out here," she replied. "Just kidding, it's stronger than you think. But when are you going to invite me in?"

"Is that like the third time you've asked me that?"

"It was only the second time. Will you let me in?" Karolina asked again.

"No, I'm pretty sure it was the third and that was the fourth," Steve said.

"No, just now that was the second time," she teased.

"You know, I'm not that stoned."

"I know. I've been watching you, and I know you want me to come in. So just say, Karolina you're invited into my room."

"If you know I want you to come in, why don't you just come in?"

"It doesn't work that way. You have be 100 percent committed. It's a covenant. You have to invite me in, you have to consent. So invite me in."

He shook his head. "I still don't understand why I need to invite you in."

"If you want to fuck me," she said, "you'll invite me in."

"Did somebody hire you? Do you work for the hotel? I'm not complaining. You're hot as hell." Steve was starting to notice just how attractive she was—dark-brown shoulder-length hair, about five foot five, a nice hard body with small breasts, and beautiful almond-shaped brown eyes that almost seemed to glow as she watched him carefully. She was that perfect image he had of the hot-as-hell Euro girl, attractive with little or no makeup, wearing a black top, faded designer blue jeans, and black pumps, already off her feet and on the balcony.

"Fuck you," she said. "I don't fuck for money. I'm getting bored, I think I'm going to leave now."

"No, no, don't leave. It's just not every day a hot woman materializes outside my window. Did you fly up here like a bat, like Dracula?" Steve asked.

She smiled. "Something like that. So are you going to invite me in?"

"You seem assertive enough. I don't understand why you just don't come in."

"I told you, it doesn't work that way. It's a rule, you have to invite me in."

"Whose rule, the hotel?"

"No, the covenant that was created by the council of elders. We have to follow it under the threat of true death," she replied.

"Who the fuck are the elders. Are there other rules?"

"Just two main ones. Everything has to be consensual, and you can't kill more than one person per century."

"Kill? Per century? You mean the 'elders,' whoever the fuck they are, let you kill one person in a lifetime? Is this some sort of Dutch thing? Are the elders those guys in funny black hats from the church over there?" He pointed at the "new church" across Dam Square, which was only about six hundred years old, compared to the "old church," which was about eight hundred.

"No," Karolina answered. "I'm not Dutch. I'm *bohémský dívka*, I mean Czech girl, and the elders created the covenant in 1733, 280 years ago, to end the deaths and upir terror."

Steve shook his head in confusion. "The what terror?"

"Upir. You call it *vampír*, I mean vampire, the un-dead," Karolina replied, staring straight into Steve's eyes. "We call ourselves the almost dead."

"You're fucking saying you're a vampire come to suck my blood? You must think I'm really high, or maybe you are."

"You won't die, and you get to fuck me if you just let me in," she replied.

"Okay, come in," Steve said, and she hopped over the windowsill landing on the hardwood floor with a feline grace. *At a minimum*, he thought, *this was considerably more interesting than the warm-blooded blowup dolls he could fuck for fifty to one hundred euros in the red-light district.* "So how does this work?" he asked in a somewhat joking way, wanting to humor the girl in her vampire fantasy.

"I let you fuck me, and right when you come, I'll bite your neck and feed on your blood. Then in the morning you won't remember anything—what I'm telling you, what I did to you, or that you ever met me," Karolina replied soberly. "The reason I bite you right as you orgasm is that the hormones make the blood two to three times more nutritious for me."

"And then I'll turn into a vampire." Steve said jokingly.

"No. Only .0001 percent of the population has the upir gene. For the rest, the virus or whatever it is gives them amnesia," she said.

"Virus! What the fuck? Now you're going to give me an STD?"

"*Like* a virus," she lied. "I don't know what it is."

"Okay, we both know I want to fuck you, so just tell me the truth," Steve asked.

"All right, you won't remember anyway. They say it's a blood disease. If you have the upir gene, it feeds on your blood, and in the process, as a waste product it produces an enzyme that gives you strength, agility, clearness of thought, greatly decelerated aging, and the ability to heal very quickly. The problem is that in about two weeks it will churn through all your blood, stop producing the enzyme, and as a result you will die unless you feed on human blood. The good news is the virus, or whatever it is, feeds on the blood in your digestive tract first. For the other 99.999 percent of the population, the enzyme that the virus produces causes a fever that lasts four to six hours, and amnesia of the previous twelve to twenty-four hours. That's going to be you.

"For the few that have the upir gene," she went on, "the first exposure to the virus also causes a fever, but then as it feeds on your blood, the enzyme is produced, and you begin the change. At first it's just light sensitivity. Light hurts your eyes and makes you very weak. Then as the sun goes down, you start to feel an energy, a clarity of thought, and a physical strength like you never believed was possible.

"I won't kill you. I could but I won't. I'll take just enough blood to survive." She giggled. "Or maybe a little more."

NIGHT

For ten minutes Steve pounded Karolina's bald pussy. He knew what he was doing and figured he would give her the fuck of her life, or at least the year. The whole time he felt like he was in a dream, fading in and out of a third-person perspective, still amazed at the events that had led to this point. Her strange appearance at the window, her crazy story, his half believing it, and the fact that every time he looked down at her, she seemed even hotter. Maybe it was just the Afghan Kush. She came once, twice, and then the third time her pussy got so tight, he was coming himself despite trying to go on. She pulled his head down, and he felt her soft hair on his neck. Then in the next second, needlelike fangs sank into his flesh with a sharp pain. Any other time he probably would have freaked out, but with the story she'd told, it all seemed so natural. Maybe he really had taken ten hits and passed out dreaming on the bed; he still wasn't sure. She was almost suckling at his neck like a baby. It hurt and somehow felt good at the same time. Then she was done.

Steve rolled off her and looked over. She wiped his blood off her lips, "Thank you," she purred. She seemed energized and almost glowing. She sat up after a few minutes, and her stomach muscles flexed like nothing he had ever seen. So tight and animal like, the most toned he had ever seen, but not in a bodybuilding sort of way.

"So how was it fucking a six-hundred-year-old woman?" she asked.

Steve had almost forgotten her story, the bite, the whole thing. He felt his neck, and his fingers found two tiny wounds, like he had had some sort of medical procedure.

"You're six-hundred years old?"

"Actually, closer to seven-hundred. I was born in 1447 in Praha. I mean, Prague."

Steve was starting to come down from the weed, and as his head cleared, he became increasingly skeptical of her story. He started to get up, wanting to check his neck in the bathroom mirror.

"Stay in bed," Karolina said. "Get some rest, and in the morning you won't remember any of this."

That Steve doubted, but what if she was telling the truth. Could this all be real? Were vampires real? Was she actually 667 years old?

"One more thing," she said. "If by some obscure chance you remember all of this, you probably got turned. If you did, wait at the old church in the red-light district tomorrow night. I just need to warn you. You probably won't make it on your own."

Turned into a vampire? Was that what Karolina just said? Steve was getting tired now, his head heavy, and he wanted to sleep.

"Sleep, my American prince. Sleep, and it will all be okay in the morning," she said.

Steve conjured a last burst of energy to push himself up with his weakening arms and walk to the bathroom. He looked in the mirror and saw two red marks like large insect bites.

He walked back into the bedroom, saying, "So you really are a vampire," but she was gone. He barely made it to the bed on wobbly legs, somewhat pissed that Karolina hadn't revealed how she had managed to materialize on the faux balcony. Within sixty seconds of hitting the mattress, he was out cold.

THE DAWNING

S teve awoke late, naked, and on top of the covers. He felt like shit, and the light coming through the windows hurt his eyes, making his headache that much worse. He got up and closed the drapes. That was better, but he barely made it back to bed. *I'm sick, the flu or something*, he thought. It was Saturday, he was pretty sure, so he had a couple of days to recover before he had to work. He would get room service in an hour or so and some coffee. He had been looking forward to breakfast in the winter garden. Maybe tomorrow. His whole body felt so heavy. He dozed off again, waking every couple of hours, still feeling sick. Late in the afternoon he was still in bed, trying to remember what the hell happened last night.

The next day Veronica and her friends woke up early and had room service for breakfast in Veronica's room. Afterwards, they walked down to P. C. Hooftstraat, the high-end shopping street. After a couple of hours there, they went to Kalverstraat, the famous pedestrian shopping street, and shopped their way from one end to the other for six hours, before reaching Dam Square. There they spent another two hours in de Bijenkorf (the Beehive) department store. Finally, they ended up at the Green House coffee shop on the edge of the red-light district. They bought some weed for ten euros, and some German guys helped them roll a joint. They got high, fended off the advances of the German guys until they lost interest, and compared bags of loot from a day of shopping. More than half would go to charity in the next six months—maybe never worn.

ANOTHER NIGHT

That night, Veronica, Lauren, Sophia, and Carol had room service for dinner, then went to Club Paradiso near their hotel. An up and coming Canadian DJ was spinning house music and electronica that none of them had heard before. They danced with many somewhat attractive European men, and accepted gin martinis with Tanqueray only. Which somewhat annoyed the mostly continental crowd, but impressed a couple of overweight British guys. The more they drank, the better the guys looked.

Later in the evening, Carol met a Spanish guy who barely spoke English, but that didn't seem to matter. After they'd danced a few songs together, Veronica saw them off to the side making out. *At least Carol might get lucky*, she thought. About 12:30 a.m., Sophia said she was feeling sick, unable to hit that magic ratio between enough booze to make the room more attractive without having to pray to the porcelain god. Veronica tracked down Carol while Sophia waited near the door. Carol, just half a drink behind Sophia, said she was going to stay and fondled the Spanish guys bulge.

"This is Robert," Carol slurred. Or was it Roberto? Veronica could barely hear over the music.

Veronica looked for Lauren, but couldn't see her in the now frantic crescendo of the witching hour crowd. She headed toward the door, bored or not drunk enough. She wasn't sure which. She texted Lauren and started walking back to the hotel with Sophia. About halfway there, Sophia puked in an alley while Veronica held her blonde hair. When they got back to Veronica's room, Sophia got sick into the toilet for another forty-five minutes, gripping the cool porcelain with both hands and praying for the room to stop spinning. This time a tie held her hair back, provided unnoticed by Veronica. As always, the porcelain god had no use for her soul, and let the room spin despite the offering. She would spend the night in Veronica's room passed out, which was how a night out usually ended, unless one or the other of them went back to some guy's room or brought a guy to their room. It was the only reason they had separate rooms.

About 8:30 p.m., Steve started to feel better. He took a shower and got dressed. By 9:15 he was down on the street, figuring on just a little walk in the fresh air and a bite to eat. The night air, or something, energized him like cocaine back in the day in Marin County. At least for the first few times he tried it, before it started making him paranoid. *Never should have smoked it, lesson learned,* he thought. He wasn't that hungry either. Maybe he had a fever that was making him feel so weird. He cruised the red-light district, checking out the girls behind the windows of their rented rooms, all types of girls, and 10 to 15 percent actually worth fucking. It was high season, and every alley he walked down was packed. Three separate groups of thirty to fifty tourists on red-light district walking tours got in his way, speaking all different languages and, surprisingly, no English. He could imagine Americans loving this sort of thing, but it seemed to be mostly Europeans. He was also in more of a looking mood. After all, he was sick.

When Steve finally looked at the Rolex Submariner his father had given him when he graduated from high school, he was shocked to see it was 3:30 am. Had he really been walking around for six hours? *Better get back to the hotel and get some rest,* he thought.

As he walked back, he felt like he could hear people breathing in their bedrooms above the street. Maybe he really did have a fever, or was it an acid flashback? That elusive side effect they had learned about in middle school drug-education class that neither he nor his friends had ever experienced. Still, the city felt alive, with a dark Gothic energy emanating from the old buildings and the cobblestone streets, like this was its true time to shine. Or whatever the opposite of shining was.

The hotel lobby was empty, including the check-in counter, although as he walked past he thought he could hear a couple having sex behind the counter. Instead of continuing on to the stairs in the middle of the hotel, he took a quick look behind the counter. Nobody was there. Was the noise coming from a room behind the counter? He wondered. He really must have a fever.

Up in his room, Steve still wasn't tired yet. He opened the drapes and one of the windows out to the faux balcony. The joint he had partially smoked the night before was still on the round glass table, right where he had left it. He felt fully justified in taking ten hits now. It was like medicine for his flu, or whatever it was, and then he could sleep. He greedily smoked the whole thing down until it burned his fingers, and ran to the bathroom to run cold water on his stinging fingertips. Taking a quick look in the mirror, he thought he didn't look that bad for being sick. Or maybe it was the weed. He looked away quickly in case the weed made him look worse or maybe freakish in the next turn. He was stoned for sure, but not completely gone, and not that tired yet. He was surprised. *I thought I had smoked enough weed to put down an elephant.*

So he spent the next few hours hanging both feet out the window and gazing over Dam Square. Not much going on, except he occasional bike or two zooming by. Where were they going; home from partying, or to an early job? Despite the lack of people, he could still feel the nocturnal energy of the city, feeding off it somehow and experiencing a contented feeling of wellbeing.

Carol brought Roberto back to her room. It was close by, and from what she could tell from his broken English, he was sharing a room with friends. They were both fairly drunk, but she was not as drunk as she acted. She could beat Veronica at something, she thought. Roberto actually looked better in clothes than out of them, with a slight belly and soft look to his body, despite being only twenty-two. Carol did not have that problem. The less clothes she and her friends wore, the better they looked. She hoped Roberto appreciated her concession to international relations, or at least would someday. *Maybe he'll remember the hot American girl on his deathbed in seventy years or whatever,* she thought. After brief foreplay, it was over in a few thrusts. Like most women, Carol was used to this. She just wished she could tell the talkers from the real men. Maybe if she stopped drinking so much when she went out, she would make better choices. Maybe.

As the sky started to lighten to his right and behind the hotel, Steve was finally tired. He closed the window and drapes, took off his clothes, and climbed into bed, arms and legs heavy, like he was underwater.

SUNDAY

About 9:00 a.m., housekeeping woke Steve despite his do-not-disturb sign. "Sorry sorry," the woman apologized. She was overweight and not attractive, and could have been anywhere from her late twenties to fifty plus. *Why was the maid never hot like in the movies or a porno flick?* Steve thought. Then a memory flashed into his head, so startling that his mind told him to sit up, but his body was too lethargic. He must still be sick, he thought. But the image in his mind flashed again like a bolt of lightning, and wouldn't go away. *Karolina! Holy shit!*

Through the haze of his "flu," Steve remembered everything. Actually, it wasn't like he hadn't remembered all day. It just seemed like something that had happened Friday night, but had been obscured by the fog of his fever. Now, his brain suddenly connected the dots, the implications and, most importantly, the woman. He mustered his strength and pulled himself out of bed, stumbling toward the bathroom. He looked in the mirror, first one side of his neck and then the other; nothing, no marks, a fever dream, a nightmare, the weed, exhaustion? He sure felt tired now. *That's it I have Mononucleosis,* he thought as he fell back into bed. The beautiful Karolina's image swirled through his head as he fell quickly into a deep sleep.

Sunday morning, they quizzed Carol on all the details about Roberto. All talk, what she could understand, it turned out. Another day of shopping lay ahead. After all, a Southern girl just doesn't understand the phrase "all shopped out."

Steve fell in and out of sleep, sick as a dog all day Sunday. About 8:00 p.m., as the long summer gloaming was again upon the city, he started to feel better. He took a shower and got dressed. He still couldn't believe he'd stayed up all last night after all the weed he had smoked. He glanced at the glass table where his weed was sitting, and saw his phone. He hadn't looked at it since Friday night. A quick glance and he saw fourteen texts, eleven from Suzy. <Where RU>, etc. He quickly texted her back and agreed to meet for dinner at a trendy Mediterranean restaurant called Envy, a few blocks away, in about thirty minutes. Jim and Suzy had gotten in Saturday afternoon apparently.

At the restaurant, he saw that Suzy had light brown hair now, a change from the dark brown she'd had when he last saw her and the blonde when they had first met at school. Jim was the same: short brown hair, steely blue eyes, and the massive look, at least, of an ex-football star. At dinner, Suzy wanted to know where Steve had been Saturday. Had he met a woman?

"Actually I did," Steve replied, thinking of the stunning Karolina. "A Czech woman, really hot and smart." Why did he think she was smart, considering how little he really knew about her, he wondered?

"Where did you meet," Suzy asked. "A bar?"

"No, no, I met her in the hotel lobby, and we really hit it off right away." Why am I lying, Steve wondered, the real story was even better, but who would believe it? "Then I got sick and slept all day Saturday and today, but I was fine Saturday night, and I feel okay now."

He chatted with Jim and Suzy over dinner about new stuff and old, but he still wasn't hungry, just pushing his food around the plate. When was the last time he'd eaten? He wondered. At some point he started to focus on a vein on Suzy's neck. He could see her heartbeat, the blood literally flowing through the vein. As he stared, he became obsessed. He started fantasizing about fucking her brains out like back in the day, and then biting her neck like Karolina had bitten him.

Karolina, I have to see her again, but how? Hang out on my balcony all night?

Then he realized, as if he had been in denial since Saturday morning, I'm turning into a vampire, or what did she call it upir,

Karolina turned me, he realized. He had to meet her at the old church, or de Oude Kerk, as the Dutch called. He must have walked by it about twenty times last night going from one side of the canal to the other in the red-light district. It was supposedly the oldest building in Amsterdam, built in 1306, and Steve imagined a massive underground complex of stone-wall tunnels underneath the church, cool and dark during the day, and filled with sleeping vampires. He couldn't stop thinking about it. "You won't make it on your own," she had warned.

I have to get there. I have to meet up with Karolina!

Sunday night, Veronica, Lauren, Sophia, and Carol had a late dinner at one of the Argentinean steak places on the narrow street called Damstraat between Dam Square and the red-light district, after getting high at the Green House again. This time they had done very little shopping, having bought it the day before, and were thus unencumbered by shopping bags. As they sipped lattes after dinner, they tried to decide what to do next.

"I have an idea," Lauren said, smiling.

"What?" Carol asked.

"Let's go to a sex club."

"Oh no. I could never have sex in front of everybody with a stranger," Sophia said.

"It's not that kind of sex club. Other people have sex on stage, and sometimes they pull people out of the audience, I think. I read about it online."

"I don't know," Carol said, and they debated, leaning toward a no vote for a few minutes.

Finally Veronica looked up from her phone. "Let's do it, it sounds like fun," and so they all agreed. Of course, she had put the idea in Lauren's head that morning after getting an email from the company that ran the travel app she was blogging for.

DE OUDE KERK

Steve was getting desperate sitting with Jim and Suzy at the restaurant. He had to get to the old church, he had to see Karolina. He feigned sickness, not hard since he obviously had not touched his dinner. They said their good nights, and he headed back to his hotel. When he got there, he just kept going, walking straight to the old church. It felt like it took forever as he was so on edge and impatient, then he realized it had taken less than fifteen minutes. He didn't feel sick at all. On the contrary, he was energized, felt like he could have run the whole way, but didn't want to draw attention.

Standing by the old church in the middle of the red-light district, he thought what a high, his head was so clear, and he felt like he could fuck ten women. Maybe he should stop by one of the hookers. The windows were just across the square from the church. He looked over, but knew from experience these were not the good ones. *But there might be a hot girl on the other side of that building, down that skinny alley that started next to the original Bulldog coffee shop,* he thought. He could just take one lap and see what was available. No, I have to wait here; I have to wait for Karolina. Those girls are nothing compared to my Czech vampire girlfriend, he thought.

But wait where, by the front door, the back? She'd never said. She'd never said when, either, but it couldn't be all night. Was it near dawn? It couldn't be too close to dawn. It was 10:30 now. How long would he have to wait?

He tried calming himself by walking slowly around the old church. Wondering if he had imagined the whole thing, *there is no such thing as vampires; Karolina was just messing with me,* he thought. He walked around and around as it got later and later, trying to look casual.

Maybe he wouldn't be meeting her. Maybe it would be another

vampire. He started checking everyone out, wondering if each person looked like a vampire. But Karolina hadn't really looked like a vampire. *But she didn't not look like a vampire either,* he thought.

Surrounded on all sides by the unique baroque architecture of Amsterdam and standing outside an eight-hundred-year-old Gothic church, Steve could definitely imagine the city was full of vampires, but how could you really tell? He didn't feel his fangs. In fact, he never saw Karolina's fangs, but he was sure he'd felt them.

Veronica and her friends had to wait in line at the Casa Rossa, along with other people who actually seemed normal, not perverts, just tourists, and many of them groups of women like themselves. Inside, the theater was dark, but it seemed clean from what they could tell, with comfortable cloth theater seats with armrests and drink holders. The walls were painted vermilion, the stage a more feminine light pink. The first "act" was a hot black guy, oiled down with ripped muscles and a six-pack. He asked a girl to volunteer from the audience, and a drunk British girl with blonde hair was pushed onto the stage by her even drunker friends. The act was fairly tame, and although it seemed like it would get racy, he never pulled his cock out. After a short break, a good-looking couple came out and quickly got naked. Club music was blasting as the woman sucked the guy's cock, which was definitely larger than average. Then they started having sex on a round bed that slowly rotated like a giant turntable. Veronica and her friends were shocked, as the couple seemed to be having sex in time with the beat, switching positions in what looked like choreographed movements. They had never seen anything like this; it was shocking to see two people having sex right in front of them, just twenty-five feet away. Then it was over. Well, not exactly over, neither of them finished. They just stopped having sex. That was maybe the most shocking part of it; and after she got over her surprise, Veronica realized this was all just a show.

Steve was still waiting and walking around the old church, oscillating between being sure the whole vampire thing was all bullshit to being sure he was turning. It was well past midnight and the crowds had finally started to thin out, making it easier to fully inspect anybody walking by to see if they were a vampire. He started trying to make eye contact, still not sure who would meet him. Then he saw four women on the far side of the bridge across the canal. They were coming from the other half of the red-light district where the sex clubs where. As they walked toward him, Steve noticed one of them appeared to have Karolina's shoulder-length dark brown hair. He walked casually toward the bridge to meet them as they crossed over. When they got close, Karolina hair girl turned her head. It wasn't her.

He was still looking straight at her. Their eyes met, so he smiled and said, "Hi."

"Hi," she said with a Southern drawl as the women walked by. She wasn't Karolina, but she was gorgeous.

"That guy was kind of cute," Lauren teased Veronica. "Was he British or American? I couldn't tell."

A TURN FOR THE WORSE?

Another three hours went by and still nothing. *Should I go back to the hotel?* Steve wondered. Was this just a waste of time? Fuck it, he finally thought. This is bullshit.

He walked briskly back to the hotel, through the lobby, up the main staircase, and into his room. What now? He wasn't tired, so he decided to hang out on the faux deck again. Maybe smoke some weed. He was still debating as he watched over Dam Square, just after 4:00 a.m. "You won't make it on your own," Karolina had said. He thought about how bad he had felt during the last two days, and how good he felt at night, and especially now. He looked down on the street and Dam Square.

"I feel so energized I could easily climb up the front of the hotel if I wanted to," he said out loud.

Steve was back to the old church ten minutes later, but he didn't see anybody. He started taking a counterclockwise lap around the building. He had been wondering if there was some sort of entrance into the secret undercroft, or would he have to go inside the church to go down below into the tunnels? He came back around the church, opposite the prostitute windows. He was starting to get desperate.

I should have been waiting here Saturday night. Now maybe it's too late. Should I try to drink somebody's blood?

He was moving into survival mode. He didn't feel like he had fangs, though. Maybe he should go to a doctor? But could this be cured?

Over by the bridge where he had seen "Karolina hair" girl and her friends, there was a guy, early to mid-twenties, on a mobile phone. Steve wandered in his direction, expectations low. Speaking German, the brown-haired man, about five feet eleven with a trim athletic build walked toward Steve. *Don't be some gay guy*, he thought as he noticed the man's blue jeans, black button-up shirt, and pointy black shoes. Steve tried to act casual as the guy finished his call with, "*Auf wiedersehen*," and then pulled out a cigarette.

"Do you have a light," he asked Steve in English tinged with an old-world accent. Steve fished through his pockets, not sure if he had brought his weed lighter. "Never mind," the man said. "I don't really smoke. I just use that as a pickup line sometimes."

Steve tensed. Growing up in the bay area, he was long used to dealing with gay guys who suffered from signal processing issues.

"To pick up women," the man added. "I'm not gay, if that's what you were thinking." He reached out to shake Steve's hand. "I'm Valentin."

LADY KATE

Kate Wydville's flight from Barcelona was about forty-five minutes late when it arrived at Amsterdam Schipol at almost 11:00 p.m. Annoying, but she had traveled so much, she was used to it. She just had one more day left of work, Monday, before her holiday officially began, and she would meet up with her mates from London. All of them from good families, Oxford or Cambridge graduates going back generations. She was the only one still single by choice, due to her career according to her and being too picky according to her friends. An international barrister specializing in corporate mergers and acquisitions law, she was constantly traveling in support of deals that could take more than a year before they closed.

A company-supplied Mercedes whisked Kate to the Hotel Grand Krasnapolsky. Not as nice as her father's Bentley, but it would do. Being senior partner of a big London law firm paid her father well, but with his inheritance, he could have done nothing for a generation. And she too.

She looked out the window as the outskirts of the city passed by, thinking that she had a good life. It was hard to tell sometimes, hard to stop and smell the roses when you were "Super Kate, star lawyer," and everybody wanted a piece of you. Hell, she couldn't even slow down and smell the roses as they flew by. The blonde-haired blue-eyed Kate was by far the smartest and prettiest of her friends, and that was saying a lot. She was part of the next generation of London high society. Range Rovers, hunting dogs, good schools, and generations of family portraits on the walls of the country home. Sienna Miller would play her if there were ever a movie about her life, but she was far too reserved to do anything that would make her that famous. A few times a year she cut loose when she hooked up with her old friends, but mostly it was hard work and keeping up appearances.

As Kate unpacked in her deluxe room at the Krasnapolsky, she thought about the pressure in her life—family, work, and friends married with kids who wanted to live vicariously through her. It was all too much sometimes. *Thank God for a good single malt, highlands preferred*, she thought. Well, that would come tomorrow night, along with a transfer to a suite at the Waldorf Astoria. But tonight was late, and tomorrow work was early.

THE TOWER

"I'm parked right over here," Valentin said to Steve as he started walking toward the one-way street with three Bulldog coffee shops on the west side of the Oudezijds Voorburgwal canal. Steve was confused. What about the secret tunnels under the old church? Valentin pulled out his key, and the lights of a midnight blue Porsche 911 Carrera S blinked silently as the car unlocked. Steve looked at Valentin, confused.

"You're turning," Valentin said. "Let's get indoors before forenoon. I know you have many questions, and I can give you a lot of answers in time," he went on as he started up the Porsche and pulled out of his parking spot, more rare than a supermodel on the streets of Amsterdam centrum. "It's best that I keep things simple for now. Survival, feeding, and the two main covenants."

The covenants. That again, Steve thought. "Karolina mentioned the covenants, something about the elders. By the way, I can't wait to see her again."

"Ha ha. You and every guy she's ever fucked, except most can't remember in the morning. You won't be seeing her anytime soon. It's just you and me while I show you the ropes. For now, you're my apprentice." Valentin drove briskly toward their unknown destination, shifting often to keep the flat-six engine at around 3,000 RPM.

"First of the two covenants, only drink enough blood to survive, never kill. If you do, there will be a counsel of three elders to determine your punishment, if any. If you kill twice in a century you will be given true death, nonnegotiable. You will be tracked down and killed, end of story."

"Once a century. Vampires can't die, you live forever right?" Steve asked.

"Being a vampire is not about living for eternity, or being invincible. It's about more opportunities to survive, mitigated sometimes by more threats," Valentin replied. "The upir gene— Karolina told you about the upir gene, right?— combined with the virus gives you strength, accelerated healing powers, and greatly decelerated aging, but it doesn't make you immortal."

"The second covenant is that it has to be consensual. No rape, no forced blood sucking, you have to be invited in. We were slaughtered in the old times, and we slaughtered in kind, never realizing we could survive without killing. It was simply thirst and slake for most, but when the vampire hysteria hit its peak in the early eighteenth century, a few started to realize something had to be done. In 1733, the covenant was established, and that began the great war between the vampires of old and the new breed of forward thinkers. The combination of vampires killing one another and mortals killing vampires led to a huge drop in the European vampire population. Some fled to America, but most moved west, here to Amsterdam and also London. In the end, around thirty thousand European vampires were reduced to under one thousand in just twenty-five years. Every day we live with the risk of being discovered by some self-righteous group, hunted down and slaughtered as of old. But here, here in Mokum, I feel safe. At least today."

As he finished speaking, Valentin maneuvered his car down an alley and stopped at a closed roll-up door. He tapped a code into a keypad, and a few seconds later the door started to open. Valentin pulled the Porsche into a warehouse space turned into a parking garage. He parked among the assortment of Porsches; BMWs, including a few 2002 tii; older Mercedes SLs, and even a 1955 Mercedes 300 SL gullwing. Not a single car was less than five years old. As Steve got out, he noticed a silver '58 Porsche 356 Speedster convertible. *There's some money here*, he thought.

Valentin walked over to a dark wooden door that looked like it belonged to a mansion. "Does that lead to the tunnels?" Steve asked.

"Tunnels? There are no tunnels in Mokum. We are below sea level. If you dig down, you hit water."

"Mokum, what's Mokum?" Steve asked.

"It's an old name for the city, like *zufluchtsort*. I mean haven. Haven from the hordes who would kill us. When I was turned, the covenant had only recently been created. It was a hard time. It was 1769, and I was at a party for my cousin Maria Antonia, at Schloss

Schönbrunn in Wien. My cousin and I were close. I went out to the garden to meet her, but instead I met a woman I had never seen before, beautiful with long blonde hair and a perfect body, definitely my type. I just couldn't resist. Her name was Carina. I didn't really believe the tale she told until it was too late, and I never saw her again after that night. After hiding out and barely surviving in Wien for a year, I left Österreich and followed my cousin to Paris to see her wed, the Dauphin of France, in 1770. I don't know what I was thinking. I couldn't go out during the day, but I saw her one night just before the wedding and said good-bye. I was chased all over Paris by the hordes, and had to flee. Eventually I came here, to Mokum. That was the first time I felt safe since my father tried to kill me in Wien when he realized what I had become. Little did I know that a few years later, the hordes would turn their wrath on my sweet cousin. Our best defense now is letting people believe we don't exist."

"You're from Austria?" Steve asked, understanding just enough German to put Valentin's story together.

"Another time, another place, yes," Valentin said.

"So, if vampires go out during the day do we die, or catch on fire?"

"No, that's just a myth. But at night we are stronger than mortals, and during the day we are weaker, much weaker. It's when we are most vulnerable. That's why we need to sleep in secure nests during the day. I can dispel all the other myths you may have heard as well. We can look at a cross, or anything for that matter; we have a reflection in mirrors; we can't pass through keyholes, although I'm not sure there are very many of that type of keyholes left anyway; garlic has no effect on us; we can't fly like bats; and although we're much quicker than mortals, we can't move so fast that they can't see us. On the other hand, a stake through the heart can kill us in many cases, but the surest way to kill a vampire is decapitation."

"What about silver, can it burn our skin?" Steve asked.

"Karolina," Valentin responded.

"What?" Steve asked, confused.

"She started that rumor in the sixteenth century, or so she claims. Hey, it's not a bad thing to trick mortals into throwing silver at you, although I would have gone with gold," Valentin joked. "The truth is, vampires probably started all of those myths just to throw the mortals off. Also, and you probably figured this out already, we don't need to eat food like mortals, just their blood."

"By 'them,'" said a man as he walked up to them, "he means the herds of blood cattle out there."

After unlocking the door, Valentin led Steve into a lush dark grotto. It was like the lounge of some secret private club for old-money types, low light and the high life, with a spiral staircase in the center of the room. The furniture was a mix of styles in rich leather and ornate upholstery, all old but in excellent repair. On the wall, Steve was sure he was looking at a series of van Gogh paintings he had never seen before in any book or museum. His mom was a big contributor at the SFMOMA and De Young museums, and he knew or could at least recognize most well-known paintings or series of paintings from the last 150 years plus, whether it hung in Paris or a private collection. These paintings looked to be from van Gogh's asylum phase, but darker. In one, a dark-haired woman stood in front of a house in the typical baroque architecture of Amsterdam. She looked a lot like Karolina, but maybe he was just projecting. The other thing Steve noticed was that there were no windows. The structure was really a building within a building.

"Welcome home," Valentin said. "We call this the tower. This is where we sleep during the day. Everybody should be getting here in the next few minutes. Tomorrow night we will start with your first lessons in survival. You'll sleep up here."

Valentin led him up to the fifth floor, the top level, of the building. Each floor had a number of sleeping chambers connected by hallways and nothing else, like some sort of hive. Steve could hear cars pulling in downstairs, including the distinct exhaust note of a twelve-cylinder Ferrari.

Well, at least the vampires have money, he thought. *Or do they just steal everything?* His chamber was the farthest from the front door downstairs—due to his lack of seniority, he assumed—and had a queen-size bed, no coffin, and a bathroom with a shower. Steve was exhausted, and fell asleep quickly.

When Steve awoke, he wasn't sure what time it was. A quick glance at his Rolex on the side table told him it was 8:15 p.m. He wondered how his body knew the sun was going down when there were no windows. He took a quick shower and went downstairs. The place was full of people, vampires, hanging out and chatting, but nobody really looked up at him. Right away Steve noticed that about 70 percent of the vampires in the lounge were female. He looked around for Karolina or Valentin, but couldn't see either one. As he kept looking, a young guy about nineteen walked up to him.

"I am Otakar," he said in a faded eastern-European accent. "We need to go over some logistics."

"Sure," Steve responded.

"First, what hotel are you staying in and for how many more nights?"

"The Krasnapolsky, and I'm booked through Friday night. I'm supposed to fly back to San Francisco Saturday morning."

"Good. Bring your stuff over here before morning, in case your work misses you and calls the hotel." Otakar was about five foot eight and muscular, with curly brown hair, and wore a black T-shirt and jeans. He really looked young to Steve, and he thought he must be the intern assigned to do orientation for the newly turned vampires. "Next, what job did you have before?"

"I was a network engineer for a financial institution," Steve said.

Otakar nodded. "We need somebody like you. The last two computer engineers got themselves killed. We could really use you, if you survive the first week that is."

Well, that was ominous, Steve thought. The questioning went on for about twenty minutes, ranging from where he lived and grew up to sexual orientation, since Otakar had not heard it was his old friend Karolina who had turned him yet.

Eventually Valentin walked up. "Are you ready for your first lesson?"

"Sure, where are we going?" Steve asked.

"Out to find a woman for me to feed on," Valentin said.

"What about me?"

"All in good time. You will still survive a few more days," Valentin said. He and Otakar exchanged glances and laughed.

As they walked out the heavy oaken door with a group of other people, Steve asked, "What did Otakar mean when he said if I survive?"

"Don't worry about that, just watch and learn. I'm the best teacher you could possibly have, ask anyone," Valentin said.

A woman walking out with them piped up, "He's the best at what he does, but probably not a good teacher. Just make sure you do as he does, not as he says," she said, and laughed.

They walked past all the cars in the warehouse, straight out onto the street and the warm summer night.

"We don't need a car," Valentin said. "The more women we see, the better my chances."

THE FRAY

Veronica, Sophia, Carol, and Lauren were at the Hard Rock Café near their hotel, drinking and preening, although not successfully. It was about ten o'clock, and so far the night had been mildly entertaining. How they expected to meet any intriguing European guys in a bar frequented by Americans was a mystery. The crowd was composed of mostly young American men afraid to be away from home and looking for something familiar, and rowdy Brits. They wondered how the British had somehow become more obnoxious than Americans. The British guys were all sloppy drunk, singing football songs, and seemingly oblivious to the attractive American girls. Some of them weren't half bad looking, so the women decided they might do in a pinch.

Steve and Valentin got to the Hard Rock an hour later. "It's generally easy pickings about now," Valentin said. "The key is to strike between about 9:30 p.m. and 1:30 a.m. After that your odds go way down as the crowds thin, or just pass out drunk. You will only need to feed every seven to ten nights, so you don't have to panic if you strike out one night."

"How does it work? I mean, when you drink blood. I don't have fangs?" Steve asked.

"I'm sure Karolina gave you most of the details. You'll grow fangs in the next few days. If you don't, you probably won't survive, but don't worry. That's extremely rare. You won't know you have them until the moment, if you know what I mean. Now, let's scope out the room for likely candidates. This is just picking up women, but with a little help."

"What do you mean, 'a little help'?" Steve asked.

"Any good vampire should be able to sorcerize their intended target."

"Sorcerize? What the fuck is that?" he asked, now getting nervous. What if he couldn't grow fangs? What if he couldn't "sorcerize," whatever that was?

"Sorcerizing is what Karolina did to you. You're still thinking about her, right? That's just not natural. I can make a woman think I'm the best thing that's ever happened in her life, and the great thing is, she won't remember any of it in the morning." Valentin started explaining. "There's something about vampire physiology that sort of hypnotizes mortals. They become almost mesmerized by us, turning into our biological puppets. I've heard cats can do the same thing with their prey."

"You mean we can turn mortals into our personal thrall?" Steve asked.

"It's more subtle than that. They won't jump off a bridge at our command, although there are some vampires that could turn any mortal—or any vampire, for that matter—into their thrall if they were so inclined, but that has nothing to do with them being vampires."

Across the room, Steve saw "Karolina hair" girl and her friends. He was sure it was her. "Over there, those four girls. I saw them the other night."

"Are they American?" Valentin asked.

"Southern girls, I think."

"That's exactly what we're looking for. Now, when we get over there, just watch what I do. Don't try to pick another one up tonight. You're not ready."

They threaded through the crowd, at peak capacity and frenzy at this hour, tourists on holiday trying to forget their real lives, perfect fodder for hungry vampires.

When they got over to the women, "Karolina hair" girl was gone, so Valentin walked right up to the prettiest woman left, the blonde-haired blue-eyed Lauren.

"Hi, I'm Valentin," was delivered in a perfect moneyed accent, but with a hint of being more than a little dangerous.

"I'm Lauren," she said in her southern drawl as she looked into Valentin's piercing green eyes. She held out her hand on a limp wrist for Valentin to kiss, which he obliged like the perfect European gentleman he was.

Watching, Steve realized this wasn't all an act for Valentin. He was the real deal. His limited German was coming back to him,

"Schloss" that means castle or palace or something I'll need to look it up later when I get the charger back for my phone. *If he was going to parties at palaces and castles he must have been some sort of old European aristocracy before he was turned,* Steve thought.

"This is my American friend Steve," Valentin said, and Carol went right on the attack when she saw the suave Valentin was already in the grips of Lauren. A guy like Valentin was the reason Lauren came to Europe.

"What state are you from?" Carol asked.

"California."

"Oh," Carol and Sophia exclaimed in unison. Valentin gave Steve a quick look as if to say, "You're in, but remember, not tonight."

Within a few minutes, Valentin whispered, "de Oude Kerk, two-thirty," to Steve as Lauren told her friends she and Valentin were going for a "walk." *That was quick,* Steve thought. He chatted with the other women for a few minutes. Carol nervously asked Sophia where Veronica had gone, afraid of the competition if Veronica returned too soon.

"She had to make some calls back home," Sophia answered.

Veronica, Steve thought. *That must be "Karolina hair" girl's name.* Perfect.

"I've never been to the Amsterdam Hard Rock before," he said, "and I haven't been to the one in San Francisco since it moved to Pier 39 years ago." He was at that point where he had to make a move, but figured he would heed Valentin's advice. He excused himself to the bathroom and slipped out of the bar.

When Veronica got back to her friends, Lauren still hadn't returned.

"She left with a hot European guy," Carol told Veronica. "He was like some sort of count or something I think."

"Yeah, you missed out," Sophia said. "But his friend from California is coming back in a minute."

THE BITCHING HOUR

S teve wandered the streets of Amsterdam with a new perspective, like he was a predator one rung up on the food chain from the people that passed by. He felt quicker and stronger than any of them as the enzyme, a byproduct of the upir virus, coursed through his veins. He was excited and nervous about his first time. It didn't feel like before the first time he'd had sex. It felt more like he was going to be born, born as a vampire. He knew there was risk, no fangs, he needed to feed in the next few days, and he wasn't sure exactly when as nobody was being completely honest when it came to that. Karolina had said it took about a week before the virus churned through all your own blood. He was pissed at that condescending punk Otakar. "If you survive the first week that is," he had said.

"Fuck you," Steve said out loud.

He thought he would swing by the hotel so he could recover his clothes, laptop, and phone chargers. Fortunately, he had remembered to bring his card key with him so he could get into the room. He cruised through the lobby and went up the main staircase. Really seeing the old wooden carvings of figures between the railing and the stairs for the first time, looking like something out of the Middle Ages, he felt akin to them now, as if he too was part of something ancient.

Steve turned the corner and looked down the hall. The door to his room was open. Was it housekeeping? He'd thwarted their efforts the last few days; maybe they were just making up for lost time.

He walked toward his room and heard a man say, "Call the bank and let them know there's no sign of him, but his luggage is still here." He walked by casually, then made a U-turn at the end of the hall and quickly got out of the hotel.

That was fast, he thought, but no surprise. He hadn't showed up at the partner bank that Monday, and it made the company look bad. There wasn't much room to screw up at SKF. He had really wanted to grab the charger for his iPhone so he could listen to some music. He still had a work phone, turned off, and an HTC One with a European SIM card the bank didn't know about that still had a little juice. He was afraid even to turn it on and browse the Internet, as the battery was down so far.

He walked out of the hotel and turned left, then left again, down the alley that led back to the red-light district. A buzzing crowd of people hung out drinking in front of Wynand Fockink as he walked by. He figured he would cruise the prostitute windows to kill time. He walked down past the first Bulldog coffee shop, then at the second he had to maneuver around a group of about twenty-five rowdy Brits singing football songs and looking for trouble. Steve avoided looking anyone in the eye. He was sure, he could beat any one of them now with his newfound strength and agility, but he didn't want to draw any attention. One guy called after him, but didn't follow.

When he got to the third Bulldog, Steve turned left down the skinny alley between two buildings, only wide enough for one person. It widened after a few feet, and then opened up a bit more before the first window. There is something so ancient about this alley as if it's the birthplace of the oldest profession, Steve thought. He knew that wasn't true, but girls had been selling their services here for hundreds of years. The girls with a customer had their curtains drawn; the others generally had their doors open and tried to get men to come in. "Fifty euro suck and fuck," was the usual line. Some stayed inside, door closed but tapping a coin on the glass to get your attention, especially if Steve had already walked by. The girls were from all over Europe, all over the world, for that matter. They came in all shapes and sizes, but for the most part they were decent looking. A few would actually be considered hot by any standard. He started to wonder if prostitutes were an option if he couldn't sorcerize a woman in order to feed.

He went across to the wider alley. The few windows on the left all had the curtains drawn. A room on the right had several more windows. He had fucked a Polish girl in one of those rooms, which were just big enough for a bed, a sink, and little more, about two months ago, when he started his European project for SKF. He turned the corner to make a counterclockwise loop and saw an interesting blonde, one foot out the door and a cigarette in her hand.

"Suck and fuck fifty euro," she said as he approached. He walked up to her to get a better look and maybe flirt. She backed away into the room. "I know what you are, stay away from me," she said in a thick eastern European accent, and quickly closed the door and curtains.

Steve was shocked. Did she actually know he was a vampire? Could all the prostitutes tell? He doubted that and continued to walk around, heading to the other side of the canal, over the bridge where he first saw "Karolina hair" girl, Veronica. He passed more windows until he saw a decent-looking brunette and walked over for a closer look. She was super flirty, flashing her perfect medium small breasts and trying to get him to come inside.

"It's nice in here," she said, playing on the phrase to imply both the room and her pussy. She grabbed his hand and tried to pull him in. "Be my temporary boyfriend."

"Maybe later," Steve said, thinking that at least they couldn't all tell he was a vampire. A few more similar encounters led him to believe the first woman was a fluke. Maybe she had been high on mushrooms and just hallucinating. Or maybe when she said, "I know what you are," it just meant she hated Americans.

He was getting increasingly curious, and decided to go by the blonde girl's room again. He crossed the bridge once more and headed down the skinny alley. When he walked into the big room, the blonde and a brunette were talking in a foreign language. He was fairly sure he heard the word "upir," so he quickly turned around and left.

It was getting close to 2:30, so he looped by more windows and behind some buildings as he headed over to the old church to wait for Valentin. He checked his watch and it was exactly 2:30, but there was no sign of him. Then he saw the silver '58' Porsche 356 Speedster, its top down, slowly driving down the one way street, which was much less crowded with people at this hour. He quickly recognized Valentin and walked over.

"Wow, this is your car too?" he asked.

"I went back to Österreich in 1963 and bought this off a guy with gambling debts. I can't really park it on the street because it's a Cabriolet, but I like to drive it around in the summer after I've fed."

"Valentin, I was walking around the red-light district, and this woman, I think she knew I was a vampire. She had an eastern-European accent."

"Be careful. Her uncle or whatever is probably a vampire hunter. I'm not kidding. Stay away from here for a few weeks. She will likely be gone by then. Best-case scenario, she had some contact with vampires back home in Romania or wherever the fuck she's from, or she could just be bait set by her uncle."

"I doubt she was bait. She seemed afraid of me and backed away."

"Well, either way, she likely will tell someone who could be trouble."

"Oh, the other thing," Steve said. "I went by the hotel. My bank already called them since I didn't show up today. Or is it yesterday now?"

"That's not good. You should swing by after midnight tomorrow and try to get your stuff," Valentin said.

For the next few hours, they cruised around in the vintage Porsche, seeing and being seen. About 4:30, they got back to the tower and walked in, past Otakar on the lounge floor.

"Still alive, I see," he said sarcastically. They sat on the other side of the lounge, which was about three thousand square feet of open space with the spiral staircase in the middle.

"I don't like that guy," Steve confided to Valentin. "He's such a punk."

"Remember, it's not a vampire's age when they were turned that matters. It's their real age. He's actually a good guy once you get to know him, if a little too pragmatic at times," Valentin said.

"He still seems like a little bitch to me," Steve said cockily.

TUESDAY NIGHT PARTY NIGHT

The next evening, Steve came downstairs and tracked Valentin down. He seemed distracted. "I need to get some work done tonight. I fed last night, so I'm good. I'll take you out tomorrow night for some more mentoring."

"Work?" Steve said. "You have a job?"

"Some of us have jobs of one sort or another. At a minimum, we manage our investments. It's a lot easier when time is on your side. And after a century or two, you start to see the same cycles repeating over and over, and know what to do. Boom or bust, war and peace, I've seen it all. It's about parsing the available data and making decisions. No day trading. It's more, when to be in what type of investment. The Internet just makes it that much easier. You should swing by the hotel later, but don't try to feed yet. You're not ready."

"When will I be ready?" Steve asked.

"You'll know. It won't be any mystery."

"Or you'll just lie down and die like a little bitch," Otakar said as he walked by.

That punk really doesn't like me, Steve thought. Well, the feeling was mutual.

☥

Kate Wydville and her friends took an Uber from Amsterdam's Waldorf Astoria down to the red light district. They were Bulldog bound, the de facto destination for most Brits looking to party hard in Amsterdam. They got a table across from the middle Bulldog coffee shop on the one-way street called Oudezijds Voorburgwal right on the canal, and started drinking and smoking.

"So how's work, 'Super Kate'?" Chelsea asked.

"You know, the same long hours and secrets I can't tell you now, that will bore you to tears in six months when I can," Kate said.

She and Chelsea had been thick as thieves growing up together in town and country, and finally all the way to Cambridge. Chelsea had married soon after school, her huge wedding preceded by a bachelorette party off the coast of Spain on her father's yacht, to the promising son of a member of the House of Lords by peerage. Promising led to disappointing by the measure of most friends and family. He was not interested in politics, in making a living, in making a difference in any way, or in Chelsea after their second child was born. He was drunk by noon most days, hanging out at the country club drinking with his similarly minded buddies, and on occasion playing some golf. Of course, he didn't really need to make a living as long as he didn't do something stupid like divorce Chelsea and lose his inheritance. Chelsea looked good for having had two kids, and Kate was often prodding her to take a lover, but sex was not Chelsea's priority.

"We need to find a guy for Kate," Hedley said.

"Maybe an Italian guy or an American, but definitely not a Brit," Chelsea added, laughing.

They spent the rest of the evening hunting for a suitable prospect for Kate. Kate, for her part, saw more eligible men at work than they saw that entire evening, but she knew the other women needed a distraction. She wasn't against meeting a sexy guy; she was just being pragmatic. Four days prior she had sat in a conference room with a man that looked like a younger, hotter Antonio Banderas, smoldering in his Armani and confidence.

Veronica was still pissed at Lauren for not giving her more details about the suave European guy she had hooked up with the night before. The truth was though, she couldn't remember his name until Carol said it. Lauren figured she must have been really wasted, which wasn't like her. Maybe it would come back to her later, but she had been sick all morning, skipping shopping with the girls, which was a big deal. She couldn't even remember what the man looked like, despite Carol's vivid descriptions. The other women had hung out at the Hard Rock looking for "Count Valentin" and Steve, the guy from California. Veronica was interested in Steve. She had met a guy in California when she was interviewing and auditioning in LA. His name was Michael, and he had definitely known how to please a woman. She got wet just thinking about him. Steve had never come back from the bathroom last night, but he had said he hung out at the Green House coffee shop in the red-light district. Their destination determined, the women proceeded out into the night.

After smoking some weed and not seeing either the "count" or Steve, they decided to check out the girls working in the red-light district. They crossed over the canal and walked past the first Bulldog, and then the second. The coffee shop had a patio with tables encircled by a clear Plexiglas railing overlooking the canal. Veronica looked over and saw a group of women, the nucleus of which was a stunning blonde. One look and Veronica hated her.

When they got to the third and original Bulldog, they saw the skinny alley they had read about online. It looked a little scary, but just then a group of about thirty men and women on a walking tour came through. If the group felt safe, it must be okay. They walked down the alley between bare walls covered with sporadic graffiti. Then the alley opened up to reveal women behind glass, all the way down on both sides.

"Look at these skank girls," Lauren said condescendingly.

They worked their way along the alley, until Veronica saw a brunette with a pretty face and tight body telling an average-looking man in his twenties, "Fifty euro suck and fuck."

Holy fuck, Veronica thought. The prostitute wasn't as beautiful as Veronica, but she was pretty hot. Veronica's world was turned upside down with this realization. She had expected the girls to be ugly, or at least not hot. This was something she had never really considered, that a guy could pay a small amount of money to fuck a hot girl. She had imagined a girl who looked as good as she did would cost ten thousand dollars.

Steve hung out for a few hours after waking up, watching people in the tower lounge working on their laptops, chatting, or listening to music. At the far end of the lounge, about ten vampires were watching a movie on one of the five flat-screen televisions. Finally, a little after midnight, Steve headed over to the hotel. He passed the impressive car collection in the warehouse parking area on his way out, access codes memorized.

He walked toward Dam Square, ever aware of potential women to feed on. He didn't feel weak, like he needed to feed. On the contrary, he was energized, especially out in the night air.

He walked past Madame Tussauds wax museum, and crossed the street to Dam Square. As he walked toward the phallic war memorial across Warmoesstraat from his hotel, he heard someone call his name. It was Suzy.

"What are you doing out at this hour? Where's Jim?" he asked.

"We got into a little fight, I'm just out for a walk. What are you up to?" Suzy asked.

"I'm headed back to my room right now. Do you want to get high? My room is right over there." He pointed to one of the faux balconies on the front of the Hotel Krasnapolsky.

She grinned. "So, you're going to get me stoned and try to take advantage of me, are you?" she teased.

"Oh, no, I would never do that," Steve said with fake sarcasm, since he really wasn't interested under the circumstances.

He led Suzy through the lobby and up the stairs. He was nervous that the card key had been changed, or that somebody would be waiting for him, but the hall was quiet. His key worked fine, and upon entering the room he saw all of his stuff was still there untouched, or at least with the appearance of being so. The room was a little warm as usual in the summer, so he turned on the AC.

After opening the drapes to show off the view and one of the windows out to the faux balcony, he checked the glass table. His bag of weed was still there. He rolled up a skinny joint from the last of his bag and ushered Suzy over to the open window. They smoked, talked, and people watched, careful to avoid the topic of Jim and her marriage.

After a few hits of the Afghan Kush, Suzy was high as a kite. Steve had been a little more conservative, not wanting to fall into a weed coma with a guest in his room. Suzy started to get flirty, moving over to the bed. Steve had never noticed how emotionally vulnerable Suzy was until now, or more likely had chosen to ignore it. He remembered he and his friends back in school had called emotionally needy girls *wounded minnows*, easy prey. Out of respect for Jim and Suzy, of course, he didn't make a move. That and the fact that he was turning into a vampire, something he kept forgetting. He didn't want to kill Suzy, he didn't love her, but he didn't want to kill anyone. Could he fuck her without feeding? he wondered. She had been a fun girlfriend, but neither one had thought of the other as "the one," which was probably why they were still friends.

Steve joined her on the bed, and he knew from their past as a couple that he was in for sure if he wanted to be. He still kept his distance as they talked, but soon he started to notice the vein on her neck, pulsing with blood. It looked tempting again, just as it had the other night at the restaurant.

He tried not to obsess, and kept steering the conversation away from not-so-subtle comments like "We used to have a lot of fun, didn't we?"

Suddenly Suzy exclaimed, "We were meant to be together," and pulled up her blouse to reveal she was using the birth control patch.

Holy shit, Steve thought. Was he sorcerizing her without even trying? Suzy would never say something like that. Maybe it was the weed talking.

What if he could just fuck her without feeding? He wondered again. He was really starting to want her now; and truth be told, he was still obsessed with that rhythmic pulse in her neck. He thought his first time should be with a stranger, but this would certainly be consensual, so he didn't think he was breaking any covenants. That was unless he killed her. He was terrified of that. If he fucked her and fed now, he would likely leave a blood-drained corpse in his room. That would bring the authorities and the vampire hunters—whoever they were—after him, not to mention the elders. He imagined the three white-bearded old men, infinitely wise and sitting in judgment of his fate. Not something he was looking forward to. Better to get rid of Suzy now before things take a turn for the worse, he thought.

Decision made, Steve turned to Suzy, ready to deliver the "I'm tired, work in the morning, blah blah blah," bullshit speech, but her lips were on his before he could make a sound. He was gone. He had to have her now, the elders be damned. They were both on fire, ripping each other's clothes off, rolling on the bed, and Steve was inside her within two minutes.

They knew each other well, and Steve fucked her slowly, enjoying the familiar closeness that they both felt. After a few minutes, though, Suzy gently dug her fingers into his ass cheeks, the unmistakable sign that she wanted him to fuck her brains out. She was in a frenzy. It seemed like she was going to come faster than ever, but it had been years since they broke up. *Maybe she was just getting better with age*, Steve thought. He knew her so well and was ready to time his orgasm with hers. Then they were both coming, and in that moment Steve felt his fangs extend. His head snapped down, and his mouth was suddenly on her neck filling with blood, delicious blood, warm with hints of salt and copper. All in a single reflex movement that shocked him more than it did Suzy. She gave a little cry, but was so high she probably thought he was just playing. *Holy shit*, Steve thought again, afraid of his animal like instinct to drink blood, so fast and uncontrollable.

After a few seconds, he reluctantly pulled his mouth off her neck, panting. Had he killed her? How long was he drinking her blood? Thoughts raced through his head, just as the blood reached his stomach and gave him a rush like the best energy drink in the world. He could sneak Suzy's body out of the hotel later, he thought. Maybe Valentin would help him. For now he luxuriated in the rush of energy from drinking her blood, and the familiar feeling of being inside her. Then he remembered she was dead. Repulsed at the idea of having sex with a corpse, he rolled quickly off her.

"I really needed that," Suzy said, still very much alive.

"Me too," Steve said with so much more meaning.

He was a vampire. He knew it for sure now, and his life would never be the same.

He surreptitiously checked out Suzy's neck. Two holes and a little blood dripping down, but the bleeding had stopped. He wiped the blood off his lips, but his fangs were still extended so he kept his mouth closed. He hoped Suzy wouldn't notice her neck. Hoped it would heal quickly as his had. The rushes he was getting now from drinking her blood were better than any drug he had ever sampled in his youth, suffusing him with energy but without being jittery. His head was not swirling either. In fact, his thoughts had never been clearer.

They chatted for a while enjoying the post-coital peace and sense of wellbeing, although Steve's sense of wellbeing was in turbo mode. He was a vampire, and he wasn't going to "lay down and die." *Fuck you, Otakar*, he thought.

Eventually Suzy got up to pee. Steve thought nothing of it. She left the door open, still comfortable from days past. Then Steve panicked. What if she noticed her neck? Maybe she wouldn't look in the mirror. But if Steve knew one thing about women it was that she was going to look in the mirror. *Maybe her hair will cover up the bite marks*, he thought.

"What the fuck, Steve? What did you do to my neck?" Suzy

stormed out of the bathroom and confronted him. "Did you bite me? I thought I felt something. What the fuck is wrong with you?"

When he was finally able to get a word in, Steve decided to tell her the truth, hopeful she wouldn't remember in the morning. He knew he was supposed to explain the process before feeding, but things had happened too quickly. Still, had he broken a covenant? He didn't think so, but what would the elders think? It had to be consensual, and it had been. The question was, would it have been if she had known he was a vampire? Steve did not want to face the old judging men in a trial for his life he knew that. The best plan was to talk her down until she fell asleep, then hopefully she'd forget everything in the morning.

He explained everything, the way Karolina had told him in this same old room. Looking around, he realized Karolina had not been the first vampire in that room, or any of the rooms in this old hotel most likely. Suzy thought it was bullshit, but after all, so had Steve. Eventually, she started to calm down, and then she fell asleep. And Steve thought, that Afghan Kush was definitely worth eighteen euro.

THE LIFE

After Suzy fell asleep, Steve quickly packed, staging his black rolling suitcase and laptop carry-on bag over by the door, and then checked the room for anything he might have left behind. Next he went down the stairs and checked the lobby. Nobody was at the desk that he could see. It was almost 3:30 in the morning, so he wasn't surprised. He was sure the desk clerks knew exactly when the first flight of the day got into Schipol, and how long it would take guests to get from the airport to the hotel. He walked back to his room, brought his luggage to the small elevator to the right of his door, and pressed the button. He remembered how long it had taken when he checked in, and was anxious wanting to get through the lobby before anybody got back to the front desk.

He could just hear it. "Are you checking out, sir?"

"Ah no," what would he say? Suzy was still in bed passed out with two bloody holes in her neck from his fangs.

The door leapt open, welcoming him, and Steve was out of the hotel without being noticed, home free.

He pulled his rolling bag through the thankfully empty streets of the city, bound for the tower nest. He hated having to pull his bag around outside an airport or hotel. It made him feel vulnerable somehow. He didn't feel vulnerable now, though. He felt like he could handle anything that was thrown at him. He was a vampire. He couldn't believe it; the whole thing seemed like a dream. It was only five nights since the mesmerizing Karolina had turned him, and until the moment when he sank his fangs into Suzy's neck, he hadn't really believed it himself. He had successfully fed, despite Valentin's warnings. Maybe he should keep this a secret, let Valentin feel like he was a good mentor and all that.

Steve got back to the large warehouse and entered the code for the outer door, then the code for the dark hardwood door to the tower. As he opened the door, he immediately heard what sounded like Nirvana's "Sifting," from their album *Bleach*. Was that their first album? He wondered, he couldn't remember. He had that CD back home, but wasn't sure if he had ever ripped it to iTunes. The woman who had made the sarcastic comments about Valentin the previous night walked up to him. As he got a better look at her, he realized she was very attractive. She had strawberry blonde hair, was about five foot four, with medium small breasts, and was really skinny. She could have been a model if she were taller. She wore blue jeans and a black top with a black bra that was strategically exposed at the top.

"Well, done," she said in what he now realized was a British accent, patting him on the ass.

Was she congratulating him for getting his bags out of the hotel? If Karolina didn't show up soon, maybe this woman would make a good girlfriend.

"Valentin got a phonograph," she said, pointing to a group of about twenty vampires dancing in a makeshift mosh pit on the other side of the lounge.

He walked over, curious and drawn by the raw rhythm of the Nirvana song, strangely in sync with the energy he felt from feeding for the first time. Expecting to see some vintage record player to match the general decor of the tower lounge, Steve instead saw a modern black turntable that, upon further inspection, had a carbon fiber tone arm. Then he was pogo dancing with the rest of them, spurred on by the rushes he was feeling from the blood in his stomach. He wasn't surprised to see Otakar dancing too, and he disliked him less in that moment, although he still thought he was a bit of a brat.

After about half an hour in the impromptu punk club, Steve decided to get his luggage upstairs.

Valentin walked up to him and said, "Congratulations."

"For what?"

"Everybody can tell you fed. That's not something you can hide. Just like I could tell you were a vampire from across the bridge. I spotted you a couple of hours earlier, but wasn't ready to come back to the tower yet. How did you like that fine Österreich engineering?"

"What?"

"The turntable."

"Oh." Steve knew vinyl was making a comeback, but hadn't really looked into it. When he was a kid, compact disks had hit the scene and were billed as the greatest thing to happen to music since the electric guitar. Vinyl just disappeared, except for DJs and hip-hop samplers. Then it was MP3 players and the convenience of the iPod. These days Steve preferred downtempo music like Thievery Corp or old Zero 7, but in high school he'd leaned toward punk and grunge groups like Nirvana.

He looked over at the crowd dancing, now to the Sex Pistols' "Pretty Vacant," and realized they looked different, somehow glowing. He gradually realized that they had all fed that night, not just him. Strawberry-blond Brit walked over as he dragged his luggage to the bottom of the stairs.

"I'm Steve," he formally introduced himself.

"I know. I'm Sarah. Everybody knows your name. It's not every day that somebody gets turned. In truth, it's not even every year. You won me one hundred thousand euro, by the way."

"How's that?" Steve asked.

"We had a wager on whether you would survive or not. Everybody bet no, except Otakar and I. Only about 60 percent of vampires survive after being turned, and as you can imagine, the percentage is much lower than that for men."

"Otakar, really? What about Valentin?" Steve asked.

"He couldn't participate, since he's on duty this year to watch for newly turned vampires and mentor the men. Put your bag over your head whilst climbing the stairs. It's the easiest way, and you're strong enough now. I'll carry this one."

She picked up his carry-on, and he followed her up the spiral stairs to the fifth floor. They walked along the snaking hall to Steve's chambers, where Sarah gave him a hug. "I'm glad I met you."

"Thanks for betting on me." *Sarah would definitely make a good girlfriend*, Steve thought. She had fed that night too, he could tell. He still had a ton of energy, and his cock started to harden as she held him just a little too long. Thinking there was no time like the present to make his move, he turned his head to kiss her.

She backed away. "You don't want to do that. Vampires should never be together. It just leads to tears and true death. We just don't have what each other needs." She turned and walked away. "But I still like you."

Great, Steve thought. They could "just be friends."

As he unpacked his suitcase, he started to get tired again and knew the sun was coming up. When he finished, a few minutes later, he got in bed and was out cold in less than sixty seconds.

The tower could sleep about one hundred and twenty, but only held ninety to one hundred on any given day, depending on who was there at sunrise. Most floors had enough chambers for about thirty vampires, some of which were for guests. The city itself had two other nests, one of which had similar unique interior architecture to the tower. Curved hallways snaking to and from the sleeping chambers and a center spiral staircase gave the nest an organic hive-like feeling. The design roughly emulated the feeling of the ancient stone-walled tunnels beneath the Mother of Cities, home of the primal vampire nest. The warehouse surrounding the tower had been built in the mid-sixteenth century during the Dutch golden age, as had much of Amsterdam's city center. Around 1775, the owner extended himself, allowing one of the elders, who had fled the vampire cleansing in the east, to purchase it for a bargain. They used it as it was until about 1785, when increasingly more vampires fled west and space was running out. They then had the tower built within the warehouse.

Suzy woke up alone in a hotel room. She couldn't remember how she had gotten there. Oh my God, she thought, what am I going to tell Jim? She felt like shit and didn't even know what hotel she was in. Had she gotten so wasted the night before that she couldn't remember? A quick look around determined two things. The first: stationary confirmed that this was the Hotel Krasnapolsky, Steve's hotel. Second: there not only was nobody there, there was no sign of anyone. No luggage, no toothbrush drying by the bathroom sink, nothing. She decided to make up a story she thought might be at least partially true. She knew Steve was staying in this hotel, so maybe this was his room and he was already flying home. She would tell Jim she had met Steve, stayed with him overnight, and nothing happened, they had just talked. Maybe he would believe it, or at least convince himself it was true. Maybe it was even true. She would never know.

When Steve came downstairs after sunset one evening about a week later, vaguely familiar South American downtempo music was playing in the tower lounge. Valentin held court over by the sound system as usual, so he asked him who was playing.

"It's Federico Aubele's classic *Gran Hotel Buenos Aires*, produced by Thievery Corp," Valentin told him.

The sound system consisted of a Mac mini connected to a digital receiver via HDMI, tower speakers, and a sixty-five-inch flat screen TV used as a monitor. It also had a Blu-ray player, or they could stream movies from the Mac.

Valentin, Steve, and Sarah hung out browsing the Internet for a couple of hours, as they had done the previous few nights. Valentin controlled the sound system using the remote app on his iPhone, changing up the sound to suit his mood, mostly downtempo electronic music, and coming back to selections from *Gran Hotel Buenos Aires* often. As Boards of Canada's "Dayvan Cowboy" started playing, Sarah began getting restless. It had been five days since she or Steve had left the tower to feed or otherwise. Valentin went out every night; since he had to go down to the old church looking for newly turned vampires.

"I saw my twin down at the middle Bulldog about a week ago," Sarah said. "Either of you want to give her a shot?"

Steve said nothing, not wanting to seem too eager, but he thought Sarah's "twin" might be an interesting distraction.

"It's about time I take Steve out for some more mentoring," Valentin said. So it was decided they would head over the few blocks to the red-light district. "Stay away from those prostitutes, though, Steve," Valentin added. As he explained to Sarah that Steve had seen a woman who knew he was a vampire.

Out in the garage warehouse area, they tried to decide whether to walk or drive. Steve was starting to feel more like one of the gang, being included in the decision-making, however trivial. They lingered by Sarah's Range Rover.

"Thing is, I'd rather drive my new Jag," she said, pointing to her slightly used dark-green F-Type bought from the spoils obtained by betting on Steve, "but it only seats two. Let's walk. I'll drive it later if I feed."

Admiring the new Jag, Steve thought that he needed a car, something nice. Back home he had a leased BMW 3 Series, partially paid for by Sterling Klein Financial, but he wanted something more exotic to compete with his new housemates, maybe a BMW M3.

The three vampires ambled down the cobblestoned streets of

Amsterdam City Center; the humid summer evening enveloping them as they traveled the few short blocks to the red-light district. When they arrived at the middle Bulldog, they bought weed and a beer each, just for show, then sat at one of the tables overlooking the canal. At one table Valentin saw a sophisticated-looking blonde, but no sign of Sarah's "twin." Steve saw the same beautiful blonde and definitely had an interest in her as well. She was casually yet well-dressed, wearing designer blue jeans, a white top see through enough to reveal a light-blue bra covering her medium large breasts, and a string of pearls around her neck. An Italian guy, good-looking well dressed with strategic stubble on his face, was making his case, while essentially being interviewed by three of her friends.

Just then Sarah said, "There she is." Across the road was a near twin to Sarah, strawberry-blonde hair a little shorter than hers, and not quite as skinny, like she'd had a kid. She could pass for Sarah's older sister, and she made a beeline toward the group of women with the beautiful blonde.

"Hiya," Sarah said in her London accent, and the other woman stopped.

"Do I know you?" she asked. "You look familiar."

"It's because you look just like her," Steve said. "I'm Steve, this is my cousin Sarah, and that's my buddy Valentin visiting from Austria."

"I guess I do look like her. I'm Hedley," she said, thinking that this American could be a good prospect for Kate. "My friends are over here."

Both Steve and Valentin noticed she gestured to the same table the blonde was at, and noticed each other noticing.

"She's my type, Steve," Valentin said under his breath. "Watch and learn,"

Introductions were made, and Kate assessed both men. They each seemed exotic in opposing ways. Valentin was like the continental prince of Kate's dreams, not at all like the real princes she had met— pale, sickly, with fortunes ruined. Steve, for his part, was from California. The word alone sounded so enticing, a dream, a promise.

Kate's friends all started to think maybe this was that fling of a lifetime. They turned on the charm going into maximum flirt mode, forgetting their husbands. Living vicariously through Kate just wasn't going to cut it tonight, but under her breath Kate mumbled sarcastically, "The pretty bird gets the worm."

This was Valentin's world; this was where he had excelled for the last two hundred and fifty years.

"Valentin's going to show me his Porsche," Kate said abruptly, and they disappeared into the night. It happened so quickly, it took Steve and Kate's friends by surprise, but the only thing to do was act like it was perfectly normal.

I really do need a nice car, Steve thought, and wondered which Porsche Valentin was going to show Kate; the '58 Cabriolet, most likely. The five remaining women circled Steve, leaving the Italian guy abandoned.

"I have a Ferrari back home," the Italian blurted out, but everybody suspected he was lying. Sarah swooped in and saved him. His night was about to get interesting; too bad he would never remember. Sarah would, though, but she would never mention that maybe he did have a Ferrari back home and that it was three weeks before she stopped thinking about him.

Watching Sarah go off with the Italian, Steve felt a pang of jealousy, and then realized he had to make a choice. Not hard really. Chelsea and Hedley were pretty, the others a bit plain. Hedley, though, was the clear leader with Kate so suddenly gone, and she knew it, rubbing Steve's bicep from time to time. The idea of Sarah's "twin" being a stand-in for the sexy Sarah didn't hurt either.

When she asked if he'd ever seen the Waldorf Astoria, he answered honestly that he hadn't. Soon they were walking back toward the Krasnapolsky to catch a cab.

Valentin and Kate reached the warehouse in a few minutes by foot. He let her into the garage area, exposing a veritable car show, but not the hidden truth behind the oaken door of Karolina's tower. "This is mine," he said, walking up to the silver Speedster. "I've never been to the Waldorf Astoria," he added for what, he guessed, was the thirty-first time. "I'll give you a ride over."

"Thanks!" Kate said, truly feeling he was doing her a huge favor.

They sped through the warm summer night, top down, breeze in their hair. Kate imagined she was the princess she had thought she would be when she was a little girl. People on the street turned and stared with jealousy and admiration as they drove past. Were they famous? The Porsche went by too fast to tell, leaving just a lasting impression of something to aspire to.

At the hotel, Valentin let the valet take his car, then walked through the lobby with Kate, their arms interlocked, letting her lead and yet giving the impression both to her and anyone watching that he was leading.

Her room could only be described as money. It had that old money feel, a suite about a thousand square feet in an already expensive hotel. Valentin had to admit this was the nicest room he had seen, and he had been in many of the rooms in the Waldorf. How much it cost, he could only imagine; five thousand, ten thousand euro a night? He doubted even an attorney could afford this, and suspected Kate must have family money. They sat together on a richly upholstered couch, befitting of the hotel and room, kissing gently. Kate thought she had finally found her prince. She wanted to know everything about him, but that could wait. She even wanted to show him just how good a wife she would make. All those other men she had known had just been practice for tonight.

"I have a confession," Valentin said.

"What, my prince?" Had she really just called him "my prince"? *How cliché*, she thought. But she didn't have that feeling of dread like she did when a man was about to reveal some deliberately withheld fact and she knew she had made a horrible mistake.

"To start off, I'm a little older then you probably think."

How old could he be? Thirty-seven at the most, but he looked more like twenty-seven, like a good twenty-seven, she thought.

"I have to tell you this, so you know," he went on. "I'm not like you. I'm an upir, what you call a vampire."

Kate laughed. Thank God his "confession" was just a joke.

"I was born in 1747, and was turned in 1769 at Schönbrunn Palace. I need to drink your blood to survive. But don't worry, it won't kill you. I'll stop before that happens."

"So you're the spawn of the devil come to ravish me," Kate said, playing along.

"To tell you the truth, I don't feel Satan, just as I didn't feel God before I was turned. So just to be clear, you're okay with this, right?"

"Of course. Can I call you Count Valentin?" she said, still joking.

"The other thing is you won't remember any of this, but if you do, that means you've been turned. In that case, go down to the old church in the red-light district, just past where we met. You won't survive on your own, and you will need to feed within two weeks. Remember, if you recall any of what I'm telling you now, go down to the old church, because you've been turned into a vampire."

"How do I get turned? Can't you just turn me tonight and make me your vampire wife?"

"No, it doesn't work that way. It's a virus, and you need the upir gene to turn. It's very rare."

Valentin led Kate over to the bed and started to remove her clothes, kissing any newly exposed flesh. For her part, Kate wanted to show off her oral skills, just to make sure he knew this would not be a boring marriage like her friends'. You get what you give, after all.

"I think I'm falling in love with you," Kate murmured when he slid inside her. The illusion was in full force now, except that Valentin was caught up in it himself. As he looked into her clear blue eyes full of emotion and intelligence, he thought, She really is my type. Being a vampire was great and all, but would he give it all up for the love of a woman like this? He knew this was just a moment in time, and that mortals' breakneck race toward true death meant these moments were fleeting.

Female vampires had an advantage in that their prey usually had an orgasm, increasing the nutritional quality of their blood ten to twenty times. That meant they didn't have to feed as often as the men. For Valentin, tonight was going to be one of the better feedings. He felt her close, then as they both came, he sank his fangs into her neck. Sweet blood filled his mouth as he fed, and as an act of discipline—and was that love?—he stopped short of killing her.

"You really are a vampire," Kate exclaimed. "I can't believe it. I think I'm in love with a vampire. I hope I turn into one too."

"Not likely," he said. "There is less than a 1 percent chance of getting turned. In all likelihood, you will forget everything, and I'll be gone in the morning."

"Well, we have now, I guess."

As she snuggled with her newfound vampire boyfriend, Kate wasn't sure what to believe. She felt sleepy post sex, and blood reduced. Valentin on the other hand felt energized. He hadn't had good blood in six weeks, and this would last him ten to fifteen days. In the more than two hundred years since he had been turned, he had learned a lot about women, but still had more to learn about himself. He more often than not chased the fake blondes, and not just in hair color, wasting his time looking for the real thing. Or was he just chasing the ghost of the Proto-Germanic blonde beauty who turned him so many years ago? Kate was the real thing. He knew that as he looked down at her as she drifted off into a deep sleep.

What would my life have been like if I hadn't been turned? If I had married a woman like Kate and lived a normal life. Instead I'm almost dead, having to feed every few days just to survive.

Valentin stayed in Kate's room until just a half hour before daybreak, risking delay in getting back. He wanted to cherish his time with her. She had been right when she said they had now, but that was it. Tomorrow she would be just a lonely memory, like the rest. He got the Porsche from the valet, tipped him, and headed back to the tower. He drove briskly through the predawn streets, hoping he would not run into any trouble. That had only happened once back in the 1980s, and it hadn't ended well for the police officer that had tried to arrest Valentin for speeding. For a year and a half, the city was on alert for the depraved cop killer who had literally torn the officer to pieces. He pulled down the alley street, quiet as it should be, a faint light appearing east of the city as he entered the code to open the door. Five minutes later, Valentin was sound asleep in his own bed.

The next evening, Valentin, Steve, and Sarah hung out in the lounge having all fed the night before.

"Accalu is coming tonight," Valentin said. "He is one of the elders, more than two thousand years old and the oldest vampire in Amsterdam. The elders trade places between the nests every five months. Usually one of the three elders in the city will be at each nest at any given time."

Steve wondered who had been the elder when he first got to the tower. He was likely hiding in luxurious chambers upstairs.

About 3:00 a.m. Valentin got a text and said they had to assemble for the arrival of Accalu. Everybody at the tower went down to the garage area. The roll-up door started to rise a few minutes later, and a 1997 red Ferrari Testarossa pulled into the garage, its twelve-cylinder engine rumbling as it pulled to a stop.

These vampires sure like their sports cars, Steve thought.

The driver's door opened and out stepped a guy who looked about thirty, black hair and olive tan skin. Steve was confused, watching as the man walked straight up to Valentin and shook his hand.

Then turning to Steve, he reached out his hand and said in a faded

Middle-Eastern accent, "I am Accalu." Steve had thought an elder would look, well, old. He had pictured something like a ninety-year-old Moses when he first heard the term from Karolina. This was not what he had expected. Accalu walked around, greeting everyone and shaking hands like a politician. When he went into the tower, everybody followed.

After that, Accalu seemed like everybody else, hanging out in the lounge, listening to music, and working on his laptop. Steve started to wonder what the other two elders looked like. Had he met them and not known they were an "elder"? *How could you tell?* He wondered.

THE MORTAL LIFE

Hedley awoke alone in her bed when Chelsea called on her mobile the next morning. She wanted to know how it had gone last night with Steve, the guy from California.

"It went great, he was amazing," she lied, only because she couldn't remember anything, not even leaving the hotel last night, nothing. "He's a total stud," she added. "I came twice." She was on a roll now, but she also felt like shit. "I need to run. I think I'm going to be sick."

Hedley got off the phone, but didn't get sick. She ordered breakfast from room service and felt better, but still could not remember a thing from the previous night. Had she been drinking Scotch again with Kate? she wondered. She just couldn't remember.

A few doors down in the hotel, Kate was awoken by the insistent double ring of her hotel phone around 10:00 a.m., her mobile being off. It was Chelsea wanting to know how it went with Valentin. Kate remembered the Austrian, and somehow that they had hooked up, but not actually doing it. She had this feeling, an impression at least, that she was in love, but it was hazy, like a dream. She also felt like shit. Just the light peeking in through a slight opening of the curtains in her room was like ice picks in her eyes, poking into her brain. She needed water; she needed ibuprofen.

"I need to go," she told Chelsea. "I think I'm going to be sick,"

Kate crawled into her bathtub just to get away from the light, and waited for the ibuprofen to kick in. Around eight that night she woke up when Chelsea finally convinced hotel security that they needed to check on her, as she had not responded for hours. After being woken up for the second time, Kate started to feel much better, and after a shower she was ready to go out and tear up the town. She was eager to meet up with Valentin again; she was sure she had given him her mobile number.

KAROLINA

A few minutes after sunset, Karolina requested an Uber from her iPhone, checking her phone with anticipation every minute or so until the app told her the car was on her block. Then she descended the stairs of a somewhat dilapidated but grand manse in heels and a little black dress, a small overnight bag over her shoulder, meeting the driver at the curb. He drove her to Amsterdam Schipol, through the private aircraft gate, and onto the tarmac and a waiting Dassault Falcon 5X. Twelve minutes after that, with only Karolina and the two pilots on board, the private jet was in the air.

One hour and fifty-seven minutes later, Karolina descended the steps of the plane onto the tarmac at Peretola airport in Florence, Italy. Fifty meters away, Laurent stood waiting in a charcoal Armani suit and white shirt with no tie, leaning against a blue and white Smart car.

"How many of these things do you have?" Karolina asked, teasing.

"I think two or three. Maybe I gave one to my sister," he replied in his thick French accent. He kissed her on the cheeks and held the passenger side door for her.

"I have one in Paris, one here, and maybe one in Saint Tropez," he added as they drove off.

"I never really understood these cars, except for parking I guess. I prefer walking or something faster," she said.

"It comes in handy in Paris with my commute, and I have my Lamborghini if I want to drive fast."

"What, your commute is only three kilometers. What does your wife drive?"

"She is all French, unlike me. She has a Peugeot RCZ R. It's sort of like a French Audi TT."

Twenty minutes later they pulled into the courtyard of an eight-bedroom villa in the historic central district of town. They walked together, arms entwined, into the opulent seventeenth-century three-story residence and sat in one of the two large living rooms on the ground floor. The air conditioning kept it comfortably cool in the lingering summer heat of Tuscany.

"So, you said you needed some business advice," Karolina started.

"*Oui*. I am thinking of selling off some of my company, then merging with our closest competitor."

"Tell me about it, the details."

"We have three main divisions. Retail banking is checking and savings accounts; investment banking sells retirement instruments mostly; and what we call boutique banking, a hybrid of both, but for higher-end clientele. A number of those clients have been with us for generations. The boutique banking is really the business that my grandfather built. My father and I expanded into the retail side and grew the family business very well, allowing us to do a public stock offering and make some serious money. Now the retail side has stopped growing, and we can't compete as well for high-end clients because we are perceived as lower end."

"So you want to get back to basics and sell off the retail side, move up market again?" Karolina asked.

"*Oui*, and merge with a competitor to build economies of scale. We can continue to manage the finances of high-net-worth clients, build a brand around that."

"Then you can grow by adding upwardly mobile clients like football stars based on your brand," Karolina said.

"Exactly, but it's a lot more than just the obvious nouveau riche. I meet many people at parties back in Paris. They are right at that line, the line where the government takes almost all of your money in taxes. They need tax advice, investment advice, even advice on how to get their kids into a good school. In my grandfather's day, we only dealt with people from a certain background. Now I see it's all so clearly. Why discriminate if someone has the money?"

"Which brand would you use?" she asked.

"That's one of the big questions. Ideally, we would sell the retail and keep our old family name. It's tarnished. We played on the banker-to-the-rich while catering to the middle class for decades. It would take us five to ten years to repair the brand. The other options are less ideal, using the brand of the company we merge with, or creating a new one, which is not easy in France."

"The brand is worth a lot. I'm sure whoever purchased the retail side would want it."

"That's the problem. I will need to sell it to the board. Less money now for more in the long term, measured in years."

"You drove the expansion into retail that grew the company many times over. Won't they respect that?"

"I continued the expansion after my parents were killed in a boating accident. It wasn't my idea, it wasn't my vision, it was my father's."

"How did your parents die?" Karolina asked. "You never told me?"

"You know my mother was Italian, my father French. This villa was from my mother's side of the family. We also had a home on a cliff overlooking the sea on Corsica that came from my father's side of the family. My grandfather had it built. We had a speedboat, a thirty-eight-foot Cigarette that we kept at the marina in Livorno, just on the coast from here. We would take the boat over to Corsica for long weekends with the whole family. One Saturday morning we left early, my parents, sister, and a younger brother I never told you about. About halfway between the mainland and the island, a gunboat started to chase us. It was unmarked, but looked like it was military. There was just no way to tell which country. Our boat was one of the fastest on the Mediterranean, a race boat really, so we pulled away easily, but it was a trap. We raced right toward another gunboat. They didn't try to board us, they just started shooting, and used I think a torpedo. Our boat exploded. My sister and I were thrown free, but my parents and brother were never found."

"I'm so sorry, I had no idea," Karolina said.

"They never found out who it was or why, but I have my suspicions. I think we got too successful, and one government or another wanted to take our money. I was already almost thirty, and having worked at the bank since graduating university, I took over as CEO right away. We didn't miss a beat, never faltered, which is at least some consolation."

"It's almost sunrise," Karolina said. "I need to get some sleep."

"I'll tuck you in."

Laurent led her down into the cool basement and a storage room in the back. Inside was a luxury coffin, rose wood with red satin lining, which he had bought two years prior for Karolina to sleep in.

The next evening, Karolina and Laurent continued where they had left off. She felt safe around Laurent; he exuded that perfect handsome fiftyish Euro-executive look, and was wise for a mortal. Laurent obviously knew what Karolina was, and he craved the wisdom of her years. He knew she held some sort of position of power, just not exactly what, nor the details of her history beyond Prague and Amsterdam, but knew she needed her secrets too. He had remembered everything after she fed on him ten years ago in Paris, and had thought that he had turned, which would have been highly inconvenient for a man in his position. But he had no light sensitivity or other ill effects the next morning.

"I think above all you need to keep your brand," Karolina started. "You also need to consider other options in M&A after you sell the retail business."

"What do you mean?" Laurent asked.

"Without selling the name, you may not get as much as you want. It will simply be the accounts and some branch offices. That may leave you in a weaker position with your competitor. If you merged, the board would be diluted. They may not even let you keep your sister on as an executive. By buying a few smaller boutique financial services companies, you could keep control. And don't just think about France, think Pan-European. There may be some small guys out there, relatively new, without the brand power you could bring. Maybe even with some fresh ideas."

"That's interesting, I never thought of that. This whole thing started over lunch with the CEO of my biggest competitor. He's older and wants to retire, but has no clear successor. I need to keep the bigger picture in mind." Laurent smiled at her. "I knew you could impart some good wisdom."

For Karolina, this was nothing. Her best work, she knew, had been in 1771, getting the newly turned Valentin to go back to Austria soon after he showed up in the Mother of Cities, and convince his aunt, the empress Maria Theresa, to have her personal physician Gerard van Swieten, declare, after a mock investigation, that vampires did not exist. That essentially ended what the mortals called the Vampire Controversy, and the vampires called the Vampire Terror.

They continued discussing Laurent's business and other topics for the next few nights. Karolina would wait to feed on him until just before she left for Amsterdam on his company's jet. He considered the arrangement fair, his blood for her wisdom, and she made a great mistress, something every successful Frenchman needed.

SOME HISTORY

A few nights later, Steve was in the tower nest lounge and started talking to Accalu. "How old are you really, and where were you born? Valentin said you were over two thousand years old."

"Two thousand six hundred years," Accalu said. "I was born in Babylon in 593 BC, neo-Babylon really, the second reign of that empire. At the time the city was swarming with Lilitu, female demons that fed on the population at night. They killed almost every man they seduced, drinking his blood; often more than a twenty a night since there were so many of them. Where they came from nobody knew. They were demons unto themselves, most believed. Unlike today, Babylonians had no single god or devil, but many gods and demons, and they were used to explain everything from the sun to the sea. If anything new came along, good or evil, it got its own god or demon in turn.

"I was young and naive, but thought otherwise, as the young do. One day I was walking home in the evening and met Shala. She was beautiful and young with long dark hair. She looked nothing like the demons my mother had warned me about. She didn't try to seduce me that night, just talked, which was momentous for me at the time. A few nights later I saw her again. This went on for about two moons. When she finally took me to her bed, I thought I was in love. At first when she bit me, I was in denial, but as my life started to drain along with my blood, I pushed her off. She let me go, perhaps out of pity. I woke up in my own bed not knowing how I got there. I almost died in the next few days, but somehow lived two weeks, my health waning and waxing with the rise and set of the sun. Then by instinct I knew what had happened, what I had become, and what I had to do to survive. When my older sister came into my room to take care of me, I raped her, drank her blood, and left her for dead. I was a demon now. That's all I knew, that demons were pure evil. I'm ashamed of the monster I was then, but it was a brutal time. Life was cheaper than you can imagine.

"A few years after I was turned, the city turned against us. A priest came to Babylon who could tell who had been turned into a demon, and the eradications began. I fled to Persia, and then fled Persia, fleeing repeatedly through the years until I got to Rome. Over the centuries I saw the fall of the Republic and the rise and fall of the Empire. Our population was low then, but we killed in numbers that stagger the imagination, but in Rome it was barely noticed along with all the other brutality. There was no cooperation among us, just solitary brutal predators seeking and killing their prey. We were truly the monsters of a child's nightmare, primitive, like animals really, but with time came wisdom for some of us. Discovery and a disrupted feeding, later followed by a chance sighting of the victim alive, gave some of us the idea that we could survive without killing, but that took centuries.

"At some point during the Roman Empire, awareness of the *venatores* among them gave rise to massive eradication efforts, led by the new Catholic Church. I fled north and east, ending up in the lightly populated hills of Bohemia around 850AD."

"I discovered a cave with a matrix of tunnels as ancient as man himself. It was said that the first men of Europe had settled in these caves, but when I got there a nest of vampires already populated it. It was hard to tell if humans had carved the tunnels or if they had started as caves, but every wall was finished smooth and carved with ornate designs. Not some troglodyte cave drawings, but not carved by the vampires either. When I got there, the city above was already growing. At the time it was already populated by the Slavic people, but it was said it had existed for a millennia prior. Along with the growth in population, our food source grew. In the fourteenth century, the growth was incredible as the city became preeminent as the seat of the Holy Roman Emperor. We slept during the day in the nest, and came out at night to feed. Many of us at the time were feeding without killing, but this had the unintended effect of causing an increase in the population of vampires.

"In the late seventeenth century, the upir gene seemed to become more prevalent, and not just in the Mother of Cities. The population of the nest increased to almost three thousand, and many of them were newly turned, with no discipline not to kill. The times were still relatively brutal with people dying all the time, but by the eighteenth century, mortals started to notice. By 1729, the 'upir hysteria' was at its peak, and another eradication naturally followed. I had seen this many times before and fled, but this time decided something had to be done. We couldn't fight; we had to evolve. Some of us formed the first council of elders. Over the course of a few years, through informal and then formal deliberations, we established the covenant in 1733. At first the majority of vampires rejected it outright, but as the number of vampire hunters grew and many vampires met with the true death, many considered the benefits of the covenant. In 1734, we sent emissaries out into the world, visiting all the known nests and bringing the philosophy of the covenant with them. To many, it was obvious we had to evolve to survive. To others, though, we were simply predators one rung up on the food chain with no natural obligation to give quarter to our prey. I had already lived that way for over two thousand years, and it hadn't worked.

"We fought the mortals and we fought each other until thirty thousand vampires in Europe were reduced to under one thousand. Many fled west with the covenant as their new guide, to Amsterdam and London, and some from there to America. I was one of the few members of the original council of elders to survive. Today, usually the oldest three vampires of a nest or city form the various councils, meting out decisions on the covenant and assessing the general wellbeing of the nest or city. Here in Amsterdam we have three nests, each with an elder in residence. London has four nests."

THE CANAL NEST

Valentin, Accalu, Sarah, and Steve left the tower early with two other vampires, Viona and Hubrech, six nocturnal creatures blending into the warm summer evening. They felt free and alive, all having fed in the last few days. They did not feel the burden of being almost dead. Their destination was just a few blocks away on the Singel Canal, where Valentin met a trendy, intellectual-looking Dutchman who was selling a small motorboat with an inboard engine. The boat could hold up to six comfortably, had a white hull, and a brown awning in case of rain.

After a little haggling, cash payment helping, Valentin purchased the boat. They spent the next few hours tootling around the different canals and the Amstel River, where they cruised by the decks of the NH Doelen and Pulitzer hotels, checking out the crowds for future reference, and being checked out in turn. They dodged tour boats until 9:30 p.m., and the higher-end hotel party boats, with their wine and cheese spreads, until 11:00.

Viona and Hubrech were both Dutch. Steve hadn't really noticed before, but all the vampires he had met so far had been from somewhere else, like him. Hubrech was tall even for a Dutchman, six foot four, and had blue eyes and light brown hair. He'd grown up in the countryside near Nuenen. A big farm boy, he'd been destined to a life in agriculture like his father, and his father before him. He came to Amsterdam with friends in the summer of 1993, and on a fateful night, his path changed forever. He had resisted at first, gone back to the countryside to be with his family after the first time he fed, but he could not change his new nature. He tried to feed in his hometown, and killed a woman. The elders keeping an eye on him brought him back to the city. The council voted two to one to spare him true death, but he had been a poor advocate on his own behalf. He rebelled against the idea of being a vampire, his will finally broken at the prospect of true death at the age of twenty-one.

The blonde-haired blue-eyed Viona was a completely different story. She was born in Amsterdam in 1754 to a wealthy family. Her father was a physician, and her mother from money. Viona went to the best schools and studied art in preparation for a desirable marriage. The only problem was it was more desirable to her parents than her. She was a wild girl, having lost her virtue at sixteen, but she kept up appearances for her family's sake.

In 1772, during a party for an art opening, she met a boy she had to have. He was older at twenty-two, she being just eighteen, and an officer in the Royal Dutch Navy, which made him seem a little dangerous. He too came from a good family, although they had never met. She knew her parents would like him, but the bad-boy persona just below his façade of the well-bred gentleman made him attractive to her. He had been all over the world, and could talk about his adventures for hours. She was just about to suggest a walk in the garden that she hoped would lead to more, when a beautiful Bohemian woman walked up to them. She was exotic, with dark brown hair that contrasted with Viona's blonde, and she transfixed the boy. Not to be outdone, Viona upped her game, whispering in his ear what she wanted to do to him and rubbing up against him in not so subtle ways. The Bohemian woman, Karolina, had just moved to Amsterdam after her family had died in a horrible fire. Or so she said, telling her tale of woe. The two women campaigned for the boy's attentions with all they had, until first Karolina then Viona realized he did not want to choose, he wanted them both. Karolina's need to feed and Viona's try anything once wild side made it a reality.

Karolina an early proponent of the covenant, having witnessed the slaughter of vampires in the Mother of Cities firsthand, explained everything to them. She said she had never fed on a girl before, but was willing to make an exception. The worldly boy and Viona doubted her story, but went along for the fun of it.

The boy never remembered his great adventure, but Viona was turned. She didn't know what to do, and had no one to show her. She rented a window in the red-light district the first time she fed, but killed the man. She lived in the shadows, telling her family she was sick during the day and going out at night to feed. She learned not to kill the way Karolina had done, but her so-called life was headed for disaster as her family and friends grew increasingly concerned. She had fed on every boy she knew, when by chance she saw Karolina again. Knowing Viona intimately, Karolina thought she would make a good vampire. So she took her in and mentored her over the years, a process that eventually evolved into the loose support system the Amsterdam vampires employ today.

Just before three, Valentin brought the boat up the Oudezijds Voorburgwal canal in the red-light district, and Steve recognized the old church. Valentin held the boat against the dock and asked if he could do the duties. Steve realized Valentin wanted him to check for newly turned vampires waiting by the church. He got on shore and started to walk around the church, not sure if he would recognize a vampire. At the northwest corner farthest from the canal, he saw a black guy, dread locks and bright Jamaican shirt, standing alone, facing the other way. Steve couldn't be sure so walked about five feet from him as he made his circuit.

"Charlie?" the guy asked, and Steve knew he was just a coke dealer. He returned to the boat. Steve was the first person in seven years who had been turned in Amsterdam so expectations were low to find anybody, but this year it was Valentin's responsibility to check, and mentor them if they were male.

About thirty minutes later, Valentin steered the boat up another canal in the red-light district, stopping at a point where the houses on both sides came to the edge of the water. In most other canals, a street separated the buildings from the water. They tied the boat to a small overhang, and Accalu punched a code into a keypad on the wall. A door that was not immediately visible to the casual observer opened. Once inside, it was obvious that this was another nest.

"The nest continues below three buildings all owned by the vampires for over two hundred years," Valentin told Steve. "We sleep in the bottom level and rent out the three floors above. Similar to the tower, there's a lounge area, and tunnels lead to the chambers, only here they feel a little more like the caves beneath the Mother of Cities."

Otakar got up from one of the sofas and greeted Valentin warmly with a big smile. "So you got us a new boat." The two went outside and checked out their new acquisition, taking dimensions so that they could order online a full cover that would protect the boat from the almost daily rain of Amsterdam. Like everybody, they considered the

Internet a great invention, but for vampires it meant not having to wait for winter when the sun set before 5:00 to go shopping. "There is no better time to be a vampire," Valentin had said to Steve. For now, though, they would have to bail the boat out every day or two until the custom cover arrived.

"Two kids, teenagers it turns out, stole our previous boat," Otakar said to Steve. "They went out into the bay and accidentally sank it, barely getting rescued before they drowned."

Accalu continued the story. "The covenant has exemptions for crimes against vampires, up to and including death on rare occasions, although not for many years, at least here in Amsterdam. Self-defense, a verified threat to a nest, or an active vampire hunter. The boys had the terror of their lives as Sarah and Viona first seduced them, and then told them they would die. They kept this up for a few weeks, feeding every few nights, leaving them with just enough blood to survive, and a hazy unfocused fear of something they could not quite remember."

An hour before sunrise, Valentin, Accalu, Sarah, Steve, Hubrech, and Viona walked back to the tower nest just twelve blocks away, climbing the stairs to their respective sleeping chambers and a good day's sleep.

REMORSE

Valentin followed a group of women down an alley. In the shadows lurked a fell creature, and the creature was he. *Am I really that monster, the character in the tales that give children nightmares?* He wondered. He didn't think so. He considered himself a refined gentleman, the count of Europa, he liked to call himself. *I'm tough. I'm a survivor, so why can't I get the thought of Kate out of my head?* He wandered the streets of Amsterdam for hours, thinking and wondering what could have been, and what could be. *Could I be with a mortal? Do I even want to be? Am I in love with Kate?*

Before being turned, Valentin led an aimless life. He was born cousin to royalty, the first son of a count, at the acme of the Habsburg dynasty. Educated, comfortable, and wealthy, he had never felt need of anything, but had no real purpose or direction either. At age twenty-two, he was never going to be a great man, although he dined and feted with the empress and various kings and princes on an almost weekly basis. Being turned gave him something, made him something more, and even gave him a need, the primal need of the almost dead to feed on human blood.

I need more. I need the love of a woman for more than just a night. Would I give this life up for it? Not likely. Do I crave the true death? Never. In his two hundred and fifty plus years, Valentin knew one thing for sure—every man rebels against the idea that this is it, regardless of what it is.

⚚

Kate and her friends sat in the Waldorf Astoria's Vault bar at the end of another long night of partying and searching. Kate held a whiskey glass containing the golden liquid poured from a bottle of fourteen-year-old Oban, her third.

I'm tough, she told herself. Much tougher than my friends, or even my mother who has never held a real job, she thought. *You can't count all the charities she's funded and worked on. Good work all, just not the real work that I do.*

Kate knew that despite being born to the manor it was people like her that made that sort of good work possible. She was super Kate, after all, and traveled the world working on corporate deals, as many as twelve in parallel that took months to gestate, all the while managing intricate details of advantage and liability for her firm's clients. She was able to answer the most esoteric questions on the precedent of one country's laws over another's without missing a beat, and on only three hours of sleep. Yet she felt whipped by a common continental playboy, who had played her for sure. She wasn't ashamed that she had fucked a stranger on the first night; she was ashamed that she had fallen for his bullshit on any night. Her phone had no calls or texts from him. The callous loser had probably forgotten her name already. He had gotten her wasted, that was clear due to her lack of cognitive focus on the details of the evening, and then taken advantage, pure and simple. Yet what she did remember, her feelings, her sense that he was not like that … He was more of a gentleman, like a duke or a count of old.

Stop it, Kate, she told herself. *It was all an illusion.*

Valentin looked at his phone, wondering why he had even put Kate's number into it to begin with. He knew he would never call her, and she wouldn't even remember him if he did. Did I think she had been turned, nobody can tell right away not even the eldest of the elders. So why am I so tempted to send her a text right now?

New message to: Kate Wydville.

<What RU doing?> His finger hovered over send, then after a long pause hit cancel.

The next morning Kate was sick again. *The six glasses of Oban most likely,* she thought. The light was a killer, and she definitely lost a little weight in prayer to the porcelain god. This time, though, her friends knew to let her sleep all day, waking her only after the sun had started to set.

FEEDING FRENZY

Steve and Sarah left the tower together at about nine thirty, stepping into yet another perfect summer evening that enveloped them with a blanket of warm, humid air. It had been raining hard for the last two hours, keeping all the tourists and locals cooped up inside. Ungrateful for their chance to catch up on email and sports scores back home, almost every tourist in the city felt like they had to be outside, thus creating a swarm-like buzz in the streets. Sarah and Steve had not fed in about ten days, and for the first time since being turned; Steve finally felt hunger, a real need for human blood. They went to a few coffee shops, as Sarah said it was easier to sorcerize somebody after they had had a few hits of weed. They did a quick survey of each and rejected them in turn due to a lack of prospects.

About eleven, they found themselves on the canal side patio outside the Bulldog Energy coffee shop, where Steve got to have a little taste of what Sarah might be like in bed, with her "twin" Hedley. No sign of Kate, Sarah would report to Valentin later. She had never seen Valentin like this before, so affected by a woman, so off his game.

Within a few minutes, Sarah had a strapping British guy—football smart real life not, in the grips of her charms. Full-on sorcerizing was taking place right in front of Steve's eyes. This one was sharing a room with his buddies to save money, and Sarah convinced him he needed another room for himself and her, his new girlfriend.

After Sarah left with her dinner, Steve felt like a fish out of water. He was an American, not very welcome at a British coffee shop. After a few huge wannabe footballers gave him a stay-away-from-our-birds look and broke into some unrecognizable football song, he decided to cut his losses and try the Green House just up the road, still his favorite. These guys would rather fight him than fuck women, from what he could tell.

On the short walk to the Green House, Steve got increasingly ravenous and nervous. He had only fed twice, once with Suzy, whom he had fucked hundreds of times before. The second time, he had wondered if Valentin's presence hadn't somehow helped with Hedley.

What if I don't have it? What if I can't sorcerize a girl to do what I want, no matter how dark the tale I will eventually be compelled to tell her?

Veronica, Sophia, Carol, and Lauren were out for their last night in Amsterdam before taking the train to Paris. They didn't have a set time to leave the next day, and could pay a little extra to check out late if they had to. Tonight they were going to party hard, like the true Southern girls they were. Veronica still had not found a suitable candidate to hook up with, despite her friends all doing so on one or more occasions. She was being picky, and was still comparing guys to the pretty boys she had met in LA. But if she didn't find someone here, she still had Paris, Barcelona, or London.

Steve walked into the small coffee shop and immediately saw Karolina-hair girl, Veronica. She was sitting with her three friends, the women he had already met. He walked over and said, "Hi, remember me?"

"You're Steve from California, right?" Sophia said.

"Yea, that's right," he replied in that flat national-news-anchor non-accent that people from northern California cultivated naturally.

"This is Veronica," Carol said.

"Nice to meet you," Steve replied, trying not to seem too eager. *She's the one*, he thought as he looked at the attractive brunette, and tried to turn on his sorcerizing power, however you did that. It had seemed to come naturally the other night, but maybe that had been Valentin's.

Veronica thought *he's the one; I'm going for it*, as she looked at the perfect geeky California guy in his Levis and blue plaid shirt, six feet tall, with medium brown hair, blue eyes, and a hard body. After a little flirting by everybody, it was clear Steve was interested in Veronica and she in him, so the other women backed off. Within a few minutes they were in a cab heading back to her hotel. Steve felt relieved. Being both hungry and on his own for the first time trying to feed had made him very nervous.

In Veronica's room, they tore each other's clothes off, and any resemblance to Karolina and her hard, skinny body was gone. Steve looked over Veronica's curvy body—large breasts with large nipples, and landing strip trim accenting her brown hair perfectly.

He had the vampire discussion with her, telling her she would forget, but that if she was turned she should go to the old church, and did she still want to have sex after all that? All of which she believed just as much as he had, which is to say, not very much.

Then he took one then the other nipple in his mouth and suckled until she moaned and grasped for his cock. Soon hard as a rock, he rolled on top of her and sank his cock inside her.

Steve fucked her hard, out of passion and out of a need to feed. He was extremely hungry for blood now. It took some doing, but he had her close to coming, so he timed his orgasm with hers. Then they were both coming, and he sank his fangs into her neck. Blood delicious blood gushed into his mouth, salty warm and coppery, and he thought, *I'm finally feeding what a relief.* He drank the elixir of life, feeling the energy starting in his stomach, the warmth, the power. He kept feeding, his head spinning with pleasure. He lost all sense of time and place only knowing the life preserving blood flowing into his mouth with each beat of her heart. Then she made a faint noise like a sigh that brought him out of his feeding frenzy and back to reality. He knew he had to stop feeding, so he did.

Steve rolled off Veronica and looked over at her lying on the bed. She was very still, and paler than he remembered. He lay there for a few minutes, and then thought it was time to leave, as she was obviously sound asleep. He was pleased with himself; he had fed on his own, and had bedded a super hottie as well. Then he looked a little closer. Was she still breathing? He put his ear next to her face and listened. She definitely was not breathing. He tried shaking her awake, but it was no use.

She's dead. I killed her.

Steve panicked. For the first time since he had been turned, he felt like a monster, a killer, a predatory animal. How could I have done this? I never wanted to kill anyone, especially not Veronica.

Then his thoughts started racing.

I need to get rid of the body. Will the other vampires know? Somehow he thought they would.

Should he text Valentin for help? What was the protocol?

This was only one. As long as I don't kill anyone else for at least a hundred years, they won't kill me, right? Oh my God, I just killed someone.

The remorse was overwhelming, gnawing away in the pit in his stomach like guilt with teeth.

DAMAGE CONTROL

Valentin slid his dark blue Porsche 911 Carrera S into a sharp turn at twenty-seven miles per hour, letting the rear end slide out, on the throttle just a little too much before backing off and catching it. He knew this car well, and knew its limits as he accelerated to 133 miles per hour, and then he was downshifting and breaking for the next turn. The Cabriolet was all about style. This car had its own modern style, with an almost golden natural-leather interior and an assortment of other high-end luxury features, but it was also a serious performance car at close to 400 horsepower and a top speed of just twelve miles per hour shy of 200.

A few minutes later and he was outside of the city on the highway from the airport. His phone vibrated with a text, and he wondered if he had given Kate his number. *No, I never do that, ever,* he thought. He slowed and checked the text.

<HELP! @ Amsterdam American –Steve>.

About twenty minutes later, Valentin parked a few blocks from the hotel, texted Steve for the room number, and moved into fixer mode. He had been here before over the years. The key was to fix the evidence, removing any sign that vampires even existed.

When he got to the room, Steve was a mess, pacing back and forth and freaking out, but Valentin was calm and calculating. What he learned from Steve was not promising, though. This woman was popular, with a big family and many friends. She would be missed, so the body couldn't just disappear.

The secret Valentin had learned over the years was to cultivate a medical examiner with a secret addiction, preferably an addiction that cost a lot of money. The best place to do that was just a few blocks away at the Holland Casino. Gambling was by definition an expensive addiction. There wasn't even a buffer, something in the middle, like cocaine. Cocaine was the addiction and the cocaine cost money. With gambling, you gambled your money directly; a bet was for money. Sure, casinos had chips as a sort of faux buffer, but everybody knew chips were money. The denomination was stamped right there for all to see. A well-paid medical examiner could gamble more than most, but when you don't win for a while, and then maybe lose big in an off-books high-stakes poker game, you can end up underwater quickly.

Viona had found Jacob a few years previous, when he was desperate, owing three times his substantial annual salary to Russian gangsters. She quickly realized that the long game was not to feed that night, but to help him out. So Jacob met Valentin, who gave him the money in exchange for receiving favors for life. It was amazing what a man would do, despite not having a venal disposition, to avoid seeing his family killed in front of him before he dies, so Valentin seemed like a good guy compared to that.

"There may not be any favors," Valentin had told him, "there may only be a few, but if there are any, they will be big favors."

Jacob got Valentin's text and told his wife he had to go into work. There was some sort of death, a wealthy tourist, he wasn't sure. He knew he would get his story straight for tomorrow when Valentin told him what it was so he left it vague for now.

When Lauren, Sophia, and Carol found out that Veronica had died of an aneurism that morning, they couldn't stop crying. They had just seen her and she was fine. Hotel housekeeping had found her in the hall, dead already. She must have been trying to get help. They asked if she had been doing cocaine, and they said no, but she had left with a guy, Steve from California. Inquiries would be made, and nothing determined.

Lauren called Veronica's parents, and they cried together on the phone for an hour. Lauren thought this was the worst summer of her life. Then she remembered her own tragedy, the car crash, waking up in the hospital, arms, legs, and ribs broken, and Dale dead. It was like she kept having nightmares. She would think it was over, that the darkness was finally behind her, but it wasn't. She collapsed to the floor, curled into a fetal position, and cried.

THE ELDERS

Steve sat in a small room on the ground floor of the tower, himself, a table and a twin-size bed, a jail cell by any other name he knew. His trial would be within the next three days, he had been told, as one of the elders was out of the country and had to get back. He wondered who the other two were, other than Accalu.

Were these his last days on earth, after getting turned and thinking he could live hundreds, if not thousands, of years? He couldn't believe his run had ended so quickly.

"Nobody lives forever, not even the almost dead," Valentin had told him.

There was no such thing as immortality, Steve thought. *It was always something. If mortals weren't killing vampires, vampires were killing each other.*

On the second night, Valentin came to see him. "Otakar is here. It should only be about an hour or so before your trial," he told Steve.

"Otakar? He's one of the elders? But he's just a kid," Steve blurted out.

"Remember I told you it's not your age when you were turned but how many years since you were born. Otakar was born in 1402. He fought with Jan Žižka's army in Bohemia during the Hussite Wars. The pope sent his armies against the Czechs three or four times and got defeated every time. It was the beginning of the modernization of Christianity, and warfare at the same time. Otakar was a fucking badass knight, fighting to end the tyranny of the church, more than you or I could ever claim. The guy is older than even Karolina."

Steve wasn't sure if Otakar liked him or not. He had been so sarcastic and callous about him living or dying. You don't want someone who says you will "die like a little bitch" to decide if you should live or die. On the other hand, since I fed the first time,

Otakar had been friendly enough, he thought.

Three hours later, Steve was summoned to trial by the elders of Amsterdam. He was led into the lounge by vampires he did not know, and was seated in a chair that faced a couch. Beyond the couch, everybody in residence at the tower, except Valentin, was there to witness the spectacle. Like gawkers at a hanging, Steve thought. His tension built as first Accalu walked in wearing a dark suit and tie and sat on the couch facing him. After a few minutes Otakar joined him, also wearing a suit and tie, a change from his usual jeans and 150-dollar T-shirts. They talked, but in voices so low, Steve couldn't hear a thing.

About ten excruciating minutes passed before there was a commotion and a buzz in the crowd. Then a woman said, "Get your ass in there, Valentin. *Schnell.*" and in walked Valentin, like a dog with his tail between his legs. He sat on an empty couch to the side that Steve thought might be for witnesses. He looked down, as if fearful of a beating or Steve's gaze, he couldn't tell which.

About a minute later, Karolina walked in wearing a mid length dark gray skirt and black top that showed off her hard body, but it was still a conservative businesslike appearance that made her look like a first-year consultant. The one in a hundred new grad job candidates that don't get cut after their first year, and make senior partner a few years later. She walked straight to the couch and sat with Accalu and Otakar, and then all three stared at Steve. Any hope he had was gone in that moment. Of all the people to judge him he couldn't believe Karolina was an elder. This was just not what he had pictured when he'd first heard the term *elders*. He felt like he was going through a horrible breakup, with the woman he had a huge crush on now accusing him of atrocities. Except that he had committed those atrocities; he had killed an innocent girl out of lust and hunger. All hope gone Steve thought maybe he deserved to die for his crimes.

"You have been accused of killing a mortal in the act of feeding," Karolina started. "When I turned you, I specifically said vampires could only kill one person every one hundred years. Do you remember that? Don't answer, I know you do. When the covenant was created, it was debated whether we should allow a vampire to ever kill in the act of feeding, not even once in a thousand years. Do you know why that is? Don't answer."

Steve couldn't believe how much of a bitch Karolina was now

compared to the sweet vampire who had seduced him just a few weeks ago.

"The reason we allow one every hundred years," she went on, "is to account for accidents. Was this an accident? Don't answer that?" She turned to Valentin. "Valentin, you are on duty this year for anybody who is turned, and you are supposed to mentor them if they are male. Yet when Steve went out to feed for just the third time, where were you? Don't answer that, I know. You were moping over some mortal bitch you thought you were in love with. That shit just gets old. She doesn't remember, she didn't get turned, move on."

"Now, Karolina," Accalu said, "I remember back in the Mother of Cities, you were like an animal, killing once every few months. If Steve kills one person a century, he still won't catch up to you in a thousand years."

The three elders then talked quietly amongst themselves, again too low for Steve to hear.

After about ten minutes, Otakar started to speak to Steve. "As you know, we take this very seriously, and the covenant is very specific in this. If you kill more than once in a hundred years, you will be sentenced to true death, no exceptions. This means that you need to be extremely carful for the next one hundred years, despite the fact that Valentin may have been remiss in his duties. Ultimately, you are responsible for your own actions."

So the judgment, or non-judgment, depending on how you viewed it, was passed down. A tongue-lashing really, and from the one woman Steve had a huge crush on. As the crowd got up and started talking among themselves, Steve saw Karolina and Viona embrace and kiss the air next to each other's cheeks, the way Europeans do. He started to work his way through the crowd, trying to catch up to Karolina. When he made his way to Viona, Karolina had already walked outside of the tower with a group of people, each seemingly trying to curry favor with the powerful elder. Or they were just being friendly, he couldn't tell which. By the time he got out to the garage, the roll-up door was already open and a black Porsche GT3 RS was just starting up, its exhaust note like twenty Ducati Panigale motorcycles strapped together. There are exotic super cars and there are racecars. The GT3 RS is the latter. Then she was gone, racing into the night with a roar and a screech of tires.

"Don't look so sad," Viona said to Steve.

"I thought I was going to get the true death," he said.

"I didn't mean that. You know you can never be with her, right? Didn't anybody tell you the tale of Adam and Eve? They were the first vampires to fall in love. They spent all night making love and all day sleeping. After two weeks they died in each other's arms because they had not fed, too in love to sleep with anyone else."

"'Adam and Eve'? That sounds more like fable or allegory to me," Steve replied.

"It sounds so romantic, but you need to survive first. Just don't go there, ever," Viona replied.

MISSED RENDEZVOUS

Steve, Sarah, and Valentin left the tower a few nights later. Nobody really wanted to talk about the trial, so they didn't. Valentin wanted to go by the Bulldog Energy—"Because it's close to the old church," he said—but Sarah and Steve knew he was hoping to see Kate again. Nobody really knew if she and her friends were still in the city, and even if Valentin found her, what could he do? He couldn't risk feeding on her again so soon; and if she had been turned, well, there was "Adam and Eve."

They got a table on the patio overlooking the canal, party supplies in hand. Not for themselves per se, but to share if need be. There was strength in numbers, and Sarah was British, so Valentin and Steve looked like the Austrian and American friends hanging out with her. None of them really needed to feed, but didn't rule it out either since they would be hungry in a few days. Steve knew he should try to feed when he wasn't so hungry.

Just before midnight, Valentin said he wanted to check the old church for anybody who had been turned. He acted like he was taking his duties more seriously after the tongue-lashing he'd gotten from the elders, but they knew he hoped Kate would be there.

After about forty-five minutes, Valentin had not returned and Steve had a blonde woman, Kimber from Manchester, England, under his spell. She was attractive enough and had a nice body, but maybe not the brightest bulb in the lamp and just a little trashy. He didn't know the British well enough to tell if she was playing trashy, like an American girl emulating a Britney Spears look, or if it came naturally.

He was close to persuading her that they needed to go back to her room, when he heard Kate's voice. "Sarah, hi. Where's your friend Valentin?" she asked in a half-demanding, half-belligerent drunk-girl way. Steve and Sarah shared shocked looks that she could remember their names, and Steve wondered if she had been turned.

"He'll be back in a few minutes," Sarah said. Thankfully for Steve, Kate was just with her best friend Chelsea, as Hedley and the others had already gone home.

"You're Kate Wydville, aren't you?" Kimber asked excitedly. "You dated Derek Jones from Man-U, didn't you?"

"For like five minutes. What of it?" Kate said dismissively as if Kimber were a beggar asking for change. Steve wasn't sure if she was being dismissive because she knew he had fucked Hedley, or because she thought Kimber was low-class trash. Probably both, he thought.

After about twenty uncomfortable minutes of waiting, with Valentin not returning and Kate and Chelsea refusing to acknowledge the existence of Kimber, Sarah volunteered to wait if Steve and Kimber wanted to "go for a walk." So off they went back to Kimber's room in a sketchy nearby hotel in the red-light district.

Valentin drove his Silver Porsche Speedster by the Waldorf, top down and stereo blasting, for the fifth time. Hoping if Kate walked out, he would get her attention with the music. He thought this was the best idea he'd had in a while.

Steve and Kimber rolled on her bed kissing and getting cozy. The hotel was a dump, and he hoped nothing of the multi-legged variety tried to feed on him.

"You seem nervous," Kimber said.

He was, for obvious reasons. One too many gulps of blood and it would be the true death for him. He wondered if they had a bet on that back at the tower. *Two and out, too stupid to live was what they would be saying*, he thought.

"It's just that I'm a vampire," he said, and Kimber laughed.

He told the tale, leaving out the part about Veronica, and got the "yeah right" back at him. *At least she was informed*, he thought. He pulled her top off and took off her bra, and she had nice small breasts with puffy nipples. Her skin was so white, he imagined she looked like he had already drained her blood and killed her, but put the thought out of his head. She slipped out of her jeans to reveal a pink thong. Steve pulled off his shirt and jeans, leaving his black boxer briefs on, then he slid off her panties to reveal that as trashy as she seemed, she was at least a real blonde, trimmed two fingers wide and waxed bald on her pussy lips.

When the time came, he sank his fangs into her neck. She was startled, but didn't resist. After a few gulps of delicious life-giving blood, he stopped. Probably too soon, but definitely sparing her life. She was surprised he really was a vampire, and excitedly asked a bunch of questions he knew she would never remember the answers to in the morning. She happened to mention, getting sleepy now, that she was sharing the room with her mates, and Steve left as soon as she was asleep.

About 2:00 a.m., Kate and Chelsea decided to give up their vigil and go back to the hotel. "Tell Valentin I'll be in the hotel bar tomorrow night at nine," Kate told Sarah, and immediately regretted saying it.

SORROW

The black hearse rolled slowly down a narrow tree-lined road, followed by dark luxury sedans, as the funeral procession proceeded toward the final resting place of Veronica Thompson's ancestors. Sophia and Carol rode together, but Lauren rode alone, too high on her meds to really interact with anybody, and just out of the Institute for the day.

When Sophia and Carol had found Lauren lying in a fetal position on the floor of her hotel room, they had thought she would be okay in a few minutes, or at the worst a few hours. Hours later, the Amsterdam paramedics took her away. She spent a few days in hospital before her parents had her transferred to a mental health facility back home in Montgomery, Alabama, where she had stayed until now.

Lauren rode in her grandfather's Rolls Royce Silver Cloud, old but solid and stately, toward the darkness that lay ahead. She was so high on meds that, she barely knew what was happening, too high to cry or laugh for that matter. Deep down, though, she knew Veronica was gone.

The private service at the funeral home for family and intimate friends had been gut wrenching. Before it started, each mourner had filed past the open casket. Veronica looked as beautiful as always, like she was just sleeping, but they all knew she would never wake up to fulfill the promise that had seemed so bright and shining just a few weeks earlier.

Now four hundred of Montgomery's old-money whites, some with family names dating back to the early 1800s, and a handful of influential blacks were converging on the cemetery to pay respects to one of their own, stricken down too soon. The sorrow was palpable, not just among the old oaks and somber stones of death, but in town, among the rest of the populace. Sorrow for the beloved girl who never hurt anyone, and who was the last person in the world who deserved to die from something so random.

GERLACH

A few nights later, Viona and Valentin were at a large party thrown by some spoiled rich Dutch girl. Champagne, cocaine, and super DJ Hardwell providing beats. Viona was from a different time, but the music spoke to her, at least when I'm on the hunt to feed, she thought. The majority of the crowd, though, were kids in their late teens and early twenties, and were annoying her tonight with their selfies and self-interest, easy to turn to her purpose but boring nonetheless.

Gerlach was older, thirty-one, and feeling as annoyed by the crowd as Viona, or so he said. He was saying all the right things, and had an interesting background. He was ex-military, still kept his light brown hair cropped short, and had been in the Dutch Army with a tour in Afghanistan. Hell, he said. Now he worked security for high rollers, wealthy Dutch and foreign nationals, but most of his time was spent coordinating not being the muscle. By the look of him, Viona thought he could be if the situation required it, and she was anticipating an athletic fuck. He was done working the event, although still on call, and he lived close, so they left.

Gerlach had the top floor of a converted warehouse, about three thousand square feet. He could afford it not from his job, but from family money. It looked like a place vampires might live, Viona thought, except for the large windows that would let in light during the day. They lay together on his bed in the middle of the loft, kissing and caressing. As things started to heat up, Viona told her tale of necessity, and he agreed, but something about him was different. He seemed to expect the story, almost anticipate it, but Viona was hungry and horny.

Gerlach had gotten lucky, the break of a lifetime. When a contact of his at the police department had filled him in on the dead

American woman, he had also mentioned that a man named Steve who matched the description of the guy from California had been reported missing about five weeks before the recent suspicious death. Gerlach put two and two together, and now he was out for revenge.

Gerlach came from a long line of vampire hunters, his grandfather and namesake being the last, as his father was never a complete believer. The stories from his youth had propelled Gerlach on a journey that led to tonight. Joining the army and being trained as a disciplined killer, despite the opportunities of working in his father's firm, were all part of his long-term plan. His current job in security brought him into the sphere of high-end parties that he suspected would be prime opportunities for vampires out to feed, and he had his finger on the pulse of anything strange going on in Amsterdam. He had mapped a few of them—Valentin, Sarah, and Viona—of whom he was almost sure; and a few others he suspected. He thought he knew where their nest was, or one of them anyway. His grandfather had always told him there were three nests in the city, but not where. That sort of information was just too dangerous for a kid, his grandfather had told him. Until a few days ago, he had never been sure, but the guy from California disappearing and then reappearing in connection with a suspicious death, and now Viona confirming everything he had suspected, gave him the impetus to move forward.

He slid his hand under his pillow for the hypodermic filled with a sedative.

Viona awoke in what seemed to be a cage with rusty iron bars that she could only feel because a black cloth covered the bars. She thought that was good because she could tell it was day now, and fell back asleep.

At about nine that night, Gerlach pulled the thick black cloth off of her cage and said in Dutch, "I know you're a vampier."

"*Neuken u,*" she replied.

"I've been watching you for a while. I know about Valentin and Sarah too."

"Who are those people? You're just some psycho who has kidnapped me. Let me go now and I won't tell the police. You don't have to go through with your sick plan. I was just joking when I made up that vampire story last night."

Viona spoke convincingly, but Gerlach was not fooled.

THE HUNT FOR THE HUNTER

Two days after Viona went missing, Sarah found the note tucked into a seam in the wall of the warehouse that surrounded the tower nest. A vampire not returning for one night was not necessarily cause for concern, as they might be hunkered down someplace safe, a closet or a basement. But two nights and not showing up at another nest was concerning, and now the note.

"I have your vampire Viona, and will trade her for the brutal killer Steve. Leave a note here with your response. -The Equalizer"

A new vampire hunter had emerged, smart enough to use a handle and not his real name. A chill went through the tower as many remembered the infamous Dutch vampire hunter Gerlach, long dead at the hands of Otakar. Valentin and Accalu went through the previous day's video from the tower security camera, finding the image of a man about six foot one with brown hair, but a baseball cap obscured his face, and he kept his head turned away from the camera as he left the ransom note. So they had no clues. Because of his height, he might be Dutch, but that was just an educated guess. They had watched Gerlach's son Hendrik for a number of years, but he showed no interest in vampires, and seemed to be in denial of their very existence after the disappearance of his father. That left an enormous list of suspects, which included Amsterdam residents and foreigners visiting the city.

Steve got his first chance to earn his keep as a network engineer. Sarah had procured a copy of Viceroy, the latest NSA snooping software, from a CIA agent visiting Amsterdam. How he had gotten the software from another agency he wouldn't say, and he never remembered how he lost it. They had tried to get it to work, but nobody in any of the nests had the skillset necessary.

Sarah handed Steve a black cloth bag with nine USB flash drives, and he started trying to figure it out. He was not a security guy, although he had configured his share of firewalls and had a basic understanding. Eight of the flash drives seemed to be empty, but one had some executable files and documentation. He read through the PDFs, but was getting nowhere until he made one of those giant leaps in understanding. The other eight flash drives contained an ARM processor, and thus could boot a stripped-down version of Linux with just one driver for USB. The kernel could boot in under five seconds when inserted into a USB port, immediately deploying Viceroy to the host system and then to any IP address on the same network behind a firewall. This allowed the person deploying Viceroy to remove the USB stick in under sixty seconds. Another hour, and he thought he had everything figured out.

Steve already had VMware running on his MacBook, and added a Red Hat Linux virtual machine (VM), along with the rarely used Windows 7 VM. It took his dual core MacBook Pro what seemed like hours to calculate the 2048bit encryption key that would be used during the compile of the Viceroy distribution kernel. That done it was only a matter of seconds to compile the actual kernel. Once Viceroy was deployed, he could use a Windows-based console to browse the compromised computer systems, using the encryption key he had already generated over the TLS protocol on a randomized TCP port after the initial handshake. He could request any file or run a program remotely, like the front end to an SQL database that could browse or query records. The distribution kernel installed the actual snooping software on virtually any operating system on a private network inside a firewall. A different key was generated for each site to be compromised using the Viceroy system.

Next they needed to get one of the USB drives onto the police computer systems and on all three of the common reservation systems used by most Amsterdam hotels. This was a job for Sarah and Evette, a Frenchwoman who came over from the museum nest to "distract and deploy," as Steve phrased it. Evette was a stunning brunette with curly shoulder- length hair that played a perfect contrast to Sarah's strawberry-blond locks. She had been turned during the French revolution while working for the faceless masses, a thing that Valentin could never reconcile in the 120 years he had known her. Together, Sarah and Evette covered all the bases in the distraction game.

The night after they had deployed Viceroy, Steve was overwhelmed by the amount of data. On the police systems, he found the report on Veronica, with the narrative as synthesized by Valentin in the dawn hours of his accidental homicide. He also found a missing person's report on himself filed by his employer, and token inquiries by his self-absorbed parents. *At least they wanted to give the outward impression that they cared about me,* Steve thought. They used the data from the hotels to cross-reference any known foreign vampire hunters, and see if it raised red flags. Everybody spread out trying to gather information. Some hotel guests had already left the city, others had not arrived yet when the note was found, but the sheer size of the list was still daunting. Steve continued to mine data, but it was hard when he didn't know exactly what he was looking for, or if it was even on a computer system.

Suspects were interrogated, and then fed on so they would forget, but nobody was killed, and nobody yielded any useful information. The one thing the vampires did not do was respond to the ransom note. As the elders often said, the best defense was to let people believe vampires did not exist. That was a lot easier in these times, with science explaining almost everything, and all superstition being explained away. Today only kids and the insane really believed in vampires. Even most descendants of real vampire hunters took the old tales with a grain of salt.

Four days and nights passed without a real lead, when Valentin found a Czech woman, mid forties dark brown hair and the body of someone who took care of themselves, back to the tower for further interrogation. She was a professor at Charles University in Prague, and she specialized in paranormal phenomenon. She was the best lead they had found so far, and all present where convinced she would at least know whom The Equalizer was, if it wasn't her.

By dawn, Accalu was 99 percent sure she knew nothing. She was book smart on any number of topics, but viewed vampires as purely folk legends, easily explained by disease and superstition. They would keep interrogating her another night just to be sure, Accalu doing an abbreviated feeding so she would forget, but they all knew time was running out for Viona—if it hadn't already.

They had placed spies on the doors at every nest to supplement the security cameras, but they could only watch at night. Valentin and Otakar considered hiring private security during the day, but thought it may arouse suspicion. That evening, though, with no viable clues, they changed their minds and procured daytime guards for all three nests, with a twist.

STALEMATE

Viona knew she had to feed soon or she would die, and Gerlach knew it too. She had not fed for fifteen days before she had met Gerlach, and that had stretched out to eighteen with her captivity.

"Please," she pleaded. "Just chain me up. You can fuck me and let me feed, but I won't get away."

"I won't remember anything, though," Gerlach said.

"You will when you see me chained up in the morning."

He just shook his head and walked away.

Things hadn't gone Gerlach's way either. He always had a plan and executed it precisely, so this situation with Viona was outside his comfort zone. The other vampires had not responded to his demands. They hadn't even acknowledged them. It was like they didn't exist, but he knew they did. Viona had confirmed that three nights prior. He also knew from what his grandfather had told him that she would not live much longer, and he would lose any leverage he had to get to the homicidal vampire Steve.

Gerlach seriously considered Viona's offer, his cock getting hard at the prospect of fucking the sexy blonde. But honor and duty forbade it, along with the stories related by his grandfather. He lived by the same code of honor, or at least tried to. He only had the oral history to go by as nothing was written down, but he knew that when a vampire killed, he had an ancestral duty to give the vampire the true death, and so he would. He also knew that because of what they called the covenant, vampires didn't kill as a rule. But he was sure Viona would try given the chance, and thought it better not to let her feed on him.

Gerlach had learned to ignore pain even before his military training, but he had to make sure he didn't insert the knife directly into an artery and bleed out. The yield was less than he expected, but he handed a lowball glass a quarter full of his blood to Viona. She grabbed it out of his hands and gulped down the life-preserving fluid.

"Thank you," she murmured, still weak. It was not much, but it would keep her alive for a day or two. If she fed properly, it would be ten to fifteen. "That wasn't enough," she said. "Please let me feed, I promise I won't hurt you."

He ignored her.

Gerlach got a text from his buddy Jan from one of the other security firms in Amsterdam. He had put out the word to be on the lookout for any strange security jobs guarding seemingly random buildings. Jan's firm had just been hired to guard three sites, one of which was the warehouse where Gerlach had left the note. Now he was sure he had the address of every vampire nest in the city. Besides the tower, there was one in the red-light district, and the Rijksmuseum, a location he had suspected for some time due to its age and underground architecture.

Although Gerlach was relieved that his theories had panned out, the fact that guards would be installed at every vampire nest made communicating that much harder. He needed to leave another note, in case they hadn't found the first one—a possibility he thought increasingly likely—to let them know Viona was still alive and they had a chance to turn the rogue vampire Steve over to him. Jan happened to mention on the phone later, when Gerlach called him back, that he was assigned to the museum nest the next morning. Gerlach thought Jan was a bit of a loser, he would never do a job like that, but in the interest of his goal of gathering valuable vampire data, he had never blown him off completely.

The next day around noon Gerlach, was down at the museum. He was sure he could determine where to leave his new note by learning what and where they had asked Jan to guard, but after twenty minutes of talking to Jan, he was no closer to finding the entrance to the nest. Jan was stationed behind the museum, near the lily pond at the southeast corner of the building. He'd been told to look for anything suspicious, anybody looking around or leaving a note. After an hour and a half surveying the area, Gerlach gave up, defeated, but he had one bit of hope. Jan would be stationed at the red-light-district nest tomorrow. He didn't think Viona would live that long, so he spent the rest of the day trying to procure some human blood.

⚑

The next evening yielded no more useful information from the Czech professor, and Accalu resisted the urge to spend time juxtaposing for intellectual reasons the reality of vampires versus her theories and interpretation of folk legend. Time was running out. Viona could only be alive if her captor had let her feed on him, which was not likely. Vampires left the nest again with lists in hand as they tried to find the perpetrator, but with over two million people in the metropolitan area, that was difficult. They could eliminate a million and a half, but that left more than half a million people. They couldn't even be sure that the figure in the security video wasn't really a tall woman, although they doubted it.

⚑

Gerlach almost snagged the IV bag of a patient getting a blood transfusion in the hospital, but was noticed by someone he knew, an ER doctor. That evening he extracted more of his own blood, thinking that he looked like a pathetic teenage girl into cutting herself. He was disappointed in himself for not having a contingency plan; he was smarter than this. The modest yield of blood kept Viona alive, but he could tell she was getting weaker by the day without a proper feeding.

The next day Gerlach went down to the address in the red-light district that Jan had given him, and was relieved that this time Jan had a specific point to guard. Along with the stairs going up to the front of houses on the street, there was also a door below street level, accessed by another set of steps. He left his note in the crack of the door along with a burner mobile phone, and then reiterated to Jan that he could not tell anyone.

After that, Jan clearly expected a favor, or at least to hang out. Gerlach didn't particularly want to hang out with Jan when he had time, and he didn't have any time right now since he needed to find blood for Viona. Then he got an idea. Jan frequented a place called The Dungeon a few blocks from there. It wasn't like the several Amsterdam dungeon and torture museums for tourists. This was a hard-core bondage and S&M club. He had been there once with Jan but it wasn't his thing. Jaded by combat, nothing really shocked him, and he preferred his women more willing. He had pretended he was into it a year or so ago, partly because he thought he might be and partly to humor Jan.

So he told Jan to come by his place that night. "I've got this crazy submissive girl into bondage that I'm getting bored with."

When he got back to his loft, he told Viona he was going to let her feed that night, not on him but a friend of his. By nine o'clock, he had her chained up bondage style. "Whatever you do, don't kill him," he said when he was done.

When Jan arrived, his expectations were surpassed as he surveyed his perfect fantasy girl, blonde and shackled the way he liked. Had Gerlach kidnapped her off the street? He doubted it, but he could fantasize. Most of the girls he had met who were into this sort of thing had dyed black hair and too many tattoos. He liked them more innocent looking, like this one.

"You two have your fun," Gerlach said, checking his grandfather's watch as he headed down to the street.

Viona had never allowed herself to be chained for fear of being exposed at sunrise, combined with the fact that she never wanted to be, but she had engaged in light bondage and role playing as a means to an end. So she played along with Jan, especially since she was now fully in survival mode. She was so weak, she wasn't sure the chains were needed to restrain her. She also neglected to follow the decrees of the covenant. This was war against the vampires, and she believed an exemption was justified.

When the time came, she sank her fangs into his neck. He flinched a little but didn't realize she had actually broken the skin. The life-giving blood gushed into her mouth, warm and coppery, with each beat of his heart, and she felt the energy radiate from her belly. After a few minutes the blood stopped flowing, and she knew he was drained, and she knew he was dead. She felt little emotion, mostly the recognition that she could survive another fifteen days plus on this much blood.

When Gerlach got back, he saw Jan's bare ass still on top of Viona and thought he had returned too soon. He had been gone almost two hours if only to avoid seeing just such a scene.

"Sorry, I'll come back," he said as he slipped out the door and went downstairs. Forty-five minutes later he returned; they were still in the same position.

"Shit. Oh shit," he exclaimed as he realized what he was looking at. Jan's pale, blood-drained corpse was still on top of Viona, who was unable to push him off due to her restraints.

⸙

Sarah read the new note found at the red-light-district nest out loud. "'I'm having trouble keeping Viona alive. You need to hurry. Hand over Steve. It's your own covenant I'm trying to fulfill. He killed and now he deserves the true death. Call the number programmed into the phone.'"

"Don't blame yourself," Sarah told Steve, but that was hard for him not to do. He was the cause and this was the effect, Viona captured by some psychopath. Otakar and Valentin, on the other hand, knew that they were dealing with a real vampire hunter now, someone in whom had been handed down the traditions and practices of that vile guild. He knew about the covenant. Not many mortals did, not even the Czech professor they had released that evening. Steve checked the number of the phone that had been left and the one number programmed into the address book. Both were burners, the minutes purchased with cash.

"What happened with the security guard? Why didn't he report anything?" Otakar asked.

They called the agency, but got no information. Then they scoured the video from the security cameras and found the perpetrator, this time wearing a black hoodie, as if protection from the summer showers typical of Amsterdam. His face was obscured, but they were convinced it was the same guy.

Then they got a break. After placing the note, he started talking to the guard as if he knew him. That explained why nothing had been reported. They had already deployed Viceroy at most of the security firms in the city, and Steve quickly had a name—Jan Vos—and then a picture to match their video.

Steve got Jan's home address, and Sarah and Valentin went out to investigate. Sarah, with Valentin hanging back in the shadows, knocked on his door. A blonde woman in her early twenties answered the door. Without thinking, Valentin joined the two women; standing next to a somewhat surprised Sarah. The woman said her name was Johanna. She was Jan's sister, and she hadn't seen him since yesterday, but didn't think anything of it. Valentin and Sarah posed as friends who owed Jan money for a bar tab he covered, but she seemed to doubt their story, because her brother didn't have much money as a rule. Valentin left his number, thinking that he needed to feed in the next few days, and with Johanna he could kill two birds with one stone.

Sarah read Valentin's mind. "I know she's your type," she said as they walked away, "but don't complicate things."

Sarah felt guilty about not telling Valentin about Kate waiting for him at the hotel bar, but it was for the best. If she didn't show up at the old church turned, there was no point in pursuing her.

Valentin didn't answer Sarah. He was thinking that if Jan hadn't shown up by tomorrow night, he'd interrogate the girl fully and feed. In times of war, the covenant held exemptions for situations like this.

Gerlach had a problem. Well, actually two. He had a dead body he needed to dispose of, and people would quickly start to miss Jan, especially his employer. It was Viona's fault Jan was dead, and he already planned to give her the true death, after using her as bait. He knew the vampires had to have gotten his note this time, so all he had to do was wait for his burner phone to ring.

THE CALM BEFORE THE STORM

Viona, back in her cage, looked through the bars at Gerlach's open loft. *I staved off the true death for another two weeks or more from over feeding, but I'm still a captive.*

Gerlach looked at his prisoner. *She will live for another week or two, giving me more options and flexibility with my plan.*

He was closer to his goal, but as sunrise neared and the phone didn't ring, he grew increasingly pensive.

☥

The next evening, Valentin slipped away, thoughts of Johanna in his head, and the task of getting information on her brother Jan. His plan was to seduce her, feed—letting her know he was a vampire and that this was serious—and then interrogate her. Jan could be a vampire hunter or just a "person of interest," and by midnight he would know which.

Johanna was home when Valentin got to her house, but there was still no sign of her brother. After he fed, Valentin began his interrogation, telling her she would die, telling her that it would hurt. She was not all that smart, spending her days hoping to meet a rich man who would take her away from this. *Whatever the fuck "this" is,* Valentin thought. Her brother was a loser in her eyes. He had a low-paying job, and she knew he was into S&M porn, which she thought was creepy. Still, she was starting to get concerned, as he hadn't returned. To Jan, a long-term relationship was two days, so she doubted it was a woman. Valentin wondered if he was guarding Viona as well, but he had only disappeared two nights prior, right after they saw him on the security video. *Maybe he has been recruited by the mastermind, the real vampire hunter,* he thought. Valentin spent the rest of the night waiting for Jan.

He returned to the tower nest just twenty minutes before dawn with no real information on Jan, who had not returned.

"I checked the computer system at Jan's company with Viceroy," Steve said. "He didn't show up for work today."

"I didn't get much from the sister either. I suspect he is with the vampire hunter, but we have no way knowing where."

With nothing else to go on, they made a plan that they would execute the following evening, just after sunset. They needed to flush this "equalizer" vampire hunter out, and they had an idea. They'd use good old-fashioned intimidation.

THE SHOWDOWN

Steve was still learning the Viceroy system, and had recently discovered a feature that allowed him to spoof any phone number while making a VOIP call. He dialed the number of the burner phone and Hubrech, impersonating a police officer, demanded Gerlach come down to the station for questioning, right now. "We can get a warrant in the morning, but I'm sure you want to clear things up before it comes to that," Hubrech said.

They hoped that Gerlach might have committed other crimes, not just kidnapping, and the shock of the police calling his burner phone might throw him off his game.

"How did he sound?" Valentin asked. "Do you think he will go down to the station?"

"Hard to say, but I can tell you one thing, he's Dutch for sure," Hubrech said, knowing his native accent.

Gerlach debated blowing off the police, but he didn't need any more trouble than he already had. He had to dispose of Jan's body later. If the police came to the loft now and found a kidnapped woman and a dead body, he would almost certainly go to prison. He called his buddy on the force, but he didn't know anything. He checked the system and found out that they wanted to interview Gerlach in relation to a missing person, Jan. Steve, who had planted the data, was watching and now had Gerlach's contact at the police station.

Otakar assembled a team of both reconnaissance and enforcers at the tower. Each vampire was fitted with Dutch Special Forces communication systems, small wireless earpieces with encrypted audio capability. They had procured them a few years prior for just such an occasion. Nobody knew what the vampire hunter looked like, so people were placed at the main and employee entrances to the police station, along with the streets leading up to the building. They expected a single male about six feet one with brown hair, but they didn't know if he was bald on top as his head has been covered in both videos. Inside the police station, Sarah tried to identify the mystery vampire hunter's inside contact, Gerrit Jansen. She walked by his desk, saw his nametag, but he wasn't there.

Gerlach walked slowly toward the police station, wary of a trap, but only a few people were out. He quickened his pace as he neared the front door. The vampires keeping watch spotted a man about six foot one with short cropped brown hair were sure they had their guy. They started to move in, flanking from all sides just as Otakar had recommended. Valentin and Otakar blocked the front door, walking toward him. Then from behind them they heard somebody shout, "Gerlach look out!" and both Valentin and Otakar went down, tasered from behind by 50,000 volts. Gerlach ran past the men and into the station with Gerrit.

"That's not possible," Valentin exclaimed as he pushed himself back up. "Gerlach van Meer died years ago."

Steve pulled an Android tablet from his bag and Googled the name. The results quickly showed the truth. Gerlach the vampire hunter had a grandson who apparently had taken up the family obsession. Steve had an address and photos to go with the name, but they had more to deal with right now as both Gerlach and Gerrit emerged from the front door with a Heckler & Koch MP5 submachine gun in each hand, four guns total. A vampire could recover from a gunshot wound more quickly than a mortal, but a gun like that could cut you in half. The three vampires rapidly retreated. Not that Gerrit intended for either him or Gerlach to discharge a weapon in the middle of Amsterdam. The guns were just to intimidate. After scattering, each vampire took a different route back to their respective nests, arriving at different times and making sure they were not followed.

MAD SCRAMBLE

Gerlach moved quickly when he got back to the loft. He had put off getting rid of Jan's body, and was not looking forward to hauling a corpse down the street, especially since it was already emitting the foul scent of corruption. He needed to move Viona too. He knew where to take her. His buddy had a greenhouse for growing marijuana just outside the city, and he had a key. It was automated and generally there was only somebody there once a week, until it was time to harvest the buds.

It took hours for everybody to get back to the tower and reassemble. It was truly shocking, considering how organized they had seemed just three hours earlier, but a vampire's survival did not depend on cooperation on a daily basis. The ancient nest model was more about shelter and trust than cooperation. They needed a place to sleep during the day, and they could really only trust other vampires. In the act of hunting and feeding, a male and female might go out in a group to put mortals at ease, but the act of closing the deal, so to speak, was generally a solitary one.

With just twenty-five minutes until sunrise, they planned their next move. They had the vampire hunter's address, and come gloaming next, they would execute their assault, free Viona, and kill Gerlach.

Gerlach didn't even have time to weight Jan's body before he dumped it in the canal, but the neck wound would raise suspicions by those in the know, pointing them in the direction he desired. Moving

Viona was more difficult. He had to chain her since he couldn't bring the cage with him, but he soon had her properly restrained and in the trunk of his BMW.

A quick forty-five minute drive and he was at his friend's greenhouse. They could stay there a week or two at most, so he needed a plan beyond calling in sick to work. He found an empty equipment shed that he hoped wouldn't be checked by anyone who came by to care for the plants, and Viona was sound asleep in there a half hour after sunrise.

As the sun set on Amsterdam, Accalu, Otakar, Valentin, Steve, and Hubrech headed directly to Gerlach's loft. They climbed the outside wall on the alley side, easily entering through a window. Once inside they immediately knew they were too late. Nobody was there. An old, rusting cage like a giant antique birdcage, round and pointed at the top, likely once used in a circus sideshow, made it obvious they had the right place. They spent a few hours looking for clues as to where Gerlach had taken Viona, and waited for his possible return. About 1:30, they decided to check every known van Meer property, including anything Steve could find online.

Gerlach's father Hendrik's house was their first stop. They again got in through an upstairs window and quickly checked every room, careful not to wake anyone. In one bedroom Gerlach's younger sister Tess, blonde and lithe slept, and if Valentin hadn't fed in the last few days, he would have taken her right there as retribution. The house had a large garage with three cars, but there was no sign of Gerlach or Viona.

The next stop was the more likely old workshop of Hendrik's father, Gerlach the Senior. With Hubrech's translations, Steve had learned through online searches of old news stories that this had been the home base of Gerlach's vampire hunting activities. Once again they came up with nothing. The floor was dusty, with most things covered in drop cloths. They did see a relatively dust-free circle from where the younger Gerlach had removed the rusty iron cage, but no other sign that anybody had been there for many years.

That left only one other location, the site of Gerlach the Senior's demise. The family cabin in eastern Belgium was outside the small town of Voort, a three-hour drive each way. They couldn't make it that night, but tomorrow, they decided, Accalu, Valentin, Otakar, and

Steve would make the drive.

NOTHING FOR IT

Sophia and Carol drove down the long twisting driveway of the place everyone called the Institute, a catchall facility for the seriously wealthy of Montgomery, treating anything from dementia to mental disorders. Some would say it was used to put people away and out of sight, but they also had their successes, taking people traumatized by life events and making them whole again.

When they got to Lauren's room, she seemed better, not as drugged out as she had been during Veronica's funeral. She had a private room the size of a studio apartment, with a bed and a couch, but no kitchenette. They all sat together on the couch and chatted about this and that, trying to avoid the subject of Veronica.

Then in a clear voice Lauren started, "I remember everything now, what Valentin did to me, all of it. When we were alone, he told me he was a vampire. I thought he was kidding, playing on the European count persona he had, but while we were having sex, when I … you know, he bit my neck and drank my blood. He said I would forget, and I did for the longest time, but now it's coming back to me in my dreams. It's all so real. I'm not crazy." Talking faster, she went on, "I think Steve is a vampire too, and I think he killed Veronica. I don't know why Valentin didn't kill me. Sometimes I wish he had."

Sophia and Carol looked at each other, then at Lauren. "It's going to be all right, Lauren," Carol said. "You just need some rest."

"Yes. You're just tired. You need some rest, and this is the best place for you right now," Sophia said. Both were trying to make themselves and Lauren believe everything would be all right, but deep down they knew they hadn't just lost one friend in Europe that summer. They had lost two.

THE ENCHANTED FOREST

They planned to take four cars: Accalu's Ferrari Testarossa, Valentin's Porsche 911, Otakar's Ferrari 250 GTO, and Karolina's Porsche GT3 RS. She had overruled their original plans; she was coming along with Hubrech. She had turned Viona and felt responsible, and Hubrech, massive at six foot four and 230 pounds, was Dutch like Viona and had convinced Karolina he could help. When Otakar started to say maybe it wasn't a good idea for all three elders to leave Amsterdam and put themselves in harm's way, Karolina dismissed the idea with a wave of her hand and a look of anger. Her anger was not at Otakar, but at the situation itself. Steve thought for a moment that he would ride with her, but she quickly told Hubrech to get in her car, and Valentin said he wanted to drive alone. Otakar motioned Steve over to his red 1964 Ferrari.

"Do you want to drive?" he asked.

"Sure," Steve said. The 250 GTO was considered one of the first super cars for Ferrari, or anybody else for that matter. Steve knew it had to be worth millions. He just didn't know how much for sure.

The drive was long and monotonous, but as Steve got just a few miles outside of Amsterdam, he felt a sense of anxiety and had the strong desire to return to the safety of the nest.

"The feeling will pass soon enough," Otakar said. "Most vampires find it hard to travel at first." He knew the feeling of dread would have been tenfold if Steve had been in the passenger seat with nothing else to concentrate on. To help Steve take his mind off his travel anxiety, Otakar started telling him stories about the old days.

"Did I ever tell you how I was turned?" he asked.

"No," Steve replied.

"In December 1421 and January 1422, I fought in the Battles of Kutná Hora and Deutschbrod in Jan Žižka's army against the forces of Pope Martin V. After they burned Jan Hus at the stake, creating a martyr, his followers grew, so in 1415, the Catholic Church declared war on us. By this time, those in the church reformation movement were called Hussites. They sent their army against us, German and Hungarian troops of the Holy Roman Empire, but Jan Žižka had us prepared. We used horse-drawn war wagons with cannons mounted on them. I carried a long, thin hand cannon called a snake with a load that would slice right through the armor of their knights. After a month of getting ass kicking after ass kicking, the Pope's army retreated from Bohemia. On the night of January 7, after the battle of Deutschbrod, we were camped on the edge of a forest celebrating another victory. I was taking a piss not far from our camp when what I thought was a camp follower, this beautiful girl, walked up to me. Her dark hair and fit body immediately transfixed me, and we went into the forest. I'd been with girls before, but she was something special. I didn't know if she was a whore or my future wife. I'm sure she left me for dead—this was long before the covenant—but I survived somehow, and the shade of the trees helped me get through that first day. We didn't have the support systems we have today, but I made my way to the Mother of Cities and, based on rumors I had heard on the street, found the entrance to the tunnels under the city."

After three hours of brisk driving, but not so fast as to arouse local law enforcement, they arrived at the van Meer family cabin, little more than a brick shack on the edge of a small forest among farms that spread out in every direction. The property had been in the family for generations. A quick inspection of the cabin revealed nothing, but the family also had an illegal underground cellar behind their property in the forest, which unknown to the family was near the final resting place of Gerlach the Senior. They found the door, but it appeared nobody had been down there for some time.

"Six hours total driving and nothing," Valentin snapped. He had been on edge since before Viona's abduction, and was clearly at the tipping point now. Steve thought Valentin was starting to act like the vampires in horror stories, just one wrong glance away from going on a wilding spree and leaving a trail of bloody carnage.

They drove back to Borgloon, hoping to find an open petrol station on their way to the A13. They found one on the edge of town and started filling up the cars, none of which had a particularly long range or could be considered fuel-efficient.

It was just past midnight and the station had a small store, one of the last places open at that hour. Some teenagers, three boys and a girl, all wearing neo-Nazi garb, walked out of the store, looked at the vampires, and gave a Heil Hitler salute before sauntering off toward a nearby orchard.

"Easy, Valentin," Accalu said. "We don't need any more trouble here."

Valentin often felt that he was misunderstood, that others believed he preferred his women with blonde hair and blue eyes. But his "type," so to speak, was a much more complex combination of features, including personality.

In the spring of 1939, Valentin met a woman named Gisela, a brunette whose curls fell past her shoulders and framed a round face with big brown eyes. She had an alluring body, and that something else he could not, after all these years of living, name. As with Kate, he had thought he was in love with a mortal. The catch was that Gisela wasn't a tourist. She had been living with relatives for the past two years, having fled Germany and its increased hostility toward the Jewish population. Valentin had not paid much attention to the Third Reich and their politics, living in his vampire bubble, until May 10, 1940, when four days after the Germans invaded Holland, the Dutch Army surrendered. After that the Nazi presence was in Valentin's face and not something he could ignore. Apparently they blamed some sort of Jewish conspiracy on all of their troubles, which Valentin knew were mostly the result of the treaty of Versailles.

Gisela did not get turned, and she could not remember Valentin every couple of months when he fed on her again, but now he also protected her, lurking in the shadows to strike down any German troops doing night raids. She never knew he was there, and that was the way he preferred it, a selfless act for his lover. He could not protect her during the day, though, which tore at his heart. In 1944 they took her. Not satisfied with the ever-increasing restrictions levied against Jewish population, they transferred more people to the camps.

When they took Gisela, Valentin lost control. He felt so helpless since it had happened during the day. He went on a wilding spree that lasted for weeks, killing Nazi soldiers by the dozens, but never telling anyone in any of the nests, although Accalu suspected. This quickly brought increased troop presence to Amsterdam to quell the perceived resistance; and with their arrival, more Jews were removed to the camps. Valentin was racked with guilt. He hadn't protected

Gisela, and now he was responsible for more innocent people being taken away.

Valentin was gone before anybody could do anything. Kate, Viona's abduction, and their failure to do anything about it had his anger at a boil, and now he had a target for that anger. The group of teenagers was walking on a footpath between fruit orchards when he apprehended them, fangs visible in anger.

When Accalu finally caught up to them, the three boys and the girl were cowering under a pear tree in terror while Valentin, a real life *vampier*, lectured them on the evils of the Nazi philosophy. Accalu held back, relieved not to have found three bodies that looked like the product of a meat grinder, arms and legs detached like the wings of a house fly, and Valentin draining the last drops of the girl's blood. After about thirty minutes of lecturing and imploring the teens, with the occasional snap of his fangs, Valentin ran out of steam. The four ran off in the naïve belief that they could outrun him.

Then Steve got a text from Sarah.

<Help @ van Meer cabin police –S>

They raced back to the cabin to rescue Sarah, who had apparently followed them in an attempt to help. When they got there they saw a police car, two other vehicles, and Sarah's Range Rover, but no sign of Sarah.

The police officer had initially claimed he was going to write up Sarah and Evette for trespassing, but when he heard Evette's French accent, he decided they needed another form of justice. His buddies arrived fifteen minutes later, and now they were going to have a little fun. They stripped the women and tied them up, unaware that any attempt to rape them would be a quick death sentence. They all had guns, but Sarah and Evette were patiently waiting for their opening, but it had not come yet.

After the other vampires had assessed the situation at the van Meer cabin, Valentin spoke from reason, past the peak of his anger and lust for violence. He told the group they needed to strategize, and Otakar told them he had learned well enough in the fifteenth century that the more angles you came at an enemy, the quicker they would fall. Flanking on all sides, they moved in quickly, and no mercy was given. They left the bodies and the vehicles, thinking that leaving the van Meer cabin as the scene of a gruesome crime that included the mutilation of a police officer would help discourage Gerlach's vampire hunting activities.

BACK TO HAVEN

W ith all that extracurricular activity, there was no way they could get back to Amsterdam before dawn. Karolina called Fallon, the resident elder in Antwerp, and the oldest native vampire still alive in all the "low countries," which included the Netherlands, Belgium, and Luxembourg. She had been turned around 100 BC when the Romans invaded what would become Belgium. She liked to say Accalu had turned a woman in Rome who had turned a man who had then turned her. It was also rumored that the Romans had had a "night platoon" of vampires as part of one of their legions.

They got to the nest about forty-five minutes before sunrise, a large building within a building similar to the tower in Amsterdam, but horizontal, smaller, and crowded. Otakar and Hubrech got their own sleeping chambers, but the others had to share: Valentin and Karolina, Accalu and Evette, and Steve and Sarah.

Fallon, who was twenty when she was turned, stood about five feet zero out of her heels, and had brown hair and a curvaceous body. To Steve, her face was somehow different, like something he had only seen in paintings by the Dutch masters. She truly had a look from another time, but her Chanel clothes and Prada heels were clearly of the now.

"Are you okay?" Steve asked Sarah when they got in bed together naked.

"Yes, I trust you," Sarah said.

"I meant from the forest. Are you okay from that?"

"Yes, they were going to die one way or another," Sarah said.

They had undressed together naturally as if they did it every night, and her pale skin, her landing strip of strawberry-blonde pubic hair and bare pussy lips were everything Steve had dreamed of. Now in bed, as they cuddled naturally as if boyfriend and girlfriend, he was hard as a rock, and he knew she knew. She acted tough, but he sensed from the way she relaxed in his arms that she was glad she wasn't alone.

The next evening Fallon announced, "No feeding in my city." It was obvious to Steve that her bossy manner annoyed Karolina, but Karolina let it go. Steve hung out with Fallon in the lounge area of the nest as they waited until 10:30 to start their journey back to Amsterdam.

"I was in Antwerp earlier in the summer on business at two banks," he said.

"Yes, we have lots of banks here," Fallon said. "Karolina told me you just got turned."

"Yeah, just this summer. I understand you got turned more than two thousand years ago. I'm sure you've seen a lot."

"It was way back around 100 BC, when the Romans first came. When I was turned, there were maybe 10 percent the amount of people as there are today, and they found so many ways to get themselves killed that I learned early to feed without killing. They certainly didn't need me thinning the population, and I needed to have a blood supply. Let me tell you, cities are the greatest invention for vampires."

"That's funny. Valentin says it's the Internet," Steve said.

"That too." She let her leather pump, clearly bought online, dangle from her toes. "But he was born long after cities started springing up everywhere. Here in the Low Countries, the good times for me were when we got invaded. I fed on Napoleon not once, but twice, and on his brother too. He was a puppet king for a few years in the Netherlands until he tugged too hard on the marionette strings and was forced out."

About eleven, they finally got their act together and headed out into the night, four sports cars and the Range Rover. Steve rode with Sarah, as he felt closer to her now, in an easy but somehow deleterious way. They arrived home at the tower nest around three, happy to be back someplace familiar, but disappointed at having achieved nothing in their efforts to rescue Viona.

That morning, Steve and Sarah went to their own chambers, both wishing they had an excuse to fall asleep in each other's arms and both knowing neither could give the other what they needed. In a day or two, they would need to feed on human blood, and both felt a tinge of jealousy.

LAST GASP

Viona had not fed for seventeen days and had never felt so weak. She could not stand up and was slipping in and out of consciousness. She knew she would have the true death if she didn't feed that night, and she wasn't sure she had enough strength to do so. She had been on this earth for 318 years, maybe this was enough. She had never felt invincible, never thought she would live forever, and had always felt a little uncomfortable as the future constantly came rushing at her like an express train.

Gerlach had heard his buddy's voice during the day, calling people on his mobile to work a harvest the next day, and knew he had to be out of the greenhouse that night. He also knew Viona couldn't walk, and he was trying to decide if he wanted to leave her or not. It would be difficult for him to find human blood at this point, and he doubted she could feed on her own. She was lying on the ground, limp and helpless. He could carry her, or he could just leave her here to die for killing Jan. She deserved it. His plan was disrupted, but he could come after Steve again when the vampires least expected it.

Suddenly, a feeling of hate and lust swept over him. *I'm going to have this vampire bitch before she dies.* He pulled off her jeans with no resistance from her, and raped her. He was fast, using her for himself and coming quickly.

When Gerlach came, the instinct to feed and survive sparked in Viona. Even though she had given up all hope and accepted the true death, her fangs came out and her head snapped into position to feed on Gerlach. He was as surprised as she, but didn't struggle. Somehow he wanted to experience the thing he had learned to hate from an early age; and maybe he wished he would be turned too. When he finally lost consciousness from blood loss, he wondered if he would even remember this., forgetting that no vampire would follow the covenant under these circumstances.

Refreshed and energized, Viona went through his pockets and found the key to the manacles on her wrists and ankles. She pushed his body off and released herself from her restraints. It was only about 9:00 p.m. so she headed outside. Seeing his car, she went back to get his car keys. She had never been comfortable driving, one of those things in the modern world that she neither appreciated nor mastered. She did make it back to the city, though, despite getting honked at several times for driving too slowly, and left the car about five blocks from the tower. By now she was full of energy and life, euphoric from overfeeding, but when she walked into the tower lounge, she broke down in tears when she saw the other vampires. Having faced the certainty of true death, and with Gerlach finally dead, she couldn't control her overwhelming emotions.

THE MUSEUM NEST

The vampires of Europe rarely throw parties anymore, feeding or otherwise. There was a time in the Mother of Cities, starting in the fifteenth century, when they threw elaborate balls at a palace they still own, designed to lure in unsuspecting mortals for feeding. The scheme was so effective; they had a party almost every week, but eventually the vigilant vampire hunters of that age figured it out. The slaughter of vampires in one night was their most effective operation ever. It was a night of infamy for the vampires, and a night of celebration for the hunters. Seeing the incident as an allegory to the dangers of greed, they ended the practice of throwing feeding parties, and initiated the endeavor to create the covenant, the process of conscious evolution.

The daily existence of the almost dead—feeding to survive and acting out of necessity, the pure pragmatism of that existence—means that they have little reason to throw parties for themselves, but the escape by Viona and the execution of the first legitimate vampire hunter in Amsterdam in twenty-five years, even before his first real success, seemed reason enough.

The museum nest is the vampires' most prized possession in Amsterdam. It was not named for its location under the Rijksmuseum, where it most certainly is not, but for its priceless treasures of antiquity. The museum nest is a mansion, somewhat rundown, among several other mansions on Koningslaan a mile and a half southwest of the Rijksmuseum. Karolina had bought the house soon after arriving in Amsterdam, and it was the vampire's only nest until purchasing what would become the tower.

The walls were covered, in most cases from floor to ceiling, with paintings spanning from the Dutch masters to van Gogh and beyond. Vermeers and Rembrandts were everywhere, including a giant Rembrandt, about fourteen feet by eleven feet, that dominated the mansion's large living room and rivaled the more well-known "The Night Watch," the centerpiece of the Rijksmuseum. Similar to that painting, this one featured a number of people in a room that could have been the very room in which the painting hung. Those people included Accalu, Otakar, Karolina, and a few others standing on each side of a man about fifty-five-years-old with olive skin and salt and pepper hair. It was painted in a style similar to "The Night Watch" which made it appear three-dimensional. The painting, older than both Viona and Valentin, had been commissioned from Rembrandt by Karolina, Otakar, Accalu, and several others who were either no longer in Amsterdam or dead. More than twenty van Goghs also hung in the mansion, including paintings that looked like they could have been of either Karolina or Viona. There were also more modern works, including Impressionist paintings by Monet, Cezanne, Pissarro, and Renoir; and Expressionist paintings bought by Valentin from Schiele, Kandinsky, and, of course, Munch. There was also the missing masterpiece, "The Just Judges" from the "Adoration of the Mystic Lamb" altarpiece.

The treasures didn't stop at the paintings; they included actual treasure. Gold coins from throughout history, some going back to the days of Babylon; twenty-five million by weight in Roman gold coins, worth many millions more due to their antiquity, that Accalu had brought with him to Bohemia, traveling at night with a train of wagons from Rome. The Florentine diamond entrusted to Valentin for safekeeping by relatives now dead, and three of the lost Imperial Faberge Eggs. Some of the jewelry boxes containing these treasures were worth hundreds of thousands of dollars on their own, but the total value was only 2 percent of the real vampire treasury beneath Luxembourg City, which was ruled by the ancient elder Ambre.

The mansion itself, unlike the other two nests, had been left intact except that all the windows were blacked out with what looked like drawn curtains from the outside. The mansion simply had its original fourteen bedrooms, unlike the cave-like architecture of the sleeping chambers in the tower and canal nests.

Karolina held court near the large Rembrandt in the mansion's spacious living room. Looking around the elegant space, she thought of how much she missed throwing parties like the old days. Every vampire in the city was there, emboldened by the execution of Gerlach the Junior, whom they now referred to as Gerlach the

Abridged for his short reign as a vampire hunter.

Viona, for her part, had a revolving crowd of well-wishers around her, sympathetic and secretly glad it had not been them, as she told her tale repeatedly. Vampires as a rule have more time to learn, but the oldest vampires pay particular attention to optimizing feeding opportunities, and the detection and elimination of threats, so this was more than just idle cocktail chitchat. As a mortal, Viona had been raised for such parties, and she basked in the attention. Secretly, though, she wanted to share her ordeal with her closer friends— Valentin, Accalu, Karolina, Sarah, Otakar, and the newly turned American Steve.

Valentin used these types of events, rare as they were, to consolidate the financial plans of the continental vampires of Europe. He had grown up in a family that had mastered the art of holding on to its wealth. The nasty business of attaining it was never a concern for his family by the time Valentin was born, as that had happened more than a century prior. Growing and holding on to that wealth was the primary directive of the family's existence, and all were trained for that eventual responsibility. Valentin had learned well, and his extended years had only served to sharpen his acumen and steady his long-range patience. Most of his family had fled Austria for America for political reasons in the early twentieth century, and most were now ruined. Some of the family's real estate had fallen to Valentin: the aging palace in Vienna that he had grown up in, a financial money pit for decades until after WWII; a three-thousand square foot "cabin" near Axamer Lizum ski resort, built of old spruce and oak, that had been the summerhouse of his youth. The increased popularity of skiing over the decades, and the fact that the 1964 Winter Olympics had been held there, had increased its value.

In the 1950s, Valentin started to refurbish the rundown palace in Vienna, a project that took fifteen years. He toyed with selling it, convinced he could smell a foul stench left by the Nazis who had occupied it, along with the rest of the country, during WWII. The value kept going up, though, now possibly as high as 135 million euros, so he kept it and for a time rented it out at a loss. Then in the 1980s he tapped into the foreign diplomat market. Now he rented it for 42,000 euros a month to a merry-go-round of diplomats looking to entertain on a grand old-money scale.

He had a similar experience with the former hunting cabin near Innsbruck. He had never been able to rent it until the two golden weeks during the 1964 Olympics. After that, he broke even renting it until 1976, when he made more in rent in the two weeks during those Winter Olympics than he had made to that date combined. From there, with improvements and refurbishing, the cabin was booked three years in advance both winter and summer, for a huge profit. He, of course, like many property owners in the area, rolled some of that money into financing efforts to get the Winter Olympics back, which everyone knew was only a matter of time. This was the Austrian Alps, after all.

Otakar and Accalu were off to the side talking to Radek, a surprise visitor from Bohemia. One of the elders in the Mother of Cities, he had been turned in 837. He had seen many of the original Bohemian vampires killed during the eighteenth century in a series of upir cleansings, even as the entrance to the tunnels under the city remained a secret. Any sniff of vampire-hunter trouble usually brought him out to investigate. Most recently, that had been London in 1998 with two vampires killed, Munich in 2001 with four killed, and now Amsterdam. All had been dealt with quickly, but none being resolved as quickly as the Gerlach the Abridged incident.

Satisfied with what he learned, Radek led Otakar into a discussion of one of their favorite subjects, Italian sports cars. Otakar was obviously a Ferrari aficionado, with his iconic '64 250 GTO. Radek had a 1980 Lamborghini Countach, and an extremely rare '65 Lamborghini 350 GT, bought simply to counter his friend's classic Ferrari super car. Radek had driven neither car to Amsterdam, instead traveling the old fashioned way: by train, resting safely in a coffin.

Steve and Sarah tried to avoid each other, but not very successfully. Eventually Karolina motioned Steve over. "What's going on with you and Sarah?"

"Nothing. Why?" Steve asked.

"Because you're obviously trying to avoid each other. Just don't go there. It never ends well, ever."

Several hours into the party, Karolina brought Viona to the master bedroom to reveal her present— a tall young man on leave from the Dutch Navy, and sorcerized out of his mind. He would have done anything for anybody at that point. Since she hadn't fed in twelve days by the time they threw the party, Viona was thankful for what turned out to be quite the physical specimen. While the others partied in the rest of the mansion, Viona and Karolina undressed their sailor and themselves, then started kissing in front of him, not because it particularly excited them, but for the effect it had on the sailor. He was overwhelmed by his good luck at being with both a beautiful brunette and blonde and couldn't decide which to have first.

Karolina pushed him on top of Viona and said, "It's her turn tonight."

Like that fateful night more than three hundred years ago, she guided his cock into Viona's blonde pussy to get things started. When Viona finally fed, she felt like a princess being catered to. As the warm energy started radiating from her belly, she couldn't believe she'd almost welcomed the true death less than two weeks earlier. She felt so alive and happy now; so glad Karolina had turned her all those years ago.

About an hour before sunrise, the hired valets started to bring everybody's car around. Steve and Sarah left together in her green Jaguar type F as "Lebanese Blonde" from The Thievery Corporation's *The Mirror Conspiracy* was playing. Karolina and Viona pulled away with the loud exhaust note of her black Porsche GT3 RS. Valentin raced off into the night in his silver Porsche, Speedster "Nocturne In Paris" performed by the Usual Masters from *Buddha Bar IV* playing loudly. Accalu brought Radek back to the tower in his red Testarossa; and as Otakar drove into the night in a red flash of Italian style worth thirty to fifty million American dollars, he decided he needed another car so he could drive his Ferrari 250 GTO less.

Karolina pulled into the garage of the tower and dropped off Viona before she headed back to the mansion. Maybe it was time to move Viona there, she thought. It seemed to suit her more than the tower. When she got back to the museum nest, she pulled into the two-car garage—one of the drawbacks of the mansion that didn't affect her as an elder. There was room for five more cars behind the house, but since some vampires had at least two cars, the place really needed twenty-eight parking spaces.

ROAD TRIP

As part of his mentoring, Valentin planned to take Steve on a business trip across Europe with Karolina and himself. The trip was intended to take care of business in Belgium, Luxembourg, and Austria, and would conclude with a meeting of the elders at the primal nest beneath the Mother of Cities. Since they wanted to travel with as low a profile as possible, they chose to take Karolina's Mercedes S500. She had picked it up used about five years ago, but it had low miles.

They had four primary objectives for this trip: try to return the stolen "The Just Judges" from the "Adoration of the Mystic Lamb"; meet with their banker, Dieter Hahn, in Luxembourg; check on Valentin's properties in Austria; and in the Mother of Cities, Karolina would attend the council of elders while Valentin attended some business meetings.

The night before they planned to leave, they all went out and fed, just to be on the safe side in the first week of their trip. After sunset the next day, with goodbyes they departed for Antwerp, the first stop on their trip.

THE ART DEALERS

In the spring of 1934, Fallon, the elder of the Antwerp, Belgium, nest, was in the city of Ghent for a few weeks. On the night of April 11, she fed on a man who had just stolen "The Just Judges" panel from the Ghent Altarpiece. After she was done feeding, she thought the right thing to do was return it to the Saint Bavo Cathedral, but was unsuccessful. Soon after, another man, Arsène Goedertier, tried to ransom the artwork. It was never clear if he was an accomplice or a fraudster.

When Fallon claimed she could return the panel, the police were secretly contacted. When she arrived at the cathedral, she discovered the trap and had to fight her way out, killing two police officers. The incident was kept quiet, but the police continued to believe some sort of political organization, possibly German in origin, had the artwork. This theory continued over the decades with a detective still assigned to the open case.

The unique feature of the panel was that it was believed to contain self-portraits of both Jan and Hubert van Eyck, as the third and fourth judges on horseback. The panel itself was somewhat of an anomaly, as the other panels could all be directly attributed to the Bible in one way or another or were representations of saints. Historians have debated the depictions in "The Just Judges" over the years.

Every ten years or so, the vampires attempted to return the piece, trying to find someone who could help who was not either the police trying to arrest them or a thief trying to steal it.

The traveling vampires got to the Antwerp nest in good time, at about 3:00 a.m., so they decided to walk around the city, taking in the sights and scoping out the place they would meet the art dealers who claimed they could return the stolen panel. Since they had all fed two nights previous, there was no sense of urgency, and they simply enjoyed the warm fall night. Steve thought Karolina had seemed less standoffish than in the past month, which was nice, but he still felt somewhat obsessed with her and wondered if it was the lingering effects of being sorcerized.

That morning, they all got their own chambers in the nest, since there were fewer of them. Steve had wanted to share with Karolina, though he'd known that would never happen. At the same time, he thought his day sleeping with Sarah in his arms was more real than his infatuation with Karolina. Not that Karolina wasn't still an irresistible woman, with or without sorcerizing. Her toned body and eastern-European super-model sexuality were the real deal.

The next evening, they planned their meeting with the two highly successful art dealers Valentin had been in contact with over the past two years. They were mostly legitimate, but from time to time dealt in black market art. If not stolen, some of it had questionable ownership, or owners that did not want to be known, or didn't want the world to know they had to sell part of their collection—again.

Conner Chaten and Claude Moreau lived in a gray area, art dealers to the rich and famous and about 98 percent legitimate. When collectors dealt with them, the one thing they knew for sure was that they were not getting a fake. Sometimes that meant that a painting hanging in a museum was the fake. They worked equally well with two distinct markets: the new-money ultra rich and the old-money rich. Sometimes the old-money rich were also ultra rich, but that usually wasn't common knowledge. The ultra-rich, on the other hand, mostly from America and the Middle East, were in your face with their money and you knew their names. The old-money rich were generally embarrassed by the ultra rich and didn't like to deal with them directly. This was perfect for Claude and Conner.

Claude Moreau grew up in Paris. His father was an art dealer, and his grandfather had been a very successful investment banker. Since the family already circulated with the wealthy collectors of Paris, his father's job was relatively easy. He grew the family fortune modestly, keeping them in their "comfortable" lifestyle. Claude went to exclusive schools, matriculating with his future clients. In fact, he went to most of the exclusive prep schools in Paris, getting kicked out of one quietly and attending another in turn, all on a two-year cycle. It wasn't a plan. He just got caught doing any number of improper things, creative cheating being his favorite. But this also greatly increased his contact with future clients, especially since he never ratted out any of his coconspirators. When it came time for him to enter the family business after his father's sudden death from a heart attack, Claude wanted to go big. He was looking to be international, not just Pan-European. That's where Conner came in.

Conner Chaten grew up on the wrong side of the tracks in Atlanta, Georgia. A city where poor blacks got the empty words of sympathy and little else, and poor whites were all but invisible. Born Dale Connors, he reinvented himself after moving to New York City, changing his name and his accent. He was a natural con man, but got a job in a large art gallery and was able to survive legitimately in an unforgiving city. He too had bigger aspirations, and after two years, New York seemed just as small as Atlanta. He wanted the world.

Conner worked a long grift with an old pro he had met in a café, netting $75,000 when it was over. He decided to spend the summer in Europe so he could stop pretending he had been to all of the cities his clients had vacationed in.

In Paris, he met Claude, and a partnership that was now going on twenty years was formed. Claude was the smooth old-money European type, and Conner the closer. They typically did a great deal of research on their clients, so they could play the deal to their favor. With social media, that was easier to do now when it came to the ultra rich, but harder with the old-money types. Generally, Conner was the lead with the ultra rich and Claude with the old money.

Valentin was an enigma to the two men. His only social-media presence was on LinkedIn, where he billed himself as a real estate investor and CFO of a company they had never heard of. That sort of profile typically meant wannabe loser, but he was trying to give away art, so he had to have some money.

When they found out the artwork had been stolen decades ago, they thought they finally had a way to get out of the pickle they were in. Three years earlier, they had been arrested by INTERPOL while trying to sell a stolen Monet to a Saudi prince who, it turned out, was an undercover agent. They had made two mistakes. That Saudi prince had had way too much social media presence for a royal; and they hadn't investigated fully whether the painting had been stolen. They still were not sure if the whole thing hadn't been a setup, with INTERPOL on both sides, but now they were confidential informants, which was preferable to being prison bitches.

THE DEAL

The plan was to meet Claude and Conner at a small café, bring them to a hotel suite Valentin had booked for the night, and work a deal to return the stolen art work. The panel was still safely back at the mansion in Amsterdam, so this was just a preliminary meeting to make sure they could trust the art dealers. They had learned the need for such precautions the hard way.

They had also brought the Dutch Special Forces communication earpieces they had used in the Gerlach operation, and all of them were fully charged, from last day while they slept. Wearing the earpieces, Valentin, Karolina, Steve, Fallon, and several other vampires from her nest took up positions around the café. Once they were satisfied there was no law enforcement presence, Valentin and Karolina went into the café, which was full of old-world charm, with dark its wood and aging photos. They looked like an ordinary couple as they ordered cappuccinos before sitting at a table in the corner with a view of the whole room. They couldn't spot anyone who looked like the art dealers, and they scoped the room for police. On one side of the room sat a blond guy about thirty, short hair, with an ex-military look. On the other side of the room was a brunette woman around the same age who looked a little frumpy despite being attractive with a firm body. Neither one was definitely a cop, but both in the same place looked suspicious.

"I'm thinking of taking the train," Karolina said clearly, the code for the others to be even more on the lookout for law enforcement, if that were at all possible.

About fifteen minutes later, Claude and Conner walked in, and Valentin and Karolina knew right away they were the art dealers. Claude was about five foot eight, one hundred ninety pounds, and soft looking with longish curly brown hair. Conner was a couple of inches taller and maybe twenty pounds lighter, with cropped sandy-blond hair and a hard, lean look. Not of someone who worked out, but whose "gym" was the tension of a stressful existence and a two-pack-a-day habit.

"They make a mean cappuccino here," Valentin said, the cue to the others that the targets had arrived. The contact was the hardest part. None of the vampires felt particularly nervous about getting arrested; they could probably fight their way out. But the subsequent fallout would be hard to deal with. In five attempts to return the panel, seven police officers and four unscrupulous art dealers had died, only fanning the flames of suspicion and conspiracy theories.

After Claude and Conner had been sitting at their table for about ten minutes, Karolina got up and walked to the counter to order another coffee. She put some extra sway in her walk and added a subtle yet sexy hair flip to distract the room. In that moment, Valentin walked over to the art dealer's table, just as Steve's voice crackled across everybody's earpiece.

"I'm taking the train to Ghent in the morning," he said, code for abort, police presence confirmed.

As Valentin got to the table, he turned and muttered to the two art dealers, "You fucked up."

When they had first arrived at the café, Steve had noticed a plain white Mercedes delivery van parked nearby. He had also seen seven possible police officers walking around the area of the café. Just before he raised the alarm, he had been following a woman, late forties with greying hair, back toward the van. As she reached the van, the back door swung open to reveal an array of video screens and communications gear. In the gruff, impatient voice of someone in charge, she barked, "*Toestand!*" Steve had learned enough Dutch to recognize that she was demanding status on the surveillance.

Within a minute, every vampire had scattered in different directions. Karolina and Valentin stayed together to keep up the image of a couple simply out for coffee. They were followed for about forty-five minutes, so they decided to go to the Hotel Rubens—Grote Markt, where they had booked a suite. They had checked in earlier, so they went straight up to the room, smaller then they expected, a junior suite really, but a charming old hotel nonetheless.

About 3:00 a.m., Valentin left. About forty-five minutes later, so did Karolina. They each let the INTERPOL agents follow them.

When the distance got large enough, which was easy enough to synthesize by looking back nervously two or three times, they went down a certain blind alley and quickly climbed onto the roof of a building. Then down the other side of the building on another street, unnoticed.

Just before dawn, all were safely back in the nest. There was disappointment, but a sense of having at least tried to do the right thing. The same feeling people get from donating to charity to try to alleviate their rich guilt. In the end it was nothing really, except nobody got killed, which was more than could be said of the last few attempts to return the stolen panel.

THE MORTAL

The next evening, Valentin, Karolina, and Steve planned to leave Antwerp without feeding, with the police being on high alert. So they departed for Luxembourg, the country and city. Technically a Grand Duchy, the last in the world, Luxembourg has the second highest per-capita income in the world, and just over half a million people. In a word, it's small, much smaller than California, with fewer people than San Francisco alone. The country is dominated by Luxembourg City, which in turn is dominated by a large rock cliff in the old historical district called the Bock.

In 963, Count Siegfried built a castle on top of the Bock, with natural cliff defenses on three sides. In the rock below is a complex of tunnels and galleries known as casemates that were expanded over the centuries by the Spanish, Austrians, and a series of other conquerors. On the walls of the cliff are openings for cannon, and the castle evolved into the Bock Fortifications over the centuries; but starting in 1867, they were demolished over an eighteen-year period as part of the Treaty of London. The casemates and tunnels, however, remained open to the public as a tourist attraction.

Beneath the former location of the castle are other tunnels, unknown to almost everybody except the vampires, which make up the vast Luxembourg nest. The tunnels of the casemates proper were used as a bomb shelter, able to hold up to thirty-five thousand people in WWII. The vast vampire nest could potentially hold three thousand people, except that it was filled to the brim with treasure.

Most European vampires know the Luxembourg nest as the Treasury, as it contains vast quantities of gold, platinum, diamonds, and treasures of antiquity, the majority of the noncash assets of the vampires. If dumped at the same time, the commodities would rock world markets. The space with vampire chambers is relatively small, but so is the population of the city, so the nest can only support about twenty-five vampires.

Soon after Steve had been turned, Valentin instructed him to transfer all of his accounts to a bank in Luxembourg that held most of the European vampires' cash assets. From there he had Steve purchase some high-yield mutual funds, already on a pace to make over 30 percent for the year. Most people trying to hide money, or their existence, utilized banks in Switzerland or the Cayman Islands, but Luxembourg had a vital banking system ranked second only to Switzerland as a tax haven. When you throw in an inside man, it got even better for keeping secrets.

Dieter Hahn, a distant cousin of Valentin's, was the banker to the vampires, and a mortal. He, like his father, grandfather, and great-grandfather was one of the few mortals who truly knew of the existence of the vampires, or at least remembered, and he worked with them, for a huge profit. Someday he would initiate his eldest son into the business, just as his father did with him.

As a young man just out of the University of Luxembourg, he had met Ambre, the resident elder of the Luxembourg nest, at his father's office. She was a beautiful, playful brunette, who had looked almost the same 240 years earlier when she met his great-grandfather. She told him the unbelievable truth about the family business, and two weeks later he slept with Ambre and let her feed on him. This was done to make clear to him the danger of crossing the vampires, and to test for the upir gene. Like his father, he was not turned, but he remembered everything, a trait as rare as having the full upir gene itself.

Dieter ran a small "feeder" bank that functioned as a broker for clients wanting another layer of secrecy in their banking. It was one of seven such businesses in the city, all over a hundred years old, each typically having only three to ten extremely wealthy clients. One of Dieter's competitors brokered North Korean dictator Kim Jung Il's four billion dollars in deposits. Two others only had royalty for clients. Valentin and Dieter's great-grandfather had started the relationship and the firm, Pan Franco-Germanic Financial in 1770, when Valentin kept closer contact with his relatives. As time went by and Valentin didn't age, that got increasingly difficult, until they all died off.

Not only did Dieter know about the existence of the vampires, he also had a key to the nest, which was currently undergoing a once-in-a-century refurbishing of half of the sleeping chambers. Dieter coordinated the work during the day while the vampires slept in the other half of the tunnels. The other chambers and the treasury remained behind locked doors, away from curious construction workers. Dieter posed as a government worker to the contractors, and the one-hundred-year cycle guaranteed nobody would live long enough to compare stories.

Most of the tunnels in the casemates were raw rock from floor to ceiling, including the long stairs behind the door—three-inch thick steel with electrical closet high voltage symbols to discourage investigation—that descended down into the nest. At the bottom was the lounge, where hardwoods of different tones covered the floor, walls, and ceiling. The sleeping chambers were similar, featuring oak floors, darker walls, and rosewood ceilings. Much of the storage area was paneled with wood as well, but only a single color. The replacement cost would be in the millions today, and was not cheap when it was originally built from 1217 to 1233. The nest itself had forty sleeping chambers and averaged about twenty-five residents, so there were normally plenty of guest chambers. With the renovation work, twenty-three vampires were crammed into eighteen sleeping chambers, with only two guest chambers.

Valentin, Karolina, and Steve had left the Antwerp nest soon after sunset and arrived in Luxembourg City in good time, just before midnight. They parked on the street, and Steve got his first look at a proper vampire nest, under construction as it was. Half of the furniture was under tarps in the lounge, and construction equipment, including a table saw and a band saw, were off to the side. The place was still impressive, though, with a warm feeling of luxury that was comforting to his developing vampire psyche. He met Ambre and immediately had a mini vampire crush, and felt guilty thinking about his real vampire crush on Sarah. Ambre wore black jeans and a pink blouse that accentuated her slender body and medium sized perky breasts. Her face, like Fallon's, was from another time, but with a mischievous expression. She suggested Steve and Valentin go to a party below the Bock cliffs at a large house on the Uelzecht River to feed, but Karolina stayed behind, whispering and giggling with Ambre.

Steve and Valentin entered the party with invitations, printed on paper so heavy and thick, it felt like it was 50 percent cotton, provided by Ambre. The house was old and huge, with the unique, storybook look of Luxembourg architecture. The party was raging when they arrived just after midnight, and they both had no trouble feeding, Steve on a blonde woman in an apartment she rented down the street, and Valentin on a brunette in an upstairs bedroom he thought he had been in before, sometime in the 1790s. They went back to the party and blended with the mortals, Steve trying to follow the unique Luxembourgish language, a cross between German and French it seemed, neither of which he understood very well.

When they got back to the nest later, they learned about the sleeping-chamber shortage. Valentin had his own private chambers reserved in the nest due to his history there, three times larger than all the other ones except for Ambre's, but it was one of the ones being refurbished that century. That left two guest chambers, and Steve assumed he would get his own and Valentin and Karolina would share. To his surprise, Karolina announced, "You sleep with me tonight Steve," and grabbed him by the wrist, leading him back to a plush guest chamber, even though it was an hour until sunrise. For the first time since she had turned him, Karolina was being her old flirty eastern European self. Steve was sure it didn't mean anything, but wasn't going to complain either.

In the sleeping chambers, she quickly took off her clothes, revealing her newly trimmed landing strip.

"You like?" she said teasingly, swinging her hips, and Steve knew that's all it was, teasing.

They climbed into bed, and she immediately cuddled up to him, her lithe naked body pressing against his. He started to get hard despite himself. Then she kissed him on the lips and wrapped her legs around him, grinding her pussy against his hardening cock. He didn't know what was happening. He had already accepted that it would never happen with Karolina again, and it would never happen with Sarah, so what was this? Still, he rolled on top of her as if they did this every night, slid his cock inside her, and started fucking her brains out. He quickly realized the first time with her had not been a fluke. Sex with Karolina was if not the best close to the best he had ever had. They seemed perfect together—or was that just the sorcerizing talking?

"Karolina, am I sorcerized or is this really that good?"

"It's really that good," she moaned as she came hard on his cock for the first time. "Fuck, maybe you sorcerized me," she teased.

Around dawn, Steve decided it was time to come himself, but something was different. He didn't feel his fangs extending like they normally did. That was okay, since vampires clearly couldn't feed on each other, but it was strange. Then he was coming, and he felt Karolina's fangs sink into his neck just as they had when she turned him. He was shocked, but in that moment he would have done anything for her.

She finished feeding, and he stared down at her. "What the fuck just happened?"

"You fucked me silly," she said.

"That's not what I mean and you know it."

"I'm a super upir. I can feed on other vampires if I want to. You're going to need to feed again tomorrow night, by the way."

"Why did you want to feed on me?"

"I didn't, I wanted to fuck you. That was just a bonus. But the blood of another vampire is so nutritious to me, that I could go for a month without feeding if I wanted to."

"What about Adam and Eve?" he asked.

"We're going to be in separate sleeping chambers from now on, and I'm going to be a bitch to you for the next few months, so don't worry about that." Karolina said.

Steve fell asleep happy, confused, and a little guilty, thinking about Sarah. He had never been good at playing the field. He had usually been dating someone both before and after his failed marriage, but typically in a serial fashion, with little overlap.

The next evening when they woke up, Karolina told Steve he was one of the few people who knew she was a super vampire, and he needed to keep it a secret. He wondered who else knew, *Valentin, one of the other elders?*

⚸

Around eight the next evening, Valentin, Karolina, Steve, and Ambre met Dieter at his offices, which took up the whole top floor of a four-story office building in the financial district. Steve had expected serious business talk or some sort of crisis, but it was really just idle chitchat. Dieter mentioned his eldest son was nineteen and a sophomore at the University of Luxembourg. Valentin wondered out loud how he would take the revelation of what the majority of the family business really was. Dieter looked his full forty-eight years, about forty pounds overweight and balding. In short, he looked like a banker. Later, Steve learned Ambre didn't like to meet with him alone anymore, due to his not so subtle hints that she could feed anytime she wanted, which creeped her out. The business relationship between Dieter and the vampires was really a personal relationship with Valentin, the way of all enduring business arrangements. For most such deals, a merger or acquisition threw off the balance, ending both the personal and business relationship. With vampire-mortal interaction, this was typically a lifetime or, in this case, a multigenerational relationship.

After about an hour, Dieter's administrative assistant, an average-looking woman in her mid-thirties, with a slight belly from having two kids, poked her head into the room to announce that she was going home. Steve looked into her brown eyes, and in that instant realized he hadn't been this hungry for blood since the ill-fated Veronica incident. He quickly stood up and announced, "I'll walk you out," without breaking eye contact with the woman. She accepted as if it was perfectly natural for this American stranger to offer, and was unable to break away from his powerful gaze. Steve thought her slight belly was sexy. Somehow the act of carrying a child, all part of human reproduction, was arousing in that moment. He kept the eye contact until just before he fed on her in the stairwell.

Later, the four vampires went to another party in town. It was a young crowd, including many students from the university. None of them needed to feed except maybe Ambre, who after an hour brought a young blond guy over to meet the rest of them.

"This is Dieter's son Hans," she said with a mischievous smile.

"You guys are here for business with my father?" he asked.

"Leave this one alone for now, Ambre," Valentin cautioned. "We don't want to get ahead of ourselves."

Ambre winked, and Hans looked confused.

Back at the nest, when it was time to figure out who was sleeping with whom, Steve knew he wasn't sharing with Karolina. He thought she and Valentin would share, but Ambre quickly said, "You sleep with me tonight, Steve," exactly the same way Karolina had done the night before. She led him to her sleeping chamber, which was enormous. She had four walk-in closets filled with clothes, and jewelry boxes overflowing with pearl necklaces, diamond bracelets, and other loot. She had three sofas and a table that could seat eight, and her bed looked like something a queen would sleep in, a four-poster with a pink silk canopy.

In bed, she cuddled with Steve, and he thought maybe she was a super vampire too, but Ambre quickly put him straight.

"I'm not a super vampire like Karolina. I wouldn't mind fucking you, but it's a bad idea. You can't tell anyone about her. Not even Valentin knows."

ÖSTERREICH

Valentin, Karolina, and Steve spent a few days in Luxembourg, and then left after sunset one evening for Valentin's cabin. Normally, it was about an eight-hour drive. If it didn't look like they were going to make it before dawn, they would spend the day in the Stuttgart, Germany nest. Valentin's family cabin was on the outskirts of a village called Axams that lay below the Axamer Lizum ski resort, about ten miles from Innsbruck in the Austrian Alps.

The drive was uneventful all the way through Germany, so they didn't stop in Stuttgart. As they headed east into Austria, though, and then south toward the Alps, they hit three construction zones—one slowdown on the outskirts of Bichlbach, and two full forty-five minute stops between Holzleiten and Obstieg. Once they hit the A12, Karolina accelerated to 140 miles per hour to make up time, but as they reached the outskirts of Axams, the eastern horizon was starting to glow as the sun prepared to rise. The cabin was on the far side of town, sitting on the edge of the forest, so she risked getting pulled over by the local police and drove as fast as possible.

For the first time since being turned, Steve experienced the debilitating effects of the sun. He felt weak and nauseous, and had trouble keeping his head up. A half-mile through the village, he was sure he was going to experience the true death. The nausea got more intense each second as he dry heaved and burped out an open window. Blackness closed in at the edges of his vision, blinding him; and he grimaced as pain twisted through him, seeming to emanate from his bones.

"The first time is the worst," Valentin said, but Steve barely heard him just before passing out from the pain.

When they finally got to the cabin, Steve was still unconscious, and Valentin and Karolina had to revive him. All of them weak from the rising sun, but none more so than Steve, stumbled to the back of the cabin, where a door opened onto a stairway to a subbasement that held six coffins. They each climbed into one, closed the lids, and fell asleep immediately.

When they awoke in the evening, they took the inside stairs to the main part of the house. Steve was still feeling woozy from his first sun exposure. The cabin had an open design, the walls paneled in a light wood and with hardwood floors. Only three trophy heads remained on the walls of the fifty plus that had once been mounted, after being hunted and killed by Valentin's ancestors over the years. Two red stags and an Alpine ibex head were all that remained, just for the hunting-lodge ambience. From the back deck was an incredible view of the snow-capped Alps. Steve thought it was more beautiful than Tahoe, and the snow was probably better than Colorado in the winter. After his close call that morning, he had been thinking for the first time since being turned about daytime activities he had enjoyed, like snowboarding and mountain biking.

Valentin had a meeting that evening with a contractor who was going to do some work the next day. A cabin in the Alps suffers substantial wear and tear every winter, but it was only about a day's worth of work this year. The day after the work was to be done, the cabin was rented, as it was almost nonstop year round, so they planned to leave for Vienna the following evening.

Karolina spent most of the time on her mobile phone, but Steve couldn't hear what about or to whom she was speaking. She was keeping her distance, as promised.

"Are there any daytime activities you miss, Valentin?" Steve asked when they were out on the deck after Valentin finished his meeting with the contractor.

"Not much after all these years, but I would like to see the Monaco Grand Prix. I go down there every few years for business. I've been to the parties, which are incredible feeding opportunities, but the race during the day is something I've always wanted to see."

The drive to Vienna normally took about four and a half hours, but on the A1 autobahn at night, they made great time, Karolina keeping the speed above 100 MPH as much as possible. When they reached Palais von Hahn after midnight, there was a party raging, hosted by the ambassador to Iran, who was the current tenant. He used the palace for entertainment and meeting with visiting dignitaries, as he lived at the Iranian embassy. The palace itself was modest compared to many in the city and around the Austrian countryside, only about eighteen thousand square feet and three stories above ground. They entered the subbasement through a door hidden behind some shrubs on one side of the building; Valentin had had it installed in the 1980s after he started renting the palace out more. The subbasement, locked off from the main basement, held twenty-seven coffins and an assortment of centuries-old belongings Valentin's family had stored, including clothes in several antique armoires. They changed into formal wear in anticipation of going upstairs to the party, an unexpected but welcome feeding opportunity. The door to the stairs that connected the secret subbasement to the main part of the palace was hidden behind a bookshelf in the main basement, which is how they entered the party, on the safe side of security.

Away from home, the children of diplomats, especially from socially oppressive nations, generally go wild. Valentin was talking to an eager nineteen-year-old Persian woman when her father walked up and asked who he was.

"I'm Valentin von Hahn," he said with his ingrained aristocratic charm. "This is my palace. I am pleased to meet you."

Steve was so impressed, he thought about affecting a Texas accent just to be as obnoxiously American as possible. It turned out that the truth—being from California, and even Sausalito, for that matter—was impressive enough for anybody not from California. The two fed easily, taking turns using the subbasement, its antiques and coffins adding the proper ambience as they told their tales of necessity. Karolina, having fed on Steve back in Luxembourg would not need to feed for weeks if she so chose.

"I'm a vampire, there is very little chance you will be turned, and you will forget," not really believed times two.

The next evening, they took Steve to the Wien (Vienna) nest. Although the city had about 1.7 million residents, and the metropolitan area closer to two and a half million, the nest was relatively small, with only about 120 vampires, compared to 300 in Amsterdam. London, with over 500 vampires and four nests, had by far the largest population. Paris was about the size of Amsterdam, but the huge influx of tourists in the summer was countered by the outflow of Parisians.

They entered the nest through the basement of one of two buildings the vampires had owned for over a century.

"We converted the buildings to condominiums about forty-five years ago," Valentin said. "The land, of course, is leased from us, providing recurring income, and we kept a large penthouse in each building for ourselves."

"They use them to bring mortals back to feed, and they also hold two feeding parties a year, on Halloween and New Year's Eve," Karolina said as much to Valentin as Steve. She was again fondly remembering the feeding parties she used to throw in the Mother of Cities.

"The Wien nest is a classic underground natural tunnel complex similar to the primal nest," Valentin explained as they walked down an unmarked tunnel. "Some people think it was the home of prehistoric humans during the last ice age, the founding fathers of the city, so to speak. The tunnels of the nest itself are about five miles long in total, dry caves with unfinished rock walls for the most part. The lounge and sleeping chambers are finished in light wood mostly white oak, with darker stained oak floors. It's an exceptional nest, but I never really liked the place. It made me feel like an outcast when I was first turned. I stayed in Wien less than a year, and then followed my cousin to Paris. From there I went to the Mother of Cities and the primal nest, trying to find some meaning to my life as a vampire. Karolina sent me right back here to meet with my aunt, Empress Maria Theresa, but I went back to Bohemia soon after that. After a few years in the Mother of Cities, I started traveling around Europe, partly as an ambassador for the covenant and partly to seek out family members who had not yet been informed by my father that I had been turned into an 'abomination,' as he called me. For my first fifty years as a vampire, I struggled with that. Although my constitution and upbringing made me the ideal vampire, contact with my family during that time made me feel more civilized, more human. At the same time, I started building the pillars of the longer-term vampire financial strategy, establishing the banking relationship in Luxembourg where the Treasury already existed. Eventually I ended up in Amsterdam, which has been my home base since the early nineteenth century."

THE MOTHER OF CITIES

With security high at Palais von Hahn, and so much activity going on with the Iranian ambassador in entertainment mode, Valentin, Karolina, and Steve decided to leave for the Mother of Cities, home of the primal nest, that same evening after showing Steve the Wien nest. Although considered to be in Eastern Europe, the city was west and north of Vienna. Across the northern border of Austria, the total travel time by car was less than five hours. The trip was uneventful, and they decided not to stop at the Brno nest. Once in the city, they parked in the courtyard of their palace in the Malá Strana district, less than a mile from one of the largest castles in the world, perched on the cliffs above.

Instead of going into the palace, they headed down the hill toward the Old Town. Karolina was in a good mood, happy to be home.

"Welcome to Praha, Steve. Have you ever been here before?" She had fond memories of Prague, having lived three hundred years in the city after being turned, unlike Valentin, who had left Vienna as quickly as he could. The only reason Karolina had left Prague was the upir cleansings of the eighteenth century. She would have returned, but she had put so much into building up the Amsterdam nests, she felt that was her home now. But every hundred years or so, she thought about moving back to Prague, the Mother of Cities.

"I've never been to Prague before," Steve said. "Most of my European travel had been for work, and my company doesn't have a partner bank in the Czech Republic yet."

As they walked toward the Charles Bridge, he noted that much of the architecture was truly Gothic, and the feeling of the city was exotic yet comforting in an old way. He had thought Amsterdam looked like it was from another time, but this was much older. Construction on the Charles Bridge, which they used to cross the

Vltava River, had been started in 1357; and it was actually the "new bridge," replacing the Judith Bridge built in 1158, 150 years before Amsterdam was even founded.

Steve was amazed at Old Town Square with its massive tower and 600-year-old astronomical clock, and the Gothic Church of Our Lady before Týn. He thought the church spires look like something from a Disney movie. *Was this where Walt got the ideas for his early work?* The tower was massive and built of stone, and it looked like it wouldn't last in California, or anywhere else that had earthquakes, but that was not the tower they were looking for. That tower was just a few blocks due east.

One of the original thirteen city gates, the massive Powder Tower was built in 1475 over the main entrance to the underground caves that made up the Prague nest, commonly known as the primal nest. At the time of its construction, it was called the New Tower. Later when it was used to store gunpowder in the seventeenth century, it got its current name, powder gate or powder tower. During construction, the vampires, who numbered over one thousand then, close to 3 percent of the population, easily concealed the entrance with bribes and conspirators friendly to their cause. That same relationship with mortals backfired two centuries later when so many knew their secrets. Luckily, the entrance to the nest was never revealed, but the palace was compromised. Now, through propaganda and misinformation, they led people to believe that tales of vampires living in the palace back in the eighteenth century were just fantasy.

On the northwest corner of the tower, below the arching Gothic skyway that spans Celetná, one of the oldest cobblestone streets in Prague, is a door to a spiral staircase constructed of stone, which leads up into the tower. During the day tourists can pay a few korunas and enjoy a view from the top that could only be replicated by helicopter, or the even taller Old Town square tower. To the right of this door, along the perpendicular wall, is a hidden door that conceals an identical stone spiral staircase. It descends down, down into caves older than the city itself, the primal nest.

No one knows for sure how the nest got that name, besides the ancient population of vampires. Some think it has to do with the walls of the tunnels. On inspection, most of them are carved with so many glyphs, pre-vampiric in origin that the caves look like they may be manmade tunnels. Lacking the hardwood of many of the ancient nests of Europe, the walls nonetheless have a rich, luxurious feeling of smooth, dark, oily stone. The carved glyphs are not like anything seen anywhere else in the world; similar to Egyptian, yet, on closer inspection, different. The glyphs are from some seemingly long dead race of humans, perhaps Celtic, proto-Slavic, or not of this world. Somebody lived in the caves before the vampires, but no one knows whom.

The area has been populated for the last few thousand years, dating back to the Paleolithic era. It was historically a trade route connecting southern Europe with the north, and thus was visited by many peoples. In the third century BC, the Celtic Boii tribe settled there, and it's thought Bohemia was named after them. Starting in the sixth century AD, the Slavic peoples started to migrate into the region; and around the same time, the first vampires began living in the tunnels. It is unclear if the first vampires came with the Slavs or from somewhere else, but Slavic people, along with Anglo Saxons, do seem to have a higher incidence of the upir gene and are thus turned more often. The percent of people turned, though, is still many decimal places out.

The original source of the upir virus is not known either. Some believe it came from old Babylon, possibly brought by Lord Makru, the oldest known living vampire. Others think it originated in Egypt during the time of the pharaohs, and perhaps traveled from there to Babylon; although others argue it traveled the other way, from old Babylon to Egypt.

At 3:30 in the morning, it wasn't hard to sneak through the hidden stone door of the Powder Tower and descend 150 feet down the spiral staircase to the tunnels of the primal nest. After that, they walked about half a mile; their footsteps seemed to echo to infinity as they passed more than thirty tunnels on either side. They didn't see another vampire until they reached the lounge.

The cavern holding the lounge was enormous. Bigger, Steve judged, than two football fields, with a ceiling so high, he couldn't even see it. Vampires filled the lounge, though, probably about two hundred.

Steve followed Karolina and Valentin to the chamber of the elders, which was similar to any corporate boardroom. It contained a carved stone table that could seat twelve, but there were only five dark-wood chairs for the current elders of Prague, and all of Europe. This was the council of councils, the source of the covenant, and the birthplace of the modern vampire.

In the room stood Radek, who had been in Amsterdam at the conclusion of the Gerlach incident; his contemporary Václav, who had been turned in Prague around 920 AD; and Accalu, who had traveled by coffin from Amsterdam to Prague. Standing at the head of the table was a man who looked about fifty-five, with salt and pepper hair and an avuncular look about him, like a TV father or beloved network news anchor. Steve recognized him from the giant Rembrandt hanging in the Amsterdam mansion. Known by several names—the eldest, the seer, king of the upir, and Lord Makru among them—he was turned in old Babylon around 1740 BC, during the first rise of the Babylonian empire, making him over 3700 years old.

Makru looked right at Steve and said, "Welcome to Prague. When you get settled, you will have to meet the American." Then Lord Makru, Accalu, Radek, Václav, and Karolina took their seats at the table, which was Valentin and Steve's cue to leave.

Steve realized he hadn't met an American vampire yet, but hadn't really thought about it. He had thought of himself as "the American." Who was this one they call "the American"?

THE AMERICAN

After they exited the council of elders, Valentin left the nest on business, leaving Steve to fend for himself in the lounge of the primal nest. The lounge itself was opulent and luxurious, leather couches and over seventy-five crystal chandeliers hanging on long cables from the ceiling almost a hundred feet above. The room was massive and womblike at the same time, a haven from the centuries of violence against vampires aboveground. Everyone he met, after learning he was American, asked Steve if he had met "the American." Who was apparently out feeding or working that night, depending on whom he talked to. Around sunrise, Valentin returned and they went to their sleeping chambers. Steve had a nice enough guest chamber, and Valentin a permanent chamber, just as he did in Luxembourg. Steve had started to notice a pattern. Although relatively young at around 250, Valentin was in many ways treated like an elder.

The next evening, a Saturday night, the elders had planned a reception to be held at the palace to celebrate the end of summer and their annual gathering. Getting four hundred vampires out of the nest took some doing, but the Powder Tower entrance was not the only one. There were nine throughout Old Town and Josefov, the historic Jewish quarter, mostly in the basements of buildings, some of which they owned; and one in the building at the base of the main tower in Old Town Square. So many tourists came in and out of the building, wanting to ascend the tower to take in the view, that a few vampires coming up from the basement went unnoticed.

The reception was to start at midnight, and Karolina wanted to get there on time since she was the primary host. Steve had been advised to wear a suit, which was no problem since he had been traveling with three when he was turned and had retrieved them all from his hotel room. Until the party at Palais von Hahn, he hadn't had reason to wear one. After he was dressed, Valentin invited Steve to his chamber. The room was enormous, with a seating area and a table that could sit ten made out of dark walnut. He led Steve over to a dresser dominated by a massive eight-bay Wolf watch winder.

"Pick one out. The American is money. You need to compete with him."

The winder was black with a macassar ebony wood faceplate, and it held six watches presently. Steve was wearing his Rolex Submariner and wondered why that wasn't enough. He saw a Rolex Daytona with a black face, a watch he had coveted but couldn't afford. His father had given him his two-tone Rolex, 18 karat gold and stainless steel with a blue face, when he graduated from high school, so he technically he couldn't afford that either. Then he started reaching for another watch as if he couldn't control his hand, grabbing a black Hublot Ferrari watch with a carbon fiber bezel. He tried it on; it fit.

"What watch are you wearing?" he asked Valentin.

"This." Valentin showed him a Manual Wind Breguet Grande Complication Tourbillon. "I have one of the first keyless Breguet pocket watches from 1833 back in Amsterdam. My father had an older Breguet pocket watch, but it was lost or stolen."

The three of them strolled through the ancient streets of the Mother of Cities, the pleasant warmth of early fall enveloping them. Karolina, wearing a five year old blue Chanel dress, felt so at home here, as she soaked in the Gothic and Baroque feel, so familiar from her youth growing up in Malá Strana. When she was born in 1447, Staré Město, or Old Town, was its own municipality. It wasn't until 1784 that the four major municipalities—Nové Město, Staré Město, Hradčany, and Malá Strana, where they were headed—were all merged into Prague. Eventually, in 1850, the Jewish quarter Josefov was also included.

The palace across the river and up the hill in the Malá Strana district was sometimes called the house on the hill by the local vampires. It was only about 12,000 square feet, modest compared to many in the city; was built in the Baroque architectural style popular in the fifteenth century; and was one of the few palaces in the city still privately owned, although it had been occupied by the communist party for decades until the 1980s. It wasn't used that often by the vampires from Valentin's perspective, but Karolina refused to lease it out, as an embassy long-term or to wealthy diplomats as an entertainment base, for sentimental reasons.

By 1:30 the party was raging, full of vampires. But it had also attracted about seventy-five mortals just from the noise and crowd. It hadn't been planned as a feeding party, but Karolina was happy it had turned into one, both for convenience and nostalgia. She thought more often about bringing the infamous practice back, despite the fateful night of slaughter so many years ago at this very location. Valentin worked the sound system, playing mostly downtempo dance music, leaning heavily on Thievery Corporation and old Zero 7. The party seemed to hit its peak as Thievery's "Illumination" transitioned into "Omid," then "A Gentle Dissolve" transitioned into Zero Seven's "Destiny."

As he circulated around the room, Steve occasionally ran into Karolina. Despite her promise in Luxembourg, she was not being a bitch to him. The surprising thing that Steve noticed about the party and Prague in general was that it was full of Americans. Karolina had an older trade negotiator from the American embassy in her grips, while he was talking to two women, respectively from the nearby American and Romanian embassies. Both were young administrators working their way up the diplomatic corps. The Romanian woman was telling stories about how there used to be vampires living in the Morzin Palace where her embassy was, a slight abstraction of the legends about the location of the party. Seeing an opportunity to deflect the rumors from their truth, Steve said he had heard the same thing, and had even heard of vampires in the larger Schönborn Palace that housed the American embassy. He was thinking double feeding in one of the thirty-three bedrooms upstairs, and had forgotten about "the American" completely by this time.

A familiar song began playing. After a moment he remembered he had heard it in the Amsterdam tower earlier in the summer— Federico Aubele's "Ante Tus Ojos." Then from his side he heard a familiar voice. "Steve fuckin' Breckenridge." He turned and couldn't believe who it was.

"Trey Coleman. Holy shit, I thought you were dead."

"Not dead, almost dead."

Marin City, just on the other side of the freeway from the north end of Sausalito, was originally developed for shipyard workers during WWII. After the war, the stark apartment towers built against the hill were converted into public housing of the most notorious archetype. The level of poverty was a stark contrast to the rest of upscale Marin County, as bad or worse than the Potrero Hill projects in San Francisco that produced O. J. Simpson. When it came to high school, the kids from Marin City made up about 12 percent of the population at Tamalpais High, mixing for the first time with an eclectic blend of the spoiled rich kids of ex-hippies, rock stars, professional athletes, and executives. The majority got swallowed up by poverty, drugs, or the allure of the thug life, and ended up in prison, dead, or just disappeared. Some got out and lived productive lives. One even turned the thug life into a legitimate business, becoming the biggest west coast rapper of all time, but still couldn't manage to stay alive. Most just faded away though, victims of circumstance.

Trey Coleman had drive and promise, and didn't intend to let his circumstances get to him. He branched out from his middle school crowd when he got to Tam. *If the son of a Hall of Fame NFL cornerback can be student body president,* he thought when he first got to high school, *why can't a black kid from the wrong side of the freeway and a head full of ideas hang out with the kids that inherited the future? With a little luck, I can make that future too.*

The last time Steve had seen Trey was at a party in Mill Valley after their sophomore year of college, he at UCLA and Trey at San Francisco State, where he was getting a degree in business. A few years later when Steve got together with old friends and somebody asked, "Whatever happened to Trey," nobody knew.

Trey had learned a lot hanging out with the rich kids at Tam, and knew after he graduated from college that he needed to do a summer in Europe before he started working. He had saved up, working part-time jobs and selling weed, sometimes in partnership with Steve, enough to spend, if not a whole summer, a month traveling around Europe.

He and his friends had it all mapped out: London, Amsterdam, Paris, then south to Spain and Ibiza, but he never made it that far. Staying in hostels, he and his friends got by on very little. In Paris they heard about Prague, and half of the group of eight decided to check it out with the extra cash they had saved. In Prague, Trey met a hot Bohemian woman who told him she was a vampire and he would not remember and he wouldn't be turned; but if he was wait on the north side of the Old Town Square Tower opposite the astronomical clock in the small grove of trees around midnight.

☥

"So I heard you're hanging out with Valentin," Trey said. "They call him the 'stealth elder,' you know."

That didn't surprise Steve. It seemed like Valentin had shaped the European vampires more than anyone in the last two hundred years, at least from a financial perspective. But when you are without want, it's easier to keep the peace. Steve wondered if Valentin hadn't come along when he did, would the covenant have even held. He noticed Trey's watch peeking out from his cuff, an understated Patek Philippe. *Valentin was right*, he thought.

"So what have you been up to?" he asked.

"It's a long story. I'll show you Monday night," Trey said.

NEW YORK

On Monday evening, Steve met Trey in the lounge of the primal nest shortly after sunset. Trey showed him around, including his sleeping chamber, which was as large as Valentin's and sported the same eight-bay Wolf watch winder. Steve played it cool and resisted the urge to go over to check out all the watches.

Trey had told Steve to bring his laptop, and he led him down a tunnel heading toward the Vltava River, and then ascended into the basement of an old building. They took the stairs up to the third floor, which was taken up completely by one company. There was room for about thirty people, but there were only eighteen. The name on the wall behind the reception desk was StoneHaven Systems New York, NY.

"I have another small office about a third this size off of Wall Street with mostly IT guys," Trey said, "but the main trading operations are in New Jersey."

Trey led the way to his office in the corner. They passed Valentin in an office next to Trey's and almost as large. He was on the phone speaking in German; the name on the door read Valentin von Hahn, CFO.

"They tell me the view during the day isn't that great, but I wouldn't know," Trey joked, the name on his door Trey Coleman, CEO.

"Have a seat at the table," Trey went on. "I have a few calls to make. Here's the Wi-Fi information and a login for the company email. I already had them set up an account for you."

Steve fired up his MacBook, and after deleting his old work account to make sure it didn't show a failed login at Sterling Klein Financial, his now former employer, he started Outlook and set up his new email. He already had a few emails, including a couple of meeting invites. One titled "daily trading wrap-up" started in about an hour, at 10:10 p.m., or 4:10 p.m. in New York. The other was titled "interim CIO call," and he wanted to ask Trey what that was, but he was busy on the phone. Steve accepted the meeting.

After a couple more calls, Trey joined Steve at the table. "Have you ever heard of high-frequency trading?" he asked, running his fingers through a short trimmed beard that made him look more male model than CEO, especially combined with the two-day stubble on his shaved head.

"Sure, but I couldn't tell you exactly what it was," Steve replied.

"Basically, it's automated trading based on an algorithm. The individual trades may not make that much, but overall when you add up the high frequency of trades, you can make some real money. After I got turned here in Prague, I started doing research into how to make money remotely at night. When I came up with the idea, your buddy Valentin was in town, so I pitched it to him and asked for ten million to get started. He refused, but after two months he called me from Amsterdam and said he wouldn't give me ten million, but he wanted to get involved. He said he had looked into it and thought the trading needed to be in New York or New Jersey, and it would cost twenty-five million to get started. He raised the money from several other vampires, the general fund, our banker in Luxembourg, and five million of his own money. That was five years ago, and today our net worth is 650 million, give or take. I expect to exceed one billion in about nine months."

Steve didn't know what to say and forgot to ask about the meeting invite.

"Oh, and one other thing," Trey said. "The people out there in the office and the people in New York and New Jersey, they're all mortals. They have no idea what we are, and we need to keep it that way."

A few minutes later they got on the conference call with the New York and New Jersey offices, and various managers went over the daily numbers from the different trading strategies they ran. Statistical arbitrage, event arbitrage, and order properties were doing well, but the low latency unit was still doing poorly due to technical glitches. The total take for the day was thirty-eight million, but that was against substantial expenses, including almost five hundred highly paid employees worldwide.

After the trading wrap-up call ended, Trey briefed him on the next one. "Our last CIO left for a competitor who gave him a one million dollar signing bonus. We had brought him in to build up the low latency business, but he actually made it worse with bad equipment buying decisions. I'm not sure exactly what the problem is, but the New York guys will know. Oh, yeah, one other thing," Trey said as he connected the Skype call. "I need you to be interim CIO until we find a replacement."

On the next call, Steve learned that the primary issue was the storage system. It was a low-latency all-flash storage array from a small startup, but it rarely made it through a complete day of trading. In low-latency trading, the trade offer price at one exchange gets intercepted and the spread played for a small profit on another. The trading strategy relies on low-latency communication on the network and in the calculation to do the trade. Besides the storage being unavailable, it had also lost data on the trades they had made more than once, which could be disastrous with the SEC and IRS. The other thing Steve learned was that Jim Knowles, a guy he had worked with at Sterling Klein Financial was now the trading manager for low latency. He had left at the beginning of the summer just as Steve had gotten to Europe, so he didn't know Steve had "disappeared" in Amsterdam. Additionally, he had been walked out the day he resigned due to company policy, and had not had time to catch up with anyone at the old firm. Good news for Steve, as he had always gotten along with Jim, but there could be trouble in the future if he talked to anybody back at SKF.

After the conference call, Trey showed Steve an office down the hall from his—modest, but more than his cubicle at SKF back in San Francisco. The rest of the night, Steve researched solid-state storage systems and asked more questions via email and Skype chat with the guys in New York. Near morning, he was leaning toward an all-flash array from HP/3PAR. A few minutes before dawn, Steve, Valentin, and Trey walked back to the nest, as Valentin reiterated the point that except for the three of them, everybody was a mortal. And unlike Dieter, nobody at SHS knew they were vampires.

THE DEAD GIRL

She was a sister, a daughter, a friend, a smart girl; she was a party girl, a popular girl, and she was drunk girl. Whitney had come to Europe the summer between her junior and senior years of college for fun and adventure. She had partied more and seen more than most Americans did in a lifetime, but was little effected or just didn't notice. She and her friends all came from Portland, Oregon, and like their parents all attended the University of Oregon in Eugene, and belonged to the same sororities and fraternities. In Whitney's case, that was Delta Gamma. When they graduated many of them would go on to graduate school for law or business, and like their blue-eyed ancestors, they would eventually run Portland. Not as mayors or any other elected politicians, but as members of a handful of exclusive country clubs and, of course, the Multnomah Athletic Club known as the MAC club; all institutions where behind closed doors and on the golf course, the real decisions were made. They would pull the strings and make the deals that kept their way of life alive for a few more years, if not another generation.

Whitney and her friends had been bouncing around Europe all summer, as far south as Greece and as far north as Norway, the birthplace of many of their ancestors. In the last week of their holiday they had visited Prague, and now in the middle of September all but one of her friends had gone home, heartbroken at the loss, or more precisely disappearance, of their friend. The hardest part was not knowing what had happened. Was she dead, did she run off with a boy, would they ever know? Her best friend Susan had stayed behind, hoping for some news, checking with the authorities every day, but she would give up eventually too. She had to.

"Steve, can you talk to this American girl?" first Valentin then Karolina asked. "She was turned about a week ago, but she is in some kind of denial."

Steve had been spending almost every night of his last few weeks in Prague at the office with Trey and Valentin. Eager for some distractions and the possibility of a feeding partner, he took up Karolina's challenge. He found Whitney on one of the sofas in the lounge where she had apparently stayed since she had been turned. Jan, a Czech guy on call that year, had brought her back to the nest. A Russian girl who called herself Vampire Anjelica and who styled herself after the porn star of the same name and similar look—waif skinny with small breasts—was supposed to be her mentor. Anjelica loved to fuck and drink blood, and just couldn't understand any girl who didn't, so she made little effort to get Whitney out of the nest to feed. Steve had noticed when he had been turned the general lack of empathy by other vampires toward anyone who had recently been turned. They didn't seem to care if you lived or died, not until you proved on your own that you could survive. He couldn't tell if they were being pragmatic or just resented the competition for "blood cattle."

He sat down next to the American girl on one of the sofas in the lounge, where she had stayed, curled up with her knees pulled up to her chest, since being turned. "My name is Steve. What's yours?"

"OMG, you're American. I'm Whitney. You have to help me. I just want to go home. I don't know what's going on," she exclaimed breathlessly. Steve wondered right away why she hadn't left the nest to feed. She was attractive enough, blonde hair and blue eyes with the toned body of a coed.

"I'm sure Anjelica has told you we're vampires, although they call them upir here in Czech. You're a vampire now, and you need to drink human blood to survive. You can't go home. Maybe someday, but right now you need to learn how to survive."

As he said this, Steve realized this was the first time he had really thought about going home or missing it. Maybe it was because he had traveled so much already in his life, or maybe because he had already been in Europe for nine weeks before being turned. He had thought about mountain biking and snowboarding when he was at Valentin's cabin. Not from the perspective of missing home, though, but more from the perspective of missing a daytime activity, especially in the Alps.

"Do you know Valentin?" Whitney asked. "He's the one who did this to me."

"I do. He's my friend, but he left the city for a few weeks," Steve lied, knowing from personal experience that the emotion of interacting with Valentin would not help her now. "Why don't we go up into the city and you can learn from me? I need to feed anyway, and I'll see if I can get Anjelica to come with us."

Anjelica, however, had fed the previous night and was not interested in the "boring American girl."

Steve had had all of his feedings at the palace since he'd arrived. There had been two parties so far, not officially feeding parties, but by any other name they were, and they'd been hosted as in centuries past by Karolina. Trey also had a large guest list of Prague's rich and beautiful mortals.

"A rich man can attract people," he told Steve, "but a man who makes other men and women rich is the one that entices the most real friends. Everybody at StoneHaven Systems makes a good salary, and a twenty to thirty-thousand euro bonus every quarter, and they have friends."

Once out on the street, Steve thought he knew why Karolina was throwing the parties. The cold of an early autumn was on the city, a chill that had driven the number of tourists down by 70 percent. By the time the snow came, the streets would be reduced to only locals in heavy coats walking briskly from one warm building to another. *Well, at least there's a party in two days,* Steve thought.

He decided to walk east, once they found that Old Town Square was almost empty. He had heard about a place called the Buddha Bar, and wanted to check it out. Valentin had been playing some of the Buddha Bar albums at the feeding parties. Some of the songs he liked and some he thought was just okay. Once they arrived, the bar—which was in a hotel of the same name—was dead like the rest of the city, and Steve started to think he should just bring Whitney to the party.

"How are you feeling?" he asked. "Are you weak, do you feel like you need to feed?"

"I don't know," Whitney said wistfully.

They started on a slow walk back to the Powder Tower, and not far from there they saw her, Susan.

"OMG, Whitney! You're alive! Everybody was so worried about you," Susan said as she hugged her lost friend as if she had come back from the dead.

Steve immediately was concerned, and for good reason. Whitney started telling Susan everything, about being turned into a vampire, how she hated it, how she wanted to go home. Steve knew there was only one option. Well, two really, but only one that he preferred. Susan was a pretty, although frazzled from her weeks long vigil, early twenties college girl with medium brown hair and blue eyes so Steve quickly hatched a plan.

"Whitney, you like boys, right?" he asked.

"Yes, of course."

"And you too, Susan."

"Yes."

"It's cold out, so let's go to your hotel, okay," Steve said.

"Sure, it's close by," Susan said. "But first let me call Whitney's parents, they're worried sick."

She pulled out her phone, but Steve grabbed it. "That can wait until later. Let's have some fun now." He hoped he was playful enough and sorcerizing enough so that he could get her back to her room and feed. Whitney would learn something, and Susan would forget everything.

Back in Susan's room in a small boutique hotel called the Hotel Maximillian, things went smoothly. Susan was adventurous, not really believing the tale, but Whitney was uncomfortable and tried to leave several times. When he was done, he was relieved that Whitney at least knew what it would be like when she fed. The party would be the place for her to feed, but she was already at twelve days or so since being turned, so that would also be her last chance.

Friday night, two nights later, Steve, Valentin, Karolina, Anjelica, and Whitney dressed like the European aristocracy at least some of them were walked up to the palace. Valentin was starting to like Anjelica; she was playful and could make a good feeding partner. About two hundred vampires were in attendance at the party, and about three hundred mortals. These were odds everybody liked, the perfect setup hosted by Karolina, with Valentin as DJ. Valentin was getting tired of his DJ duties, and he and Karolina started talking about hiring some professionals. Anjelica knew a Russian guy from the university that they had never heard of, but they thought it would be a good idea to mix things up too.

The parties at the palace were becoming increasingly popular with mortals, more than just the diplomatic crowd that lived in the neighborhood. Finance people associated with StoneHaven Systems started showing up, along with a younger crowd from Charles University that Anjelica had tapped into. It was the perfect night for Whitney to feed for the first time. She was that blonde blue-eyed American coed who was the object of many a fantasy, and that worked on men's subconscious even before she started sorcerizing.

By one the party was raging, and Steve had lost track of Whitney. He finally had the brunette from the Romanian embassy whom he had met at the first party as the focus of his sorcerizing. Her name was Petronela. She wore a little black dress that exposed her neck and the tops of her large breasts, and Steve tried not to stare. Caught up in the moment, he wasn't sure who was sorcerizing whom.

Valentin and Anjelica, who liked girls almost as much as boys, had some Czech twins from the university in their grasp. Valentin had queued up a playlist that would last three hours, so his DJ duties were over for the evening. As they headed for the bedrooms, Anjelica saw Whitney taking an American man who was visiting Prague on business upstairs. Anjelica didn't really care what happened to Whitney, but she did feel some relief that she wouldn't be blamed for not trying hard enough to mentor the boring American girl.

After feeding at the Prague palace, the vampires would tuck their dinners in, wait for them to fall asleep, and then some would go to four bedrooms reserved for the vampires to hang out in before returning to the primal nest near dawn. Karolina's inner circle, which included Valentin, Trey, Steve, and Viona—who was now in Prague—along with a revolving group of seven to ten other vampires—which included Anjelica that night—had gathered in the large master bedroom. Karolina slept in one of several coffins in the basement most days along with Viona, whom she had called the night after the first party and invited to Prague. Steve kind of wished she had invited Sarah as well, but Karolina was not as close to her, and he wondered why he missed her so much anyway.

Valentin, Trey, and Steve talked business, as Valentin and Steve would be heading back to Amsterdam soon. Steve had gotten the low-latency trading team in better shape technologically, so he felt like his work was done, but Trey and Valentin said they still needed help. So he would keep working at least part-time from Amsterdam as Valentin did until they found a full-time CIO.

"For like a hundred years," Trey mumbled to Valentin too low for Steve to hear, and they both laughed.

The women were making fun of the noises the guys they had fed on had made when they came, and Karolina complained that she hadn't had an orgasm in weeks, something Steve found hard to believe, knowing her.

About forty-five minutes before dawn, they all headed downstairs, Karolina and Viona to the basement and the rest back to the nest. When they got to the ground floor, there was a crowd of mortals and vampires around a sofa in one of the living rooms, along with emergency medical personnel. Everybody got nervous trying to figure out what was going on. Valentin and Karolina shouldered through the crowd just in time to see the paramedics giving up on the dead girl on the couch, Whitney. She had failed to feed earlier, and had simply run out of time and had met the true death. The assembled vampires felt little emotion about her death. She had known what she had to do and either hadn't believed it or hadn't cared. Steve gave Anjelica a look as if to say, we did everything expected. *I even fucked and fed in front of her,* he thought. *I thought it would have been hot with two girls, but it just felt like work at the time.*

The crowd of people and paramedics, on the other hand, were a huge problem. The parties would be over for now, and they would need to retrieve the body from the morgue before an autopsy was performed. There was nothing obvious about the biology of a recently turned vampire, but an expert on the subject could tell if consulted about any anomalies, and the highest concentration of such experts were in Prague.

SUMMER IS OVER

"Summer's over, dude," Trey lamented to no one in particular as they walked back to the nest, in a group that included Karolina and Viona. The palace was not a place for vampires right then. The party planning company would clean up as they always did, but inquiries would be made, people questioned.

"All the usual questions," Karolina said. "Did you see her taking drugs? If you did, who gave them to her?" She knew she would need to lay low and leave the city within the next few days as she had been the high-profile hostess at the palace, but she always told somebody different at every party that she was thinking of jetting off to anywhere she wasn't—Paris, Monaco, or London—just in case. This just wasn't the contingency she had expected; an accidental feeding death was the more likely scenario.

Saturday night, Valentin and Trey used a secret tunnel to gain access to the city morgue. It wasn't connected to the nest tunnels, but it had been there for over two hundred years in case of accidental feeding deaths. They doubted there would be any vampire-hunting trouble, and there was no blood draining evidence in this case, but they didn't want to take any chances. Luckily, the autopsy wasn't scheduled until Sunday, as it was the weekend and the coroner needed to return from his country house.

They slid Whitney's body into the cremation oven and forged documents that showed the cremation had been scheduled for the previous day. Worst-case scenario, there would be confusion and somebody would get in trouble.

An hour later, Trey retrieved Karolina's Mercedes from the Palace courtyard. If anyone questioned him, he would act like he was trying to steal it and run. He hated to play the race card like that, especially after rising to CEO of a high-frequency trading house from the brutal reality of his youth in the projects. He had volunteered, though, thinking it was the best plan, and swallowed the bitter taste willingly. This time anyway.

Soon after, the Mercedes left Prague for Vienna, slightly more crowded with Viona in the backseat with Steve. As they reached the outskirts of the city, an early snow started to fall, melting in seconds on the windshield, not heavy enough to stick to the road, but giving a light frosting to the dirt shoulder and tree branches on each side as they passed.

By the time they got to Palais von Hahn in Vienna, a few hours later, there was more snow on the ground, and the palace was completely silent, the opposite of their previous arrival when a party had been in full swing. It was about two hours until dawn, but they snuck into the subbasement anyway, preparing for a good day's sleep. All four of them had fed the night of the dead girl, so they would try to make good time getting back to the Treasury in Luxembourg. Valentin said they would need to stop at the Stuttgart nest as his cabin was rented, even though it was cold and the ski resorts didn't open for a month at least. Valentin was on his laptop using his phone as a portable Wi-Fi hotspot, and then he looked at his watch and frowned. He sent an email off and then Skyped with Trey to see if everything was clear back in Prague. It was.

Steve chatted with Viona, especially since Karolina was now ignoring him as promised. Viona seemed to have a glow since the Gerlach incident back in Amsterdam, her life seemingly new and full of promise. Nobody talked about the dead girl, but it was on everybody's mind, especially Viona's. Not so much that she was dead, but why hadn't she wanted to live? Where was her survival instinct? For the almost dead, the routine for staying alive was so immediate and had to be actively engaged by feeding. The thought that someone would give up and embrace the true death was chilling. *I guess the dead girl had never really started that cycle, but did she choose or not understand?* Viona wondered. Either way, the thought was so unsettling that she tried to push it out of her head.

Later Steve shared Valentin's Wi-Fi, and purchased a blade server, another storage system, and Oracle database software with money from the general fund. He, Trey, and Radek had discussed setting up a data center in the primal nest underneath a building they owned so they could get more electricity. Radek wanted to create a database of all known and suspected vampire hunters in every city so they could be better prepared.

The next night they left at 11:00 p.m., arriving about seven hours later in Stuttgart, forty-five minutes before sunrise. The nest was in an industrial area, gray and dirty. The snow had turned to rain in the past hour, and what little snow remained, already stained shades of brown and black, would certainly melt before noon the next day. The nest was beneath a large two-story warehouse jammed with cars. About 60 percent were Porsches of various vintages; almost all of the rest were German luxury cars. They were met in the garage by Heinrich Spreckels, an old friend of Valentin's, and quickly retired to guest chambers.

Heinrich was German American and had been turned in 1847 in San Francisco, and thus spoke fluent English. He had eventually come back to his homeland in 1939, trying unsuccessfully to guide his ancestral land away from the brink, but decided to stay anyway after the war.

The next evening, Valentin asked Steve if he wanted to come along on some errands. They drove to a residential area, where they met a man selling a silver 2006 BMW M3 Competition Package. The car was almost the limited edition CSL, minus the carbon fiber roof, which meant it had a sunroof, but it did have the brakes, wheels, and suspension of the CSL. After negotiating in German, a deal was made, and Valentin handed the keys to Steve.

"Do you want me to drive it back?" he asked.

"No, it's yours, your first bonus from SHS. You need a car and you said you liked the M3. This is the last of the great six cylinder sports sedans. This one has the six speed manual and not the SMG II, which sucked."

They drove back to the nest, packed their stuff in the two cars, and then Valentin and Karolina left in her Mercedes, Steve and Viona in his new M3. In less than four hours, they would arrive at the tempest that was the Treasury and the Luxembourg nest.

THE MORTAL'S SON/STOYRIDGE
TERRACE

After parking on the street—one of the downsides of the Luxembourg nest unless you rented a parking space somewhere nearby—the four traveling vampires descended the long stairs into the lounge. The construction that had been going on during their first visit had been completed, with all the drop cloths that had covered the furniture and the power tools removed, but that wasn't the first thing they noticed. The first thing they noticed was the unavoidable spectacle of Ambre screaming at the top of her lungs. Then to their shock they realized with whom she was arguing: their mortal banker Dieter's college-age son Hans. She had seduced him despite Valentin's warnings, and now Hans knew everything about the vampires and his father's business—but was also "in love" with Ambre. He couldn't accept that she needed to sleep with other men to survive.

"I'm a fucking Vampier! Why can't you get that through your head? I can only fuck you once every couple of months, and I can't survive on that."

The fight went on for about twenty more minutes before Hans finally ran out of steam. Valentin had an idea. He conferred with Karolina and then left to check out his newly refurbished chamber.

Valentin's Luxembourg chamber was significantly larger than all the other ones except Ambre's, and was similarly configured to his chamber in the primal nest of Prague: a seating area large enough for eight or ten people, a table that could seat eight, and a king-size bed made from oak and trimmed in dark brown leather. The walls were customized now to his specifications. The one with the door was the standard two-tone dark hardwood, and the other three were of leather, dark and light. Finally, in the corner was his luxurious "travel" coffin, in case he needed to get somewhere farther than a night's drive. He hadn't used this coffin in over a hundred years, instead using an ugly gray shipping coffin he kept back at the tower nest in Amsterdam whenever he traveled by plane or train. This one scratched too easily, and drew too much attention.

He booted up his laptop, intending to get some work done, and then quickly the room, annoyed. "Is the mobile service down?" he asked as he entered the lounge. Being underground, they needed to extend the service from the surface and through a repeater antenna in the nest.

"It will be fixed in the next few days," Ambre replied. "The construction workers broke the cable."

Frowning, Valentin grabbed his laptop and headed out, hoping to find a café open all night, but expecting his temporary office to be a bench at the top of the Bock overlooking the city as it slept.

Outside, Valentin settled for a bench after looking at his watch. It was already four, and he didn't want to just walk back anyway. It was cold, about forty-two degrees Fahrenheit, and clear, as the early autumn storm had passed through. He replied to a few SHS-related emails and started to write one to Dieter informing him of the situation with his son and Ambre, but couldn't find the words. The fact was, Dieter still harbored feelings for Ambre, despite the gap in their physical ages that had grown with each year.

Valentin closed his MacBook with a sigh, and from his seat on high gazed over the city, barely illuminated by the silver light of a low-slung crescent moon. He inserted his Shure earbuds and started playing *Frequent Flyer: Departure Lounge*, his favorite album of the last ten years, and for a moment velocity was suspended, a welcome respite. *My life has been a sprint played out over two and a half centuries, since I was turned,* Valentin thought. He'd spent the first thirty years running from his father's attempts to have the monster his son had become eradicated, while at the same time applying the lessons he had learned from him to set up the financial foundation of the European vampires. Now he spent much of his time maintaining his wealth and the wealth of the general fund, often without much notice from most other vampires. At least the elders that mattered gave him some credit and rewards, such as his chambers in the rock below, in the primal nest, and at the tower of Amsterdam. This work was juxtaposed against the constant need to feed on human blood every week or so, with the all-consuming compulsion of a junkie competing for his time.

Valentin's drive, coming partly from his need to prove that he could survive without his father's help, had propelled him into a position of transcendent power recognized by only a few elders. In many ways, the wealth he had created was the fabric that held the Continental vampire community together, the glue that kept them from the centuries of violence prior to the covenant. The covenant was words; Valentin was about following them up with actions. He had a natural refinement indistinguishable from his persona as a vampire, and although he sometimes called himself the Count of Europa, he was years—if not centuries—away from becoming an elder.

He knew others called him the "stealth elder" behind his back if only out of jealousy. But the elders that mattered, the ones that sat the table in the primal nest beneath the Mother of Cities, they all knew how much he had contributed. Still, that could only go so far.

Before he was turned, Valentin's life could only be described as that of the idle rich. He worked hard, studied hard, learned Latin, English, French, and Italian, along with his native German, but that hard work was never from a position of want. His back was never against the wall. He would always live in a palace; the first son of a count, his life was set. It was that fateful night, that fateful bite from Carina in the gardens of Schloss Schönbrunn that accelerated his trajectory and changed his life forever. Now almost dead, he had everything he had sought: wealth and wealth for his people. He had some of the most beautiful women in the world on an almost weekly basis, but that was from the perspective of survival, not as the international playboy he appeared to be. His life from some angles was a dream, but he knew there was a blind angle too, and not just the light of day. Could he ever experience true love and not only the evening of illusion he was the master of? The women he had loved over the years had never remembered, and never lived long enough, due either to the passage of time or misadventure. He had never felt anything for another vampire, someone on his time scale, although that would only bring another form of sorrow.

The lights of the city and the stars above all seemed to signify the multitude of living and long-dead mortals, all with the capacity to live and love for a normal lifetime. Then, as one of the stars fell from the sky in a streak of silver toward the horizon, he remembered the other thing that was missing. The fear of death rushing toward him as it did for those sparkling symbols of normalcy out there. No, death was something he increasingly thought would not come for many, many centuries, but there was something he needed now, something to halt his current existential crisis. A new car!

Back in the lounge, Steve was talking to Hans, a setup really, but he tried to talk him down.

"You will meet someone else, a mortal, get married, and have kids. Ambre can't offer you any of that, no vampire can. You remember Karolina from the party last month? And this is Viona."

With the two women sitting on the leather sofa opposite Hans and Steve, the setup was complete. Karolina would make him forget Ambre, and Steve knew that afterwards she would disappear or be a bitch or both like no other woman he knew. As Karolina and Hans started to talk, Steve noticed a tattoo on Viona's ankle. A pre-Christian cross that looked possibly Egyptian with a rounded top, but the cross bar was blood red with what looked like barbs or a representation of fangs.

"Where did you get that tattoo?" he asked.

"Oh, Karolina has one, so I got the same one a few years ago. She got hers in Prague before I was born I think."

A few minutes later, Steve excused himself and went looking for Valentin aboveground. Steve, like Valentin and his old friend Trey, all had trouble standing still. Steve complained about the overwhelming crush of work before he was turned, but the truth was, he welcomed being the guy who was sent off to Europe for the summer. Now he had SHS emails to respond to, responsibilities as acting CIO. For all of them, the life the majority of the almost dead led, hanging out, chatting, listening to music, and watching movies in a nest somewhere between feedings was not enough. They needed to keep busy, they needed to work and be successful to feel a sense of self-worth.

In the rock below, Karolina took Hans inside her. She knew her old friend Ambre would have taught him well and was not disappointed, which quenched any thoughts of feeding on Steve again. A bad idea, she knew.

When she was done, she assessed Hans. He might miss a semester, or he might die. He'd already looked anemic from Ambre's too frequent feedings. But he needed to move forward now and for the next fifty years as their future banker, if that was at all possible.

⚴

Ambre and Steve converged unplanned on Valentin's vista at the same time.

"I don't know how you guys do it," Ambre said. "I could never travel like you do. It's just not natural for a vampire, and I have no desire to do it at all. It's so dangerous too. You hear so many stories of vampires getting killed or not being able to feed when they're away from their nest."

Valentin had never really understood that attitude. He didn't know if he was different because he had traveled so much before he was turned, or because he had felt so compelled to travel so much in the first fifty years after he was turned. He was conscious of the lack of desire and fear most vampires had of travel, and he had deliberately exposed Steve to travel early on, before he got set in his ways. Most vampires stayed in the city they were turned in, out of habit and a fear of the unknown, of getting caught outside at sunrise, of running into vampire hunters in unknown lands, or of not being able to feed.

HOME

The trip home over the next two nights was uneventful. Karolina fed in Antwerp despite Fallon simply because she could, but the rest waited until they got back to Amsterdam.

Upon returning to the tower nest in Amsterdam, Steve parked his new car in the garage for the first time and immediately went looking for Sarah with tales of adventure. They hadn't talked or texted, but he had missed her.

Karolina dropped Valentin off and headed back to the mansion along with Viona to drop off her Mercedes.

Valentin immediately got on a call with Trey to catch up on business and see if there was any further fallout from the dead girl. He trusted Trey completely and had never been let down. Sure there were problems, but Valentin had known the success of StoneHaven Systems would never be linear. He knew the concept of linearity was manmade and could only be replicated with a manmade tool, a straight edge ruler or a computer. In nature, there was only random creation, and that was never linear.

The news about the dead girl was not good. According to some chatter Radek had heard from his contacts, the guy she had failed to feed on but had told everything to was possibly in contact with a vampire hunter. The SHS news was better. The low-latency trading unit had stopped bleeding cash thanks to Steve's efforts, but it still had a long way to go.

Steve found Hubrech at the tower nest, but not Sarah.

"She's gone to London," Hubrech said simply.

"To visit or did she move there?" Steve asked.

"I'm not sure," Hubrech mumbled.

Steve sent her a quick text.

<Hey, what's up I was looking forward to seeing you when I got

back>
He got no immediate response from Sarah.

Back at the mansion, Karolina was trying to figure out how to tell Evette that she had to move to the tower nest. She liked Evette, but she liked Viona more, and Viona was Dutch, had grown up in Amsterdam, and so deserved to live in the mansion more than the Frenchwoman. Karolina was worried how Valentin would take it too. He had never really liked Evette due to her association with the French Revolution, but he had to get over that someday.

Karolina was also trying to figure out how to convince Valentin that she should throw feeding parties at the mansion. She was a chosen elder and technically outranked him in the loose vampire hierarchy, but like most of the elders, she lived somewhat in awe and fear of the one they called the "stealth elder," "the player," or simply "bank." She knew Valentin was not trying to be any of these things. He was just doing what he did, the same way he always did, even before he was turned, but he could sometimes be too careful and conservative, especially with that annoying Radek back in Prague encouraging him.

She had become preoccupied with the idea of having feeding parties after their visit to the Mother of Cities. The night of infamy was not something Karolina had put behind her easily, in a few short decades or even a century or two, but 285 years was, she felt, finally enough time. So in Prague she had conveniently forgotten to instruct security to deny access to anyone without an invitation, thinking a few mortals would spice up that first party; and opening a few windows of the palace to let the music out had been just a convenient "coincidence." The results had far exceeded her expectations, with the bored diplomatic staffs checking out the party, and then texting and calling each other to come to the palace.

Karolina felt her persona as a vampire revolved around the parties she had hosted at the palace in the Mother of Cities for almost three centuries, from 1467—shortly after being turned—until 1729 and the night of infamy. She had escaped the slaughter by the vampire hunters, but many had not. Before being turned she had thrown similar parties at her ancestral home and loved being the hostess and planning, although she'd always hired professionals to carry out the details. For a time before being turned, she would sleep until four in the afternoon, waking only to get ready for the next party, whether she or one of her friends was throwing it. After she was turned, her family knew she was a vampire and let her sleep in the basement of the palace. There had been a history of family members supposedly being turned for the previous two hundred years, but nothing substantiated until Karolina. Her family loved her and tried naively to protect her, not realizing she would outlive them all, now going on centuries.

The next morning when Steve woke up, he had a text on his phone from Sarah.

<Why didn't U text me when U were gone, U suck>

Later he got another text. <Sorry I was such a bitch. I just had to get away>

<Are you coming back?> Steve sent.

<Yes, but I don't know when, it's so weird here in London, everybody seems so desperate>

BRUNO

Within a few of weeks of their return to Amsterdam, the post-dead-girl situation back in Prague was deteriorating rapidly. Valentin had nightly status calls with Radek now to keep up on the situation. In turn, he updated Accalu, Otakar, and Karolina.

The American guy Whitney had failed to feed on named Jeff Laird was from Chicago. He had left Prague, but not before telling his tale to several legitimate and wannabe vampire hunters in the city. One in particular was a savage man called Bruno, whose day job was bouncer and general enforcer for local organized crime types, gangsters. Bruno came from a long line of hunters of upir—father, grandfather, and beyond—and he had been initiated into the lore and traditions of that ancient guild.

He actively hunted when he became an adult, successfully from what Radek had learned, going to clubs and bars to pick up women. Whenever the woman was a vampire and began the requisite tale of the covenant, he was ready and killed her quickly with a short sword he always carried with him. Three times he had been successful, but now forty-six and married with kids, he was greatly diminished and longed for a greater success. The stories the American had told him, although perhaps distorted by the absinthe the man had been drinking that night, fueled a fire in Bruno that had if not been extinguished was reduced from his younger days. The story of the palace, something he had thought was only legend, spurred him with a new purpose. Bruno, if not intelligent, was highly driven when motivated, especially on his terms.

His younger nights of scoping out bars for vampires had evolved into an excuse to drink. Drink to help him forget the things he had seen in his job, the constant threat of violence and potential retribution if he pissed off the wrong guy. Drink to help him forget the woman he had married, now a bitter shadow of her former self, built like a hard sack of potatoes, and whom he was afraid would slit his throat one night while he slept if she was so inclined.

Now reenergized, he staked out the palace in Malá Strana every night he wasn't working, but had not seen a thing. Nobody seemed to go into or leave the building from what he could observe. He wondered about secret tunnels, another legend he had heard; tunnels that were not on this side of the river but under Staré Město, Old Town.

A few more nights of nothing led Bruno to the other side of the Vltava. He stalked Old Town Square looking for anyone suspicious. The streets had become emptier with every one-degree drop in temperature. So now he could focus on any suspected vampire and follow them. He figured that if he was patient, he might find the entrance to their long rumored underground nest below Staré Město.

LORD MAKRU

They say that humans only use about 10 percent of their brains, but this is just a myth, an urban legend. The truth is, we can't even measure it, but it is generally thought that we use all or most of our brains for one thing or another. After all, it would take an incredibly powerful computer to walk, run, and accomplish all the athletic feats humans can perform, and that doesn't even include the literature, painting, sculpture, dance, and other artistic endeavors, along with science and mathematics that humans can create utilizing other parts of their brain. If you study a subject over time, math or science, you will know more and more about it. The same is true of playing a musical instrument or painting, an artistic endeavor. In this way, humans train their brains.

Some people, using this technique, have developed what we call psychic powers. The CIA has used some of these people, nurturing their talent over time to fine-tune it. They have—or had, depending on who you talk to—a group of remote viewers, people capable of seeing events in another location, sometimes on another continent. The Russians have the same clandestine programs. Many of us have some psychic abilities but never put the effort into increasing their effectiveness. We just don't have the time.

If somebody had over 3700 years to improve their psychic powers, what could they achieve, remote viewing, telekinesis (the ability to move objects without touching them), levitation, precognition (the ability to see the future), and telepathy (mind reading and control)?

Lord Makru had honed all of these skills both before and after being turned around 1740 BC. In the great city of Babylon, there were several practitioners of these arts, and before being turned he had studied with one of them. But they were amateurs compared to what Makru became centuries later. He continued to study with all the masters of the psychic arts in Babylon after he was turned; and with five generations of masters after that, until the Babylonian empire collapsed and he fled the Middle East for Europe.

Lord Makru sat on a large pillow in the small anteroom of his chambers, in the primal nest beneath the Mother of Cities. He concentrated on a point in the energy field, which he could now see in three dimensions. It was a rift of negative energy and it was near, above him and a half-mile east. He sensed a dull man, a man who worked with his hands. Not to create, but to intimidate the weak and innocent. Makru immersed himself in the flow of his thoughts like a reed that had fallen into a stream. Bruno was his name, and he was looking for vampires. He was the son of a hunter, and he would show everyone who had doubted him that he could be as successful as the hunters of old and could kill at least as many vampires as they had in 1729 at the palace.

Lord Makru followed the stream of thoughts around a bend, but it turned around and faced him. *I'm going to kill you all when I find your nest, for I have done it before,* the consolidation of energy having no shape analog in the physical world told him. This one was not just powerful physically, Makru realized. He looked out of Bruno's eyes and saw a dark street. U Prašné brány, Makru could tell by a storefront, so close to the Powder Tower. Makru looked for a reflective window so he could see Bruno's face, but Bruno did the psychic equivalent of a shrug to get Makru out of his mind. Powerful indeed, Makru thought as he returned to his physical location in the primal nest. He knew a great deal about Bruno now, but lacked the crucial piece they needed: Bruno's physical description.

At the main Prague train station, a white Mercedes van took delivery of two coffins off-loaded from the 9:07 from Amsterdam. After the back doors were closed, the coffin doors opened and Valentin and Otakar emerged, looking tired and rumpled after a poor day's sleep traveling the old-fashioned way. The van drove a few blocks before stopping in an alley, where Valentin and Otakar quickly got out and made the short walk to one of the buildings that housed an entrance to the primal nest.

Below ground, Otakar walked straight toward the lounge, and Valentin to the basement of the building that held the offices of StoneHaven Systems.

Otakar met with Lord Makru in his chambers, away from prying ears. No reason to alarm everybody unless it was necessary. It turned out it was necessary.

Valentin met Trey in his corner office before he got to work making calls. The last ten trading days had been the worst in SHS history; they had lost $101 million, like a kid losing a helium balloon at the fair. One minute you have a firm grip on it and the next it's gone, gone forever. They needed to figure out what was going on and quickly, or they would have to shut the whole operation down.

"We're fucked, Valentin," Trey said. "I'm not sure what's going on, it's like somebody knows our every move."

"What about the guy Steve replaced? Could he have stolen our algorithms?" Valentin asked.

"It's possible, but nobody would be that stupid. Once exposed, you would be dead to Wall Street."

"Let's have Dmitri in the Wall Street office test it tomorrow," Valentin said.

Dmitri was their algorithm guy, a Russian Jew who had immigrated to America with his parents when he was twelve. An MIT dropout and just twenty years old, he had made $2.5 million the previous year working for SHS. He was young, felt guilty about dropping out of school, and had a propensity for existential crises, but Valentin liked him and could always talk him away from the edge.

Soon after Otakar arrived, the resident elders—Lord Makru, Radek, and Václav, along with Otakar—presided over a general assembly in the lounge. Almost everybody was there; Valentin and Trey would get an update later. Lord Makru explained the situation with Bruno.

"He appears to be working alone, but the man the dead girl failed to feed on talked to several people about what he learned from her at the palace. Everybody needs to be vigilant, as we don't have an exact physical description of Bruno. We have a rough idea of a hard man of forty-five to fifty with a working-class mentality, but Bruno is in truth likely a violent man who works for one of the gangster families that tries to control and profit from crime in the city."

The vampire-hunter protocol that Radek had spearheaded was only twelve years old. Every confirmed kill by a vampire hunter, or cluster of unexplained disappearances, was met with equal violence. This included being proactive, as was the case with Bruno, whom they now knew had killed vampires in the past. The database Radek had recently set up also tracked the children and associates of vampire hunters, ranking them on a scale of one to five for risk. Bruno's name was added to that database.

When the assembly was over, Anjelica slinked off to her chamber, feeling guilty for not having mentored the dead girl better. Poor decision-making skills before getting turned didn't automatically improve when someone became a vampire, and Anjelica now needed to sneak the mortal boy she had brought back to the nest out before dawn.

As she got to her door, she heard someone behind her. Turning, she saw Lord Makru floating about two feet above the ground as he often did when tutoring a younger vampire, an irrefutable display of superiority from a gentle man who only chose violence when all other options had been exhausted.

"You need to get the boy out of here now," he said. "I detected him while I was meditating earlier."

"I'm sorry. I met him at the university and he remembered me from when I fed on him last month. I wanted to bring him here in case he was being turned," she half lied.

"He's not being turned. It's rare, but some mortals can remember. Our banker in Luxembourg is one. Don't worry. He won't tell anyone after you make it perfectly clear he will die if he does."

"No, I don't want to kill him please," Anjelica, pleaded.

"You won't have to. I will, but I don't think it will be necessary. Who knows? Since he is studying finance, this one may be useful to us after he graduates, and us useful to him, but if you keep feeding on him so often, you will end up killing him anyway. He's not your fuck toy Svetlana," he finished, using her real name.

CRISIS MANAGEMENT

By the end of trading that day, a Thursday back in New York, StoneHaven Systems had lost another $11 million. Valentin and Trey sat huddled in stunned silence in Valentin's office after the daily trading call.

Finally Valentin said, "I'll call Dmitri in an hour and see what he has." Then they went to their planned meeting with the elders, walking the half-mile or so below ground to the boardroom.

"Are you guys all right?" Lord Makru asked.

"Yes, fine. Just some problems at work, nothing we can't solve," Valentin replied.

This guy is one cool motherfucker, Trey thought. Even he couldn't tell what Valentin was really thinking.

They got updated on the Bruno situation, what they knew and what they didn't know.

"We need to know what this man looks like," Otakar said, his voice getting anxious, as it did when he was frustrated. "If we did, we could take him out."

There were exceptions in the covenant regarding killing mortals, including just intent, which Makru had already had ascertained, and most of the deciders on such matters were in the room.

"We don't need to know exactly what he looks like," Valentin said. "If Makru can get a fixed location, like a club or bar he is working at, you and I can track him down."

"I want in on that action too," Trey said, now even more impressed with Valentin's cool-when-under-fire demeanor.

"Okay, Trey," Makru said. "But just observe and be backup. Otakar is the real war fighter in the room. Tomorrow evening I will start searching for Bruno. Keep your mobile phones on. We will need to move quickly when I do find him."

At midnight Prague time, six o'clock New York time, Valentin called Dmitri from his office. "Any luck on the algorithm?" he asked.

"I might have something. I'm not sure, and it will cost us," Dmitri said.

"What do you mean?" Valentin asked.

"If I create a phantom algorithm for statistical arbitrage, it won't make any money, but it will be bait that looks almost the same. If they follow it, we will go in a different direction. From there we can tell if they're somehow learning on the fly or are simply using our algorithm against us because they know it already. The only good thing is, they will lose money too."

"Okay, let's do it," Valentin said. "But don't tell anyone, not even Trey. Also, if you have time, change it for event arbitrage and order properties if you can."

"We'll just lose more money then. At least low latency is finally making some money now."

"Don't worry about losing money. We're already doing that. And $122,000 a day from low latency doesn't even pay our rent for the routers at the exchanges."

After hanging up with Dmitri, Valentin immediately realized his mistake. He walked next door to Trey's office and explained the plan.

"I guess we have no choice," Trey said.

THE HUNTED

Bruno had been shaken by the incident the previous evening. One of the upir had got into his head somehow. It had to be them, who else could it be? That night he had to work a private party at a small club that was normally open to the public. He would be bouncer and security, keeping the "civilians" out, as they liked to say, and on the lookout for trouble. His bosses were all old-school ex-communists who complained that they had made more money before the fall of the Soviet Union. They made plenty of money now, and what they really meant was that back then, they made more money relative to almost everybody else. Now they competed with legitimate businessmen and women, and had to get on waiting lists for anything from exotic cars to purebred dogs. They would fly in high-end vodka from Russia that they conveniently forgot had not even existed in the "good old days" under communist rule, and reminisce about days gone by.

Bruno did not want to take the night off from his vampire hunting, but he needed to make money and, what was more important, not piss off his bosses. They could be brutal when tested.

Lord Makru sat on the large pillow in the small anteroom of his ample chambers and again peered into the energy field, an ocean swirling around the Mother of Cities, the world, and the universe. He tried to find the one called Bruno. He sensed a woman he had fed on last week, a younger member of parliament. She was worried that she could not remember that evening and worried about the sex tape she had made with another man. *I'm a politician, a public figure. I need to be more careful,* she was telling herself.

Makru traveled in the ocean of energy, searching for that specific consolidation of energy that represented Bruno. After two hours and twenty-four minutes of time measured in the physical dimension, Makru found his prey. He quickly jumped inside Bruno to look out of his eyes and try to determine where he was. The timing was perfect as Bruno, working the door, looked both inside at the dark-wood bar and out across the street, so Makru could be sure he was at the Starý Tygr (Old Tiger) club in Old Town, a popular hangout for former Iron Curtain types.

Valentin got the text just as the trading conference call ended; and Otakar while meditating, as he always did before battle, in the lounge. Valentin walked downstairs immediately. When he realized he had forgotten to tell Trey, he hesitated, and then went back upstairs to get him.

"Just hang back and take Otakar's lead," he told Trey. "He knows what he is doing in these situations."

Otakar met them about a block from the bar.

"I already did a walk-by," he said. "I'm 99 percent sure I've identified our guy. He's working the door, about six one, two-fifty, and balding. The problem is, almost every guy I saw was carrying a gun, both inside the bar and out on the street. We need to get him away from the front of the building somehow."

"Let me take a look and see if there's any opening or opportunity," Valentin replied.

He walked past the bar, looking at his mobile phone as if distracted and not really noticing the crowd of drunken guys milling about the front of the bar, but taking in all the details. He recognized the guy Otakar had described, but they needed to be sure. The ratio of men to women gave him an idea, and he was sending a text when he got back to Otakar and Trey.

"I have an idea, a way to both verify the target's identity and get him away from the door," Valentin told them. His phone vibrated quickly. He had two texts, one from Anjelica whom he had just texted, and a longer one from Dmitri.

Fifteen minutes later, Anjelica arrived, and Valentin laid out his plan to have her get the target's name and—if it was him—to move Bruno about a half block down the street to a shop whose recessed entry created an alcove not visible from the front of the bar. Anjelica quickly agreed to Valentin's plan, but Otakar was nervous of sending her into harms way.

"If he figures out you're a vampire, he will kill you quickly," he warned Anjelica. "He likely has a large knife or short sword he always carries with him."

"I'm fine with it," she replied. "I owe Lord Makru anyway."

A few minutes later, Anjelica walked right up to the front door, and Bruno stopped her.

"Sorry, miss. Private party," he said.

"Even for me," she slurred playing drunk. "What's your name, stud?" She went on, teasing and flirting and sorcerizing with all she had, which was a lot.

"I'm Bruno. I'd let you in, but I don't want to piss off my bosses. Sorry," he said sincerely. Noticing how hot she was, and she looked strangely familiar like he had seen her somewhere.

"Are they drinking 'Putin's birthday,' limited release Russian Standard Platinum Vodka in there?" she asked. "Why don't you steal some for Russian girl and we can have private party?'

"I'd like to, but my bosses can get pissed off real easy," Bruno said.

"Oh, come on. Maybe you can get me drunk and take advantage of me." she slurred. She stumbled and grabbed his shoulder for support, still playing drunk.

She's hot as fuck or she's a vampire, Bruno thought. *Either way, I should pursue this.*

He convinced one of the younger security guys to take the door for a few minutes and hoped the wrong person didn't notice. That would get them both killed. He snagged a bottle of vodka on his way out.

A half block away, Anjelica pretended to drink from the bottle and then handed it back to Bruno. "You drink," she said, and he took a long swig. Then she did a little dance like a stripper, and unzipped his pants and started pulling them down to release his cock. "You like blow job," she mumbled, giggling. As she knelt down, she noticed the short sword in a scabbard attached to his belt.

She glanced up at him, and Bruno saw the look in her eyes. She was a vampire. He reached for the sword, thinking he had another kill—although some small part of his brain considered that this might be a trap. Still, it was too late for Anjelica, on her knees in a vulnerable position. Her head would be detached from her body in about a second.

I imagined I would live forever when I was turned just three years ago,

Anjelica thought. *How could it end so quickly?*

The violence was shocking even for a vampire—a spray of blood, the sickening sounds of snapping bones and tearing flesh. Then a foot of bloody spine dangling from the severed head like the tail of a stingray, as Bruno's body crumpled to the cobblestone street, blood spurting from the hole where his head had just been. The short sword jangled to the stones a half second later, and Otakar gently tossed the severed head into the corner, like a kid putting a ball back into the wire cage after football practice so it didn't bounce out, and take any more time away from his video games. He picked up the short sword, and the four vampires turned on their heels and walked quickly away.

"Holy shit, that was badass," Trey exclaimed, shocked that Otakar had decapitated a man with his bare hands as he, Valentin, Otakar, and Anjelica turned right at the next intersection, then left at the one after that.

Valentin pulled out his phone a few blocks later and called Lord Makru. "It's done," he said.

"Thank you, Valentin. I owe you," Makru said.

"Actually, I need a favor," Valentin replied. "A big one."

ANOTHER MISSED CONNECTION

Kate's plane from Berlin landed at Amsterdam Schipol on time for once, and the car service got her to Krasnapolsky Hotel without incident. She had a meeting with clients Friday morning and then she would be back in London by the afternoon, giving her just one night in Amsterdam. One night to search for Valentin, she didn't know why she wanted to find him—to fight with him, to sleep with him? She would play it by ear.

She started at the Bulldog Energy coffee shop where they had first met, smoking a little weed, drinking a little beer, and fending off several unacceptable suitors, coarse football fans, drunk and stupid with nothing to offer.

An hour and a half later, after getting bored with being the draw to help the women she had just met meet guys that would certainly be mistakes, she decided to search for the garage Valentin kept his car in. She was surprised she hadn't thought of this earlier, or when she had been in Amsterdam before. It did seem a bit like stalking, but she felt justified. Maybe this would turn out to be like one of those romantic comedies that annoyed her, or maybe it would be a nightmare. Either way, she was tired of being the tough, smart girl. She felt like doing something stupid for once.

You can't always keep up appearances, she told herself. And this was Amsterdam, not London, after all.

After some effort, Kate thought she had found the warehouse garage where Valentin kept his Porsche. It was down an alley, and had a regular door and a roll-up door, both with a keypad lock. She also noticed it had a surveillance camera, so she walked a half block down the alley, out of sight of the camera. She saw a few people coming and going through the door, but no cars. After about twenty minutes, she decided to walk past again. Just as she got in front the roll-up door, it started to open. A loud black Porsche with a wing on the back pulled out. A dark haired woman was driving; a blonde was in the passenger seat. They both looked at her suspiciously, but kept going. She positioned herself a half block down the alley again, this time on the other side.

After another thirty minutes, she was feeling increasingly like a stalker and decided to head back to her hotel. Before she did, she walked toward the door for one last look. Just then the roll-up door started to open again, so she turned her back and pulled out her phone, pretending she was looking at a text. Glancing back, she saw a silver BMW M3 drive off in the opposite direction, and before the door closed, she darted inside.

She looked around, surprised that she had been brave enough to pull off such a stunt. Maybe she'd had more than a little weed and beer after all. The warehouse was full of cars—Porsches, Ferraris, Jaguars—all nice and mostly sports cars. Then she spotted Valentin's silver Porsche Speedster. She walked over but didn't know what to do. She definitely had the right place, but Valentin could be anywhere. She was trying to decide whether she should wait when the other outer door opened and two women walked in, chatting loudly. She quickly hid behind Valentin's Porsche. The women didn't notice her and walked directly to another door she hadn't seen at first. When they opened it and quickly disappeared inside, Kate glimpsed what appeared to be a room within the warehouse. After a few minutes, she built up her courage and walked over to the door. Like the street door, it had a keypad lock, but was made of dark hardwood, like it had come from a house. It looked out of place and more substantial than something you would expect inside a warehouse. She wondered if this was some sort of underground nightclub, but thought Valentin would have mentioned that.

She was trying to find a way to open the door when she heard the roll-up door open again. She quickly hid and waited. A red Ferrari pulled in and parked, and the driver—a man—walked straight to the oaken door, tapped in a code, and entered.

Kate spent the rest of the night waiting for Valentin to return, crouching between parked cars whenever anyone arrived or left. Around dawn she headed back to her hotel exhausted and embarrassed, but at least she knew where Valentin kept his car, and she would be back in Amsterdam soon enough.

A REAL PROPER JOURNEY

The same night Bruno was executed, three coffins were loaded onto the train bound for Amsterdam central from Prague. Thirteen hours later, two generic white medical examiner's vans off-loaded the coffins. Thirty-five minutes after that, two of the coffins made their way to Amsterdam Schipol Airport. From there they were loaded onto a KLM flight bound for New York. Seven hours and forty-three minutes later, the plane landed at Kennedy Airport, reaching the gate at 6:31 a.m.

The two coffins were loaded into another van, which was driven to a parking lot and left there until nearly dusk. Finally, the van was driven into the city, heading to lower Manhattan and Wall Street.

The Manhattan nest had been built below one of the oldest sections of New Amsterdam, when it was founded. Not in caves, but in manmade tunnels that could hold over one thousand vampires. Today, there were only about four hundred. Another three hundred or so slept in the Brooklyn nest across the East River, all competing for the ample supply of "blood cattle."

Monday evening, on a cobblestone side street just a few blocks from the site of the World Trade Center attacks, the coffins opened. Ten minutes later, a black Maserati Quattroporte GTS picked up the two vampires and whisked them off to the New Jersey offices of StoneHaven Systems.

THE ALL HANDS MEETING

A long hour and a half later, despite Dmitri's brisk driving, they pulled up to a building in a generic office park in Red Bank, New Jersey. Dmitri used his card key to unlock the front door of the unmarked trading center of StoneHaven Systems.

Over three hundred SHS employees were crowded into the open area of the trading floor and around the low-walled cubicles, and most of them were standing. Trey and the Prague office were on the phone, and Steve had called in from Amsterdam. No one except Trey and Steve knew why they were having an all-hands meeting at 9:30 on a Monday night. There had been rumors of financial losses, so were some of them going to be being laid off? Nobody knew for certain, but they could sure throw out any number of wild guesses. Most of them were highly compensated, but they also had massive expenses—mortgage payments on at least one oversized home and private school tuition—so this was just not good timing. As if it ever was.

When Valentin walked into the room, wearing a dark Armani suit and Bally wingtips, with Dmitri following close behind, almost everyone in the room immediately knew who he was, despite never having met him in person. The buzz in the room increased to a crescendo as Valentin walked to a microphone and podium that had already been set up. He stood there without saying a word until the noise died down naturally.

"As some of you know," he began, "I am Valentin von Hahn, CFO of this company. You may have heard SHS has lost large amounts of money over the last few weeks." He spoke in his cultured accent, full of confidence and wisdom beyond his apparent years, intimidating but with a reassuring sense that somebody serious was in charge. "We discovered that someone was stealing from us. We knew they either had stolen our algorithms; somehow reverse engineered them, or used another algorithm against ours. On Friday, our analyst Dmitri at my and Trey's direction determined that the person, or persons, stealing from us have our algorithms. This means that the thief, or thieves, are either in this room or used to work for SHS. So first, I would like to give that individual, or individuals, the opportunity to step forward and confess right now. If not, by the end of the evening we will determine who you are, and the punishment will be swift and brutal."

The way he said *swift and brutal* sent a chill down everybody's spine, not only the guilty. They sensed that behind Valentin's old-world charm there was a violent streak that should never be aroused, but convinced themselves that by *brutal* he meant a school of shark-like Manhattan attorneys.

Before the sound of the word *brutal* was done echoing around the silent room, Steve got the text with the names of three guilty parties. Immediately, he started gathering as much information as possible on their families, homes, and bank accounts.

Valentin spoke for about twenty minutes, and then Trey added a few words remotely from Prague. As both men spoke, Bob Myers, Chip Talberson, and Paul King grew increasingly nervous. All three had strategically avoided each other during the meeting; and as wine and cheese were brought in, and the other employees were chatting among themselves, the three men kept themselves to three corners of the room. They thought they were clean, that nothing could be traced back to them, but they couldn't be sure.

Then, at exactly the same time, they all felt the need to go to a large conference room one floor below called Adirondack. They didn't know why, but they went as if their lives depended on it. They entered the elevator together and walked the short distance to the conference room. Sitting on the conference table was a man about fifty-five years old looking more CEO then Trey or Valentin with salt and pepper dark brown hair and a dark suit. He was meditating—and seemed to be floating about two feet above the table. The three guilty thieves rubbed their eyes, sure they were imagining, as the man sank down onto the table, swung his legs over its edge, and stepped down onto the floor.

"I usually meditate sitting on a pillow, and the hard table was starting to hurt my bony ass," Lord Makru said, as if this was a simple explanation for why he was levitating above the table, which to him it was. "I assume you all know why you're here, correct?"

They all nodded, mouths so dry they didn't think they could speak.

A minute later, Valentin walked into the room. "Thanks, Lord Makru," he said.

"No problem, Valentin. It was child's play, really. These guys put out so much guilty energy; I think Anjelica could have discovered them. My work is done here, so I think I'll head back to the city and maybe feed."

Valentin thanked him again as the ancient vampire left the room. The three thieves were now even more nervous and confused. *How had this guy Valentin called "Lord Makru" known it was them? What kind of name was Makru anyway? Had he really been levitating above the table?*

Valentin was looking at his mobile phone reading an email, an email from Steve.

He lifted his head and addressed the three men. "You all have families, that's good. I'm sure you want them to be safe and healthy, and that's possible, but it all depends on you guys. I'm going to tell you this, because tonight or in the next few days, you will all be dead anyway. Trey, Lord Makru, whom you just met, and I are all vampires. I've been alive for about 260 years, and Trey was more recently turned. Lord Makru is truly ancient. Since being turned, I've been responsible for the financial stability of the European vampires, and you three tried to fuck me. I know you don't have all the money. You spent some, and that's one of the reasons you're going to die, but we need to recover as much as possible. Do you understand?"

They all nodded as if in a dream.

"Your families will get to live," Valentin went on, "but in the next week or so, your kids will be pulled from the exclusive prep schools that your SHS salary and bonuses allowed you to afford, and placed in the system, foster care. Maybe your wives will be able to convince a social worker they can support themselves and regain custody. They certainly won't have any of the advantages though, not much chance for an Ivy League education, but they could still make it. If they're smart, some of them may live beyond their late teens or early twenties and be productive members of society, maybe," he finished sarcastically.

In the next few hours Swiss bank account numbers were provided, along with the marina and slip numbers of yachts, the addresses of second and third homes from Maine to South Beach, safety deposit boxes, and the combinations to in home safes. What they also learned is that the three had been stealing from SHS for almost a year, only recently getting greedier as they over extended themselves.

With everything checking out, Bob Myers, Chip Talberson, and Paul King were dead before dawn, and Valentin was sound asleep beneath Wall Street.

"It was a nasty bit of business, but it had to be done," Valentin said over Skype from the Manhattan nest the next evening, to which Trey and Steve agreed. None of them liked the sort of violence against mortals that they had been forced to administer on two continents in three days, but it was necessary they all knew.

THE PARTY

The penthouse apartment was crowded with more than a hundred people, a cross section of Manhattan's rich, powerful, beautiful, and famous, including about twelve vampires. The terrace above Fifth Avenue where Valentin held court had a stunning view of Central Park, which went unnoticed by the small group of upper management from StoneHaven Systems trying to curry favor with him. For the last twenty minutes, he had kept his eye on an almost famous model, with lush long brown hair and a Victoria's Secret body while people droned on at him. He knew this type of girl well, and knew most of the almost-famous models had the same vice. She would need a cigarette soon, and she would have to meet the mysterious foreigner on the terrace.

A middle-aged executive, with thinning brown hair and less fawning than the other SHS employees, walked directly up to Valentin. "I'm Jim Knowles," he said, reaching out to shake Valentin's hand.

"Ah. Low-latency trading. Good to meet you," Valentin said.

"All I can say is I'm fucking embarrassed. I thought when I took this job I could turn things around in a few months," Jim said.

"Well, the ship has turned, and the damage was done before your time by the two previous guys, the second worse than the first. We need to do better, though. I think we can all agree on that."

"Well, Steve has definitely helped with the turnaround. That guy was a great hire. I worked with him back at Sterling Klein Financial, you know," Jim said.

"Yea, he told Trey and me. He and Trey go way back, to high school."

Inside the penthouse, Lord Makru was surrounded by sleek society women, who were terminally bored within weeks of trying whatever was the newest craze in their elitist circles. Now these women were mesmerized Makru's tales of old Babylonian culture. He told of long-dead rituals, gods, and kings as powerful as American presidents in their day. He didn't need to feed that night, but he certainly had options. This was not the first time he had been to America. He always liked to meet new people and experience different cultures. Over the years, he had been to the States a number of times, both New York and San Francisco, but except for his first time, all of his visits had been after 1920, when technology started to progressively make it easier.

After getting free of the flock of women, Makru scribbled an algorithm on a piece of paper and handed it to Dmitri.

"It's for predicting the movement of a stock from those twenty-seven variables I gave you," he said. "Just model it for a while and see how it works."

"How did you come up with this?" Dmitri asked.

"Don't worry about that. I just got to thinking about your operation," Makru lied. He wasn't going to admit that he had derived the algorithm partially from reading Dmitri's mind, and the minds of a thousand other traders on Wall Street.

Outside on the terrace, "I'm Valentin" was delivered with the perfect blend of old-world charm and gravitas he'd perfected over two and a half centuries. And nuanced with a sense that he was more than a little dangerous. It was designed to impress a woman and scatter the competition, in this case three men—boys, really—and a balding real-estate magnate trying to bang a rising model before she was out of their reach.

"I'm Cassie," she replied, offering her hand.

Valentin shook her hand, holding it for a moment longer than necessary. "Cassie. That just won't do. You need a name with more luxury and distinction. What's your middle name?"

"Isabella. It was my grandmother's name." She turned her head and exhaled the smoke from her cigarette over Central Park. "You're not from New York, are you?"

"No. I'm originally from Austria, but I live in Amsterdam now. I have homes in Luxembourg and Prague, along with the family palace back in Vienna."

"That's so cool. I grew up in Iowa, but I've done shoots in London and Milan, but only four days each. I would love to spend more time in Europe."

Valentin stepped back, assessing her. "Cassie is an Iowa name. I'm going to tell you this, and I know a little something about it. You should go by Isabella from now on. You look more like an Isabella. Cassie is for a blonde girl doing Fredericks of Hollywood shoots. You're more Victoria's Secret, even in a blonde wig."

"Thanks, I think," she said. "Are you all right?" she asked as he got a faraway look in his eyes.

"I'm fine," Valentin replied. "I thought I saw somebody I knew a long time ago, but it's not possible. I think."

"An ex-girlfriend," she teased.

"Something like that."

"I'm getting a little chilly," she said after finishing her cigarette. "Do you want to go inside?"

"Sure, that sounds nice," Valentin said as he led her back into the vortex of the party.

"Do you know the guy who owns this place? Skip Talberson is his name, I think?" she asked.

"It's Chip Talberson. Yes, I know him. He works for me. I heard he's going to sell the place soon, so if you know anybody with sixty-million dollars, let them know," he said, only half joking.

"I heard he just bought it, but he's already had a bunch of parties."

Valentin knew Talberson had put twelve million down on it and had an enormous mortgage. Valentin really just wanted to unwind the place and get the money back into SHS, but knew that would likely take time.

"Have you seen the master bedroom?" he asked.

Cassie gave him a sly look. "No, it must be nice though."

"It is. I'll show you, Chip is out of town, had to fly to Miami at the last minute."

Valentin led her into the ornate master bedroom, which he considered over the top, with too much gold wallpaper and mirrors. The enormous room, larger than an ordinary Manhattan studio apartment, had a large round bed in an alcove next to windows that had the same epic Central Park view as the terrace.

"Wow, this is amazing," Cassie said, as she seemed to naturally blend into Valentin's embrace. Back in the Midwest, she had dreamed of moments like this, and she was smart enough to know it wouldn't get any better than this. After kissing by the windows for a few minutes, she started to take off her clothes, and Valentin marveled at her perfect body—skinny but with large real breasts.

"Isabella, I need to tell you something," he began, and told her his tale of necessity.

"I wondered if you were a vampire when I saw you checking me out," she said excitedly. "My friend said this was a vampire party, but I didn't believe her."

Valentin wasn't sure if she was joking, but took it as consent as he rolled on top of her and slid his cock into her bald pussy. She came quickly on his cock, but he kept fucking her, knowing that most supermodels didn't fake that intense sexuality that radiated on film and runway, and Isabella definitely had it. When he fed, she didn't seem at all surprised, but he wasn't sure if she was just New York jaded or had really known he was a vampire ahead of time.

"I just realized," he said, "that I don't know where you should go if you're turned. I need to ask someone.' He thought about it. "Is it Times Square?" he wondered out loud.

"No, it's the Trinity Church," she said. "You have to wait outside if you remember."

Later that night Valentin learned that she was right, and he really started to wonder if Manhattan was as loose as Prague had been two and a half centuries ago, with hundreds of mortals knowing about the vampires.

THE OFFER

After about thirty minutes of chatting, Isabella showed no signs of getting tired from her loss of blood or exposure to the upir virus, which surprised Valentin.

"I need another cigarette," she said. "Can I smoke in here, do you think, or should we go back out on the terrace? I really don't feel like getting dressed yet. I love being naked as much as possible."

"I should really get back to the party," Valentin said. "There are people I need to talk to before I head back to Amsterdam."

Isabella sighed. "Okay."

They emerged from the bedroom and reentered the party, still in full swing even though it was after three. They hung out on the terrace, both glowing, Valentin from the life-giving blood in his stomach and Isabella from her four orgasms. After about twenty minutes of chatting like the lovers they were, Morty Saperstein, one of the three elders of the Manhattan nest, interrupted them.

Morty had been turned in the mid-nineteenth century, and despite bearing a name indicative of a balding accountant, he was a WASPy-looking twenty-something guy, with longish curly brown hair, a rich-boy swagger, and subtle high-end low-key fashion sense.

"Can we talk, Valentin?" he asked, looking at Isabella.

"Don't worry, she won't remember," Valentin replied, verifying that he had just fed on her. "By the way, how the fuck does she know so much about the New York vampires?"

"Oh yeah. We have a few mortals sympathetic to our cause. Don't worry. These people in Manhattan are all so jaded; we have to throw them a bone from time to time. Getting bit by a vampire is just another adventure in their drug-addled YOLO lives." Morty replied with a beautiful smile emulating the spoiled rich kid spawn of Ivy League alum, he was not.

"Well, just be careful. We don't need another Prague," Valentin warned. But then he grinned. "I have to say, I'm having an excellent evening, so this can't be all bad."

Morty nodded. "I know you want to sell this place, but the potential is incredible. We could throw feeding parties like the countess did in the legends. What if I offered to go in one-third on the place with you as a long-term investment."

"It sounds interesting," Valentin replied, having trouble finding fault in something that had essentially served the next big supermodel to him on a silver platter. "It would have to be half, and I need to think about it. There would be a large number of vampires with skin in that size of a deal."

Just before dawn and resealed in his coffin for the trip back to Amsterdam, Valentin laughed to himself as he recalled Morty's words. *"The countess." So that's what they call Karolina behind her back.* And he fell asleep with dreams of feeding parties.

THE CAR

The driver of the enclosed car carrier followed the directions given to him exactly, locating the alley in Amsterdam centrum with ease and without encountering any tight corners that the truck could not negotiate. He realized it was a good idea to deliver the car at 11:30 p.m. to avoid traffic, despite having arguing against it earlier. The truck rolled to a stop, air brakes hissing as they released excess pressure. As the driver stepped out of the cab, a door in the building opened and out stepped Valentin von Hahn to take delivery of his lightly used white Porsche 991 GT3 RS. For the original owner, the purchase of the car had been the final straw in his marriage, and now he was a motivated seller. White may not have been Valentin's first choice, but for twenty thousand euro off retail, he couldn't complain, especially considering how in demand the new RS was.

The delivery driver and his assistant set up the ramps at the back of the truck and started carefully offloading the car.

Steve was a few blocks away, having just fed on a Swedish tourist. He was running a little late, but wanted to see Valentin's new car. As he rounded the corner and started down the alley, the roll-up door opened and Karolina's black Porsche 997 GT3 RS pulled out. She pulled up alongside Steve and jumped out, leaving the engine running.

"Steve, I want you to take my car. Just drive around I'll call you in a few minutes."

"Okay." Eager to drive the Porsche, Steve got in without question and drove off. Only then did he realize Viona was in the passenger's seat.

"Hi," she said, smiling.

"Hi." Steve grinned back, getting on the throttle in second gear to let the rear of the car slide out just a little as they pulled onto Rokin, just getting used to the PDK paddle shifters.

Back at the truck, Valentin's new car was on the street and he was signing all the paperwork. Patting his pockets, he realized he didn't have his phone, and he wanted to take a picture of the car. He told the deliverymen he would be right back and dashed into the warehouse.

He was coming back out when he heard the loud exhaust note of the four-liter flat six, but didn't think that was possible. It was his car. He would be the first person starting it. As he exited the door, he saw his new car drive off with a flourish. All he could see of the driver was a wisp of dark brown hair blowing in the speed-induced breeze. Hair that he knew could belong to only one person with enough audacity to pull off such a stunt. Karolina.

"What the fuck?" he said to the delivery driver. "Why did you let her take my car?"

"Your wife said she was the one who really paid for the car," the driver said impishly, coming down from Karolina's spell, not sorcerizing.

Hours later, after he'd retrieved his car and got to drive it himself, Valentin found Karolina in the tower lounge.

"I just couldn't resist," she said giggling.

"I'll get you back someday, if not this decade, then this century," Valentin joked. He told her all about his trips to Prague and New York, including Morty's offer to invest in the penthouse apartment, and feeding on the model at the party. He didn't come out, and say it was a feeding party, but she knew that's what he meant and saw her opening.

"Valentin, I've been thinking we should throw feeding parties from time to time at the mansion. I just loved hosting them when we were back in Prague, and it would really make me happy."

"I'll think about it," he said, with visions of Isabella in his head, and Karolina knew that was as close to a yes as she would ever get.

THE GUEST LIST

The museum nest, also known as the mansion, was not the palace back in the Mother of Cities, and it could hold only so many people, vampires and mortals. With just fourteen bedrooms, all occupied, and no guest rooms, something would also have to be done about feeding. A large feeding party would be about three hundred people, but that would be crowded even with the ample common space.

For weeks, Karolina and Viona, now a permanent resident of the mansion, had planned a feeding party for New Year's Eve, the first of what they hoped would be many. The guest list would have to be limited in both vampires and mortals. They would have to invite every elder in Europe since this was Karolina's first official feeding party in centuries, but most would not attend. The other vampires would be limited to their closest friends plus, three for any elder. For mortals who would be selected over the coming weeks, the invites would be plus two, which should result in an odd number, thereby avoiding too many couples. Couples could be separated with a little sorcerizing, but why make things harder than they needed to be?

Steve and Sarah were now exchanging around forty texts a day as they settled into a routine separated by the English Channel. Steve was careful not to broach the topic of when Sarah was coming back, but did ask if she was coming to the New Years party at the mansion.

<No, I'll still be here in London> she replied.

Later he learned that she had seen Kate, the woman Valentin had been obsessed with the previous summer. They had hung out together in a public house one evening. Apparently Kate came to

Amsterdam for work from time to time. Viona learned the same thing, also in a text. She was now teasing Steve, calling Sarah his girlfriend whenever she saw him, since she knew how often they texted each other.

⚱

After getting his invitation, Lord Makru decided to attend Karolina's feeding party, looking forward to spending New Year's Eve in Amsterdam. The only person he could think of to bring was Anjelica, since Trey already had an invite from Valentin, and most vampires didn't like to travel.

He brought her into his large chambers one evening to invite her. He needed to keep the party a secret within his nest, since Karolina was still so popular in Prague, and she had turned so many of the men in the city over the centuries.

He wasn't sure if Anjelica would want to go. She had never traveled, and he knew the idea of travel for most vampires was terrifying. He had never been motivated to leave Babylon until he had to. The fall of an entire civilization can be a great motivator, he thought. It was something everyone would experience, if they lived long enough.

"Do you want fuck me?" where the first words out of Anjelica's mouth as she entered his chambers.

"No, why would you think that?" Makru asked.

"It's okay, I don't mind. I know you're a super vampire."

He laughed. "Who told you that that?

"I forget. It's just a rumor. Will I have to go out and feed again right away?" She was already naked and crawling into Makru's bed.

Makru just looked at her from where he was sitting in a comfortable chair. "I'm not going to feed on you tonight. I wanted to invite you to a party Karolina is having."

"At the palace? I thought everybody in the nest could go to those."

"No, this one is in Amsterdam. We have a mansion there, much smaller than the palace."

"Oh, Amsterdam. I don't know," she replied nervously. "You travel all the time, but it just seems dangerous. I don't think I can do it. How do you do it all the time? Didn't you go to America last month?"

"When old Babylon started to fall, I knew I needed to go

someplace else, and I decided to come to Europe. Back then there was so little reliable information, I wasn't even sure if Europe really existed before I left. After taking that big of a risk, I realized traveling was no big deal."

"What was it like back in Babylon?" she asked.

"When I was born, the Babylonian empire and the city of Babylon were preeminent in the world. The Middle East wasn't as dry as it is now, and the city was incredibly rich, beautiful architecture, and gold everywhere. It was between the Tigris and Euphrates Rivers. Mesopotamia, the cradle of civilization, they call it today. The city was exactly square, and there was a moat all the way around, and high walls. Those born free inside the walls were truly fortunate.

"The Bible's Old Testament makes Babylon seem like a den of sin, and certainly there was much of that, but the real reason is people were afraid of the city. It was the first place in history with different races, different cultures, and different religions all in the same city. It was thousands of years ahead of its time. Every other civilization had a single religion. Babylon wasn't exactly secular. There was a main religion called Babylonia, somewhat based on the Sumerian religion, which had seven major gods. The four primary gods were Anu, the sky god, the king of gods; Enlil, the god of wind; Ea, the god of water; and Ninkharsag, the god of fertility. There were three minor sky gods—Ishtar, Sin, and Shamash, the god of justice. There were more than twenty minor gods, and even more demigods and heroes.

"The other religions were not persecuted, which was different from any other civilization to come before and most afterward, for thousands of years, and people spoke many different languages, as you probably know," Makru continued.

"Just before I was born, the first laws were written down at the decree of King Hammurabi. There were 282 laws carved into a seven-foot tall stone slab that became known as the Code of Hammurabi. It was the first mention of the presumption of innocence, and the right to provide evidence was afforded to both the accuser and accused.

"Babylon wasn't perfect, there were many bad men, bad rulers who were cruel and brutal, but that was part of those times. Primitive really, but we didn't have the covenant until 1733 when our backs were against the wall, so it's hard to judge."

He sighed. "It was so long ago, there were animals that are now extinct. The wooly mammoth was still around, Syrian elephants, the wooly rhinoceros, and predators like cave lions and dragons."

"There were dragons?" Anjelica asked. "No, you're just kidding, right?"

"No, they really existed. Some were up to 180 feet long, terrifying creatures, like giant flying reptilian birds, but they didn't breathe fire. That's just a myth. They lived off elephants and other large animals, including humans sometimes. By the time I left Babylon, the wooly mammoths became extinct, and soon after the larger dragons disappeared. Smaller dragons, only twenty to thirty feet, a different species I think, would still steal livestock for food, sheep and sometimes cows. Farmers hired men to shoot the dragons out of the sky with large arrows. It would take twenty or more arrows to bring one down. Other times they would use nets, but it was very dangerous work. They tried to keep some in the zoo in Babylon for a while, but they never lived more than a month or two in captivity. They needed to fly and kill their own food, or they would waste away.

"It's sad really. We saw them as monsters and did everything in our power to eradicate them, but now a majestic creature is gone. When I was a boy, before I was turned, I remember seeing flocks of five to twenty of the large dragons flying over the city. Migrating or hunting, I don't know. They never attacked people in the city, but you heard stories about them swooping down out of nowhere and grabbing someone in the countryside."

"Really?" Anjelica said, amazed. "You're not just making this up? I didn't think dragons were real,"

"I wouldn't lie to you. It's amazing how things get distorted over one or two thousand years. Every culture has legends of dragons. It's when the legends get distorted, with things like breathing fire and hording treasure, that people start to doubt the whole thing. Once something is gone, it's hard to prove it ever existed. We've used the same principle since the covenant. People think that every person bit by a vampire is either turned or dies, and when it doesn't happen, they think we don't exist. By the way, you can put your clothes back on. I'm not going to feed on you tonight."

"Does that mean you might someday?" she asked.

"Anjelica, I like you. I'm just trying to mentor you; I know it's hard being Russian here. The Czechs distrust you, due to recent history. So do you want to go to Amsterdam with me?"

"I don't know. Let me think about it. Is Trey going?"

Valentin, Steve and Evette were in the tower lounge on Christmas Eve. Valentin and Steve were working on their MacBook's, USB headsets connected for the occasional Skype call, but StoneHaven Systems was quiet, this being Christmas Eve. Valentin actually let Evette control the music from time to time, but overall she was not happy being in the tower nest, and he was not very happy to have her there. Steve thought Europeans held grudges way too long. He thought about America and Japan, now seventy-odd years after WWII and obsessed with each other's cultures.

"Can't you guys ever just relax?" Evette asked.

"It figures somebody who only knows how to tear stuff down would say that," Valentin retorted.

Two nights later, a week before the feeding party, the three of them plus Viona, whom Evette was not talking to due to their switch in nests, were at a huge night-after-Christmas party thrown by a spoiled rich Dutch girl, house music thumping as they hunted for mortals to feed on. More importantly, they were looking for potential guests for Karolina's New Year's Eve party. They all fed eventually, but not before handing out over thirty plus-two invitations.

NEW YEAR'S EVE

Karolina held court in the second floor living room of the mansion, Viona at her side and the iconic Rembrandt she had commissioned so many years ago providing the perfect backdrop. To the side, a string quartet played classical music, adding to the ambience of elegance and wealth. A steady stream of vampire well wishers, including a few visiting elders, came by, along with several mortal men making their play on the attractive hostess. Feeding would come later for Karolina. First, she was trying to identify the women who had influenced the most mortals to attend. She needed to befriend them, and make sure nobody fed on them. She wanted them to remember this party and to talk about it later. She was skilled in garnering the type of social buzz required to throw parties like this on a consistent basis, having a few centuries of experience, both before and after being turned.

A few of the mortal men commented that she looked a lot like the woman in the painting. She pretended she didn't see the similarity, but secretly thought the 1500 guilder they had paid Rembrandt, equal to about 17,000 euros today, was well worth the investment.

Before Valentin had been turned, New Year's Eve had been a big deal. Like a birthday, it marked the passing of a year, successes, failures, and time played out. Now as a vampire, he simply saw it as a prime feeding opportunity, presenting himself as the perfect opportunity to make up for a boring year. Tonight, hanging out upstairs in the mansion with Anjelica—who had come from Prague not by coffin, but on a seven-day road trip that Lord Makru had hoped would cure her of her fear of travel—he felt at ease and in his element.

He and Trey, who was also at the party, had stabilized StoneHaven Systems. They hadn't sold the Fifth Avenue penthouse yet, but after Valentin turned down his offer, Morty was trying to raise the money for a down payment to buy it himself. Part of that plan, at Trey's suggestion, was to invest some money into what was essentially their hedge fund at SHS. That killed two birds with one stone: raising capital for SHS and potentially making more money for Morty so he could eventually buy the penthouse. Valentin was still considering keeping some percentage of the penthouse, depending on how much money the New York vampires could raise.

Valentin was enjoying lounging on the third floor with the hypersexual Anjelica, who attracted just as many bisexual women as men. Karolina had hired a DJ for the dance floor setup in the ballroom on the first floor, so he was completely free. For now at least he wasn't anxious that he didn't have any work to do at a party, though he knew he would be talking business with visiting elders before sunrise. Perhaps it was the calming effect of Anjelica, he thought, or the aftereffects of so much excitement in the last few months, that had him so relaxed. Then he overheard part of a conversation between two women from the canal nest.

"Steve, Trey, and a bunch of other vampires and mortals are downstairs trying to pick up that supermodel Isabella."

Could it be her? he wondered.

"Anjelica, do you want to go down to the living room and check out the crowd?" he asked.

"Sure that sounds like fun," she said.

They made a grand entrance, Anjelica was on Valentin's arm as if they were a couple, making sure everyone in the room saw them as they slowly descended the main staircase. Once in the living room, Valentin walked straight up to Karolina and kissed the air next to her cheeks, establishing for the room that he had a first-degree relationship with the exotic hostess.

"Karolina, this is Anjelica, Anjelica this is Karolina," he said.

"I remember her from Praha," Karolina said. As the two women talked, Valentin confirmed out of the corner of his eye that the supermodel Isabella, in a little black dress studded with at least one hundred rhinestones, was in fact his Isabella from the New York party. She wouldn't remember, but that didn't concern him.

Their next step was to break through the throng of mostly men, including Trey and Steve, trying to get as close as possible to a super model. In one movement, using momentum and force of will Valentin pushed his way through the crowd with Anjelica in tow.

"I'm Valentin," he said, "and this is my cousin Anjelica." Was once again delivered with the old world charm and nuance he had perfected over two and a half centuries.

"I'm Isabella," she replied, clearly not remembering, but narrowing her focus for the first time that evening on the mysterious foreigner and his skinny "cousin."

"Would you like to meet our hostess, Karolina?" he asked. "I'm sure she would like to meet you."

"Sure," Isabella said, and Valentin broke her out of the circle of admiring men. Steve and Trey knew the game was up, and Valentin was in. She had seemed totally immune to sorcerizing anyway, something neither had ever seen.

"Karolina," Valentin said, when they reached her side, "this is Isabella, the girl I was telling you about from New York."

"Nice to meet you," Karolina said to the model.

"We met before, Valentin?" Isabella asked. "Oh, I knew it. This is a vampire party, isn't it? Karolina, that's you in the painting. Everyone has been talking about it."

Karolina turned to Valentin, her eyebrows raised. "You weren't kidding, Valentin," she said.

Isabella smiled at him teasingly. "Did you feed on me in Manhattan?"

"I did. And I wouldn't presume anything, but you are the loveliest woman at this party, more beautiful than I remember, if that's possible."

"Thanks and maybe. I quit smoking. That's done wonders for my complexion, and I have more of a glow, I think. Were you the one who told me to stop?"

"No, I was the one who told you to go by Isabella and not Cassie." Valentin guessed Morty, the waspy looking Jewish elder of the Manhattan nest, had probably been the one who told her to quit smoking.

"Oh, yeah," she said. 'I sort of remember waking up one morning after a party, not remembering much but thinking I needed to go by Isabella from now on. It really helped my career. I'm making more money in a week now than I used to make in a year. I guess I owe you."

"Who's managing your money?" Valentin asked.

"I have an investment manager in New York. I'm trying not to spend much, and it's easy to get guys to spend money on me now. I know this won't last forever."

"I might have some suggestions. Perhaps we could lower the minimum investment in our hedge fund at StoneHaven Systems and you could park some money with my banker in Luxembourg just to diversify."

Karolina rolled her eyes. *He's gone again; reverse sorcerized by a mortal once more, or whatever he chose to call it.*

Valentin was in complete control this time, though. He knew exactly what he was doing, and feeding on a supermodel every couple of months was something he was going to make happen. It wasn't that he didn't like Isabella, he did. She was beautiful and smart enough to be hyper successful, but he was only impelled into a Kate-style existential crisis every one or two decades, and he wasn't entirely sure he was over Kate yet.

He was about to lead Isabella away to discuss her financial situation, when Ambre from the Luxembourg nest walked up, shocking both him and Karolina,

"I made it," Ambre said. "Can you believe it? You guys inspired me to travel. I can't believe I did it. This party is awesome, Karolina."

Karolina and Valentin shared a look and then surreptitiously gazed around, making sure Ambre had not brought the mortal Hans. They were relieved to see no sign of him, and Karolina was pleased that the Hans situation was finally behind them.

Late that night a group of vampires—the elders Otakar, Accalu, Karolina, Ambre, and Lord Makru, along with Valentin, Steve, Trey, Viona, Anjelica—and the mortal Isabella all stood beneath the giant Rembrandt, which contained the images of not just Karolina, but Otakar, Accalu, and, of course, Lord Makru at the center. Without saying a word, the vampires all knew it was time for business, time to feed. It would be midnight in forty-five minutes, the start of the new year and prime time for mortals to couple with mortals, and vampires to couple with mortals. Karolina turned to the string quartet and requested, "Eine Kleine Nachtmusik," and the musicians started playing Mozart's iconic composition.

"Valentin introduced me to Mozart, you know," Karolina said, smiling.

"You knew Mozart?" Steve asked Valentin.

"Yes, from Wien when I was at court. After I was turned, believe it or not, I didn't have that much money at first, and I asked Karolina if she would help support him. She commissioned this composition, and was one of the backers of the opera *Don Giovanni* back in Prague."

"He tried to give me this piece," Karolina said, "but I paid him anyway. Mozart was a terrible businessman. He was supposed to write many more pieces for me, but he was a mortal and didn't last long enough."

Steve gestured to the Rembrandt. "Does this painting have a name like 'The Night Watch?'"

"No, we still haven't gotten around to naming it," Karolina said.

"Maybe in another one hundred years," Trey joked.

"How about 'The Night Creatures'?" Viona said, only half joking.

"You know, that's not even the real name for the painting in the Rijksmuseum," Makru said.

"I think I knew that," Steve said. "What's the real name?"

"'Militia Company of District II under the Command of Captain Frans Banninck Cocq,'" Makru replied.

"That's a mouthful," Trey said. "How about 'The Feeding Party of Karolina, Otakar, Accalu, and Lord Makru'?"

"How about 'The Feeding Party of the Elder Lord Makru'?" Anjelica suggested.

"Hey, it's my feeding party," Karolina said, feigning affront.

"Sorry," Anjelica said.

"She was just kidding," Valentin said. "Karolina doesn't give a fuck that you're Russian."

Karolina nodded in agreement. "I lived here in Amsterdam during the Cold War, so I don't have any of those issues. Except maybe that they occupied my families palace for a few decades. On second thought, guards, get this girl out of here, just kidding."

"Who's the guy in the painting standing next to Karolina with the long blond hair?" Steve asked. "He looks familiar."

"That's Lord Koenraad van Laar. He was the original elder here in Amsterdam when I arrived, from before the covenant," Karolina said.

"What happened to him?" Trey asked.

"Nobody knows. He just disappeared in 1744."

"It's time, I believe," Valentin said. He led Isabella upstairs by the hand, and the other vampires fanned out into the crowd in search of dinner.

"You can stay here, Anjelica, Karolina said, inviting the skinny Russian girl to remain with her and Viona. "They'll come to us."

Trey had had his eye on the woman who brought Isabella to the party all evening, not a model, but a pretty makeup artist, an American woman named Lisa. The thing he liked best about her was she never mentioned that he was black, hadn't made him feel like the "ghetto experiment" that white women often saw him as. In a pinch that was fine, but it was tiresome.

He was often in a pinch back in Prague, working too many nights in a row running StoneHaven Systems and forgetting to feed. He had been going to Charles University parties with Anjelica lately, especially since the tourists had disappeared for winter, but that still took half the night away from his responsibilities.

Lisa was blonde, about thirty, and had a curvy body with enhanced breasts. Trey wasn't normally a fan of fake tits, but they balanced her "Kim" figure well. She wore a light pink Chanel skirt and black top that had a conservative but sexy look. The color—Trey knew it had a name other than "light pink"—looked good on her pale skin.

"How long are you in Amsterdam?" he asked.

"Just three more days for a shoot with Isabella. The holiday took one day out of the shooting week, which is normally six days, so two more days of shooting here after tomorrow. After that, I fly to Milano for two more weeks of spring shoots. Then I think London or Paris. I can't remember now."

"So your pretty good at what you do?" Trey asked.

"Yeah, I'm at the top of the food chain. I'm good and get along with most of the models. They know they can't pull any bullshit with me. What do you do?"

"I'm the CEO of StoneHaven Systems, a high-frequency trading house out of New York."

"Wow, you look so young. You live in Manhattan? So do I."

"No, I live in Prague. We're international. Do you want a tour of the mansion?"

"I'd love that. Are you friends with Karolina?"

"Yeah, I've known her for a few years. She grew up in Prague and visits all the time."

Lisa frowned. "Did you used to date her?"

"Oh, no, nothing like that. Just friends, and I manage some of her money," he said as he led her upstairs to the bedrooms, doing a quick glance to see if one was available. There was one and only one was available. Karolina's room was already in use most likely by Valentin Trey thought.

Steve met Nancy in the kitchen, and he recognized her accent immediately. She was an "ABC"—American born Chinese— from the Bay area.

"I'm Steve. Where are you from?" he asked, already knowing the answer.

"I'm Nancy, I live in Paris," she said.

"You're a student?"

She nodded. "How did you know?"

"Your accent. I think you're from the Bay area. I grew up in Sausalito."

"Wow, I grew up in Palo Alto. You're good with accents," she replied.

Steve had a thing for Asian women. How could you not, going to UCLA? Or did they have a thing for him? He wasn't sure, and the only white girl he had dated in school was Suzy. In the case of Cantonese-speaking women like Nancy, he was always the white-boy experiment before they married someone their parents approved of. He never complained about being a temporary boyfriend, and Nancy was a perfect example of the girls he dated—skinny, small breasts, and hard to get into bed. Back in school it usually took a month or two to gain their trust, but Nancy, currently residing in Paris, was more adventurous than most; and he had sorcerizing to accelerate the process down to fifteen minutes.

Otakar met Maria as the men walked away from Karolina's circle, literally running into her since he was staring at Isabella on Valentin's arm. He wasn't jealous or obsessed; she was just the nicest thing he could see in the room at that moment, until he saw Maria.

Maria was Italian, a model like Isabella, with dark hair and a curvaceous figure. She was wearing a white blouse with a black bra deliberately showing underneath, a black leather miniskirt, and two-tone black and charcoal Prada heels. She had come to the party with Lisa and Isabella. She wasn't as famous as Isabella, but she was doing fine, and was on the spring shoot with her for the Amsterdam fashion house Scotch and Soda.

He apologized for bumping into her and introduced himself.

"I think I caught you staring at Isabella," she replied.

"Do you know each other?" he asked.

"Maybe," she teased, flipping her long thick hair.

"Do you have a name?" he asked.

"Si."

"Are you going to tell me what it is?"

"I'm not sure you're worthy. Where are you from? Not Amsterdam."

"I'm *Bohémský člověk*. I mean, Czech man."

"Soviet what? What language is that?" she asked.

"Czech, not Russian. What soviet?"

"You said bombsky soviet."

"No. *Bohémský člověk*, Bohemian man," he said.

"Bohemian? Are you like a hippy. You don't look like it. Your look is very conservative and clean," she said.

"No, I'm ethnic Bohemian. It's what most of the Czech Republic used to be called," he said.

"Oh. Well, your word for man sounds like soviet."

"No, it's *člověk*," Otakar replied.

"That's sounds like soviet to me."

"Are you trying to mess with me?" he asked.

"Maybe a little. I'm Maria by the way," she said, reaching out to shake hands with the six-hundred-year-old vampire warrior, now fully sorcerized.

"Nice to actually meet you finally. Do you want a tour of Karolina's house?" Otakar asked.

"That would be nice. You're such a gentleman."

Up the stairs they went in search of a free bedroom. Not finding one, Otakar texted the valet for his car. After a bit more of a tour, he guided Maria downstairs and to the front door where they retrieved their coats from the mortal coat check girl.

"Do you want to go for a ride?" he asked just as his blood-red Ferrari pulled up. Again, he thought he needed another car. Using a fifty-million-dollar vehicle just to get around town was a little ridiculous. Then again, for a night like this, maybe it was perfect.

"Wow, that's your car? You must be somebody," she said as he held the door for her.

"We are all somebody," he teased as he pulled away from the museum nest. In about twenty minutes, they were on a dirt road in the massive city of greenhouses south of the airport with no one in sight. Otakar got out of the car, walked around to the passenger side, and let Maria out.

"I like to come out here sometimes when the city gets too much for me. It's so quiet and you can see the stars," he said, and she looked up into the crisp, cold night sky of January. Otakar looked at his watch and saw that it was tomorrow and the next year. "Happy New Year," he said, turning to her. They started kissing. He held her close, enjoying the feeling of her warm blood just beneath the skin.

"I need to tell you something. I'm not human. I'm an upir, what you call a vampiro," he said, using the old world mortal upir delineation he had grown up with. Separating himself and moving up the food chain from mortals, Otakar was always aware he could kill a mortal at any time, for feeding or otherwise, and still felt separate despite the covenant. He wouldn't kill Maria, or kill for no reason, because like any well-trained war fighter, of today or six hundred years ago, he knew there was a time and a place for violence.

After he'd delivered the speech prescribed by the covenant he had helped envision and had received skeptical consent, Otakar removed her white blouse and black bra, exposing her large, natural round breasts. He began suckling at her hard nipples while he reached under her black leather miniskirt and fingered her pussy. After a few minutes, Maria was on her knees sucking his hard cock. After letting her show off her expert oral skills for a while, he pushed her over the hood of his Ferrari and took her from behind without removing her leather miniskirt. He fucked her hard until she was close to coming, then flipped her around, ass on the hood as he leaned over her, neck within striking distance, fucking her hard, bringing her to the brink. Then they were both coming, and he was feeding, life giving blood, hot and salty gushing into his mouth.

Before they got back to the city, Maria was sound asleep, and

Otakar had to wake her twice. Once to find out which hotel she was staying at, and the second time to bring her up to her room.

"Stay the night," she said, before falling back into a deep sleep.

"Of course," Otakar lied, but stayed until forty-five minutes before dawn, watching her sleep. Then he returned his car to the tower nest warehouse and walked briskly the few blocks to the canal nest, where he was the elder in residence.

Farrah was an intern for Al Jazeera based in Berlin. She had grown up in Paris, not the Middle East. Her father was from Iraq, her mother from Qatar, a distant cousin of the House of Thani, the ruling family, and she'd been able to get Farrah the job. Farrah's film crew had been in Amsterdam that day covering a story, so she came to the party with an acquaintance.

"Are you from Iraq?" she asked Accalu. "I can't place your accent."

"I suppose many years ago my family was from that part of the world," he replied, "but I spent a great deal of time in Rome, Prague, and now Amsterdam."

"Oh, my father is from Iraq, but left for obvious reasons long before I was born."

"Are you a reporter?" he asked.

"No, I'm just an intern for now. I do everything from get coffee to hold cue cards," she said.

"Well, I'm sure you will be on air soon enough."

"I'm not sure I even want to keep doing this, If I was on air, I would have to wear a burka and I'm just not a burka kind of girl, having grown up in Europe. God is great and all, but I'm more of a practical Muslim, if you know what I mean."

"I think the Catholics call it a 'reformed Catholic.' Me, I'm not very religious in any direction, but I'm open to spirituality," Accalu said.

"Who do you know at the party?" Farrah asked.

"Oh, I know Karolina our hostess, and maybe half of the other people, though some just in passing."

"It's kind of a strange crowd. I can't really put my finger on it, but many of the people seem, I don't know, sort of sinister in some way. Except that guy Makru, he looks like he could be a news anchor from work," she said, laughing.

"I'm sure you're tired," Accalu said. "Do you want a tour of Karolina's house, or we could just go for a drive?"

She was a little too perceptive, he thought, and needed to forget about the evening. Fortunately, he knew just the way.

"A drive would be nice," she said. "I'd like to get away from these crowds. It has been a long day."

So Accalu texted the valet, and a few minutes later after retrieving their coats, his red Ferrari Testarossa sped away into the night.

When the party was just fifteen minutes away from its peak, this being New Year's Eve, four mortals walked up to Karolina's circle of friends. Kevin and Scott were male models working with Isabella and Maria on the Scotch and Soda shoot, along with Zalika, a model from Africa by way of France. Right away Anjelica noticed how attractive Zalika was, jet-black skin, medium Afro, and a skinny body like hers, only taller.

"I'm Scott," one of the male modes said. "This is Zalika, this is Denise our boss, and Kevin is the straight one."

"So you're all gay except Kevin?" Anjelica asked.

"No, Denise is straight and Zalika goes both ways," he said.

"So do I," Anjelica blurted out, then grinned. "Oops did I sound too eager?"

"No, that was totally subtle," Zalika said, smiling big at her. Then she giggled. "Okay maybe not subtle."

"I'm the gay one," Scott said.

"Yes, we know," Karolina said somewhat sarcastically. "What do you all do?"

"We're models," Scott said, again stating the obvious.

"Does Kevin ever get to talk?" Viona asked.

"Not very often when I'm out with this one," Kevin said. "What's your name?"

"I'm Viona, this is Karolina, our hostess, the skinny one is Anjelica, and this gentleman just walking up is Lord Makru," she said.

"Hey, I'm skinny too," Zalika joked. Makru walked straight up to Denise, a thirty-something blond who quietly held sway over the others.

"I'm Lord Makru," he said. "You must be the cat herder,"

"Something like that. I'm vice president of content for The Pretty Day Agency."

"Lord Makru is kind of like the president of Europe," Anjelica said.

"Watch it, Anjelica," Karolina said.

"I'm not even European," Makru said, "so that's impossible anyway. Although I have been here for several years."

"Amsterdam?" Denise asked.

"No, I have a home in Prague," he said.

"Oh I love Prague. It's so beautiful."

"It has a certain comfortable old charm," Makru said.

"So you're American?" Viona asked Kevin.

"More or less. I grew up in LA, but traveled all over the world with my family. My father is in the industry."

"I've mostly spent my whole life here in Amsterdam," she replied. "What industry do you mean?"

"Sorry, the film industry. LA jargon. I love this city; it's one of my favorites. Maybe you could show me around."

"How about a tour of the mansion to start?" Viona asked.

"That would be great," he replied, and Viona led him upstairs and to the secret stairs that led to the roof and the finished deck area after retrieving their coats.

"The view is amazing up here," he said.

"Yeah. I like to come up here at night when I'm stressed and just relax."

"It would be a great place to get a tan during the day, it's so private."

"I'm pretty pale. I don't really like the sun," she said.

"Your pretty and pale," he joked, and she fell into his arms.

"Thanks. You're the prettiest boy I've seen in a long time," she said, lifting her head to look into his blue eyes from up close. He was perfect, light brown hair, six foot one, and a natural hard leanness that more often than not was airbrushed.

"Thanks," he said. "I thought I was more handsome."

"English is my second language," she said, hoping she hadn't offended him.

"As long as you like me, you can call me whatever you want," Kevin said, thinking his life was awesome since he had this hot woman hanging on to him. Viona was happy to let him feel like he was the one in control as they started kissing.

☥

Anjelica looked down between her legs. Zalika's hair obscured the view, but this was more about feeling anyway. She felt a tightening of suspense, then quivered as the contractions radiated from her pussy. As her orgasm subsided, she moaned, "Again." Sometimes she thought only girls could understand just how many orgasms she was capable of. She looked down again, the view still obscured by Zalika's little Afro. She liked her hair, though, and wondered why so many black girls thought "good hair" was straight hair. Zalika had "good hair." She had good everything, and a great tongue!

After her turn was over, Anjelica worked the tip of her tongue expertly on Zalika's clit while sliding a single finger in and out of her. Giving her what she had just received. Always being one to bend the rules, she waited until Zalika was close before giving her speech of necessity.

"Of course I consent, just finish me off, bitch," Zalika said while pushing Anjelica's head between her legs but not fully believing the tale.

When she was done feeding Anjelica gazed at Zalika's body, thinking Valentin was on to something with these models.

"Do all top models look this good without clothes?" she asked.

"*Oui*, I think it's a thing," Zalika joked.

By 4:00 a.m., all the mortals that had not been fed on had left and only a few of the ones that had been remained, sleeping upstairs or on couches. Karolina held court once again in the living room. Or more precisely, still held court.

"No, I didn't feed," she told Viona. "This party was about setting up the future, so these parties run themselves. Now with just a few texts and emails, I can fill this place with mortals."

Gradually Valentin with Isabella, Trey, Steve, Accalu, and Makru returned to the living room. Anjelica and Zalika came downstairs, both still naked, while a mortal girl somebody had fed on earlier wandered around naked as well, looking for her clothes. Makru relaxed floating four feet off the floor on a pillow from one of the sofas, his head at eye level as he took in the scene.

"This party rocks, Karolina," Trey exclaimed.

"Has anybody seen Otakar?" Viona asked.

"He's with Maria, one of the girls I'm on the shoot with," Isabella said. "She texted me a few hours ago."

"Karolina," Makru said, "did I tell you that Anjelica recently fed on a boy going to Charles University who remembered everything?"

"No. It seems to be genetic, from what we can tell with our banker and his son in Luxembourg," Karolina said, glancing around to make sure Ambre wasn't in earshot. She turned to Anjelica. "Is he sympathetic to our cause?"

"He likes to fuck me, if that's what you mean," Anjelica said.

"No, I mean can he keep a secret and do our bidding if asked?"

"I can't seem to sorcerize him, but he hasn't told anyone yet. And he will do anything I want just to get a piece of this hot Russian ass."

"Well, be careful," Karolina said.

"What is he studying?" Valentin asked.

"Finance. Lord Makru says we can use him in the future," Anjelica said.

"Maybe a job in the SHS office to keep an ear to the ground with the mortals," Trey said.

"Tell him you can get him an internship next summer," Valentin said, thinking about Kate. She remembered, but from what Sarah had told him, he wasn't sure if she was sympathetic to their cause or wanted to kill him. She didn't seem to remember everything, but unless he saw her again, he could never really be sure.

"Trey, has Dmitri tried the algorithm I gave him?" Makru asked.

"What algorithm?" Trey and Valentin said at the same time.

"I gave him an algorithm derived from reading his mind and the minds of a few thousand other traders on Wall Street," Makru said, and Trey was sending a text before Valentin could even get his phone out of his pocket.

Shortly before dawn, all the vampires headed back to their home nest; or to either the tower or canal nest if they lived at the mansion. They'd had to move out of their rooms during the party so everybody could feed. Viona rode back to the tower with Steve. They would share his room, as there was not enough space for everyone. Karolina shared with Valentin, but slept on one of the four couches in the massive chamber Steve had only recently learned he occupied in the tower, almost a third of the second floor. He wondered if Karolina chose to sleep on the couch because she would feed on him if they were in the same bed, and she didn't want Valentin to know she was a super vampire.

As he and Viona cuddled in his bed, he was hard as a rock.
"Watch it there," she joked.
"I think it's because I just fed," he said.
"Yeah sure. I bet you wish I was Sarah."
"I do miss her sometimes," he said.
"Me too."

SPRING

The night after the first feeding party in Amsterdam, and the first fully planned feeding party hosted by Karolina in nearly three hundred years; Trey was already on a train, safely in his coffin, heading back home to Prague. Lord Makru and Anjelica stayed for two more weeks before gassing up his dark blue 1974 Tatra 603, with it's three headlights and air cooled rear engine V8, and began a circuitous route home.

In those two weeks, Anjelica fell in love with Amsterdam, its constant flow of hard-partying tourists and Dutch pragmatism toward all things sinful. The coffee shops and sexual tension created by the ancient red-light district made feeding easier than even Prague during summer.

"I may come visit in summer," she said excitedly as she and Makru said their good-byes in the warehouse-parking garage of the tower nest.

"Be careful, Karolina," Makru said as he looked into her eyes, not needing to say anything more. The events that had led to the night of infamy at the palace were unique to that time and place. Hundreds of mortals had known and were sympathetic to the vampires in eighteenth-century Prague, and hundreds of others had vowed to eradicate the vampire infestation that plagued their city. Today, fewer than ten mortals knew about the existence of vampires in Amsterdam, and they were all sympathetic in one way or another.

Karolina still felt guilt about the slaughter in Prague, even though she knew she had not been the sole cause. And the covenant had been her idea as much as anyone's. In fact, not killing mortals was what the feeding parties had been about in the first place.

And with that, Karolina, with Viona at her side, planned to have a feeding party about every month. She collaborated with the rich and beautiful of Amsterdam so as not to conflict with other parties; and, of course, attended those other parties to feed while bringing a handful of close friends.

Valentin and Evette finally came to terms with their new situation after the elders did their every-five-months switch of nests. Karolina went to the tower, Accalu to the canal nest, and Otakar to the museum nest. Karolina finally got sick of hearing their bickering and got in a yelling match with Valentin one evening, in German, that he knew he would never win, and that forced his hand.

☥

In early March all anticipated spring and with it the increase in tourists and feeding opportunities. Valentin, Karolina, Steve, and Evette were in the lounge, listening to music while working on their laptops, a few nights after the second feeding party of the year, when Steve got a text from Sarah.

<It seems like they don't really follow the covenant here –s>

Steve read the text aloud.

"What the fuck does that mean?" Karolina said.

"I'm not sure," Steve said.

<What do u mean? > he texted.

<There is this guy Trevor, I think he killed a bunch of mortals> Sarah texted, and again Steve read it out loud.

"That's not possible," Karolina said. "What about the covenant, what about the elders?"

<What about the elders? > Steve texted.

<Nobody can find him and the elders are weak here, I don't think they try>

London had its issues; everyone knew that. In 1998, one of the four elders had been killed by a vampire hunter. With Radek's help, the vampire hunters, two brothers, had been tracked down and killed, but not before another vampire had been killed. After that, the choosing of a new elder had taken some time, during which some vampires developed a more hawkish view against mortals, but eventually stability returned.

The rest of the texts between Sarah and Steve were more of a personal nature and really about nothing. They generally avoided talking about who they'd fed on out of an unspoken jealousy, and Steve started to appreciate the fable of Adam and Eve that much more.

Later that night, Karolina dragged Valentin up to the elder's chambers in the tower for a conference call with Otakar and Accalu in Amsterdam, and Lord Makru, Radek, and Václav in Prague. They discussed the situation in London, what it meant, if they should do anything, and if so, what. Karolina was surprised that even Radek was preaching a wait-and-see attitude, but knew his obsession was with eliminating vampire hunters, not defending the covenant. She was disappointed that neither Lord Makru nor Valentin sided with her.

"All I heard was a text read by Steve," Valentin argued after the conference call. "I'm not sure what it really means. Are you proposing we send an invading army of vampires over to London to fix them?"

About a week later, it had been one of those unseasonably warm days that gave a hint that spring was just around the corner, and warmth lay on the city even as evening fell. The city would be swarming with locals and tourists alike, as if somebody had poked a beehive with a stick. Every vampire from every nest would go out to feed that night, and most would be successful. They knew this was a one-day and one-evening event, because a glance at their smart phones told them so.

Then Steve got another text.

<Trevor killed another mortal, they say he is going to Amsterdam –s>

Steve debated telling Karolina and Valentin, considering Karolina's reaction to the earlier texts, but thought the repercussions of withholding that sort of information would be worse in the long run.

"Wait and fucking see," Karolina said calmly when he told them, clearly addressing Valentin.

TREVOR

Trevor Smith grew up in the London neighborhood of Tottenham, at a council estate called Broadwater Farm, or simply the Farm. A failed social experiment in public housing that really only produced more criminals, its other nickname, bestowed by law enforcement, was the Criminal Farm.

It was one of the most dangerous places in greater London, but if that was all you knew because it was where you grew up, that was your normal. Violence, drugs, prostitution, and more violence were all Trevor knew. He was lucky to make it to twenty, not dead or incarcerated, but his time was running out. He ran a small gang of mostly younger kids dealing drugs, shaking down people for cash, and protecting their turf. Getting turned in 2001 was the best thing that could have happened to him, and at first he thrived as a vampire.

As time went by, though, he and what many upper class vampires of London maliciously called chavs and chavettes, working-class young adults, had trouble assimilating into the four largely upper-class nests of London. The empty promise of riches, expensive cars, and the high life left them bitter and disillusioned. The fortunes of the London nests had faltered in the wake of the stock market decline of the early 2000s, and those troubles were exacerbated by the global financial crisis of the late 2000s. Within ten years, Trevor had reverted to his old ways, rejecting the sophisticated, low-key approach to feeding his mentor had taught him.

It started with brazen robberies of high-end clothing stores, Burberry, Ted Baker, Louis Vuitton, and escalated from there. He took what he wanted and threw it away when he was done. The elders suspected, but were too embarrassed of the chavs and of themselves for allowing the London nests to be ruined, and so did nothing.

Trevor had grown up on the Farm, and he knew the toughest, strongest, meanest geezer always won, and now he was stronger then almost any mortal he would ever come up against. He was the lion on the Farm now, and all of London, all of the world was the Farm.

⚑

After the text from Sarah, the Amsterdam vampires were on high alert. Steve resurrected the Viceroy system and was monitoring all police communications, but after two weeks, nothing out of the ordinary was discovered. No out-of-town vampire showed up at any of the nests, and nobody on the street had heard about Trevor or any new vampire. Steve continued to check with Sarah, and Trevor definitely seemed to be gone from London, from what she heard.

"Maybe the elders did the right thing and they're just spinning a tale that he left London," Karolina said.

"That seems the most likely," Valentin said. "They would uphold the covenant after all, wouldn't they?"

After a few more days of calm, Karolina finally sent several texts to Nigel Wentworth, the elder of the Temple London nest. He had been at the original council of elders, helping to create the covenant, and she knew him fairly well. After a day of getting no response from Nigel, she texted Sarah directly to see if he had changed his mobile number, Sarah texted back from the Chelsea nest that he had not, but Karolina still got no response.

Halfway into the third week, with no sign of Trevor, Otakar decided to travel back to Prague and possibly buy a 2013 Ferrari 458 Speciale Aptera. He had been looking for a more "practical" car, and the Spider version of the top-performing 458 was perfect. The car, red of course, had just gone on sale, so he was eager to check it out and pay in cash before anybody could get to it before him. He planned to travel by train and drive the car back to Amsterdam. Karolina was not happy about it, but was starting to think the whole Trevor situation was overblown and the elders had already given him the true death, although she wished Nigel would text her back.

That morning, Otakar was on the first train to Prague out of Amsterdam Centraal. The next evening Karolina had a text from Nigel.

<We can't find Trevor in London. I guess he's your problem now>

Karolina was so mad she didn't reply, but they still had not seen any sign of Trevor in Amsterdam. They wondered if he had only said he was coming to Amsterdam and gone somewhere else, perhaps Manchester, just to throw them off. Later, though, Sarah sent Steve another text.

<They say Trevor went to Amsterdam the year before he was turned and loved it. He thinks he will be more appreciated. I guess he just doesn't know K>

With that Karolina went ballistic. "I fucking need Otakar back right now," she said, but he had not turned up in Prague that evening. She kept texting Lord Makru, but he had no good news. She even had Valentin get Trey to walk back from his office to the nest to check if he had arrived. He had not.

Then Steve got the message to all officers from the Amsterdam police department over one of his Viceroy spy nodes. <Homicide being investigated in the red-light district. Nineteen-year-old female believed to be an American tourist. Victim appears to have died from blood loss due to what appear to be bite wounds of the neck. Autopsy pending>

"Valentin, call Jacob and make sure he determines it was an ice pick," Karolina said, but Valentin had already texted Jacob, the chief medical examiner who owed him favors for life. They could deflect this one, Valentin thought, but if the bodies started piling up, there would be repercussions.

Valentin cleaned up the mess, and Karolina traveled to each nest in turn, giving an impassioned speech to the assembled vampires.

"This is a threat to our way of life, our very existence. I was there for the upir hysteria in the eighteenth century. Take a look around you, because this may be the last time you see most of the people in this room. We need to find this Trevor, stop him, give him the true death, end of story."

Every time I try to throw feeding parties, something bad happens, she thought. Even in Praha last summer with the dead girl. She felt like she was hexed, but had lived long enough to know that was an empty superstition.

A week later, despite maximum vigilance by every vampire in Amsterdam and constant surveillance of the authorities by Steve, there had been no sign of Trevor.

There had also been no word on Otakar's arrival in Prague. He too seemed too have vanished.

WHAT CITY IS THIS?

Otakar awoke in a mortician's lab. The tools, the deadly formaldehyde injection system, and funeral makeup, all archaic, indicated he was not in a major city. He was still in his coffin, which was open, and he could tell it was day. As he sat up, a man he had not seen over the side of his sarcophagus of travel, as he liked to call it, was startled and ran to the door. He closed it after him, thus locking Otakar inside. He knew most of these labs were in the basement of mortuaries, out of the way of grieving relatives who didn't need to see the process of their loved ones being prepared for an open-casket service. Two of the walls would be earth, and the others likely reinforced due to tradition and superstition, superstition of what, in fact, Otakar was.

After he'd inspected the door for about thirty seconds for a weakness, it swung open and two enormous police officers burst in, Tasered Otakar, and had him subdued in fifteen seconds flat, handcuffs and leg irons. It was partially the Taser, but mostly the fact that it was day. During the day, Otakar was greatly diminished, weaker than an average man, and these were not average men. The final humiliation was a dark hood being pulled over his head.

Otakar was walked, hobbled as he was, upstairs and out the front door to a waiting car. After a short drive, he was walked into another building and put in a holding cell. The dark hood, handcuffs, and leg irons were removed. It was still day, late afternoon, and he was so weak, he lay on his side upon the bench, trying to focus on what he knew would be an interrogation of sorts.

"Kakvo strying za kontrabanda?" one of the two men—who now looked to Otakar more like organized crime enforcers than cops— asked. What language were they speaking? he wondered. Not Czech. Where was he?

"Kakvo strying za kontrabanda?" was asked again, with more authority.

Was it Romanian? He only knew a few words and this didn't sound like it.

"Ce ai strying de contrabandă?" the other one asked, and Otakar knew that was Romanian. They were asking, What are you … something. He wasn't sure about that last word.

"English?" he asked.

"What you try smuggle?" the first one asked in broken English.

"I'm not trying to smuggle anything," Otakar said.

"Then why in coffin?" This was asked with a knowing grin, as if they had caught him in a lie.

"What city is this?" he asked.

"What city. Ha ha. Very funny. What you try smuggle, joke man?"

"I'm not trying to smuggle anything, really. What city is this?" Otakar asked again.

"This not city. Is town. Krapets."

"In what country?" Otakar asked.

"Very funny. This is Bulgaria. You no smuggle here without pay," one of his captors said.

"I wasn't trying to smuggle anything. I got locked in the coffin and ended up here," Otakar said.

"Ivan will sort you out when he gets here," one of his captors who could have been brothers told him.

Otakar figured Ivan was either the police chief, local crime boss, or both, but didn't want to find out.

After that, he was left alone in the cell. There was a woman at a desk just around the corner, out of sight. He could hear her phone conversations, but the two cops who had brought him in were gone. Otakar had never heard of Krapets and had no idea what part of Bulgaria he was in.

Several hours later he woke up, and knew it was night. His strength was back at about 95 percent. Now he could easily overpower the two "beef" brothers when they returned.

Two hours passed, and no one came to check up on him, although a new woman was answering phones now. Like the first, they all sounded like personal calls.

About an hour later, a man appeared outside his cell who made the first two seem like wimps. He was a super heavyweight, and Otakar guessed this was Ivan. He was around fifty, and instead of a uniform he wore street clothes, wool slacks and a white linen button-up shirt open at the collar. The man gazed at the much smaller Otakar for about thirty seconds before opening the cell and saying in English, "Now we get truth."

Despite, and also because of, Ivan's size, Otakar simply pulled him into the cell, pushed him into the corner, stepped out into the hall, and locked the door behind him, all in one smooth motion. He then startled the front desk woman, a fortyish looking local who spoke no English.

"Where is my mobile phone?" he demanded, his fangs now exposed in anger, but got only blinking surprise in response. He pushed her chair, which was on wheels, gently to the side and started to rifle through her desk drawers. Not finding his phone, or the small bag he had brought with him, he asked again, "Where is my mobile phone?" This time she glanced at a black wooden cabinet with locked doors against the wall. Otakar quickly got the door open, easily breaking the cheap lock. Inside were the belongings of at least ten people, and his bag. Most of his stuff was missing, except for his phone, but no charger, and a Rolling Stones T-shirt that didn't even belong to him. His extra black shirt and his passport were gone, and Otakar was glad he traveled light, still having clothes stored in his old chambers in the primal nest. He rifled through a few of the other boxes and bags, but only found cheap stuff and dead mobile phones. He guessed the phones would be sold in bulk at some point in the future.

By this time Ivan was starting to make a lot of noise, swearing loudly in Bulgarian, and the woman at the front desk was getting nervous. Thinking it was time to get out before somebody else showed up, Otakar walked out the front door, free.

A block away, he powered up his phone and opened Google maps to see where he was. The town of Krapets was in the north of Bulgaria, on the Black Sea coast, not far from the Romanian border. Then his phone shut down the battery dead.

Otakar started to walk briskly away from the police station, in case anyone was coming to search for him, and looked for the beach. The town was flat and appeared to be built on sand dunes that gently sloping toward the sea. For the most part the single-story houses were older and rundown, not particularly charming. Not ugly exactly, more of a stark, working-class utility feel. As he got closer to the beach, he saw a few newer and nicer two-story homes that looked to be owned by retirees or were maybe vacationers' second homes, but not locals.

Lord Makru had an old friend who lived in a small village called Sighisoara, somewhere in the Carpathian Mountains of Romania. Otakar could look him up if he found a car, but there was a nest in Bucharest, which was closer. He couldn't remember where, but could probably figure it out once he got there. Bucharest was probably only a three or four-hour drive away; from what he could tell from the ten-second glance he'd got off the map on his phone. That would give him another four hours or so to find the nest.

I haven't been there in 220 years, but how much could the city have changed in that time? After that I can ship myself to Prague, and hopefully the Ferrari will still be for sale, he thought.

THE WAITING GAME

Spring seemed so distant now, it was hard to believe it would ever come, or ever had. Unseasonably cold and frequent storms swept through the Benelux region of Belgium, the Netherlands, and Luxembourg, bringing cold winds, late snows even at sea level, and leaden skies day after day. A pall had fallen over Amsterdam, and not just for the vampires who dreaded the possibility of Trevor killing again, but the mortals as well. Daily news stories on TV, warnings at all the hotels, and a constant chatter on everything Internet from social to conspiracy bloggers warning of the possible serial killer loose in the city. He had only killed once, but Karolina and the other elders doubted that would hold. Though it was still early in the tourist season, high hotel vacancy rates were blamed on the senseless murder, along with the weather. That single murder had insinuated itself so completely into the psyche of the populace, the prospect of another was terrifying to all the vampires.

Karolina's next party was canceled, although feeding on the general public was encouraged as a way to keep an eye out for Trevor; and everyone was on high alert for the emergence of the next vampire hunter, either from Amsterdam or elsewhere.

Steve was so busy monitoring the situation, crosschecking hotel check-ins and police communications, he had reduced his StoneHaven Systems commitment to a single brief meeting per week. He had recruited Evette to help parse the data, and she was surprisingly—to Valentin at least—a big help, working on her laptop throughout the night alongside Steve. All the data was transferred to servers he had set up in the primal nest with Radek and imported into an SQL database. From there, every name that showed up in airline manifests, hotel reservations lists, and police reports was crosschecked. In Prague, Anjelica had recruited some students from

Charles University to write the front-end application, including mobile versions for both IOS and Android that made it easy for even Radek to run SQL queries based on different assumptions.

It seemed like every evening when the nests awoke, the tension had increased. They all dreaded Trevor's next move, but two weeks had passed with nothing. He would have had to have fed in that time, but no reports had come through of a new murder. Vampires in all the nests started to doubt whether Trevor was even in Amsterdam, or if he really existed at all. Karolina became obsessed with the disappearance of Otakar, wondering if it was related. She couldn't imagine anyone getting the best of him, mortal or vampire, but there has been no word from him since his coffin left the train station two weeks ago.

"He picked the worst time possible to disappear on us," she lamented more than once to Valentin.

Then, on the first Saturday night of April, it happened, two bodies, a man and a woman, found in an alley in the red-light district, both British nationals. The man's head had been almost ripped off of his body, as if he had encountered a brown bear, 2000 pounds and eighteen feet tall if it stood on its hind legs. The woman was found about seventy-five feet away down the same alley, Steve read in the police report. Likely cause of death: blood loss, possibly from puncture wounds to the neck. It was clear to the vampires what had happened. Trevor had seen something he wanted and taken it. The man no doubt had resisted, being an enforcer on his local amateur rugby team, and had paid the price. Trevor then raped the terrified woman, feeding until no more blood could be extracted from her body, and then left the carnage strewn in the alley, like dirty dishes after a meal.

THE PLANNING

Karolina and Accalu held a conference call with Prague on the Trevor situation. A quick vote was taken as a prescribed formality of the covenant. The vote was unanimous. True death. Radek would leave that night for Amsterdam to help with the situation, as Otakar was still missing.

Otakar was the perfect person to carry out the sentence and everyone knew it. The great military leader, Jan Žižka, had trained him as a disciplined killer, always using the same two-step strategy that the Hussites of fifteenth century Bohemia had used when engaging the superior armies of the Holy Roman Empire. The first step was to provoke the enemy into attacking, assuming a defensive posture while weakening the attackers. After the enemy's morale was sufficiently lowered, the offensive phase began, which had included the first use of gunpowder-based weapons, with devastating effect. Žižka is still considered one of the greatest military leaders in history, having never lost a battle, an exclusive list that includes the likes of Alexander the Great. But nobody even knew if Otakar was still alive. And if he was alive, where was he?

Every vampire in Amsterdam carried a picture of Trevor with instructions to text one of the elders if they saw anybody who looked remotely like him. Radek assumed the position of elder in residence at the mansion and continued to coordinate with Steve and Evette. His concern that the murders by Trevor would bring out vampire hunters from all corners of the earth reached a fever pitch.

If Otakar was still missing when they finally located Trevor, Valentin, Steve, and the big Dutchman Hubrech would execute the sentence. Everybody was aware of how dangerous a job this was. There was a strong possibility that one of them would be killed.

Sarah was so terrified she would never see Steve again; she

decided it was time to return to Amsterdam. The decision was made that much easier with the rapid descent into disarray of the four London nests. Not only was the discontent of the more recently turned chavs high, but Trevor had his sympathizers who started to believe that mortals, were simply a food source, like beef had been before they were turned. Not blood cattle, but truly just cattle.

Two nights after the elders voted for execution, Sarah arrived back in Amsterdam, traveling by way of coffin.

"Sarah, it's good to see you," Steve said, and gave her a big hug.

"It's good to see you too," she said. A little coolly Steve thought.

He wondered at her chilly tone, and asked if she had left because of him.

"The question you should ask is, why is a British vampire living in Amsterdam and not London," she replied.

Before she left London, she had been able to get several more photos of Trevor, despite many of his supporters refusing to help. Valentin noticed one particular photo and got a brilliant idea. Evette would go to the police and claim she was a possible witness to the most recent murders, and show them the photo. Trevor was not the main subject of the picture, but somewhat behind two other people, as if he had photo-bombed a picture of strangers. The background was generic and blurry enough so that it could be in any bar or coffee shop. She would claim she took the photo and later noticed him follow the couple out of the bar. Once she gave them the picture of Trevor, it would be spread throughout the city, the Internet, and on TV. They would continue to monitor all police channels and shadow any investigations into any persons of interest.

THE SEARCH

And then Trevor disappeared. The vampires expected him to lay low for the first week to ten days after he killed the British couple, but as the third week began, there was still no sign of him. Karolina called all the elders on the continent, warning them he may have left Amsterdam. She even texted Nigel in London to warn him he may have returned.

<Bullocks, I have enough trouble as it is > he immediately responded, which pissed her off.

The city and all its mortals were in a perpetual state of foreboding. Hotel occupancy plunged to the lowest levels in over sixty-five years, back to when Europe was recovering from WWII. Everyone seemed to think Amsterdam was now the place where you went to get killed on holiday, forgetting that murders happened all the time in cities all over the world. Yet something about the nature and seeming inevitability of the second murders sent a chill throughout the world, not just Amsterdam. In the same five weeks, twenty-nine murders were reported in New York City, four of tourists, but they just didn't resonate.

Within the three nests, the tension was high, with bickering, open hostility, and a search for someone or something to blame. Steve couldn't figure out what was going on with Sarah. Was it him, was it the Trevor situation, or was it something back in London? The more he probed, the colder she got. He couldn't believe she was the same woman he had had such a connection with last summer, and blamed himself for not staying in contact during his road trip with Karolina and Valentin. At least, he was busy with work, and that kept his mind off it. Besides, he didn't know what he was expecting anyway. They just didn't have what each other needed.

Then, in three short days, it was spring. The weather turned, the cold storms giving way to the normal rain and cloudiness of the region, but warmer. It lifted the spirits of the mortals a little, and the vampires in turn, who found it slightly easier to feed.

"The police have a suspect," Steve announced after reading an internal email from the department. He was sitting in the tower lounge with Valentin, Karolina, Evette, and Sarah.

"Where is he?" Karolina asked.

"It looks like the address is just three blocks from the canal nest. They're planning a raid for 10:45 p.m. tonight, since that's when he was sighted last night."

"It's eight o'clock now," Valentin said. "Evette, can you track down Hubrech? We need to get there within the hour."

"*Oui,*" she replied.

Ten minutes later, ten vampires assembled in the garage area of the tower to see Valentin, Steve, and Hubrech off. Steve looked for Sarah to say good-bye, but there was no sign of her. *Why did she even come back from London?* he wondered.

With the short good-bye and good luck that always come to those going into battle before they expected, the three headed toward destiny, each prepared with a concealed short sword and incipient resolve.

THE NEEDFUL, THE WRONG, AND THE
TRUE DEATH

On the way to the address where Trevor may or may not have been sighted, the three appointed executioners passed the alley that had been the scene of his brutal double murder. They all paused to glance between the two buildings. To enhance the context of what they had read so much about on their phones and laptops and thus steel their resolve to take the life of another vampire. Something none of them took lightly, especially now that it was transforming from an abstract concept to cold, hard reality.

Two people were several yards away, down the alley, and Steve recognized the woman's hair immediately. He started down the alley, followed quickly by Valentin and Hubrech. Sarah was arguing with someone, and Steve felt sick just thinking about who it was. He had a flashback to how he had felt at sunrise last summer in the Austrian Alps, and touched the wall to counteract the dizziness.

"They'll kill you if you don't run," Sarah was pleading to the other vampire.

"Too late," Trevor replied in his strong cockney accent. "'Ere's the geezers now."

Sarah sent them a quick, panicked glance. "Run, Trevor, before it's too late," she said.

"I'm not goin' ter run. I respect these guys, they 'ave a job to do. I'm goin' ter kill 'em though," Trevor replied just as the three reached them.

Sarah turned to Steve, who had regained his strength out of anger. "Please don't kill him. He's just misunderstood. He's had a hard life."

"It's dyin' time na, girl, but it won't be me," Trevor declared with the loutish insolence of the street.

"The covenant is clear," Valentin said to Sarah. "Every vampire knows it, and the elders have spoken. It's the true death for Trevor now."

"Fuck the mortals," Trevor said. "We're stronger than them. Wot 're ya afraid of?"

"I could probably take on five mortals," Valentin said, "and Hubrech here maybe ten, but there are millions, make that billions of them, and only thousands of us. I survived the eighteenth century and I was lucky. Mortals can breed, we can't. If we could, Sarah and Steve here would be picking out baby names by now."

Trevor glanced at Steve and then back to Sarah. "So this is the Yank ya were talking about. I think I'll kill 'im first."

"Sarah, get out of here," Steve said. "You don't want to see this."

He was baffled when his phone pinged, alerting him to a text message. Whoever was texting, it had to be important. He pulled out his phone and read the text from Evette.

<Another murder, two women by one of the Bulldogs>

"He killed again, two women," Steve said as they heard sirens just a few blocks away.

"It ain't killin' when it's just yer supper. Yer all on the wrong side with yer covenant bullshit," Trevor said, smirking.

Steve pushed Sarah back as the three started to circle Trevor. She leaned against the wall, sniffling back tears as she watched the scene unfold like some deadly encounter on a nature show.

Valentin, Steve, and Hubrech brandished their short swords while Trevor held a twelve-inch hunting knife in each hand. The truth was, only Valentin was properly trained with any type of sword, and Trevor's experience with his knives was only using them to threaten rivals when protecting his turf back on the Farm. But he was good at that and presented a menacing adversary. He had the added advantage of having nothing to lose, and seemed to relish the conflict, determined to take one or two lives if his was to be surrendered. If he was lucky, he'd kill all three and walk away.

The tension was palpable as each side waited for the other to make a move. Valentin knew this was the moment Otakar excelled at, provoking an attack so he could size up the enemy and counter. They couldn't get Trevor to bite, though, which was the correct strategy for the one in a three-on-one fight. Trevor waited, and waited, and then, emitting a guttural howl like a wild animal, baited Hubrech to crack and make the first move. He stabbed at Trevor but failed to turn his body so he would present as small a target as possible, the way Valentin had been taught from the age of seven. Trevor took advantage, dodging the jabbing sword and catching Hubrech in the midsection with one of his knives. It was a shallow cut, but Trevor had drawn first blood and was unscathed.

Hubrech's lack of finesse and reliance on strength alone made Valentin realize how poorly prepared they really were. He should have trained them before. Otakar would have, and in fact had, drilling Valentin and others in the tower garage for hours before even the slightest possibility of conflict.

Otakar was traveling west and north on the E81 after driving up the Black Sea coast and crossing the border from Bulgaria to Romania. The EU was great for travel. He had never needed to show his missing passport. He had laid low the first few days in one of the unoccupied two-story houses near the beach. It didn't have a basement, but he made due in a closet, carefully venturing out at night until he was sure a getaway was safe, even feeding on a tourist at a hotel in the south end of town.

The car he managed to procure was unfamiliar to him; one of those generic four-door sedans that sort of looked like a Mercedes but wasn't, a car common to Europe. It was a five-speed manual, but the engine did not rev like the sports cars he was used to driving, so he struggled at first. The gas tank was still half full, but the engine would sputter from time to time as if it were out of gas, and he suspected the car had never traveled more than thirty kilometers at a time in its twenty-odd years in Krapets.

Otakar was between small towns, probably less than forty-five minutes from Bucharest, when the car finally died completely. He couldn't tell in the dark if it was steam, smoke, or both coming out from under the hood as he rolled to the side of the road. It was still two hours until sunrise, but he needed to find a place to shelter during the day. The landscape consisted of the standard geometric squares and rectangles of any place in the world reasonably flat, not populated, and fertile, each with its own crop, but not a tree in sight. He climbed onto the roof of the car, but only saw more of the same. He considered jumping the fence and walking one way or the other on the frontage road until he found a town, but then what? He chose the other option—wait for somebody on his or her way to Bucharest to stop and help, as the car had thankfully not caught fire after the engine died. Unfortunately, at four in the morning, the only vehicles on the road were trucks that lost money every second the driver took their foot off the gas, so nobody stopped.

At dawn, Otakar's only option was to sleep under the car, despite being exposed on the side of the A81 Autostrada Soarelui. Within the hour, though, he was rousted by the Romanian highway patrol and placed into the back of a black Jaguar XFR, one of several performance cars given to them as "gifts" by local luxury car dealers. Fifty-five minutes later, he was led into the main Bucharest police station, stumbling and weak from the sunlight, which only reinforced the idea that any guy found sleeping under his car was most likely drunk.

By the time they closed the door to his holding cell, they knew the car was stolen and had traveled across the border. Now they wanted answers from the man with no identification.

This time the men who did the interrogation had no names, or at least none that Otakar would ever know. Since the crime involved crossing borders, these two were from the General Directorate for illegal immigration and organized crime. They didn't bother asking questions for the first twenty minutes; they just spent the time "softening him up." They figured if he were somebody, he would drop a name; and if he didn't, then nobody would miss a man with no ID sleeping under a stolen car.

Otakar didn't drop a name and stuck to his story, which was mostly true, excluding mention of being a vampire. He was Czech, he was just trying to get to Prague, and this was all a big mistake, which they did not believe, or chose not to. Weakened by the daylight, the punching and kicking started to take their toll. He wondered if he would make it until evening, and these men clearly didn't care.

"Who are you? Why did you steal the car? Where were you going? Why are you lying?" was followed by blows to the face and body, and then by kicks to the belly and back as Otakar fell to the ground.

This went on for four hours, the men taking turns like tag-team wrestling partners, until they got hungry and left for lunch.

Otakar lay on the ground, unable even to sit up and get back on the wooden bench in his cell. He knew he couldn't take much more. This was the closest to the true death he had been in over six hundred years as a vampire. He drifted in and out of consciousness, not sure if it was sleep or if he was passing out from his injuries.

After about two and a half hours, his eager tormentors returned, refreshed from their long lunch and ready for another round. Otakar was not, but it began anyway. It was still only about 2:30 in the afternoon, hours until sunset when he would get his strength back.

Two hours later and the blows had not subsided. Otakar could not believe he was still alive, and was unconscious most of the time. A ray of sunlight shown through the window, illuminating him and his interrogators, and making him that much weaker as one man replaced the other, refreshed and ready to punch that much harder.

The last thing Otakar saw through bloody eyes and the horrible glare was the grinning face of a man who did not care.

Sensing how tentative his three adversaries were, Trevor pressed his attack. He took swipes first at Steve and then Hubrech, but avoided Valentin, who at least looked like he knew what he was doing. Both dodged the sharp hunting knives successfully, but failed to counter with their own short swords. The fight continued for a few minutes, Valentin watching, waiting for Trevor to be weakened, until Steve tried to counter but missed. Taking advantage of Steve's lunge, Trevor cut deeply into his belly, but was stabbed in the left bicep by Hubrech. Blood stained Steve's shirt in a growing circle, and he was clearly weakened, but Trevor seemed energized by his wound. He stabbed at Valentin, missing badly.

The intensity of the battle increased, with Trevor continuing to swipe randomly at the other three, only just missing, but not getting cut again himself. All four were breathing hard as the exertion and stress set in. Then Hubrech stabbed Trevor again, this time in the torso. Incensed, Trevor went on the offensive against the big Dutchman. Hubrech was strong, but nowhere near as fast as the Brit. Trevor got in close to Hubrech, moving around him so his body shielded Trevor from Valentin and Steve. Then Trevor caught Hubrech in the belly with one of his blades, cutting deeply. Intestines glistened like giant worms through the slice in his shirt and flesh. Hubrech stumbled, groaned wordlessly, and fell to the ground in a pool of blood.

"It's dyin' time na," Trevor said again.

Despite his own wound, Steve immediately went on the offensive in retaliation. Trevor managed to cut him across the chest, but not as deep this time. Valentin closed on Trevor, intent on finishing him off, but Trevor's intensity kept the Austrian at bay, sparks flying as sword met hunting knife repeatedly with the clang of steel on steel. Then Steve was able to flank Trevor and cut his midsection, from breastbone to side deeply. Trevor stumbled, and Valentin took advantage, implanting his sword in Trevor's chest above his heart. As Valentin pulled his sword out, Trevor fell back, but got one last stab at Steve, cutting deeper this time into his gut. A long second later, both Trevor and Steve hit the ground.

Stunned, Valentin looked at the bodies on the ground, pools of blood spreading beneath them. He was unscathed, not a single cut, but three vampires were dead at his feet. Sarah was sitting on the ground sobbing uncontrollably as Karolina walked up, her Mercedes idling at the end of the alley.

"We need to get Steve and Hubrech back to the nest," she ordered. Valentin and Sarah complied in a state of shock, helping her drag the bodies, slippery with blood, to her waiting car. They at least had a few minutes to get away as the police were occupied at the scene of Trevor's earlier murder of the evening just a few blocks away. There was no room for Trevor's body in Karolina's car, so Valentin cut his head off before they left, guaranteeing what they already knew was true death.

As Karolina raced back to the tower nest, her phone rang, and she had to shush the inconsolable Sarah just to hear Lord Makru.

"I traced Otakar to Bucharest, but then I couldn't sense him anymore," Makru told her.

"What do you mean you couldn't sense him?" Karolina demanded.

"He was just gone. He may be dead, I don't know. I'll try again, but right now I'm getting nothing."

THE DEAD AND DYING

The tower nest was pandemonium. Nobody knew what was going on, except that several vampires were dead. Karolina was upstairs with Valentin, so there was nobody in charge, elder or otherwise, to tell everyone what had happened.

"Valentin, Steve, and Hubrech are dead," one vampire said. "And Trevor got away. He was helped by that Brit, Sarah."

"Karolina is dead too, I heard," another said as the information vacuum was filled with the hot air that physics theory tells us it will be.

After about two hours, Viona came downstairs. She had obviously been crying. Everyone crowded around to hear the news and secretly test his or her own theories.

"They killed Trevor," she began. "Valentin cut his head off, he met the true death." Cheers went up, but then she added, "Hubrech is dead, and Steve ... Steve is almost dead too. He has a faint heartbeat, but they don't think he will make it." She wiped a few tears from her cheek. After a long pause, she continued, "And they think Otakar is dead, somewhere in Romania."

That last one nobody saw coming, and it was a total shock. He was an elder, a true warrior, superior to everyone in the room. Everyone there suddenly felt vulnerable as the news sank in.

"What about Karolina?" one called out.

"She's upstairs with Valentin and Sarah. They're trying to save Steve."

"I thought Sarah helped Trevor!" someone shouted.

"It's complicated," was Viona's answer.

A moment later, Valentin raced down the stairs. He pushed through the crowd and disappeared through the door to the garage. Twenty-seconds later they heard the crackling exhaust note of his

Porsche GT3 RS as he pulled out of the garage.

"Where's Valentin going?" several voices called.

"I don't know," Viona said.

Every time Valentin fed on Isabella, he had to rebuild his relationship with her. She now had money invested with SHS and remembered that she knew him, just never the sex or the feeding. She knew perfectly well he was a vampire, and yet still doubted sometimes that vampires were real, since she could not remember.

Valentin needed a mortal he could completely trust. He needed to do something he had never done in over two hundred and fifty years: bring a mortal into one of the nests.

He texted Isabella at her hotel, the Intercontinental Amstel, knowing she was in town for a three-day fashion shoot. He had fed on her five weeks prior, and liked to wait eight weeks to let her blood replenish before he fed again. This was an emergency though.

He pulled up to the hotel valet, gave him three one hundred euro notes, and said, "Leave it out here. I won't be long."

"Yes, sir," the valet replied. The truth was, they left cars like this out front anyway to enhance the reputation of the hotel, and on recommendation of the insurance company not to drive them very far.

Upstairs in Isabella's room, Valentin gave her a big hug. She was still more beautiful than his memories or fantasies, he thought.

"You sounded desperate in your text. Do you need to feed on me?" she asked still not 100 percent sure he was really a vampire.

"No, I need a big favor. It's not for me. Do you remember Steve, the American?" he asked.

"Sure. Are you pimping me out? I like you, but I do have standards."

"It's not like that. You're awesome. I know you can't remember, but sex with you is just beautiful. You fuck like a princess," he said.

"Wow, the last time a guy talked like that, he wanted anal," she said, laughing.

Valentin was smooth when it came to feeding, but this was different, a life and death situation for his friend Steve, and he was nervous, babbling nonsense like she was eighteen and just out of high school, not an international supermodel hit on a thousand times a day.

"I need you to come to one of our nests," he said. "Steve got hurt, stabbed in the stomach, and he lost substantial blood. He needs some blood now or he will die."

"One of the nests? Is that even allowed?" she asked anxiously, just those words—vampire nest—creeped her out. The idea of the Euro playboy Valentin biting her, if he really was a vampire, was an adventure, but the nest she pictured was full of hungry bloodsuckers ready to pounce on her.

"It's not normally allowed, but I can do it. I'm one of the most powerful vampires in Europe, even though I'm not an elder."

"What's an elder? They sound really old?"

"They are, but remember, we're vampires. Karolina is one of the elders. She built up the foundation of the nests in Amsterdam before I got here."

"Wow. Karolina? I never would have guessed, but that makes sense since she's hosting the parties at her mansion."

"The mansion is also one of our nests. We call it the museum nest."

"Is that where you want to take me?" she asked.

"No, I need to take you to the tower nest."

She looked seriously at him, still not sure what to believe. "Will Karolina be happy that you're bringing me to your nest?" she asked.

"No, nobody will be," he said.

He could tell she was teetering on the edge of saying no. *Why would anyone say yes to a request like that anyway?* he thought. "I know it doesn't seem like it, but I'm a serious guy. I appear to be a superficial playboy sometimes, but I'm responsible for all the vampire finances on the continent. Sometimes I feel like I'm the glue that's held the vampires together for the last two centuries, and kept us from being the horrific monsters people imagine we are."

"You are a playboy," she said. "That's one of your charms. I don't know if I like you being serious, but you have made money for me."

"I just need this one favor. I don't even need to feed on you again."

"Are you breaking up with me too?" she teased.

"No, I just meant … Look, Isabella, you're in control. I just want you to feel comfortable."

"Well, I don't think I'd feel comfortable with your cock in my ass."

"Does that mean you'll come to the nest?" he asked.

"Sure, and if you're nice to me, I may have another hole you can use."

"Sarah, I need you to leave the room for a few minutes," Karolina said.

"Why?" I want to be here with Steve," Sarah said, sniffling.

"Just five minutes. It's Steve's only chance. You have to trust me."

"Do you want me to leave too?" Viona asked.

"No, you can stay," Karolina said.

"I'll be right outside," Sarah said. "Please come get me if anything happens."

After Sarah was out of the room, Karolina turned to Viona. "You can never tell anybody what I'm about to do, but it's Steve's only chance. I don't even know if it will work, but I'm a super vampire. I can feed on other vampires. I even fed on Steve after he was turned. My blood is different, it may save him."

"You fed on Steve, Karolina!"

"You can't tell anyone, especially not Sarah," Karolina warned.

"I've heard about super vampires, but I thought it was just some old vampire legend," Viona said.

"There used to be more. Lord Makru and his wife were both super vampires."

"Lord Makru had a wife?" Viona asked, shocked.

"Yes. She was the one who turned him in old Babylon. Some say she was the original source of the virus. She was the one who gave me this tattoo." Karolina pulled up her pant leg to expose the black and red fanged Egyptian ankh on her ankle. "The same one I gave you."

"So you're saying Lord Makru could feed on me, "Viona said giggling. "That's so sexy, what happened to his wife?"

Karolina looked away. "She died at the palace."

"Oh, I'm sorry," Viona said, embarrassed.

Karolina's fangs came out, but not in anger. She pierced the skin of her left wrist to extract some of her own blood, then held it over Steve's mouth, allowing a few drops to fall in. Steve had not regained consciousness since he had been brought back to the nest. They had stitched his wounds, and they had started the rapid healing indicative of vampire biology. But the healing had been arrested in the first hour as his breath became shallow, his heartbeat almost imperceptible.

"I saw Lord Makru's wife do this once," Karolina said. "My blood may have some properties that can bring him back from the true death, but he needs the nutrients from the blood of a mortal if he is going to live much longer. Unfortunately, he still can't feed." She stepped back from the bed. "Let Sarah back in."

Sarah returned to her post, sitting on the edge of the bed and holding his hand, crying softly. She felt guilty, guilty for being such a bitch and returning to London after Steve went to the Mother of Cities, and guilty about trying to help her friend Trevor. She hadn't wanted anyone to get hurt, but everybody had anyway, and it felt like it was her fault.

Then a miracle—Steve squeezed her hand, and her tears came like a waterfall. It wasn't much, but it was more than they'd had so far, and she wondered what Karolina had done.

The loud exhaust of Valentin's Porsche crackled again as he pulled into the tower garage forty-seven minutes after he had left. A minute later, the front door to the nest opened and Valentin walked in with a mortal, the super model Isabella. People gasped and immediately started looking for Karolina. She would not be happy.

Valentin led Isabella directly upstairs to Steve's chamber and burst in. Karolina stared at mortal in disbelief.

"He's too weak to feed," Karolina said. "What are you thinking?"

"Maybe I should go," Isabella said, eyes wide as she backed toward the door.

"No stay, I have an idea," Valentin said. "What if we use a needle and tube, like a reverse IV, from her arm to his mouth, and drip the blood in?" Nobody said a word for several seconds. To break the uncomfortable silence, Valentin asked, "Does anybody have a better idea?"

"She will remember everything," Karolina said.

"She already knows we exist. It's our only chance." His phone vibrated, and he looked at a text on his phone. "I have to meet Jacob downstairs."

"Great," Karolina said. "Why not bring two mortals into the nest? We could have an open house."

"He's not coming up. He has the IV, or he better," Valentin said.

Jacob's big Audi was idling in the alley outside the garage.

"What's this place, Valentin?" he asked as he handed over the IV kit.

"Don't ask questions I can't answer," Valentin said, lightly tapping the roof of Jacob's car.

Back upstairs, they started the process on a now-terrified Isabella. Her eyes kept darting around the room hyper aware of the reality as four real-life vampires were starring at her like she was dinner. Valentin rubbed her back after inserting the needle into her arm. That helped a little, but not much. As he had planned, the blood flowed from her arm to drip slowly into Steve's mouth.

"He squeezed my hand again," Sarah said.

"Let me know if you feel dizzy, Isabella," Valentin said. "I have no way of judging how much blood we're taking."

"I …I don't feel so good," she said after about ten minutes, her eyes fluttering as she sank to the ground. Valentin pulled the needle out of her arm and slapped her face, but she was barely responsive.

"Well, that's all she can give. I hope it's enough," Valentin said. "I'll take her back to my chambers and put her in my bed for now."

"Of course you will," Karolina said sarcastically. "And we will talk about this later."

"Give her a cookie to raise her blood sugar," Steve croaked.

Everybody stared at him in shock, but he immediately fell back into his coma. Valentin, Karolina, and Viona turned their attention back to the woozy supermodel, while Sarah bent over Steve.

"Steve, Steve can you hear me? It's Sarah. I'm so sorry … for everything."

Steve did not respond.

"Where do I get a cookie?" Valentin asked.

"At a store, silly," Viona said.

By the time Valentin got back from the small all-night grocery around the corner, which was heavily stocked with cookies and candies to supply the strong demand of stoned tourists with the munchies, it was almost dawn. He fed Isabella three cookies, and she smiled, but fell back asleep. He carried her to his room and climbed into bed with her, and was soon asleep himself.

Sarah was in bed with Steve now. She had thought about this moment a thousand times since she had run away to London, but certainly not under these circumstances. The whole nest fell asleep, knowing they would have to wait until evening to know if Steve had avoided the true death. It had been seventeen years since anyone had survived their first year after being turned in Amsterdam, and the person before that was Hubrech.

An hour later, Isabella sat on the edge of Valentin's bed, talking on her phone. She was so weak from blood loss she still couldn't stand. "No, I can't do the shoot today. I'm really sick, I think it's food poisoning." Her manager was insistent, but then she got an idea. "I look like shit and I'm bloated."

With that, she climbed back into bed with Valentin, the memories of the previous night swirling through her head like a hazy dream—or a dark nightmare. She wasn't sure which.

THE AFTERMATH

The next evening Steve woke in bed with Sarah. He was still weak and unable to get up. His head was foggy, the details of the last few days, the last few months, a blur. He was glad to be with Sarah, but he had that same feeling of dread, a gnawing discomfort in his gut, that he'd had when he knew he was really going to get divorced. *I'm a vampire,* he remembered, *turned last summer, and I have killed. I killed an innocent mortal and I killed a guilty vampire,* or at least tried. Sarah is not my wife, not my girlfriend. We don't have what each other needs. That was all mostly bad news, but then he started to remember the alley, Trevor, Sarah. Then he didn't want his head to clear. He wanted to forget, but he knew that would never happen.

Steve needed answers. "Sarah, we need to talk."

She sat up and looked down at him. "Steve, you're awake. I thought we were going to lose you."

"Trevor ... I mean, what the fuck?" Steve said.

"Can we talk about that later?"

"No, I think now is the time." His strength was returning, as the preternatural healing common to vampires started to take effect and he sat up. Maybe he couldn't stand yet, but he didn't need to for this. "You were helping Trevor. Why?"

"Look, Steve, I'm English. I think that's pretty obvious. I was turned here in Amsterdam, but I'm a Londoner at heart. It took me a long time to go back, really, until all of my family was dead. Now I have permanent chambers in the Chelsea nest, which is near where I grew up. Sometimes I think about moving back for good, but the London vampires have problems, a lot of them. Many are their own fault and most are about money, but Trevor and others were promised a life that they just didn't get, the life that most us take for granted here on the continent.

"Unlike here, more than sixty people have been turned over the past twenty-five years in London. They started losing patience over the last ten years or so, and took things into their own hands. They started stealing, and it escalated from there. The police became aware that vampires existed after a number of incidents, and Trevor and his friends ended up killing in self-defense during the commission of their robbing and stealing. Then Trevor started killing women he fed on, just to prove he could do it. Some people like Trevor think we're superior to mortals, above them on the food chain.

"I know what he did was wrong, but I was just trying to help, help the London vampires. Show some compassion and understanding. Hundreds in the London nests now want to vote out the covenant. That's the last thing they need. I've heard the stories from Karolina and the other elders. The covenant keeps us from being primitive beasts, and keeps us from being hunted and killed like primitive beasts."

"They're going to vote on the covenant?" Steve asked. "Does Karolina know?"

Sarah frowned at him. "Is that all you heard me say?"

"No, of course not. You care deeply about the causes of the unrest—but maybe not enough about the unrest itself."

"I just don't think killing a bunch of vampires is the answer. Trevor won't be the only one. He probably wasn't even the first," Sarah said.

When Steve made it downstairs to the tower lounge, a steady stream of well-wishers came by to offer congratulations and good luck. After Sarah went out to feed, Steve told Karolina, Valentin, and Viona about the potential vote on the covenant in London.

Karolina was dismissive. "I don't think they will have a vote. And if they do, they will be smart enough to keep the covenant."

Karolina got Radek's text a few hours later.

<It looks like some sort of vampire hunting organization is coming to Amsterdam>

<What do you mean organization? > Karolina replied.

<Like a secret society. They call themselves Lamia Venatores and they seem to claim at least that they date back to Roman times> he texted.

<How many are coming? > Karolina replied.

<Around 40 from 14 different countries. They read about the Trevor murders in the news. They seem to know or suspect it was a vampire>

<Are you sure? >

<They actually have a Facebook page and Gerlach's friend from the police department Gerrit Jensen liked it>

<Go to ground now! >, Karolina texted back to Radek, who was at the museum nest, and then sent the same message, with Radek's information, to Accalu in the canal nest.

Within the hour, every vampire in Amsterdam had the same text—Go to ground!—and within two hours not a single vampire was on the street.

"What happened?" Sarah asked Steve when she got back.

"Vampire hunters," he said, noticing with a tinge of jealousy that she had already fed.

For six days, every vampire except Karolina and Accalu stayed in their respective nest. Steve, while quickly recovering, ran Viceroy scans on the police and hotel check-ins. The elders could not find any obvious vampire hunters on their reconnaissance missions, and the police department believed Trevor's murder was the work of a right-wing vigilante group. Steve was sure Gerlach's friend Gerrit had passed this information on to the other members of Lamia Venatores, but had no proof. Slowly one by one the suspected vampire hunters left the city.

They had very little information on Lamia Venatores, and Accalu believed they were more recently formed.

"I lived in Rome for centuries," Accalu said. "There were plenty of vampire hunters before I left for Bohemia, and their organization was called the Catholic Church, not the Lamia Venatores. I think these guys just used a Latin name to make it seem like they were ancient. My guess is most of these people don't truly believe in vampires."

"I tend to agree with you," Radek said, "but Gerlach the Abridged was definitely a vampire hunter, and the guy from the police Gerrit Jansen knew him and these guys too. So there is some smoke, just not much fire."

Karolina lifted the order. The only other option was to start kidnapping mortals and bring them back to the nest so people could feed, and that would only bring more heat. Almost everybody needed to feed, but she had people stagger their feeding over three nights so as not to flood Amsterdam with hungry vampires.

SURVIVOR

D ark and cool, stone-walled tunnels soothed a vampire suffering from daylight exposure, but the sweet elixir of human blood would do more. The Bucharest nest had been established around 1450, as the population of Europe and of European vampires started to grow. About two hundred and fifty vampires lived in the nest's completely man-made tunnels beneath the capital of Romania.

Lord Dragomir, the lone elder of the nest, brought him his dinner, and her name was Violeta. Of average height, she had wavy brown hair and a tight, curvy body. Violeta was a private convalescent nurse. She never had sex with her patients, she told Dragomir as they walked down twisting tunnels beneath the old quarter of Bucharest. Dragomir had fed on her about a year earlier. She didn't remember, and he didn't need to tell Otakar.

Lord Makru had contacted Dragomir about Otakar after he could no longer perceive the younger elder's energy in Bucharest. Dragomir made some calls and, acting on a tip from a contact in the police department, retrieved from the city's morgue the body of a John Doe who died in custody soon after sunset. There was a faint heartbeat, and he gave Otakar a few drops of a restorative potion he had obtained in Budapest Hungary more than a hundred years earlier. It allegedly contained, among other secret ingredients, the blood of a super vampire.

Violeta got a bit carried away giving the bruised and bloodied, but still attractive, Czech, a sponge bath, and had to remove her wet shirt, glad she wore a sexy black bra. Three nights later, Otakar was ready to travel to his intended destination, Prague. It was then that Dragomir finally remembered to tell him that Lord Makru had called him.

"I'll surprise him," Otakar said. "Just text him a coffin is on its way." Not realizing Makru believed Otakar had met the true death.

Makru was glad to see his old friend, but not surprised. He had literally seen it all in over 3700 years, and truly knew what he had the power to change and what he did not. He sent a text to Karolina, but in the confusion of the Lamia Venatores incident, she accidently deleted it along with the hundreds of others she was getting every day.

Otakar immediately contacted the seller of the Ferrari 458 Speciale Aperta the next evening, a Saturday, and it was still for sale. He talked the guy down to 490,000 euro. The seller wouldn't go any lower, as only 499 of the cars had been built.

After driving around Prague for an hour enjoying his new car, Otakar pulled into the courtyard of the palace. He saw someone in the shadows waiting—Trey.

"Lord Makru said you were getting a new car," Trey said, grinning, and the two drove around the city for another hour. Otakar let Trey drive some of the time. After returning to the nest, Trey scoured the Internet for a used 458 Speciale coupe. He had not owned a car since being turned, and he thought now was the time to spend some of the millions he had earned running StoneHaven Systems.

A CELEBRATION

Steve was alive and well, Trevor was not, and Sarah was back in Amsterdam. Karolina and Viona started planning the next feeding party, a celebration, and considered renting a larger venue, but rejected the idea as being a little too high profile after all that had gone on.

Radek was still in Amsterdam, the elder in charge of the museum nest, and he was nervous about Lamia Venatores and vampire hunters in general. He tried unsuccessfully to talk Karolina out of having the feeding party.

"The vampire hunters came out because of Trevor, not my parties," she said.

On nights that they weren't feeding, Karolina, Valentin, Sarah, Steve, and Evette would walk over to the mansion and hang out there with Viona instead of at the tower lounge. Before dawn, they would walk back to the tower. This had the effect of reminding Radek who was really in charge of Amsterdam. Accalu avoided getting involved in the centuries-old but subtle animosity between the two elders, but reminded Karolina that the party also needed to be about their fallen friends, the elder Otakar and Hubrech.

About a week before the party, Evette was about to feed on a British tourist when he got rough with her after she told him her tale of necessity. He caught her off-guard, striking her face, but she easily blocked his subsequent blows, being more than twice as strong as the man, even though he was almost double her size. She hit him in the head, knocking him out, and then broke his arm, snapping it like a twig, in a fit of rage before feeding on his unconscious body.

She slammed the door to his hotel room when she left, still swearing in French, but by the time she got back to the nest, she was apologetic and feeling guilty.

"I'm sorry, Karolina. I shouldn't have hurt him. I don't want to bring any more trouble," she said.

"Don't worry," Karolina assured her. "He deserved it. You did the right thing."

"I'd like to hear the story he tells his buddies after he got beat up by a girl," Steve joked.

"He will probably try to tell his buddies Evette had a penis," Viona said.

"Hey, no surprises under here," Evette said, cupping her pussy over her jeans.

The next week, Valentin and Steve were walking back to the tower nest a few hours before dawn for a strategy call with Trey and Morty, vampires only. As they walked down the alley to the outer door of the tower, two red Ferraris they had never seen before drove toward them from the opposite direction. The first one, a Spider, pulled to a stop, and a skinny girl got out of the passenger side. She punched in the code and then jumped back in to the convertible, not bothering to reopen the car door.

By the time Steve and Valentin got to the front door, both cars were already inside and the roll-up door was closing. Inside, the first thing they saw was Trey standing next to Anjelica.

"What the fuck?" Valentin said. "You didn't say you were coming here for the meeting. Is that your car?" He pointed to the 458 Speciale Spider.

"No, mine's the coupe," Trey said, grinning.

"Who's is this?" Steve asked.

"Mine," Otakar said, coming into view for the first time from behind one of the shipping containers.

"Otakar! What the fuck? I thought you were dead," Valentin said.

"Me too, me too, and I heard you almost died," Otakar said, fist bumping Steve. "I need to teach you how to fight in case I'm not around next time. Here, let me show you something."

He led Steve and Valentin over to one of the shipping containers. Inside were gun racks containing various makes and models of fully automatic weapons.

"Rule number one," Otakar said. "Use a gunpowder-based weapon as your first choice. If it worked for me back in the fifteenth century, it will definitely work today with guns like these. Sword fighting skills are important too, but guns have been my preferred weapon since I joined the Hussites six hundred years ago."

"Well, we got Trevor," Steve said. "Or I should say, Valentin did, but Hubrech didn't make it."

"Well, you did. I always knew you were a survivor," Otakar said.

Steve gave him a skeptical look, thinking, *it didn't always seem that way.*

"I heard there's going to be a party," Anjelica said as Steve, Valentin, and Otakar walked back from the container.

"This weekend at the mansion," Steve said. "Your timing's perfect."

"Hey, I'm proud of you for traveling," Valentin said, patting Trey on the back.

Trey nodded. "Coming out here by coffin for New Year's was one of the hardest things I've ever done, but hearing Anjelica's tales of traveling with Lord Makru, then getting this car, gave me the idea to try a road trip."

"I'm sorry I didn't make you travel more when you were first turned," Valentin said. "But I wasn't in Prague, and then I needed you to run the business after I got to know you."

As they headed for the inner door to the nest, Valentin considered how curious it was that almost all vampires found it so hard to break the spell of place after they were turned. He had never really felt that.

Late spring, and a perfect day gave way to a perfect evening, cloud and rainless as both vampires and mortals gathered at the mansion for Karolina's celebration party. Anjelica and Trey arrived in his Ferrari, and Trey was reluctant to let the valet park it.

"Can't I park in the back?" he asked as Valentin and Isabella arrived right behind him in Valentin's Porsche GT3 RS.

"You can ask Karolina," Valentin said, "but I'm sure she'll give you the same answer I got fifty years ago," He handed his key to the valet.

"But I'm Trey fucking Coleman, CEO of StoneHaven Systems," Trey said with mock insolence.

Inside, the celebration was low-key, a secret among vampires. Viona had found an H stamp, for Hubrech, and Anjelica insisted on personally stamping it on the backs of vampire's hands only. Karolina didn't like the idea as it identified vampires, but let it go. Steve and Sarah couldn't figure out what their relationship was after the Trevor incident, but they both needed to feed, so that was maybe a good thing.

Karolina held court as usual beneath the giant Rembrandt, glad that Otakar, one of the subjects in the painting, was still with them.

"Did you tell Karolina?" Steve asked Sarah as they greeted Karolina.

"Tell me what?" Karolina asked. "She's already apologized for Trevor, and I understand what she was trying to do."

"No," Sarah said. "I just got a text from a friend in London. The London nests are going ahead with a vote on the covenant."

"You've got to be fucking kidding me," Karolina said. "How could they be so stupid?"

"Are they serious about voting it out," Valentin asked. "Or is this just to assuage the minority?"

"I'm not sure," Sarah said. "There are lot of vampires in London who think they have a right to kill, that they're simply superior creatures to mortals on the food chain."

"That works for a night, a week maybe," Karolina said, "but over time the mortals win out. Their entire history is built around them destroying what they perceive as evil. So our goal is to not be perceived as evil, or, better yet, not to be perceived at all. It needs to seem like vampires don't exist, not like we're hiding around every corner waiting to suck their blood and leave them for dead."

"I don't disagree with you," Sarah said. "I'm voting to keep the covenant, but I don't know how everybody else is voting. Many vampires in London are fed up. They don't have much money, and the elders seem weak. Everybody feels like their backs are against the wall, and many of them think they should fight their way out."

"You have a vote in London?" Karolina asked.

"Yes, because I was born there. And when I'm back, I try to help them."

As she finished speaking, Accalu and Radek walked up and Karolina turned to them. She was truly angry now at what she perceived as a threat to the concept she thought of as her life's work.

"They're going to vote on the covenant in London," she said. "Can you fucking believe it?"

Accalu stared in shock. "You're kidding. I didn't even know that was a possibility."

"I forgot to mention it during all the excitement with the Lamia Venatores because I thought there was no way it would really happen. We should call a meeting with Lord Makru right now."

"This will bring out every vampire hunter in the world," Radek said nervously.

"Don't worry," Valentin said, trying to lighten the mood with a touch of humor. "I'll have Luxembourg go long on London hotel stocks if they vote the covenant out. The vampire hunters need to stay someplace, right?"

"Very funny," Radek said obviously not amused. "This is serious."

Karolina winked at Valentin, showing she at least appreciated his humor. "It is serious, but this is just speculation right now, I seriously doubt they would vote out the covenant."

All the talk of violence and the covenant made Isabella, in Amsterdam for just the night between shoots in Lisbon and Paris, more nervous as she stood quietly beside Valentin. She still wasn't sure if she would let Valentin feed on her tonight or ever.

Their discussion was interrupted by Pieter Henny, six foot one pretty boy spoiled son of Dutch money. He was wearing a charcoal-gray Armani sport coat, a black shirt, and lighter wool slacks, with van Liers on his feet. They were expensive, but more stylish than professional, giving the impression of idle wealth rather than hard-earned money.

"This party is awesome, Karolina. I've never seen so many sweet cars in Amsterdam at the same location."

Anjelica quickly sized him up for feeding. "I can take you for a long ride in my Ferrari if you want," she said. "I might even let you drive."

Trey laughed. "Dream on, girl. That's my car and I like you and all, but you're not driving it."

"Thank you, Pieter," Karolina said. "Viona and I put a lot of effort into the planning." She looked directly into his bright blue eyes, clearly selecting him for dinner. Seeing that, Anjelica frowned. She was not as good as Karolina yet.

With Otakar still alive Radek was whisked off to Amsterdam central before dawn in an unmarked white van carrying his coffin.

Isabella eventually offered to let Valentin feed on her, but he said she needed to replenish her blood first. That made her insecure, wondering if he didn't want her anymore.

"Viona, is it true I need to replenish my blood before Valentin can feed on me?" she asked later.

"Yes, of course, especially after you gave blood to Steve. If he could feed on you any time he wanted, Valentin might marry you." Viona said *or marry Kate she thought.*

Isabella felt better after that, and started to think maybe Valentin wasn't as much of a playboy as he seemed.

Sarah fed on a blond Dutch guy who looked nothing like Steve, and Steve fed on a dark-haired curvy woman who was the polar opposite of the skinny strawberry-blond Sarah. Later they left together in Steve's BMW M3. He had decided already he needed an upgrade to compete with Trey and Valentin, but he needed more money. He had started taking a bigger role at SHS, becoming less acting CIO and more like the permanent one, and he hoped to get a sizable quarterly bonus.

Back at the tower, they shared Sarah's chamber, because the museum-nest vampires had to stay at the tower and red-light nests because of the feeding party. They cuddled, again post feeding, and Steve was aroused as he spooned Sarah. They both enjoyed the feeling of intimacy so much more than empty sex and feeding—and they both thought how much closer they would feel if Steve was inside Sarah. But they feared that intimacy too. How would they stop after that? They just didn't have what each other needed.

STONE-WALLED TUNNELS

For the week after the celebration and feeding party, everyone enjoyed the late-spring weather in Amsterdam. But Trey had a business to run, and Sarah felt compelled to return to London in an attempt to pull the vampires there back from the brink. She was to convey to the London elders a message of support from Karolina, and all the elders on the continent. Trey planned to ship his car and take a coffin via train back to Prague, because it required at least three nights driving and two days wasted sleeping in a couple of nests to get back otherwise.

At the last minute, Steve decided to go with Trey. Since he was getting more serious about being the CIO of StoneHaven Systems—and more serious about making a lot of money—working out of the Prague office would keep him more focused. He knew he would have to text with Sarah every day, which made her a bit high maintenance, but he was starting to realize that maybe they both needed more than just sex and someone to feed on.

Anjelica decided to go home at the same time, and so three coffins were pulled out of shipping containers and transported to Amsterdam Centraal one morning before dawn.

⚬⚬

A warm May in the Mother of Cities gave way to a warmer June. The tourists returned, while Trey and Steve fell into a routine of work and feeding. Steve was in charge of Anjelica's intern, Jaromir from Charles University. He put him to work doing IT tasks, mostly remotely for the New Jersey and New York offices.

A couple of weeks later, he called Jim Knowles to see if he had any finance-type work he needed done, since that was Jaromir's major.

"I think I can find him something to do," Jim said. "By the way, I was talking to one of my old buddies back at Sterling Klein Financial out in San Fran, and they told me you just disappeared last summer."

This was the moment Steve had been dreading.

"That's just a cover story," he said. "Trey and I go way back, we went to high school together, and he asked me to interview. We met in Amsterdam along with Valentin and they offered me a job on the spot. It was a lot more money, and I hadn't felt tied to the Bay Area, or even the States for that matter, since my divorce, so I took it. I gave my notice first thing that Monday morning, and they got really pissed and said that was my last day. After that, they spun stories that I quit with no notice and disappeared," Steve lied. Not many people at SKF know the real story."

"Wow, it seemed kind of suspicious, but this guy insisted that you were missing and the police couldn't find you," Jim said. "He said there was no way you were the real Steve Breckenridge. He seemed pretty convinced."

"Yea, like I said, there was a lot of spin. I think they looked bad to the customer, but they never should have let me go that day. I could have worked for another month and a half if they wanted, since I wasn't starting at SHS for a while. When they offered me the job, Trey and Valentin didn't know for sure if the old CIO was leaving or not, or what my actual job would be. The fact is, I was interim CIO until a week ago."

Jim seemed satisfied enough with the answer, and Steve sort of enjoyed the idea that word would get out that he was still alive and living in an exotic place like Prague.

He was careful to coach Jaromir not to talk about vampires, and to keep his ears open for any suspicions from the other mortals, especially about himself with all the disappearing rumors floating around now. He was also relieved to hear that, unlike their banker's son in Luxembourg, Jaromir had realistic expectations about Anjelica.

"I mean, upir or not," Jaromir said, "you're just not going to have an exclusive relationship with a girl like Anjelica. But then you have to ask yourself, do I want to fuck her. And the answer is hell yes, so you put up with it and set your expectations correctly."

Most mornings before dawn, Steve would wander the stone-walled tunnels that made up the primal nest. Inspecting the ancient carvings, he was always amazed that the tunnels had escaped becoming part of known history, and he often wished there was a Wikipedia page he could reference to answer his many questions. Perhaps Lord Makru knew their real story. The black oily look of the stone was soothing in a way he had not imagined possible less than a year ago, when bright sunny days, green trees, and colorful flowers provided a similar reassuring feeling. He was almost dead now, and had almost met the true death just a month prior. In the primal nest, though, just before he fell asleep, Steve felt safer than he ever had when he was a mortal.

☥

Lord Makru was not without emotion, but he liked to think of himself as a clear thinker. Filling in the facts you didn't know to infer something you were only guessing at was fine for creating hypotheses and scenarios you might need to deal with later, but that wasn't necessarily reality, and it could easily lead you down a rat hole. Makru, of course, had gifts that allowed him to fill in those missing facts more easily than most, and that was what he was preparing to do again that night: learn the realities of Lamia Venatores.

He sat in the small anteroom of his large chambers, allowing his essence to enter the energy field, the unseen ocean that encompassed the entire continent and the whole world. A search like this, not for a specific person's energy force but for a thought, an idea, was extremely difficult and time consuming. Every night that Makru did not feed he spent searching for that one thought, *Lamia Venatores*, and tried to associate it with a single person's life energy. An hour before dawn, he would emerge and Radek would ask the inevitable question: "Anything?" For six weeks, the answer was no.

Finally, he perceived that thought he had been searching for, and the thoughts that came after.

The master has fooled them, he is still in Amsterdam, and he will get his revenge.

This was a message someone was reading from another member of Lamia Venatores. Was the master one of their group or a reference to a vampire? Makru couldn't tell. He discerned that Lamia Venatores was working on mapping vampires, their names and locations. Everybody had a responsibility, but this individual seemed more intrigued not by the actuality of vampire hunting, but the idea of. Makru got the feeling the other members of Lamia Venatores were mostly like this one. It was a dark hobby that they would keep secret just so they could have a dark secret, harmless. The "master," though, concerned Makru. The sense he got was that this one had had some sort of success; and if he was a vampire hunter, that was a problem.

All of this Makru reported to Radek, Václav, Trey, and Steve in the lounge later that night. Over the next few days, with help from Steve and Anjelica, Radek made thousands of database queries and Internet searches in hundreds of languages for *the master* and all possible variants. Nothing specific was found, especially not in relation to Amsterdam, but that was expected from such a generic term. After all of Radek's databases had been scoured, the Prague elders held a conference call with the elders of Amsterdam. Karolina agreed there was some concern and wanted to be informed if any of the suspected members of Lamia Venatores returned to Amsterdam. She also asked them to double-check if any of them had stayed in Amsterdam, or if the police officer Gerrit Jansen had left and come back. On closer examination, nothing looked suspicious, and nothing correlated to or seemed to relate to anything or anyone called *the master*.

Makru continued to search the energy field, checking in on the one called Luca who lived in Switzerland and who had thought of Lamia Venatores and the master. All he got, though, were banal Facebook updates, porn, and more Facebook updates.

In early July, Karolina and Viona planned a series of feeding parties, alternating between the Amsterdam mansion and the Prague palace. She invited anyone who had ever been to one of her Amsterdam parties to the first of two planned at the palace, promising grander celebrations than were possible at the mansion, knowing she could deliver.

Steve was hoping to return to Amsterdam soon, and Trey planned to ship his Ferrari back and forth across Europe, depending on where the next feeding party was. Anjelica too planned to travel to Amsterdam for the mid-July party. The second palace party would correlate with the annual council of elders beneath the Mother of Cities in September. Karolina and Viona were in turn invited by various wealthy mortals to enjoy the sun for a week here and there, relaxing at private villas on the Mediterranean coast, but politely declined, citing schedule conflicts.

Karolina figured that if this Lamia Venatores group had any real intelligence about the vampires, they would find out soon enough by throwing big parties. Valentin, though, was a little nervous about the new high-profile jet-set Karolina.

HIGH SUMMER

July 17, high summer, the tourists swarmed at peak capacity, like an enormous herd of blood cattle just there for the taking by any hungry vampire in Amsterdam. Wealthy natives threw extravagant parties before and after they jetted between the city and Mediterranean escapes to the sun. A select few anticipated an invitation from the exotic Czech woman, Karolina, to parties so wild they could barely remember them, and now what promised to be the event of the summer at her palace in old Prague. If there was one thing the vampires could rely on, it was the cycles of nature; day and night, summer and winter, the earth is spinning on its axis as it orbits the sun, it has for all known history.

Pieter Henny was having a typical day, which consisted of an argument with his father and overhearing an argument between his parents about him. He backed his classic Riviera-blue 1991 Porsche 911 out of the garage, looking wistfully at his broken-down Spyker C8, whose manufacturer was now in bankruptcy. He was taking his car to get detailed in anticipation of a party later that week to be held at the mansion just down the street from his parents' home. There would be plenty of cars nicer than his at the party, but an air-cooled Porsche always got a certain amount of respect.

Pieter was wasting his summer, according to his father, not taking an internship to gain valuable business experience. But he was socializing with a whole new crowd, along with his buddy Jasper. Now that word was out that the exotic Karolina also had a palace in Prague, it only strengthened his resolve that he was on the right path to building life-long relationships with international money. Pieter came from money, as did his father and his father before him. Jasper did not, but he was going to make it himself, and everyone knew it. Unlike Pieter, he was interning that summer in Amsterdam, as well as socializing on a grand scale at night. He and Pieter suspected that the key to their new friends' wealth was the guy called Valentin who was dating that American supermodel Isabella. They had barely spoken with him from what they could remember, but would try to make up for that at the next party.

Pieter would never admit to his parents that what he really wanted to do was buy a coffee shop. They didn't even know he smoked marijuana. Most Dutch, even those born in Amsterdam, didn't, but Pieter and Jasper just saw it as a way to unwind and socialize. On the night of July 17, they were hanging out at the coffee shop Bluebird, east of the red-light district, and ran into Viona, Karolina's Dutch friend, along with an American guy, Steve.

"No, we're not a couple," Viona said, laughing along with Steve. Pieter thought Viona was a classic Dutch hottie, blonde and clearly from money, like him.

"What do you do?" Pieter asked Steve with a hint of Euro arrogance.

"I just got promoted to chief information officer of StoneHaven Systems, the high-frequency trading house Trey and Valentin founded. I live in Amsterdam, but travel back and forth between here and Prague."

Pieter and Jasper thought they had hit the jackpot. This guy worked for the enigmatic Valentin.

"So how do you know Valentin?" Jasper asked.

"It's a long story," Steve said. "But Trey and I went to high school together in Marin County back in California."

"I've heard of Marin, north of San Francisco, right? It's a nice place, right," Pieter said. "Why would you live here?"

"I really prefer it here in Europe, the older cities. It just suits me better now." Steve took another hit off the joint shared by all but Viona, scanning the room as if he were looking for someone more interesting.

"Excuse me," he said abruptly. "I need to talk to this woman." He got up from the table never to return.

"So, what do you do Viona?" Jasper asked.

"Oh not much. Mostly chill out and party," she said.

"I mean, for money," he said.

"Oh, I spend it," she said as if it was the most obvious thing in the world. She was Pieter's type of girl, the type he had grown up with, gone to school with, dated since he was fourteen.

"I'm surprised we never met," Pieter said.

"I went to boarding school in Switzerland and traveled a lot," she said, giving her standard answer to someone who would have been her peer over three hundred years ago. She knew Pieter didn't remember sleeping with Karolina, but thought it better to target the rougher blond haired Jasper for feeding anyway.

"Where did you meet Karolina?" Pieter asked.

"Here in Amsterdam, a long time ago at an art opening. At first we weren't friends, but lately I feel like she's my best friend." As she spoke, she realized how close they had become in the last year, especially since Gerlach the Abridged.

"I have a cousin named Viona," Pieter said. "You remind me of her a little, I should invite her to the party,"

"That's naughty," she flirted. Maybe Pieter was the better option. There was something hot about the acting out a latent fantasy with a guy. Most women would be repulsed or just pissed off at a guy who was thinking about another girl while they were with them, but those were mortal girls. After feeding, Viona would be done with one of these two anyway.

Later that night, after feeding on Jasper, Viona walked back to the mansion to do more party planning with Karolina. As she passed through Dam Square, four drunk British guys started to hassle her, grabbing her ass and reaching for her breasts. She employed an open palm to the solar plexus of each one in quick succession, sending them sprawling to the ground, gasping for breath. She hated violence, but these guys were stupid to mess with a vampire who had just fed, or otherwise. She felt strong and alive, giving them all a look that clearly said, Stand up if you want more. They all opted to stay down.

In the drawing room of the mansion, Karolina, Viona, and Sarah—who was just back from London—planned not only the next party, but all four for the rest of the summer. The catering, valets, and post-party cleanup would all be done by mortals.

"I have this friend in London, Cooper Morris," Sarah said. "He's a DJ, house music mostly, that goes by the name of CGI Donkey. He's getting really popular now. He gets like 25k a gig, I heard, and has been flying down to Ibiza to work, as well as in London."

"Can you get him for less?" Karolina asked. "That's a lot of money."

"I may be able to get him for less, and I can work him for a no vote on the covenant while he's here."

"He's a vampire?" Viona asked.

"Yeah. He was turned about five years ago, but he's trying to make money without taking it, and he's popular in the nest. So I hope he can be a good influence on the chavs"

"What's a chav?" Viona asked.

"It's what the media call trashy young people in England, chavs and chavettes. They say it's an acronym for Council Housed and Violent, like Trevor was, but I heard the term is really a lot older than that. It's kind of derogatory and I've been trying not to use it as much. One of the biggest problems in the London nests is they aren't inclusive enough."

"Well, if we can get him, that would be great," Karolina said.

"Hey, Karolina," Viona said. "I saw Pieter Henny and his friend Jasper at the Bluebird with Steve earlier. I almost fed on him, but chose Jasper instead," Viona said.

"It's been almost two months," Karolina said. "He should have enough blood by now."

"Well, maybe at the next party," Viona said, taking that as permission.

"Jasper. Is he a blond Dutch guy?" Sarah asked. "I think I fed on him at the last party."

Viona laughed. "He's the real player. Too bad he doesn't know it because he can't remember. There's something about that Pieter, though," she added. "I think he reminds me of me somehow."

The next week, everybody started to arrive in Amsterdam for the party. Trey came by coffin, his Ferrari by truck. Lord Makru traveled by coffin with Anjelica, but without his car. A night later, a surprise visitor from New York, Morty Saperstein, arrived.

"I decided to spend the summer in Europe," he explained as he relaxed in the tower lounge.

"And talk business I'm sure," Valentin said as he walked up. "This is Steve, our CIO. Steve this is Morty one of the elders from the Manhattan nest."

"Nice to meet you, Steve," Morty said, shaking his hand. In his faded Rag and Bone skinny jeans and an untucked polo shirt from Choate Rosemary Hall, its shield emblem of a boar and three daggers over his heart, he looked like the quintessential WASP. Of course, he hadn't attended the prestigious prep school, having been born thirty years before it was founded in 1896.

A warm July day gave way to a warm summer evening as vampires and mortals started to arrive at the mansion. Valets whisked high-end luxury cars away as everybody paraded in and out of the mansion, eager to see and be seen. Karolina as always, held court in the second floor living room framed by the epic Rembrandt.

"No, Rembrandt was like Madonna," she told one of the female guests. "That's his first name. his full name was Rembrandt van Rijn."

Later Viona corrected her pronunciation—"It sounds more like rein." Viona, born a hundred years after Rembrandt died, had studied the artist in school; as had Vincent van Gogh, who was born a hundred years after her. But it was Karolina who befriended and supported both of them when the artists were alive.

Valentin minus Isabella, who was on a shoot back in New York— Trey, Morty, and Steve headed up to the roof after an hour to talk business.

"I spent two hours on the phone with Dmitri earlier," Valentin said. "He thinks this new algorithm he developed from the one Lord Makru gave him can make us a lot of money, but only for a week or two max."

"What was wrong with Makru's original algorithm?" Trey asked.

"He kept calling it the doomsday algo. He said if we used it, we would have all the money in the world in a few weeks, but then governments would just declare it worthless and arrest us as financial terrorists."

"That guy is one paranoid motherfucker," Trey exclaimed.

"Well, he's one smart motherfucker too, smarter than any of us, even Steve," Valentin said.

"Way smarter than me for sure," Steve said. "I don't know what the fuck he's talking about half the time."

Valentin turned to Morty. "About your offer for the penthouse. I know it's not what you wanted to do, not how you pictured it, and I personally have fond memories of the penthouse, but we could really use that capital now."

"Technically, you still own it," Morty said. "We're just trying to buy it from you."

"I want you to be 100 percent behind this, but we could make substantial money, once-in-a-century money. This is the telephone in the nineteenth century, Internet infrastructure at the end of the twentieth century."

"I don't know, about all in," Trey said. "You're the one that developed the cash reserve system that has saved our asses more than once so far."

"I believe in Dmitri," Valentin said. "And I believe in Lord Makru's powers. This could be real money."

"This just seems really risky, even for me," Trey said. "I've been poor, and now I'm rich. I prefer rich any day."

"Dmitri says the algorithm will only work for ten to fourteen days, maybe less, before the market starts to react. Then it will be worthless. The question is, do you want to multiply a dollar ten times a day, or do you want to multiply hundreds of millions of dollars ten times a day. I'm even going to pull almost all the money from the treasury in Luxembourg, $655 million from the general fund, and all my own cash--$66 million. With the $63 million we would get from the penthouse, if this algorithm works for just three days, that's over $60 billion."

"And if it doesn't?" Trey asked.

"Then we're more fucked than London," Valentin said.

"Do Karolina and Ambre know about the treasury?" Steve asked.

"No, not yet. But I'm the lord of the treasury. I was the one that put those hundreds of millions of euros in there. My one regret is that I kept some in cash when I invested in early telephone companies in the 1890s, Ford, Daimler, and Boeing in the early twentieth century, Cisco systems and Juniper networks in the late twentieth century ... The list goes on. If I had gone all in any of those times, we would have billions, not hundreds of millions, today."

"I know it sounds tempting, but I like what I have now," Trey said.

"You're set in your ways already, Trey," Valentin said. "And anyway, you get the biggest share of anyone right now, so you can't really compare yourself to the continental vampires as a whole. How many vampires do you see with a car as sweet as yours who can ship it back and forth across Europe between parties? I'll tell you who. A handful of elders and me, that's it. We can barely afford Karolina's palace in Prague. Do you want to tell her we have to sell it or rent it out, like I do with Palais von Hahn? Between the spring of 2000 and when you started StoneHaven Systems, our net worth was shrinking every year. Today the annual operating costs of all the continental nests combined are over $50 million with mortals doing maintenance and cleaning, and mortals taking bribes and taxes to not ask questions. I just don't want to feel vulnerable like that again."

Trey shook his head. "I don't know, Valentin. I just don't know."

"Look, it's a big decision." Valentin looked at the other three. "I'm not saying I've made up my mind yet either, but I'm leaning towards all in."

Downstairs, Pieter Henny, sloppy drunk, high, and accompanied by his cousin Viona, was working the vampire Viona, or thought he was. Viona had already decided she was going to feed on the pretty rich boy. If Valentin could have his supermodel girlfriend and feed on her every few months, she could do the same with Pieter. She had fed on a male model who had come to the New Year's party with Isabella, but couldn't remember either his name or the sex. Pieter was more like her—Dutch, spoiled, cocky yet hapless, and backed up by his father's money so he could never fall too far. Some people made the money, others enjoyed it; Viona had always been the latter.

All the vampires were making inside jokes about the mortal Viona, and several men made a play for her, but she was standoffish and somewhat bitchy in a dismissive way. When Valentin came back down from the roof and saw her, he figured this Dutch blonde who resembled his friend Viona would make a good dinner. She looked bored in that affected way the spoiled rich did at a nightclub or big party.

"You look bored," he said to her after he was introduced. "What do you do for fun?"

"I don't just look bored, I am bored," she delivered perfectly.

"I wonder if there is anything I can do to remedy that."

"Perhaps," she said, leaving a slight opening.

Her cousin interrupted. "I'm Pieter Henny. You're Valentin, right?"

"Yes. We met at Karolina's last party," Valentin said, affecting the same bored look himself, but with the subtle message that mortal Viona was the potential antidote. Pieter tried unsuccessfully to engage Valentin in any sort of conversation as the self-described Lord of the Treasury concentrated on his cousin's blue eyes.

Breaking from their original plan to stay sober, Pieter and his buddy Jasper had started drinking and smoking heavily an hour earlier, when Valentin, Steve, and the black guy they now knew was Trey Coleman, the CEO of StoneHaven Systems, had disappeared. Vampire Viona got his wandering, muddled attention back and soon had him on a tour of the mansion. Mortal Viona left the party soon after in Valentin's classic silver Porsche cabriolet, the top down. Both Pieter and mortal Viona would have difficulty remembering the party.

An hour before dawn, all having fed, Karolina, Viona, Trey, Sarah, Steve, Otakar, Lord Makru, Accalu, Anjelica, and Morty gathered at the usual spot below the giant Rembrandt. Karolina perceived a strange tension in the air.

"What's wrong?" she asked suspiciously.

"Uh ..." Steve mumbled as he and Morty, now thick as thieves, exchanged a guilty look.

"Valentin wants to try this new algorithm at SHS," Trey said.

"So?" Karolina said.

"He want's to go all in. He thinks it can make a lot of money, but only for a few days," Trey said.

"Why so tense then? Haven't you done that before?" Karolina asked.

"Not exactly," Trey said. "I mean, he wants to go all in with everything, his money the treasury, all of it."

"And he wants to sell the Manhattan penthouse and use that money too," Morty added.

"I see." Karolina glanced around the small gathering and with centuries of experience gauged their mood in a split second. "So, you're all afraid. Valentin's made considerable money for the vampires over the years. I think he knows what he's doing."

"I know," Trey said. "But this time ... I just don't know."

"Can my boyfriend Pieter invest too?" Viona asked, giggling.

"Boyfriend now? What, are you trying to be the female Valentin?" Karolina teased.

"He's a hot guy, and he deserves a break. His father has no respect for him," Viona said.

"Is Valentin going to use the algorithm I gave to Dmitri?" Makru asked.

"No," Trey said. "Dmitri calls yours the doomsday algorithm, so he's modified it. He says if we use yours as devised, we will get all the money in the world and be declared financial terrorists, and he's not even a vampire."

"I never thought of that," Makru said. "I'll try to reveal the future it would bring when I get back to the primal nest."

"It's Valentin's final decision in the end, whatever he decides," Karolina said. "We were almost broke before he was turned. He got us this far, he saved the palace, he even bought me that Porsche."

"Karolina, that DJ was perfect," Trey asked. "Where did you find him?" a not so subtle change in subject from Valentin's plan welcome by most.

"Thanks, he's a friend of mine from London," Sarah said.

"Ha ha, did you feed on him?" Trey asked her.

"No, that's not possible," Sarah said, laughing.

"Why? Is he gay? I can never tell with you Brits," Trey joked.

"Sorry, mate, I'm straight," Cooper Morris, said as he walked up to the group. "But I'm sure you'll find a pretty boy somewhere around here."

"Sorry, I didn't mean to insult," Trey said. "You're a vampire, I see."

"Insult who, all of England?" Cooper said. "Not that there's anything wrong with being gay."

"Sorry, man," Trey apologized again.

"So what did you think, Cooper?" Karolina asked. "Will you work the party in Prague as well?"

"I guess so. As long as there are a few rich kids like there were at this party. I just got booked for three private events."

☥

Over a thousand of the rich and beautiful of Europe flew in to Prague, the Mother of Cities, from the Amalfi coast, Saint-Tropez, Nice, Monaco, and secret locations on the Côte d'Azur, filling up luxury hotels for a weekend in late July. Most had heard about the party from friends who had attended one of Karolina's parties in Amsterdam; others had heard about it third or fourth hand. Karolina didn't care. The palace could hold four thousand in a pinch, but she doubted that many would come to her party.

Valentin had his GT3 shipped by truck and traveled by coffin two weeks before the party, spending the intervening time going out at night with Anjelica and working with Trey in the office.

More vampires then had traveled in centuries also descended on the city, swelling the population of the primal nest in the days leading up to the event. As massive as it was, the nest could still hold hundreds more.

Valentin woke in the walk-in closet of some off-campus apartment, trying to remember how he had gotten there. A young coed from Charles University poked her head in the door, wearing only a pink thong, and he remembered. She was Lenka, the sister of their mortal intern, Jaromir.

"How are you feeling?" she asked. "You slept all day and half the night."

"What time is it?" he asked, still groggy. He rarely slept in. Maybe the stress was getting to him. There had been plenty of it in the last month, as he'd worked hard to convince everyone his plan was solid. Going against his own instincts had been the most difficult. He had spent hours, nights, convincing the elders that it was the right move, realizing in the end he had been convincing himself the whole time.

"It's like three thirty, I think," Lenka said.

"Shit, I need to get into the office. Why didn't you wake me?" he asked.

"I thought you were sick after you crawled into the closet at dawn. I still can't believe you're really a vampire."

She smiled at the secret knowledge, and Valentin realized that, like her brother, she likely would remember everything.

"Give me your number," he said. "I'll call you, but right now I need to talk to Trey. If it's not too late." He would call her. A mortal who could remember would either be trouble down the road or useful. Naturally, he would prefer the latter.

By the end of trading that day, a Thursday back in New York, StoneHaven Systems had made another eleven billion dollars. Valentin and Trey sat in stunned silence in Valentin's office.

Finally Valentin said, "I'll call Dmitri in an hour and see what he has." Then they went to their planned meeting with the elders, walking the half-mile or so belowground to the boardroom.

"Are you two okay?" Makru asked when they walked in.

"Yes, fine. Just some work stuff," Valentin replied.

Trey thought once again, *this guy is one cool motherfucker*, but he couldn't tell what Valentin was really thinking. They had now made about $50 billion in four days, Bill Gates money. Trey couldn't believe he hadn't trusted Valentin's plan in the first place.

"Gentlemen, I think you have something to tell us," Lord Makru said.

Valentin nodded. He knew he couldn't keep the news from Makru for long with his powers.

"The plan has worked well so far. We just need to keep executing."

"What's the plan exactly?" Karolina asked.

"We reduce our exposure by half every day for the next four trading days, then we're out," Trey said.

"It's Dmitri's plan and I trust him fully," Valentin said.

"How much did we make so far?" Morty asked, still not quite believing he was there, fully appreciating the history of the moment and place. He was in the actual council room of the original elders, the birthplace of the covenant, the true seat of power for all vampires in the world whether they knew it or not, vampire sanctum sanctorum.

"Over fifty billion American dollars," Valentin said. He smiled at Morty. "I think we can get you another penthouse if you want."

"Well, let's just hope nothing goes wrong," Radek said.

"Yes, let's hope," Karolina said sarcastically.

The night of the party, Karolina walked up to the palace early with Viona to make sure the mortal party organizers had everything under control. Valentin arrived later in his Porsche, Isabella at his side after a two-month absence. Trey came in his Ferrari with Anjelica as black Skoda sedans raced back and forth between the palace and various high-end hotels to drop off mortal guests.

Karolina had hired experts to properly light the exterior of the palace, making it look truly sensational, its fifteenth-century grand-Baroque architecture on full display. When she first saw the lighting as she walked up the hill, Karolina shivered, remembering what it had looked like during the day before she was turned. She knew even her most jaded guests would be impressed by the newly touched up gold leaf and centuries old grandeur.

Pieter and Jasper vowed they would stick to their plan this time. No booze and no smoke. They would try to get close to Valentin or the Americans, Trey and Steve, and they would remember this time. As they walked into the grand entrance of the palace, Karolina was welcoming the guests. Viona walked right up to Pieter and said, "Can I get you a drink, stud?"

"No, I'm not drinking tonight," Pieter said, resolute.

Viona gave him a little tour, and as they entered the grand ballroom, which was almost completely full, people were toasting Valentin, who in turn toasted Trey. Almost five hundred crystal champagne flutes were lifted but empty in their honor. Another three hundred, held by mortals, contained actual champagne.

The buzz among vampires and mortals was that Valentin had made a lot of money that week, but almost nobody knew exactly how much or how.

Steve squinted at his phone. There was something wrong with the balance in his checking account. He tried to work out the zeros, while getting jostled by the crowd. It wasn't six, it wasn't nine. Twelve? More? It looked like $103 million. He thought maybe Valentin was hiding money in his account and tracked him down, showing him the screen.

"Early C-Level bonus," Valentin told him. "There was a time when our systems would have crashed during a week like this."

"Thanks." Steve looked at the account balance again. "I just don't have any words."

"No SHS employee is getting less than a five-million-dollar bonus this quarter. Most will get much more. Your buddy Jim will get thirty-million, being a senior director."

When Steve ran into Trey later, he asked if he should get a Ferrari or a Porsche.

"It's up to you," Trey said. "Maybe a Lambo or McLaren, but a Porsche 918 Spyder would sure make Valentin jealous."

"The guy just made us over fifty billion, including a few billion for himself, and he has a supermodel on his arm. I don't think he'll get jealous of anything," Steve said, though he was only half joking.

A crowd of congratulatory vampires and curious mortals followed Valentin wherever he went within the palace, as if he were a famous actor, or politician.

"Now you know how I feel," Isabella joked.

"Yes." He leaned closed to her. "But I don't think they all want to fuck me."

"Oh, I think many of them probably do."

He smiled. "You're probably right."

Pieter was trying to get to Valentin, but he wasn't the only one. "Is this about that tip you gave me?" he asked Viona.

"Are you saying you didn't invest with StoneHaven Systems? I made an effort to give you that opportunity," Viona said, exasperated.

"I ... I ..." Pieter gurgled as a wave of anxiety swept over him. Why had he chickened out at the last minute? He felt dizzy with vertigo, as if he were looking down at his failed life from above.

"Thanks for letting me invest," Jasper said as he walked up to Viona and Pieter. He had only had twenty-eight thousand euros to put in, but as of the close of markets on Friday, he had a little over three million now.

"You invested? Fuck, what have I done?" Pieter realized he could have been substantially wealthier than his father now. Instead, he felt he was destined to rely on him for the rest of his life.

"Don't worry about it," Viona said. "You need a drink."

"Sure," he said, not caring that he was breaking his promise. "Something strong, like a single malt, or maybe absinthe."

Later, she brought her melancholy pretty boy upstairs for a little fun. She liked the idea of having her own private mortal for feeding every two months. This time, however, it had only been three weeks since the mansion party, so she wouldn't drink too much. Viona lay back on the bed, taking Pieter's cock inside her. In a few minutes, she would feed. Life was good. She felt like her life before she was turned was merely preparation for her life as a vampire—including her willful loss of virtue as a young girl in a time when that was considered extremely bad behavior. Being born to money and having learned how to just live without angst or guilt, she always had something to do but didn't have to do anything. She thought of Valentin, Trey, and the newly turned Steve and couldn't understand their drive. She appreciated it, since the luxury that it brought was nice. For her, the life of feeding and lounging was perfect. In that moment Viona thought she was the perfect vampire.

Steve and Sarah ran into each other after they had both just fed. Steve gave her a big hug, even though they had barely spoken since she had returned from London this second time. Not because they were fighting, but because they were both so busy. For the last two weeks, Steve had been staring almost unblinking at computer screens, both in the office and in his chambers at the nest, looking for any possible computer glitch that could ruin Valentin and Trey's plans. Sarah had been balancing her time between party planning with Karolina and Viona, and trying to influence the London vote on the covenant. Thoughts raced through their minds, driven by the hectic pace of the last few weeks and the restorative effects of human blood in their stomachs, when they both realized they were still in each other's arms.

"Watch it, you two," Karolina said, giving Steve a light pat on the ass as she passed them in hallway.

Embarrassed, they followed her to the master bedroom, where a few select vampires would hang out until near dawn. That night, two mortals also attended. Isabella, who seemed more energized than most mortals after being fed on but still would not remember in the morning; and Jaromir, the intern who was dating Anjelica. Unlike Isabella, Jaromir was looking a bit faded and pale, but he always remembered, which was why he was part of Karolina's inner circle.

Morty, as a visiting American elder, was in the master bedroom too, browsing Manhattan real estate on an iPad.

"You really want another penthouse, don't you," Valentin said, grinning.

"I just need an epic party pad so I can throw feeding parties like Karolina," Morty said. "It doesn't need to be a penthouse on Fifth Avenue."

"You can afford it now," Isabella exclaimed. "Fuck, so can I. I can't believe how much money you made for me, Valentin."

"Is that why you finally let me feed on you again?" Valentin asked.

"No. I missed you. Remember, I agreed to come up to Prague three weeks ago." She turned to their hostess. "By the way, thanks, Karolina. This party was everything people were expecting. I wish I could remember."

Near dawn, most of the vampires retrieved their cars from the valet or walked down the hill to the primal nest, while Karolina and Viona went downstairs to the basement, where they slept in coffins. Valentin and Trey left their cars in the courtyard of the palace, where they normally parked anyway.

SEA CHANGE

Saturday night, Lord Makru summoned Valentin to his chambers in the primal nest.

"Valentin, I'm proud of you," Makru said when Valentin arrived.

"I didn't do it myself. It was Dmitri's algorithm, derived from yours, and Trey's business that put us in a position to take advantage of it," Valentin replied in his typical modest manner.

"Exactly. Most vampires can't see beyond their own needs, the blood of mortals, a nest to sleep in during the day. You, on the other hand, built a team that made you and the continental vampires more successful. You made substantial money for us, mostly on your own, in the previous two centuries, but this was something more."

"Thanks," Valentin said. "And you're right, I never could have done this on my own."

"Look, just be proud of this moment. I know they call you the stealth elder behind your back, but the council really appreciates your work. You have done as much as anyone to keep us united and uphold the covenant since it was created."

"Thanks for noticing, but I'm just doing what my father taught me."

"There's something else. I entered the energy field earlier to see if Dmitri's doomsday prediction was correct. I couldn't follow that stream, but I did see Monday."

"What about Monday?" Valentin asked.

"The markets will crash. The Dow will lose 3200 points. You need to abandon your plan now."

"Thanks, but we will have to lose some money to make it look like we didn't know," Valentin said.

Forty-five minutes later, in the privacy of Valentin's chambers,

Valentin, Trey, and Steve sat around the walnut conference table, while Lord Makru sat on one of the three sofas reading an old leather-bound book. As Valentin touched Dmitri's number on his phone and waited through the international pause for the first ring, he looked around the room, thinking that this was what his chambers had been built for, the pivotal meeting, the tough decision, and the moment of truth. The room was the man and the man was the room.

When Dmitri answered, Valentin set his phone on speaker and placed it in the middle of the table. "Change of plans," he said. "Hypothetically, if the Dow goes down 3200 points on Monday, I want a plan where we only lose, say, $500 million."

"How about zero dollars," Dmitri said, "if we know it's going down that much?"

"I know it's hard psychologically to lose that much, but you know how much we've made for ourselves, for our investors. It's a drop in the bucket."

"I don't know if I can do it. I'm just not wired to lose money."

"I sympathize with you. Losing money is not in my DNA either, but we need to make a plan. I'm not saying we're going to use it. We don't know if the markets are going down right," Valentin lied."

"Sure, I can put something together, like a crash protocol that we can implement if the markets get too volatile," Dmitri said.

"But it can't work very well, we need to lose that five hundred million. We need to keep suspicion away from us. You don't want to be labeled a financial terrorist, do you, Dmitri?"

"No," Dmitri replied, his gulp audible across the Atlantic and half a continent.

"Dmitri, you know the algorithm that Lord Makru gave you? How do you think he derived it?"

"I'm not sure I want to know. It was like God told him, it was so perfect."

"Dmitri, call the crash protocol Tiger Five. If you get a text that says 'Tiger Five,' implement the protocol. And remember, it needs to be flawed. We need to lose that money."

"Okay, message received. I'll have something by Monday morning."

"Look Dmitri after we lose the money you can create a crash protocol that works better," Valentin said.

☥

Monday morning, as the rich and beautiful of Europe migrated from Prague back to the Mediterranean sun, nobody could possibly foresee the financial carnage that would be inflicted starting at 3:30 p.m. central European time, when the markets opened in New York. It came anyway as markets plunged and Dmitri received a text: <Tiger Five>

The trading call that day was tense. Trey, Valentin, and Steve each took the call from their own offices.

"We have to take the long view," Trey said, putting the synthesized situation into perspective. "We made a lot of money last week, we got knocked down today, but we need to get up again and fight tomorrow."

In fact, they had lost $1.8 billion as the markets had moved more quickly than Dmitri expected. The rest of the summer, StoneHaven Systems would trade conservatively, but it could make money on its now enormous reserves. Valentin pulled $2 billion of his own money out and $25 billion for the general fund went back into the treasury, but he personally kept $1 billion of his own money with SHS, and $2 billion of the vampire general fund invested.

Pieter lay in his bed at the Four Seasons Prague, sick as a dog from blood loss, but he didn't know that. At first he thought he was hungover, then it was the flu. On the third evening after the party, Viona had Steve track Pieter down at his hotel before she went home to Amsterdam. She wasn't thrilled with much that technology had brought, but cyber stalking, especially with the help of Radek's database, was something she could get behind.

In his hotel room, she made Pieter drink water and eat some food from room service, and he started to feel better. She realized she shouldn't have fed on him so soon, but she just hadn't been able to resist.

For the next few weeks, Valentin spent much of his time talking to every elder on the continent. Many he had never met, but was introduced to by Karolina, Accalu, or Lord Makru. He asked the same questions: What improvements did they need to their nest, what capital outlays have they delayed for years or centuries? From there he created a spreadsheet of what they all needed. The next step was to set a budget and negotiate with everyone on their priorities—what they needed now and what could wait. After that, Valentin was back in Amsterdam having had his car and himself shipped in anticipation of the next feeding party at the museum nest.

"So I heard Lord Makru has you creating a budget for all the continental nests," Otakar said when Valentin arrived at the museum nest a few nights after his return.

"Everybody has their requests in," Valentin said. "Now I need to parse them and start negotiating."

"When I was in the Bucharest nest, they didn't have a mobile phone signal repeater the way we do here and in the primal nest. I asked about it, and they didn't even know what I was talking about."

"Steve, can you set up a baseline of technology that every nest needs?" Valentin asked. "Wi-Fi, mobile phone signal repeaters, anything else you can think of."

"Sure, no problem," Steve said from where he sat on one of the sofas in the museum nest drawing room.

The conversation had shifted to other general needs when Karolina walked in with Viona and Sarah. Each was smiling and carrying six shopping bags after an early-evening excursion to P. C. Hooftstraat. Louboutin, Armani, Versace, and Prada for Karolina and Viona. Sarah had mostly Stella McCartney, Alexander McQueen, and Prada heels.

"I can't believe I'm actually the person I was pretending to be just a month ago," Karolina said.

"Steve, I heard you're getting a new car," Viona said.

"Yeah. Valentin helped me find a used McLaren 12C," Steve said excitedly. "It arrives tomorrow night from Denmark."

"A what C?" Viona joked. She didn't care about cars, but had heard all about it while shopping with Sarah.

⚜

Viona Henny—Mortal Viona to the vampires—planned to throw her second annual summer party the first week of August, a week before Karolina's next party at the mansion. She rented out the Melkweg for a Thursday night, because most of her friends didn't work anyway, and hired Avicii to DJ. Karolina had planned on attending, but at the last minute went back to the Mother of Cities. The council of elders were convening on the upcoming vote in London.

Sarah had just returned from yet another trip to London, trying to garner support for the covenant.

"Sarah, I need you to do me a favor," Viona said.

"Sure, what?" Sarah said.

"I'm going to Mortal Viona's party with Pieter, but I've been feeding on him too much. I don't want to kill him. Can you distract him so I can feed at the party?"

"Sure. Just let me know when," Sarah said.

Around midnight, vampires started to arrive at the party. Valentin brought Morty, who was still in Europe for the summer; Sarah and Steve arrived in his burnt orange McLaren 12C; and Viona came with Pieter, who drove his vintage Riviera blue Porsche 911. Viona was wearing a simple black skirt and red and black blouse with a big belt, all by Versace, along with her now favorite charcoal and red-soled Louboutin heels. Sarah wore a paisley jacquard dress by Stella McCartney paired with black Prada heels.

The party was in full swing by the time they got inside. Avicii had the crowd under his spell with almost everybody dancing. About thirty vampires attended. All but Viona and Pieter, who were dancing, hung back, surveying the crowd for potential feeding opportunities as the massive herd of blood cattle swayed to the beats.

After about twenty-five minutes, Viona and Pieter returned to the group of hungry vampires.

"I saw that mortal girl Kate last week," Viona tried to tell Valentin over the noise, but he couldn't hear.

"You what?" he asked.

She spoke directly into his ear. "I saw Kate last week while you were still in Prague."

"Really? Is she still in Amsterdam?" He tried to seem not too interested but failed.

"I don't think so. She was only here for two days on business, but she said she comes here all the time."

"Really. Thanks," Valentin said, thinking, *I need to check the Bulldog Energy more often.*

Through the undulating crowd, he saw a flash of blonde hair. Not Kate but someone from his not so recent past, a time span measured in centuries. He looked again, moving his head to change the angle, but she was gone. He walked over to the area he had seen her, but still couldn't spot anyone he could have even mistaken for her. It couldn't have been her anyway. It took him about ten minutes to work his way back to the lair his nocturnal brethren had staked out on the edge of the large main room.

"Did you think you saw Kate?" Viona asked.

"No. Somebody else from a long time ago," Valentin yelled over the noise.

"The vote is this weekend, right?" Viona asked Sarah.

"Yeah. Two nights to vote, then Sunday night to tally. We should know by sometime Monday morning."

"What vote?" Pieter asked.

"Oh, nothing, it's in England," Viona said.

Morty walked up to the group, speaking loudly to try to get Valentin's attention. "Valentin, I'd like you to meet another elder from our nest in Manhattan." Valentin turned to Morty as he said, "This is—"

"I know," Valentin said, shocked. He stood face to face with the blonde-haired, blue-eyed Proto-Germanic beauty he never thought he would see again, Carina.

"I saw you in New York at that party, but you looked busy," she said as Valentin's emotions swung from hate to lust to something else. She had seduced him, turned him into a vampire in the gardens at Schloss Schönbrunn, and left him to fend for himself. He never expected to see her again, had never expected to have any feelings like this for another vampire. *If I don't have those feelings for Karolina, how could I have them for any vampire?* he thought.

"We should feed together," Carina said to him.

"Sure," Valentin said, trying to play it cool.

"I like girls sometimes, so don't worry," she added, patting him on the ass.

"Well, I guess you two know each other," Morty said.

"Yes, something like that," Valentin said, wondering if he was keeping his usual cool and in-control exterior because he sure didn't feel like it.

Carina linked her arm in his. "Shall we?"

"Who was that?" Viona asked Morty as the other two walked off.

"Carina. She's one of the elders with me in the Manhattan nest."

"And Valentin knows her?" Sarah asked.

"Apparently," Morty replied.

"How many elders do you have?" Sarah asked.

"Three."

"And two are on another continent. You must trust everybody

there," Sarah said.

"We don't have issues like London. All we ever knew was the covenant. And believe it or not, when vampires first got to America, there weren't that many people, so they avoided killing mortals."

Carina and Valentin slowly walked through the crowd looking for their dinner, and came upon Mortal Viona with a group of friends, both close and transient.

"Valentin, right?" she said, not remembering that she had slept with him. "I'm so glad you could come. Is Karolina here?"

"No. She had to fly to Prague at the last minute, some family thing, I think," Valentin lied. He whispered "Too soon," in Carina's ear. He had fed on her less than a month ago. If they fed on her that night, she would end up like her cousin Pieter, who still looked a bit sallow from Vampire Viona's too frequent feedings. Introductions were made to Viona's friends, and Carina and Valentin focused on two sisters called Fenna and Roos. The women, twenty-four and twenty-two, were typical Dutch, blonde and tall. At six feet, they were both taller than Carina and Valentin. Fenna was wearing a classic little black dress, and Roos a black leather miniskirt and light blue blouse that almost matched Carina's.

After about an hour of socializing, the vampire pair had persuaded the sisters to take them to their parents' house. Fenna rode with Valentin in his Porsche, and Carina and Roos took an Uber. Their parents were out of town, in Saint-Tropez, so they had the run of the house. After about forty-five minutes, all four of them were in bed together. Valentin and Carina looked at each other.

"Are you going to tell them or should I?" Carina asked.

"It will sound better coming from you," Valentin said.

"Okay." She looked at the sisters. "I know you're going to find this hard to believe, but Valentin and I are vampires. Valentin is over two hundred years old, and I'm almost a thousand. We need to feed on your blood to survive, but it won't kill you, and you won't be turned into vampires. You could be, but there is very little chance of that happening. But if you do get turned, go to ... Valentin, where do they go?"

"De Oude Kerk na middernacht," Valentin replied in Dutch.

"The other thing is," Carina added, "you won't remember any of this in the morning. You probably won't even remember the party."

"Wow," Fenna said. "We heard rumors. I can't believe it's really true, real-life vampires in Amsterdam. Are you sure we won't remember?"

"If you remember, that means you probably got turned into a vampire," Valentin said. "Go to the Oude Kerk and someone will meet you."

Within minutes they were having sex. Valentin was fucking Fenna, while Roos's head was between Carina's thighs. Valentin couldn't stop glancing over at Carina, squirming under Roos's tongue.

"Let's trade places," he said, his head spinning with thoughts he couldn't control. He envisioned the sisters going at it and himself on top of Carina, two hundred and sixty years later, but nobody was having any of that. The sisters, wild as they were, had their limits, and Carina quickly wiggled away from Valentin before he could enter her. He "settled" for Roos, who was just as awesome as her sister, and started to fuck her from behind. Eventually, Valentin switched to the missionary position, more optimal for feeding.

When they were done, Valentin couldn't stop looking at Carina lying naked and glowing on her side. He wondered if this was what he had been looking for since he had been turned. It seemed so cliché, falling for the girl who turned him, sorcerized him, but he felt helpless.

"I know what you're thinking, Valentin," she said, "and you just can't go there. I won't lie I'm tempted myself. Remember, I saw you first in the gardens. But we just can't, I would like it too much."

After the two sisters fell asleep, Valentin and Carina raced through the night in Valentin's Porsche GT3 RS, arriving at the tower nest just before dawn.

☥

Through the rippling crowd, Viona saw a flash of brown hair on the mezzanine above. Someone from her past, but she knew it couldn't be him. She looked again, but he was gone. She got Sarah's attention, opened her mouth and closed it quickly like she was biting—her signal for Sarah to distract Pieter—and started off to investigate whom she had really seen. She went upstairs and saw the back of his head again through the crowd. She was sure it was him. Her heart was pounding, her head spinning with emotions. She felt like she was dreaming, but knew she was awake. She followed him down a hallway of business offices, away from the crowds of people, until the hall ended at a locked door. He spun around to face her.

Gerlach always had a plan. He had learned from his grandfather, and he knew the risks. He had had three liters of his own blood frozen over a two-year period for just such an occasion. When his lifeless body had been found in the greenhouse that morning by the crew harvesting buds, they had discovered an emergency contact bracelet with his sister's number. By the time the ambulance got him to the hospital in the city, his blood was there too. Without it, the doctors told his sister Tess, he would have died. When he was finally released, Tess pleaded with Gerlach to give up his vampire-hunting obsession, but he had learned from his mistakes, and he knew he just needed a better plan.

Viona gasped when she realized it really was Gerlach, but it was too late. In one smooth movement, he pulled out the short sword handed down from generation to generation, van Meer to van Meer, vampire hunter to vampire hunter. For a moment, panic overwhelmed Viona. The last year had been so defining for her as a vampire. Her renewed friendship with Karolina, the previous near-death incident with Gerlach, and her travels to the Mother of Cities had all combined to bring meaning to her 319 years. She didn't want the true death, she never really had. She was so contented now, her life as a vampire was just perfect.

I'm a vampire, twice as powerful as most men, and I can beat Gerlach again and for good, she told herself. She was sure of it, but it was too late. The blade swung toward her neck in a compact, efficient motion Gerlach had practiced thousands of times. He was ready for this moment; he was destined for this moment. Viona was not, but nobody ever really was, and time seemed to both pause and accelerate.

Viona's headless body crumpled to the floor, blood staining the carpet in an ever widening circle, as Gerlach held the head aloft by her blonde locks like a trophy. True death in an instant, the sudden end to 319 years. A single Louboutin pump lay on its side in the pool of blood, and Viona was gone.

THE DARKNESS BEFORE THE TRUE DARKNESS

When Valentin and Carina got back to the tower nest just twenty minutes before dawn, Morty and a generic white van were waiting. "We need to get back to New York, all this money, it's just crazy, they need some leadership. I know Morty thinks they don't need elders, but a little guidance right now is exactly what they need." Carina explained.

"Oh," Valentin said. He had hoped to spend many nights catching up with her.

"After I met you in Vienna," she said, "I traveled to the new world. New York is my home now. You understand. You settled here in Amsterdam."

He gave her a big hug, and if they held each other too long for the comfort of those watching, neither cared.

Friday evening, Karolina, Accalu, and Otakar returned from Prague with grim looks. The emergency council had gone badly, with no agreement made on what actions should be taken to persuade the London vampires to keep the covenant, and the vote was starting that evening. Karolina felt helpless, but decided to concentrate on her party, which would be held a week from Saturday at the museum nest. The actions in London would influence the actions on the continent, and though she preferred a more proactive approach, time had run out.

"Has anybody seen Viona?" she asked when she didn't see Viona in the tower lounge.

"Not since last night," Sarah said. "I think she fed on some guy she knew, but not Pieter."

"Well, tell her I'm at the canal nest if you see her," Karolina said. Being the resident elder, she was trying to spend more time at the nest she was assigned to, even though it was her least favorite.

About three in the morning a rumor started to float around the tower lounge that Mortal Viona was dead.

"We need to find out who fed on her," Valentin and Otakar, the resident elder at the tower, said at the same time when they heard the rumor. Valentin had let any interested vampire know that he had just recently fed on Mortal Viona, the obvious prize of the party being the hostess, but it must have happened after he and Carina had left with the sisters.

He turned to Steve. "Can you—"

"Already on it," Steve said as he fired up his Viceroy console and started poking around the police computer systems.

"Holy shit!" he said. "This wasn't a feeding death. It says here a young female was beheaded upstairs at the Melkweg. What's strange is they are calling her a Jane Doe."

<Call me ASAP re: Jane Doe> Valentin texted to Jacob, the chief medical examiner.

Jacob responded quickly. <What do you know? We don't have anything. The prints don't match anything on record and we don't have a head>

Valentin wondered if the London violence had again spilled into Amsterdam. Perhaps one of Trevor's buddies exacting revenge.

<I need to come down and see the body> Valentin texted to Jacob. Otakar had texted Karolina and Accalu about the latest developments, and Karolina texted Valentin in turn.

<Keep me updated. I have to let Praha know what's going on. Let Radek know that whatever it is—it's under control>

Valentin and Steve immediately set off on foot for the city morgue.

A few minutes later, Jacob buzzed them into the small reception area. A big thirtyish guy with clipper short hair and muscles that looked like they were used for something more than just lifting weights stared at them as Jacob led them back to the lab.

"Who was the guy eyeballing us?" Valentin asked.

"Oh he's just a new guy. Nephew of the police chief, just out of the army," Jacob said as they entered the sterile lab. Giant refrigerator drawers lined one of the walls, each with a number. Jacob stopped at the door labeled 3 near the far end. He slid the drawer out silently on precision ball bearings to reveal a body covered in cloth. He slid the cloth back to expose shoulders and a neck with the head cleanly removed.

"The blood has some anomalous properties," he said. "The color is still very red compared to what is typical at this stage of decay. This is a negative temperature unit which we use for unidentified bodies, a lot colder, but still, this is not normal."

"I need to see more of the body," Valentin said, and Jacob pulled the cloth back farther, to expose her bare breasts. They looked larger than Mortal Viona's, but Valentin couldn't be sure.

"It could be our Viona," Steve said as Jacob continued to pull the cloth back, and Valentin looked at him sideways.

"I need to see her clothes," Valentin said.

"Sure, they're around here someplace," Jacob said, looking in a small compartment beneath the body. "Not here. Let me have someone track them down."

"No, do it personally," Valentin said with authority in his voice. He needed to be sure, but the blood not turning black was a possible indicator that this was a vampire. After about ten minutes waiting, Valentin was starting to lose his patience.

<What's the holdup?> he texted Jacob. ,<And BTW don't involve that guy from the lobby>

Another five minutes passed before Jacob finally got back.

"They were in the garbage, the one in the break room," Jacob said holding a black plastic bag. "I'm not sure how they got there, I need to find out."

"Don't bother, I don't want to raise any more suspicions," Valentin said as Jacob dumped the contents onto a shiny metal table in the center of the lab. A black skirt, red and black blouse, and a single pump with a red sole spilled over the table. Valentin stood in shock, knowing now for sure what he had suspected but had been denying to himself for the last half hour.

He looked at Steve, who looked just as shocked. "We need to talk to Karolina." He turned to the medical examiner. "Jacob, somebody will be here to pick up the body before dawn. Don't involve the guy who was eyeballing us in the lobby or anybody else. If you do, you will have another body on your hands."

With that, Valentin and Steve walked out the side employee door that exited onto the street.

⚳

Lord Makru stood up from his large pillow in the meditation alcove of his chambers in the primal nest. He had read the vile thoughts of the one called Luca, who sat nearly a thousand kilometers away in Geneva, Switzerland, reading an email. *The master was successful in retribution; the vampire Viona is dead.* He paced back and forth across the floor, knowing he had to call Karolina immediately, but his more than 3700 years had not prepared him for this type of call. Nothing could.

⚳

Karolina was sitting in the lounge of the canal nest when her phone rang. She saw it was Lord Makru. Radek was likely getting anxious again. She was reaching for the phone as Valentin and Steve walked in, their faces grim. She declined the call and braced herself, but you can never be prepared for that kind of news, regardless of your resolve.

"It's Viona," Valentin said simply.

"Are you sure?" she asked.

"Yes. I'm sorry. She was decapitated. We're getting the body out tonight. We need—"

Karolina held up her hand, cutting him off, as she stood and walked toward the elder's chambers. Her phone was ringing again, Lord Makru.

"I know," she said as she answered.

"So it's true," Makru said.

"Her head was cut off. It has to be a vampire hunter."

"I'll let Radek know," Makru said, and Karolina was relieved for once to hear that name. The rest of the evening she was locked in the elder's chambers at the canal nest, not taking any visitors.

The rumors continued to fly around the tower and canal nest lounges. Was it Mortal Viona or the real Viona who was dead? Valentin and Steve had left the canal nest soon after talking to Karolina, and no one else, and that only fueled the speculation. A little after three, every vampire in Amsterdam got a text to meet at the tower nest at 4:00 a.m. sharp. When they arrived, no elder was in sight, not even Otakar, who was supposed to be in residence at the tower.

After about twenty minutes, Otakar, accompanied by Accalu and Valentin, descended the stairs into the lounge. There was no sign of Karolina.

"We lost one of our own last night. Viona met the true death," Accalu said, addressing the large crowd of vampires.

A gasp of shock swept through the crowd. If anybody was the most popular vampire in Amsterdam, it was Viona. She was a native, a truly nice person with no real enemies in any nest. More than half of the male and female vampires in the city had gone on feeding dates with her over the years, posing as a couple or friends to put people at ease. People looked up to Karolina, but her occasionally bitchy attitude and the fact that she was the first post-covenant elder in Amsterdam made it hard to like her all the time. A few women in the crowd tried unsuccessfully to hold back tears as the news they had all dreaded was verified.

"I heard it was Mortal Viona. Are you sure?" a voice came from the crowd, echoing the thoughts of more than a hundred.

"It's Viona," Valentin said. "I saw the body, and her clothes."

"Where's Karolina?" somebody asked, breaking the stunned silence.

"At the canal nest," Otakar said.

"Who did it?" another asked.

"We don't know right now, but we believe it was a vampire hunter," Accalu said. "She was decapitated."

"We don't have any suspects yet," Otakar added.

Accalu continued, "Over the next few nights, Radek will be bringing thirty-five vampires to search for vampire hunters and provide security. With that many guests, many of you will have to share sleeping chambers. We are taking this very seriously. An unprovoked attack like this out of the blue, we need to consider all angles."

"Was it the feeding parties?" somebody asked.

"We don't know," Valentin said, finding himself compelled to defend Karolina's parties, at least for now. "We don't know anything right now, but we will use every tool at our disposal to find the person or persons responsible. I have Steve on this already, we have technology on our side."

☥

With a history of so much death, and true death, surrounding them, vampires were conflicted on the concept of mourning the loss of one of their own, but Karolina knew what she felt. Viona was her friend and now she was gone. The hole she felt in her life was unbearable, and the one person she felt she could share that with was gone. Saturday night, she stayed in the elder's chambers at the canal nest. She didn't need anybody to see her like this, and she didn't need to talk to anybody living.

Soon after sunset, Radek and his thirty-five "warriors" started to arrive. Lord Makru had proven that Lamia Venatores was a real threat, and they needed to find the "master." Steve and Evette worked on their computers in the tower lounge trying to parse the data, find something useful. Database queries were constantly being run on the servers back in Prague, cross-referenced against almost everybody who had checked into a hotel or flown into Amsterdam in the last few days.

Sarah, meanwhile, was pacing back and forth as she talked on her mobile to anybody she could back in London about the covenant vote. Steve had never seen her so committed to anything. He had rarely seen anyone this committed, as she seemed to be trying to will a "stay" vote. So he just gave his silent support while he tried to determine who had killed Viona. He did his work with an objective efficiency, but from time to time he remembered why. Viona was gone. Radek was in Steve's ear every half hour or so looking for an update that he wished he could give. Radek wanted the true name of the master, but as before, nothing matched.

"We need to be ready for more attacks. I'm sending all my men out to keep an eye on things," Radek said.

Valentin, on the other hand, thought, they needed to use technology to pinpoint the person or persons involved, and then send Otakar with one or two others to exact justice. Flooding the city with more vampires was definitely not the low-key approach he preferred.

Rumors rose and fell as the night wore on, but none were based on truth. A few hours before dawn, Steve found an email from Gerrit Jansen; the cop buddy of Gerlach van Meer, the vampire hunter Viona had killed last summer, to somebody called Brecht Graaf. That was the same family name as the police chief.

<I can't believe he really did it> was all it said. But after their experience at the city morgue the previous evening, he was

suspicious. After a little more snooping on the city computer systems, Steve confirmed Brecht worked at the morgue. He proceeded to read all of Brecht's emails going back two months, when he first started at the morgue, but it was mostly work related. Then he tried to find Brecht's personal email account, working his way back through his work email, thinking that would be more valuable. As luck would have it, Brecht had forwarded one email, the standard admission of a Jane Doe whom Steve thought was Viona, to a Gmail account early Friday morning. The Viceroy system was useful once you had hacked into a computer network behind a firewall, as they had already done with most of the official government systems. It could not, however, hack into a commercial system without the Viceroy system being physically deployed with one of the USB sticks. He was sure that had already been done by the NSA in the case of Google, but that was no help to him without the 2048bit encryption key. He would need a password hack, and he needed some expert help. He fired up his Tor browser and went to a black-hat hacker site he knew about. There he posted his request, along with the payment available, $10,000 in Bitcoin for the person who provided him with the password.

Twenty minutes before sunrise, everybody was anxious and testy as Radek's battalion started to return from their sentry. Sarah was yelling on the phone now, and Steve—while looking for more clues—was checking every few minutes to see if he had obtained Brecht's Gmail password yet. There was little useful data, and the email angle, as thin as it was, seemed to be the most promising.

Accalu headed back to the museum nest in his blood red Ferrari Testarossa as the sun neared the eastern horizon. There had been no Karolina sighting at the canal nest or otherwise, but most were too busy to notice. Sarah and Steve had to share Sarah's chamber, but neither complained as they quickly fell asleep, emotionally exhausted, in each other's arms.

Monday evening, as the sun set the tower nest came alive. Steve woke up, hard as a rock, with Sarah in his arms. They held each other for a moment, but only a moment, as this night was so pivotal. The tally of the London vote would be known before sunrise, if they were lucky; and Viona's killer or killers were probably still somewhere in Amsterdam.

Steve's day started with a quick conference call that included Lord Makru, who unfortunately had no more information. He had failed to find any other member of Lamia Venatores during his nightly search. Steve then checked to see if he had the critical password, and he didn't. He thought this was strange. It had been almost ten hours since he had posted his request.

"Bump the payment to a hundred thousand American, it's our only lead," Valentin said.

Valentin had reduced their exposure to Bitcoin to just 50,000 euros in the general fund, no longer believing in the virtual currency except for illegal activities like this. He bought another 100,000 euros worth, just in case they needed it for any more illicit deals. Despite the increase in payment, hours went by without Steve's hack request getting fulfilled.

"I thought this would be more like Amazon," he said. "I could just order the password like a novel on my Kindle, and a minute later it would just show up."

Sarah sat in tense silence on the couch, texting from time to time for updates from London, any indication as to which way the vote would go, but none was forthcoming.

Radek sent his men onto the streets of Amsterdam again, and Valentin again wondered what it would achieve. They certainly would not encounter anyone wearing a Lamia Venatores T-shirt, he was sure, but didn't say anything. Accalu was back at the tower nest, but Karolina was not. Nor was she seen by anyone in the canal nest lounge.

The night ground by, with no new vampire-hunting information and no word on the London vote. With fifteen minutes until sunrise, Accalu started to walk toward the garage. Just as he put his hand on the handle to the heavy oaken door, Steve said, "I got the password."

"I'll stay here tonight if you don't mind, Otakar," Accalu said.

"No problem. Maybe text someone back at the mansion to let them know," Otakar said, and they both thought that would have been Viona just a few days ago. Steve was quickly reading Brecht's emails, trying to find any reference to Viona or Lamia Venatores. With just five minutes before the sun reached the eastern horizon, he found something interesting, an email sent Friday morning.

<Well done G, I knew you could do it, you truly are the "master" now.> The recipient's email address was gvmeer461. Steve looked at it. Something seemed familiar. Vmeer. He knew that name from

somewhere.

"Holy shit!" he yelled suddenly. "Gerlach is still alive. It was Gerlach. I can't believe it. I should have been following him on line this whole time. This is all my fault. Fuck!"

Valentin looked down at Steve's computer, scanning the email. "Gerlach? Are you sure?"

"It's the only explanation. Look at this email. And they're both part of Lamia Venatores. You were right about that guy at the morgue, Valentin."

"Fuck!" Sarah exclaimed, staring in disbelief at her phone. She swore again, looking at them all. "They voted out the covenant. The vote was three nests to one. I can't believe it."

In the ensuing two minutes before sunrise, the tower nest was chaos, and as Valentin walked upstairs to his chambers, he hit send on a text to Karolina.

<It was Gerlach, London vote bad>

EXPIRY

At sunset, Sarah and Steve woke again in each other's arms.

"I can't go downstairs, just hold me," Sarah said. Her whole existence over the past few months had been concentrated on saving the covenant in London. She felt only personal failure now, but she also felt safety in Steve's arms. "I just want to stay in bed for a while with you. This is the only place I really feel safe right now."

Steve didn't feel any better; he knew it was his fault that Viona was dead. Gerlach had gone after him originally because he had killed the mortal woman Veronica. Then he had stupidly assumed Gerlach was dead, ignoring the fact that every vampire had made the same assumption, including Viona.

Steve held Sarah tighter, wiped a tear from her cheek, then they were kissing like moths circling the flame, and with the same inevitable result. He needed to feel closer to her, so he simply rolled on top and was inside her. They sighed at the sensation it gave them, both physical and emotional. The world outside was gone, it was just the two of them, and that was all that really mattered. For an hour, Steve barely moved, but then he came to understand that his purpose in life was to give Sarah orgasms; and so as an expression of his love, he did. They fucked hard, they fucked soft, and Sarah melted into Steve every time she came, and she still wanted more. They experienced everything as a couple, and not as a separate man and woman. Hours later, just before dawn, Steve came as well, and they fell asleep again in each other's arms. Tomorrow night, they knew they would do the same, and the night after that, and the night after that.

☥

Karolina arrived at the tower lounge just fifteen minutes after sunset with Carina.

"I thought you went back to New York," Valentin said as he gave her a hug, which he now realized was uncharacteristic for him.

"I did go back, but I needed … I guess I needed what the mortals call closure," Carina said.

"Where is Sarah?" Karolina asked, all business-like. "I need to talk to her about London. The council has made a decision."

"I think she's with Steve. They'll be down in a few minutes, I'm sure," Valentin said.

By 10:00 p.m. every vampire except Steve and Sarah stood assembled, summoned to the tower lounge and waiting for the elders to speak. Accalu, Otakar, and Karolina descended the stairs after a short but painful wait. Karolina stood to the side and slightly behind the others, a dry-eyed look of sorrow on her face that caused many to begin openly crying over the loss of Viona. Radek and Carina stood farther to the side with Valentin, being guest elders in Amsterdam.

"As some of you already know," Accalu started, "we just discovered that Gerlach is not dead, and he is in fact the person responsible for the true death of Viona. We are currently trying to track down his location, and I have every confidence that Steve will be able to find him. This is nobody's fault, least of all Steve's. Viona herself thought Gerlach was dead. We all just failed, failed together to consider that he wasn't. We will learn from this, we will become stronger and smarter in the future. Viona's brutal murder will not be in vain, and it will not go unpunished.

"I'm sure you have also heard that the London nests have voted to leave the covenant. The first thing I would say is that this changes nothing here on the continent. The covenant remains the guide in our complex relationship with the mortals, now and in the future. We can't win a war with the mortals, so our only option is to be invisible, to not exist in their consciousness. I lived for centuries without the covenant. Every elder you see before you here tonight knew life before the covenant, and none of us want to go back, back to the night of infamy in the Mother of Cities, back to the constant fear of not just one or two vampire hunters like Gerlach, but hundreds, if not thousands. I fled Babylon, I fled Rome, and I never felt safe until I finally knew the covenant would stand. The council has met, and we have a plan for dealing with London. If you lived through it or know our history, you know the coming months—coming years—

will be hard, but for most of you, nothing will change."

As he finished speaking, the reality brought home by his speech only prompted more to cry openly at their loss, their seemingly dire situation.

Accalu looked at the other elders, feeling a bit helpless. "Do any of you have anything to add?" he said, hoping for some inspiration from the other elders.

Karolina's friend was dead. She felt a sob coming from somewhere deep within and pushed it back down. She didn't cry, ever. She looked at the women crying and the general shock in the room over Viona's death, and over London. She stepped forward, and with a clear, strong voice proclaimed to everyone in the tower lounge, "I don't want tears, I fucking want revenge."

A cheer went up so loud, Radek feared mortals on the street would hear it.

Karolina looked at Carina, her best friend from centuries past, standing with Valentin, both providing unspoken support. She knew they each needed time to work things out, but also knew this was more important. Valentin had no idea that Carina, like her, was a super vampire, or that their existence was anything more than vampire myth. Before the cheers had died down she turned to the only person she knew she could trust and pleaded, "Valentin, I need you to fix London."

ACKNOWLEDGMENTS

This book like so many things in life has been a journey. A journey played out on two continents and several countries over the last few years. I need to thank first and foremost my family who instilled a love of reading from an early age with weekly trips to the library in addition to the thousands of books in our home while growing up. Additionally I need to thank my editor Elizabeth Barrett. Kit Foster for the great cover, and interior design of the print versions. Finally I would be remise if I didn't thank John Polidori and Bram Stoker for taking folk legend and creating a genre both singular and diverse in its subsequent and numerous interpretations.

ABOUT THE AUTHOR

ML Worthingham is a dark fantasy writer and author of The Gloaming. He began thinking about the first book during a trip with friends to Amsterdam in the spring of 2002. Originating out of his dissatisfaction with the current artistic imaginings of the vampire myth he envisioned a dark alternate reality interlacing known history with the unique violent history of the continental vampires of Europe. Work on the first book The Gloaming, Rise of the Stealth Vampire Elder began in Amsterdam during the summer of 2014.

ML Worthingham grew up in Mill Valley, California where he started writing fiction as a teenager; spent time traveling all over the US for work, in Europe mostly for pleasure, and currently lives in Silicon Valley. When he isn't writing or delivering innovative new technology he can be found traveling the world, mountain biking, or just getting another cup of coffee.

www.mlworthingham.com